Seeking Haven

Book two of Atlas Cliffs series

Angela van Liempt

Dawn Publishing

First paperback edition October 2023

Cover design by Natasha MacKenzie,

Miss Nat Mack Studio @missnatmack https://www.missnatmack.com/

Editing by Kayla Ramoutar

ISBN 978-1-7782544-4-4 (Paperback)

ISBN 978-1-7782544-5-1 (E-book)

Published by Dawn Publishing

www.dawn-publishing.com

*For Lucien. My brave one. My, be-yourself-no-matter-what one.
My oldest, who exudes love and generosity. You teach me to be
gentle on myself and believe I can do anything.
Keep writing your stories.
I'm proud of you. I love you more!*

We shall not cease from exploration. And the end of all our exploring will be to arrive where we started and know the place for the first time.
T. S. Eliot

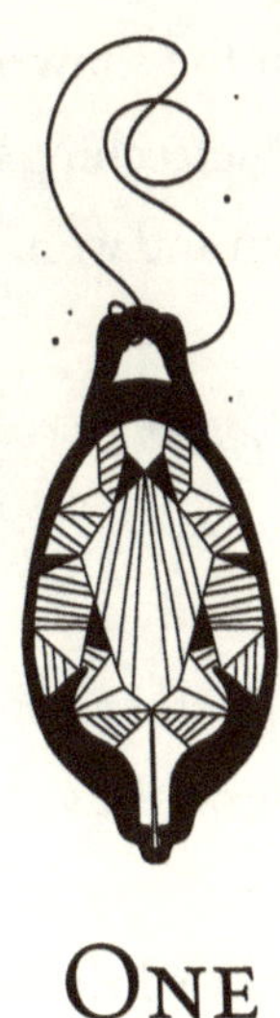

ONE

An unnerving creak echoed off the walls of the empty dorm bathroom, jolting her system like a bucket of ice water dumped over her head. Drew yanked the shower curtain aside and wiped the wet hair from her eyes as she peered around the room. It was late, and no one was around. The bright orange door remained closed, and her phone and make-up bag still rested on the vanity beside the sink. Turning the faucet off, she lingered behind the curtain, listening. The only sound reverberating off the tiles was her own panicked breaths and water dripping from the shower faucet. It must've been the pipes, making the odd screeching sound. The cool air of the room battled the hot steam and won, leaving her body covered in goosebumps.

I'm being ridiculous. Nothing's going to hurt me here. I'm safe.

She grabbed the towel off the bathmat, dried off, and wrapped it around herself before stepping out of the shower. She set the shampoo bottle on the vanity near her makeup bag and slipped her arms into her terrycloth robe. As she dried her hair with the towel, she inhaled the sleeve's soft fabric. If she closed her eyes and focused, the faint scent of home filled the air. Cinnamon and magnolia flowers. Gran had given the robe to her on her eighteenth birthday almost a year ago. As she ran her fingers over the butterfly embroidery, thoughts of home turned into a deep longing, but she couldn't pinpoint what it was she yearned for.

Nico.

Memories of him were still so vivid, even after months apart. She missed surfing at Jupiter Cove Beach, bonfires with friends, and how he used to hold her when panic attacks plagued her after the shooting. An ache settled deep in her chest. Thinking of Nico filled her with conflicted emotions.

She couldn't decide if she regretted ending things with him after prom, or simply missed his friendship. The past six months had been the longest they'd ever gone without speaking, and she worried he'd never talk to her again. But—and maybe it was her way of coping—the longer she stayed away from home, the easier she found it to forget about her lingering feelings for him.

She tried her best to avoid thinking of Atlas Cliffs, but nostalgic reminders, like her favorite pink robe, surfaced far too often since she'd begun her studies at Boston Art College. Back home, she was Drew Harlow. The girl who claimed to see dead people and had suffered a violent attack. A *victim* was the word they used. It made her cringe. If she hadn't left town and moved ahead with a career and a new life, she feared she'd end up stuck forever and filled with regret. She missed Gran and her father, but she'd made the right decision to leave. Going back home would trap her in a box, away from opportunities. She could detach herself from what Dominic Sloan—*Ben Morana* had done, and the memories of the ghosts of Neptune Point. And moving forward was the only way she could let go of what could have been with Nico, letting those memories fade into the distance. Living in a big city, she could be as anonymous as she wanted, or simply... Drew. The small-town girl achieving her aspirations. The girl who was exploring her inner artist and learning more than she ever thought possible about an open future of possibilities in front of her.

She pulled the towel from her hair and wiped the steam off the rectangular mirror until her reflection appeared. Winter weather meant her freckles had long faded against her pale skin. The jarring scrape on metal sounded again, and she whirled around, almost tripping over her own feet, but she was alone.

It's just the pipes.

She faced the mirror, eyeing beyond her reflection. Still alone. With one exception, of course. There was one ever-present problem. His name was Ori, and he was dead. The ghost who appeared on Jupiter Cove Beach, desperate for her to read her mother's letters, and never left her side. His blond hair and charming surfer boy look might be an issue some wouldn't mind, but he was like an irritating brother who never gave her a break, or what she imagined having a sibling would feel like. But he'd grown on her, almost becoming a friend like Enid had been. As long as she stayed in the dark about her mother's whereabouts, it would seem he was stuck in limbo alongside her. She didn't want to think about what might happen if she never figured out the connection between Ori and her mother. There had to be another way to help him cross over to the soul realm, and out of the in between. Nothing was going to force her back home. *Nothing.*

Stretching her neck from side to side, she grabbed her phone from the vanity, opened a music app, and turned on her favorite playlist. She combed her wet hair and sang along to the music, drowning out further thoughts of home and her mother.

A sharp drop in temperature surrounded her, sending icy air through the sleeves of her robe, and she pulled the belt in a tight hug around her waist. One of the overhead lights flickered, and a soft whisper sounded as a swirling mist behind her reflected in the mirror.

She looked over her shoulder, expecting to see Ori manifest, unsure if she should be grateful or concerned that she hadn't seen him all day.

"Ori? Is that you?"

The whisper echoed louder, and she placed the brush on the counter. She stared into the mirror as the mist spun faster, afraid to turn around and face what, or rather, who, was coming. Her rapid exhales fogged in front of her like she was outside in the dead of winter. This never happened with Ori, and he'd been her sidekick for months.

"Who's there?"

A shrill crackling cut through her phone, drowning out the music, and high-pitched enough to terrify a rabid wolf. With shaking hands, she whipped around, snatching the phone. She pressed buttons, desperate to silence the screeching device.

A spitting hiss exhaled, muttering unintelligible words as the mist turned to gray smoke. Her throat burned like the room was on fire, and an unusual heaviness pressed down on her chest.

She was used to run-ins with the wandering, but this was unlike anything she'd ever experienced with any ghost. For the first time, she wanted to yell out for Ori, or run, but the cloud of darkness in front of her blocked the only exit. But she knew this world now. They didn't want to hurt her, they only wanted help.

Biting down on her lip until it numbed, she stomped her bare feet on the floor. "Show yourself! I can't help you if I don't know what you're saying!"

In a flash, the smoke sucked up into an unseen vacuum. A cloaked figure appeared, gaping at her with glowing eyes shaded in black, peering from an oversized hood. It looked like the Grim Reaper was ready to take her to an underworld she hadn't believe existed until that very moment.

She stepped back, knocking her makeup bag to the floor, still clutching her phone. She could call for help, but no one at 911 dispatch would believe her.

The thing tilted its head back, opening its black hole of a mouth, and released a sound like a train screeching to a halt. The metal on metal screamed so loud she ducked and covered her ears. If this thing was some sort of demon creature, she didn't want to find out what it was capable of. She eyed the door behind the dark figure, hoping someone would barge through and save her from certain death. But no one came, and she scurried back against the wall to create as much space between the ghost as the small bathroom allowed.

The dead can't hurt me. The dead can't hurt me.

The shrouded figure of death knelt before her. She couldn't breathe and her muscles constricted in pain. She was going to die. It leaned close, and as its face tilted to the side, skeletal features of a man's face appeared. His dreadful voice chilled the air between them.

"Death seeks you."

The warning cut through her like a knife's blade, and she choked on frantic breaths, coughing at the taste of smoke and ash in her lungs.

"What does that mean? What do you want from me?" Tears stung her eyes as fear gripped her, clamping down onto her stomach and chest. Something terrible was about to happen. The energy from this man hovering in front of her tethered her to the floor as though it would turn to liquid and she'd drown at any moment.

Music snapped on and blared from the phone in her hand. The song, Teardrop by Massive Attack, wailed, and she fumbled, desperate to silence the haunting lyrics. The dead man stood, but his cloaked head tilted in a distorted manner to the side, like he couldn't straighten his neck. When he stepped backward, tall boots loomed from underneath the cape. She held her breath as she scrambled to her feet, sending a bottle of shampoo rolling across the floor. She was going to die, and no one would ever know what really happened to her. Her father would be devastated and Gran would spend Christmas alone for the first time. Drew had finally let her dad past her walls, and they'd built a solid relationship, and Gran was like a mother to her. She refused to let either of them suffer the pain of her loss, especially not at the hands of this... evil ghost of death.

Steadying herself, she took a few deep breaths and dared to speak again. "What do you want from me? Answer me!"

The ghost floated across the floor, his boots unmoving, and lifted a shrouded arm toward her face. With crooked fingers, and nails sharpened to points, he moved her hair to the side, reaching for her neck, and she jumped back against the wall, clenching her teeth.

"I'm here to fulfil my duty. Death seeks you." His face moved within inches of hers. Blood vessels twitched throughout the whites of his black eyes. His fingernails dragged along her neck, but when she brought her hands up to her face to push him back he lifted his other hand and rendered her helpless.

His ulcerated hand grabbed her neck, and she gasped. "Where is it!"

She pressed against the wall to support herself. Her frantic breaths turned to mist in the frigid air emitting from his presence. "Where is what?"

He released her neck. "She stole from me. I will take back what's mine, and you will die."

Her body screamed at her to run and escape, but she couldn't back down if she wanted to. He had a power over her unlike anything she'd ever experienced before. "Where did you come from? I have nothing you need! You're the one who is dead, not me!"

He released his hold on her neck. As he stepped back, her hands dropped unfrozen at her sides, leaving her gasping. Maybe he was leaving!

"You—are a witch," he spat, lunging back at her too fast for her to break free.

Smoke engulfed her, and she sucked in a gulp of air before holding her breath, searching for a way out. A tremendous force confined her between the dark smoke and the wall, and she let go of her breath, unable to hold it back anymore. She slid down the wall, choking on the thick smoke. Death was winning.

"Leave. Now!" Ori's voice boomed from the doorway as he moved through the reaper of death. A wailing like a wounded animal tore from the Reaper as he vanished, leaving a blast of black mist in his wake. Ori stood in front of her, appearing as his human self. "He's gone. For now."

As Drew stood and pushed away from the wall, the thumping pulse softened in her ears. "Who is he?" She adjusted the belt on her robe and bent down to collect the contents of her makeup bag with shaking hands. One of the dead tried to kill her; she didn't know what to do, or say, or think. The only thing she knew was that she needed to get the hell out of the bathroom.

Ori crouched and picked up the last two bottles that had rolled under the sink. "He might be dead like me, but he is nothing like me. I don't know what he wants, but he's got a fascination with you, and it's not good." He stood and handed her the bottles. "I've only seen him recently, but he knows who you are and where you live. I'm on it, Drew. I'll find out what I can."

"When were you going to tell me about him?" Drew left the bathroom, peering over her shoulder. Protecting herself from a human like Dominic was one thing, but she had no idea how to defend against the Reaper.

Ori followed her down the hall into her dorm. Her roommate had gone home early for the weekend, and the small room was quiet except for the radiator clicking under the window.

Ori plopped on a beanbag chair beside the corner desk. He sank deep into the cushion until he could rest his head against the back. Blond hairs escaped his ponytail, and he pushed them from his face. The fairy lights draped around her twin bed cast sparkles in his pale blue eyes. The light shone over bold scrapes across the side of his face, a mystery neither could figure out. He looked like an angel, and after months of frustration with his presence around every corner of her life; she was grateful to not be alone.

Still shivering, she sat on the edge of the bed and pulled a blanket over her bare legs and feet. "They've never tried to hurt me. Even Jack was harmless, and he scared the hell out of me at first. What was that Ori?" Unable to warm up, she pulled the collar of her robe tight and hugged herself.

"That, my human friend, is your worst nightmare, and the next time he comes for you, know that you can't beat him, Drew. Next time, you run."

She'd never had to run from a Wandering Soul before. *Never.*

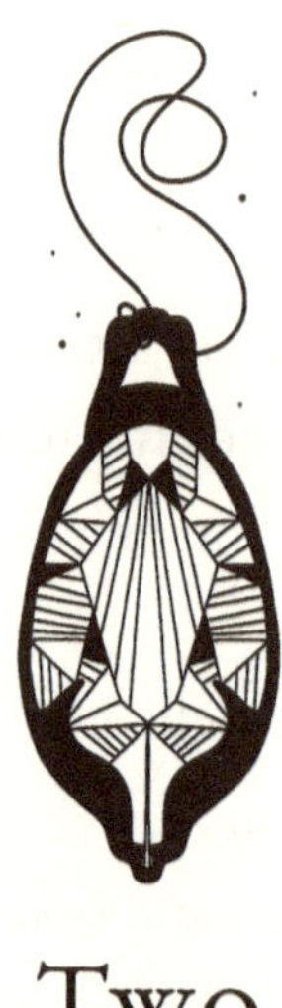

Two

With music blaring through her earbuds, Drew gulped an extra-large coffee, burning her mouth in the process as she tried to make it through Color Study class on no sleep. She'd tossed and turned, jolting awake at the smallest noise, expecting razor claws to tear her apart. The Reaper waited for her somewhere. She could still hear him uttering the words in his insidious voice that bores its way into nightmares.

Death seeks you. Witch.

She'd created theories in her head all night trying to figure out why he'd called her a witch, and why he'd said the word with rage under the surface, ready to attack. He was in the wrong century, looking for the wrong person, from a fantasy realm, with witches and vampires like something out of a movie, or he hated the occult and wanted to kill witches. But nothing she could come up with explained why he wanted to kill *her*. She could see the dead, but that didn't make her a witch—they didn't exist.

The bigger mystery was how she'd be able to protect herself if running wasn't an option, as Ori had instructed. A chill curled up her back, making her stand up straight. But the only people in the room were alive and engrossed in their painting. She turned her attention back to her own work, fueled by sudden determination. With the end of the fall term a little over a week away, she couldn't allow herself to lose sight of her goals. Maybe she'd get lucky, and the Reaper would realize she wasn't a witch and he'd leave her alone. She'd finish up strong, go home for a few days at Christmas to spend time with Gran, her dad, and Piper, and return before the winter term started. Maybe she'd see Nico.

Focus! Let Nico go.

Each brush stroke brought the painting a step closer to a disturbing reality as she applied techniques learned in just a few short months. As she cleaned her brush, the sharp smell of turpentine overpowered the intoxicating aromas of the pine easel and earthy oil paints. She shuddered as Aurora Lighthouse came alive on the canvas. Under a full moon, a blur of colors swirled together to form sea spray like a rainbow after heavy rainfall. A tiny shadow wearing a long coat and a hat stood at the gallery holding the rail.

Jack Morana.

She picked up a smaller brush as the next song on her playlist started. The echoing vocals rang through her ears singing—*"walk me home"*—as she stood motionless, staring deep into the image on the canvas. As hard as she tried to move forward with her new life at school, she couldn't deny the pull that Atlas Cliffs still had on her. She hadn't gone back to Neptune Point since summer, yet the one place she painted was Aurora.

Shaking off the thoughts, she stepped back to critique her work. Contrasting was the assignment, and her scenery piece was satisfactory enough to secure a near perfect mark.

"I'm automatically drawn to this space." A voice muffled through the music, and Drew yanked out an earbud. The teacher moved beside her and gestured a hand over the painted surf hitting the cliffs. "I like this rhythm with the line placement and shades of colors. The waves morph into abstract shapes, creating movement. Good job, Ms. Harlow." She smiled and continued weaving through the class, examining each student's canvas.

"I know that place. See? You *do* miss home. Why else would you choose to paint it?" Coming alive beside her, Ori crossed his arms and rubbed his chin. "Joelle's traveling, Drew. I can't control it; I just move around and lately it's been dumpy motels and trains next to your mother. You can't ignore her forever. I'm begging you, don't forget about me. You know, the dead guy who is trying really hard to be your friend and figure out his own shit? Can we try to find her again? Or even better, she might be on her way to find you!"

Drew finished cleaning the paint brushes as Ori paced back and forth behind her, waiting. He was always waiting for her to talk to him. How could she ever forget about him? If Drew stood conversing with Ori in public, people would gawk in wonder as she talked to herself.

And she never wanted to see Joelle again. She didn't know what she'd say to the mother who abandoned her as a kid. The mention of her mother's name made her stomach and chest tighten in dread. But she'd also accepted a responsibility to help the dead as they appeared to her—she'd just never expected one of them to have a connection to her own mother, and she'd been shoving Ori and his connection to Joelle aside for months. Neither of them could make sense of the mysterious link between him and Joelle.

She'd hit a roadblock and gave up trying… And that roadblock was the last attempt she had made to unravel Ori's mystery in California the previous July. That first day in California was the day she'd arrived at the address on Joelle's last postcard. The Victorian-Gothic mansion with its iron fence and locked gate was the last lead she'd had about her mother's whereabouts. A security guard escorted her to the front door, where an older woman with a pointed chin and stern features had greeted her. The woman's tinted glasses hid her expression as she shrugged at the mention of Joelle Marisol. Drew declined her offer of brandy and caviar—both sounded repulsive—and she'd left. It was impossible to draw any link between that woman and her mother.

She'd let all of it go, including Ori.

During their week in San Francisco, Drew said yes to whatever opportunity Piper came up with. Jasper, Piper's cousin, was twenty-two and had a flair for cooking and baking. He owned and ran a thriving bistro by the pier, but he'd dedicated that week to the position of tour guide. He loaded up his Volkswagen bus and drove them along the coastal highway. Every day was an adventure, discovering new towns, dining at seaside restaurants, and ending the day on a beach. Her journey to find her mother and help Ori had transformed into a week-long party. She had never been free of responsibility in her life.

"You're ignoring me," Ori said from behind her.

She slunk behind the canvas, lowering her voice to a whisper. "Just because you've been near Joelle in motels and trains doesn't mean she's on her way here." Students glanced over their easels toward her, their faces creased with confusion. She covered her mouth with her hand as she pretended to examine her painting and continued. "Last summer, you were sure she was in California, and we both know how that turned out. Dead-end."

Ori laughed, surprising her. "It was a dead-end because you put up an invisible wall banishing me. I couldn't get near you, or the place you were staying. How'd you do that, anyway? Can you use that power for good and call me when bad things happen like last night?"

She'd focused on keeping him away and letting him go. It had worked in California, but not since. "I don't know how it works, Ori. Believe me, I wish I knew. I think we've got bigger problems to worry about than where Joelle is on the map, don't you? Like how to keep the Reaper from... what did he say?"

"Seeking you," Ori said.

"What?"

"It's what he said. Death seeks you," Ori said, as his skin waved like water.

Dropping her hand from her mouth, she eyed him from head to toe. A pang of sadness sunk in for his predicament. His presence always shifted, unpredictable. Sometimes he appeared as human as she was, and other times she could walk through him. "He called me a *witch*. Why would he say that? Witches aren't real, are they?" She whispered out the side of her mouth to avoid strange looks as she stood talking to herself.

He stared at his hand as he tried to pick up a paintbrush from the ledge of the easel, his efforts failing. His forehead creased as he gave up and faced her. "What if they're connected somehow? Your mother and the... Reaper? Is that what we're calling him?"

"Works for me." A few people stared at her and looked away when she made eye contact. She held a hand up to her mouth again to hide her moving lips as she spoke. "Look, all I know is if I'm ever going to help you, I'll need to be alive to do it. If death is seeking me or whatever he said, I'm not going to let him win."

"Then we get ahead of him. I've been trying to figure things out for months. It's not my fault you gave up. Why did you stop trying, by the way? What's your plan, Drew? Continue like we've been doing with me as your dead sidekick? I'm hurt. It's cruel."

Despite the blurriness of his features, she could detect the shape of his smile. He was like having an annoying brother.

"I don't have a plan. I'm as stuck as you are until you can remember what happened to you. Speaking of plans, how is it that dead people can't remember the details of their life?"

Ori held up his arms as they dissipated into a mist. "I don't know. It comes back in pieces and memories. I'm working on it. We've talked about this, Drew."

"Fair point." She bit her lip and turned away from a few onlookers. "All right, you win. I'm going home for winter break next week. We keep the Reaper away just long enough so I can get through this semester. If you know Joelle is coming, I need proof of exactly where she is, otherwise it's useless. Work on remembering, Ori. I need something to go on here."

"So, if I find her, you'll talk to her? For real?"

She'd had more contact with dead people than her own mother, and the thought of seeing her again hurt her stomach. It was no wonder she'd avoided helping Ori for so long. Anything was better than dealing with her estranged mother. *Anything*. Even a Reaper who wanted her dead.

"Maybe I won't have to talk to her—"

"Oh my God." Ori covered his face with his translucent, ghost hands. "She's never going to help me. The only person in this universe who can help me is a human who would rather watch a man suffer than help." He stared up at the ceiling, talking to himself before turning his attention to her again. "If you won't talk to her and help me, I'm not helping you," he said.

Trying to be discreet as she talked to an invisible entity, she rubbed the paint off her hands as students started leaving. "You're being dramatic. If the Reaper gets me, I won't be any help to you dead. You know I'm going to figure this out and you'll be on your way. I just need a bit more time to—"

"No more time. We start this now."

"Ori, what's a few days?"

"I know where he lives."

"Who?"

"Death seeks you," Ori stated, mimicking the reaper's voice.

"You do?" She grabbed his arms and tripped over her feet as her hand traveled through his translucent appearance. When she glanced around the room, everyone was packing up their things, oblivious to her stumble.

"You do too." Ori nodded toward the painting.

Goosebumps pricked her skin as she focused on the light-house until the colors blurred together. "Neptune Point? Are you sure?"

"Let's just say it's another place I've been spending a hell of a lot of time there against my will these days. Alone, I might add. I'm not able to leave this in between place without your help." He gestured his hands over himself and, like magic, materialized into his more human form with his checkered vans and the same Sublime t-shirt he always wore. "I've been practicing. And there's more."

Ori's tone turned deliberate and serious. His voice cracked with emotion, something she'd only heard once before when he'd begged her to go to California. Until that point, she hadn't thought the dead could cry. She dried her clammy hands on her jeans and gathered her hair into a ponytail to cool her neck from the sweat that had gathered. "I'm ready. Go on."

"Like I said, I'm working on remembering. I'm having visions of what happened to me."

A couple of classmates stopped to chat as they walked by but didn't ask about her solo conversation with the canvas. No one knew about her strange gift. She hadn't kept it a secret on purpose. She never let herself get close enough to anyone to bring it up. As they made small talk, she cast a fleeting glance at Ori as he stood in human form next to the easel in silence. She had to find out what he remembered, but not here. He had done a good job of concealing his inner turmoil, but maybe he'd been too good at hiding it. Or maybe it had been right in front of her the whole time, though she had been disregarding him for months. He'd come to her rescue in the bathroom with the Reaper like a loud crash, shattering a dark presence. A wave of dread struck her as she considered the awful possibilities if he hadn't shown up. And when he needed her, where had she been? Having fun in California and escaping to a new life at college, ignoring him as much as she could.

Breaking free from the small group of classmates, she threw her backpack over her shoulder and stepped into the busy hallway with Ori at her side.

"Aren't you curious?" he said as kept pace with her. "What if Reaper comes back for you and I'm not there? I'm not too good at warping where I need to be. We need a plan—"

"I work in an hour but come to my room so we can chat, and I won't look like I'm talking to myself," she muttered under her breath, loud enough for him to hear as he vanished with a salute.

A spark of hope coursed through her. Any hints Ori remembered could be the answer to helping him get to where he needed to be. But if that happened, she'd have to face the Reaper without his help. The Reaper's power filled a room, and she didn't know how to defend against him. He not only wanted to kill her, but he also possessed the power to follow through.

Despite her attempts to ignore it, the thing that made her heart sink the most was the fear of losing Ori's friendship. Not because of any help he could give her, but because he'd grown on her like a family member she wanted to keep around.

How did I go from being frustrated with him to wishing I could keep him around?

THREE

Drew raced down the hall and outside, zipping up her jacket as she jogged back to her dorm. She was out of breath by the time she ran up the stairs and through the door. With the curtains pulled tight, and dusk falling early, darkness enveloped the room, and she searched the shadows for it... *him*.

You are a witch.

She couldn't shake his words. He was nothing like Ori, Enid, Jack, or any of the other ghosts she had met from the soul realm. She touched her neck at the thought of his taloned hands wrapped around it, and the possibility that, for the first time, one of the dead could hurt her. But if Ori could extinguish him, maybe he was the shield she needed to hold close, unless she solved his mystery and he disappeared from her life.

As she kicked off her Chelsea boots and let her jacket fall to the floor, Ori appeared, startling her. She'd never get used to his pop-ins. At least he'd been respectful of the times she'd been naked, not that he ever seemed to take notice or care. He stretched out on her bed, looking contemplative as he stared at the ceiling.

"You remembered something, but you're not talking," she said, switching the desk lamp on. She rummaged through the tiny closet for her black T-shirt and jeans she wore to work at Stargazer's Pub nearby. She unbuttoned her flannel shirt, tossed it to the side, and pulled the t-shirt over her head. As she changed her leggings for black jeans, she peered over at Ori, and as expected, she was the last thing he was focusing on.

"This is me patiently waiting for your undivided attention, not the distracted version of you," he said.

"I am paying attention."

Ori lifted his head with raised eyebrows.

"I am! Look." She sat on the edge of the bed beside him. "This is me, not distracted."

He flopped back. "I'm in this middle-ground existence on repeat and you're the only one who can help me get unstuck," he whispered.

"I know... I know you are, and I'm going to figure it out this time. I promise. You know every detail of that letter as much as I do." She got up and grabbed the crumpled piece of gold-rimmed stationery from the top desk drawer, sat back on the bed, and unfolded it, ironing it flat against her leg. A crawling sensation, like a spider scuttling along the top of her thigh, reminded her of the nerve damage, and the night of the shooting flashed through her mind. She could almost hear the gun blast in her ears again.

There was a part of her that locked away that horrible night. It had worked for a while, but as good as she'd gotten at compartmentalizing the trauma, it haunted her. She steadied her breathing like the therapist had taught her. Swallowing the lump rising in her throat, she moved the letter from her mother off her leg and onto the bed beside Ori. She read aloud again for the millionth time, straining to make out the faded cursive handwriting.

"'Drew, you're probably wondering where I've been all these years, and I wouldn't blame you if you hated me, but I have nowhere else to go. I need your help. I've called your grandmother's house and left messages. I don't have a number for your father, but he must hate me too. I know you don't want to talk to me, but I need you. Please. I'm desperate. I can meet you in San Francisco. I'll pay you back. I'll do anything. The address will be in a separate letter, with a name.'"

I'll always love you, baby girl.

She read the last sentence in her head, unable to bring herself to say those words out loud. Lies. It was all lies.

She peered over the letter at Ori. "You were with me at that house. That woman didn't know my mother."

"Agreed. But why did you push me away? How come I ended up in your hometown, and you ended up in mine? Not fair, Drew."

She'd never told him how hard she'd tried to keep him away so she could forget about everything. She still couldn't believe it had worked. "If it weren't for Dad buying my ticket and Piper coming with me—turning it into the single girl's summer, or whatever she called it—I'd never have gone at all. I just wanted to get away from Atlas Cliffs so badly. Maybe I used this as an excuse. And right now, I'm rambling on about things you already know. None of this helps us anymore, and you've got to tell me what you remember!"

"You're right. You can burn that letter. We don't need it anymore." He put his hands behind his head and crossed his feet.

She held the letter up. She'd wanted to burn it so many times. "Okay. So, if we don't need Joelle anymore—"

"I know how I died," he said.

Her body stiffened, and her breath caught in her throat. The cause of Ori's death was unknown to both. If she could get him to remember his last name, she could search for him, but he only knew himself as Ori. He often mentioned how he knew something terrible had happened but could never pinpoint the details. Enid had been the same, not knowing what happened to her until the mystery unraveled. Drew assumed it had something to do with death and being stuck between the living and eternity.

Whatever Ori was about to say had the potential to alter the course of her life.

She flopped back on the small twin bed next to him, letting her leg drop to the floor to keep from falling off. Propping a pillow under her head, she turned to face him. She might be late for work, but he needed her, and the realization of how much she'd grown to care for him gripped her.

Is this what having a brother feels like?

"What do you remember about... that night?"

"I was walking, and it was late. I was angry. I think I'd just had a fight with someone, like a lover... someone I was close to. It's so fuzzy, Drew. I just know that I had to apologize because it was my fault. I can feel this aching love for someone. You know when it hurts through your body down to your toes? That kind of love. But why can't I see their face?" He turned his head to look at her. His eyes appeared supernatural, like they had their own lights.

She knew that ache. Shane had been the one to cause pain like that. She never wanted to feel that way again. Ori's arm rested across his chest, turning from human flesh and bone to a transparent glow as he faded back to his ghostly self. If only she could hold on to him to keep him human—give him another chance at living. He started out as a ghost with a problem that she'd tried to ignore to focus on her own life. For the first time since she'd met him, her eyes were open, and not only could she *see* suffering all over his face, but his pain also seeped into her own being. He was dead, but he needed closure to move on, and she was the only one who could help... But when he got what he needed, he'd be gone from her life. Like Enid and Ezra, and Iris.

"How did you die, Ori?" she asked.

"It was pouring, and I ran. If I close my eyes and really concentrate, I can almost feel my heart beating again. But it only lasts seconds. I crossed a street in an upscale neighborhood. That time of night, it was quiet, you know? That really late, dark-night quiet. The rest is a blur and happens fast, but there's a flash of light... headlights. Stabbing pain." He closed his eyes and his body changed back to a more human appearance. "Drew, a car slammed into me, and they took off." He lifted his t-shirt, revealing purple and gray bruising covering his midsection to his chest.

As she stared at the grotesque bruises, his human form faded again, and she sat up. "I'm so sorry, Ori. I can't imagine... I don't know what to say. There must be a police report. Just tell me what to do and I'll do it, okay? If we find out who did this to you—"

"You mean, who killed me? Say it. Someone rammed into me with their car and killed me and now I'm here. You're the only one who can see me, and I can't get out. It's like those mimes who don't talk, and they're stuck in a box climbing invisible walls. I'm being thrown into all these places with no way out."

Overwhelmed by his admission, she fought back tears and got up from the bed, turning her back to him. "I promise to find out who killed you."

"Thank you," he said.

She was certain that if he could breathe like a human, he would have exhaled relief. His walls collapsed, unleashing the words he must have kept silent because she'd refused to listen. As he continued talking, she wiped her eyes and sat back down to give him her full attention. She had one connection in Atlas Cliffs who might help find out who was behind the wheel: Detective Porter. The detective had kept in touch with her since the shooting. Maybe she'd have access to police records for Ori's case.

"I've been back to Atlas Cliffs, your house, that beach across the street, all of it—your grandmother misses you, by the way. She's got lights on the porch, multi-colored because the clear lights bore you. Her thoughts, not mine."

Gran would be as excited as a kid counting down the days until Santa comes. She enjoyed nothing more than having Drew around, cooking, playing her favorite Christmas album on repeat while sipping on an endless supply of red wine, and decorating every inch of the old house. Growing up, Gran had given her a lot of freedom, and she had to take care of herself, but she was never alone. She was always surrounded by Gran's unconditional love. She may not have been her mom, but Gran was the only family she needed—and her dad was now a part of that, too. The guilt of avoiding going back to Atlas Cliffs nagged at her.

Ori continued to describe the cliffs, Jupiter Cove Beach, and the forest at Neptune Point—he even knew it was called Haven. "I met your ghost guardian when I was there."

"Jack," she whispered. She'd never thought of Jack as her guardian, but maybe he was.

"Huh. He's got a name. He doesn't say much. I barely got him to tell me who he was, but he nodded when I brought you up. I've been to the lighthouse, an old boarded-up house, all of it."

She fought the urge to stand and grab her jacket to leave. She had twenty minutes to get to work, and the walk was at least fifteen. "How is all this going to help you? You're from the west coast, not Atlas Cliffs, and we're a long way away. We need to find an unsolved hit and run that occurred where you're from, not my hometown."

Ori sat up and swung his transparent legs over the side of the bed. "Makes sense. But let's say we find out who hit me, and I get to move on to Paradise City or wherever I'm supposed to be. What will happen to you when your new admirer decides it's a good day for a visit? I think this is bigger than just finding out who killed me. Last night wasn't the first time I've seen him."

The Reaper's gray cracked skin and penetrating death stare etched themselves into her memory. Static sounded from the other side of the room, and she spun around toward the sound. Her Bluetooth speaker crackled from atop the desk like her phone had done last night, and she grabbed it, powering it off.

"He thinks I'm a witch and wants me dead. We've got to make it clear that I am not who he thinks I am. Maybe he'll leave on his own. I'm not a witch. They don't exist, do they?" She didn't believe in mystical creatures, but she could see dead people. What if everything she'd believed was wrong?

"No idea, but all that matters is whatever you are that lets you see things means I don't have to do this alone. And neither do you. We need each other if we're going to get through this, and we will get through this." He rose from the bed, fading into the surrounding air with each passing second. "Shit, it's happening. Before I go, I need to show you something. I can't explain it, but I picked it up from the guy at the lighthouse. He said you'd know." In one fluid motion, he moved to stand in front of her faster than any human could mimic. Standing at eye level, he lifted his hands to her face. "Can I?"

The last time she'd let a ghost show her anything, it was a young boy who wanted her to talk to his mom in a grocery store line. She'd followed the woman outside to the parking lot and passed along her dead child's message, sending the poor mother into tears. That was the worst part—having people look at you like you're from another planet when you tell them you've been talking with their dead loved one. But Ori's vision would be different, and maybe whatever Jack gave him would help her keep the Reaper away.

She returned the speaker to the desk, her hands leaving a sweat mark. "I'm ready. What did Jack want you to show me?" She closed her eyes as Ori put his palms on her cheeks. His hands sent an electric current zapping through her head. A metallic taste danced on her tongue as Ori unveiled a vision to her.

Like a scene from a movie, a girl Drew had never seen before appeared in her mind's eye. The girl had her hands stuffed in the pockets of a large work coat with reflector tape across the sleeves. Her face lit up with a smile as a young man flicked a cigarette and came closer. The girl intertwined her arm with his and they stood on the deck of an enormous fishing boat, overlooking the ocean. With her short, dark hair blowing in her face, she gathered it into a low ponytail. The reel in Drew's head played images, one after the other, fading to black. The next scene showed the pair talking, laughing, and kissing in a room the size of a closet with a set of bunk beds. Recognition came crashing down on Drew. Her mouth filled with saliva, and she took a few deep breaths to keep herself from throwing up.

Shane!

As she jerked her head away, hugging herself, Ori vanished, taking the opportunity to ask questions with him. He'd shown her a flashback to the time she'd believed Shane was dead!

The fishing boat... it had to be the one he'd been living on for months. Her throat burned and dizziness consumed her as she scanned the room. The vision couldn't be real!

Shane had been living in Boston with his dad, and their reconnecting had happened naturally over the past six months since her arrival at school. Their relationship had regrown to the point of friendship, something she never thought possible when they had said goodbye in Atlas Cliffs. The relief he was alive made forgiveness easy... maybe too easy. She couldn't believe he had been with someone else during all those months at sea. There was no way he could keep such an enormous secret from her. He'd told her every detail of his time away, and the conversation always ended with more apologies for the pain he'd put her through. Not once did his face give away any betrayal or cause her to mistrust what he'd said.

The more time they'd spent together, the more she could tell he wanted more than friendship. Without declarations of love, his eyes still held the same emotion as when they used to be in love. When they had been so consumed with each other, it was as though no one else existed. She'd wanted to talk to him about boundaries if they were going to continue their friendship; she wasn't in love with him anymore. As Gran would say, that ship had sailed.

But he couldn't have been with another girl while she was home grieving his death. There had to be a mistake.

Ori's wrong. He must be wrong.

Her phone rumbled against the wooden desk, making her jump. Shane's name scrolled across the screen.

FOUR

Drew hustled around the pub's back kitchen as the clanging of dishes and the sizzling of pans reverberated off the stainless-steel shelves. She rushed to bring out food, take orders, and check with the bar for drinks to serve. As the hours passed, her head swam with the visions Ori had shown her. The vision of Shane with another girl appeared so real, but it couldn't be true. How could he do that to her?

Shane had messaged her four times, wanting to meet up before she finally answered. Against her better judgement, she let him know she'd be at work until eleven. Keeping her distance to avoid having the friendship discussion wasn't working, and it was time to tell him how she felt. She'd been worried about hurting him after everything he'd been through. How was she going to accuse him of being with someone else and lying to her about it? Revealing to him that her source of information was courtesy of her dead friend, probably wasn't the best way to get the conversation started. Especially if Ori was wrong.

She finished cleaning her last two tables and dropped the forced smile plastered across her face all night. She laced up her boots, zipped her coat, and slung her bag across her body as she prepared for the fifteen minute walk home. With parking scarce and expensive, she never drove. She waved to the remaining staff as she broke free toward the double doors. An eerie symphony of sharp tapping sounded as ice and snow pelted the glass, obscuring the view through the windows. It was going to be a frigid walk home.

Shoving the door open, she paused when she glimpsed someone sitting on the long wooden bench resembling a church pew in the small waiting area. The festive lights strung along the artificial garland around the windows highlighted his dark hair in a blue hue, matching his eyes. He oozed charm as he sat typing on his phone with his legs stretched in front of him, crossed at the ankles. She couldn't deny his attractiveness, and a few years earlier, she'd fallen hard for him. But when Shane started calling her again, she responded with friendship. The romantic feelings bubbling inside were for someone else.

"What are you doing here? I thought we were meeting to-morrow?" she asked.

"I was playing pool a block over and thought I'd stop by and give you a drive home, so you didn't have to walk," Shane said, rising to his feet. He presented a bunch of flowers with every color of the rainbow, enveloped with clear plastic and pink paper. "And I wanted to see you." He smiled, handing them to her. As the sweet, powdery fragrance drifted to her senses, she had a moment of nostalgia. The smell reminded her of home, sitting on her front porch when they first started seeing each other. He had captivated her, and she couldn't get enough of him. Taking the flowers from his hands, she noticed the look of longing in his eyes. The warmth she used to feel in her chest when he'd look at her like that was gone. As she stood in front of him, the image of him kissing the other girl flashed through her mind. She had moved on from Shane before she ever set foot in Boston. Why was she so afraid to find out if the vision was true?

He placed his hands on her arms, and she flinched. "Did I lose you? You're not saying anything."

Yes, Shane. You lost me a long time ago.

The doors swung open, and guests entered the pub, bringing a wave of cold air, snapping her out of her stupor. "Thanks for the flowers, but my birthday isn't until next month."

"I don't need an occasion to give a girl flowers. Want to get out of here?"

"I just want to go home."

"It's shitty out. Let me give you a lift. I want to talk to you about something."

She could get the conversation over with on the car ride back to her place, but he was not coming inside. If she turned the conversation back to the boat, she could slip in something about being lonely and desperate for friendship.

He held the door open. "Are you coming? You're not going to walk, Drew. It's bad out." His phone rang, and the ringtone cut over the surrounding chatter. He turned it off and shoved it in his pocket.

"You could've answered that," she said, stepping outside.

He kept his gaze straight ahead as he led the way to his car. "It's just Dad. I'm parked on the side."

She hopped in the passenger seat as Shane's phone fell out of his jacket pocket. He stuck it in the center console and started the engine. The wipers sped back and forth, keeping up with the ice and snow battering the windshield. Drew placed the flowers at her feet, the scent overpowering and making her nauseous. She couldn't tell if it was the smell or Shane.

Carefully steering onto the slick roads, he drove away from the restaurant.

This would be the last time Shane would give her flowers. The friendship between them would never amount to anything, and she couldn't stop thinking of Ori's vision of the girl on the boat. There was no way she could ever return to a time when Shane was the center of her world. She'd recovered that lost part of herself, and she refused to let it go. Shane was her first love, and she cared about him, but maybe it was wrong for her to believe they could be friends. Surviving Shane's death—when she believed he was dead—nearly leveled her. She vowed to never become so dependent on someone again that losing them would destroy her.

Never again.

"Everything's working out right now, Drew. I got into the EMT program. It starts next month. I'll live with my dad until the course is over, and get a job, but I'm thinking maybe in a year or so the two of us—"

"Shane, I'm really happy for you, but there is no *us*. There never will be."

The phone lit up, the ringer on silent, and Shane flipped it over.

"Why aren't you answering it? What if your dad needs you?"

"He doesn't, it's fine. This is more important. I've already lost too much time. Drew, I love you. And when you moved here... I realized all I wanted was for us to get back together. The timing is perfect."

"There is no timing for us anymore. We're just friends, or at least I thought we were. Us being together feels like a lifetime ago." She tilted her head back against the headrest and faced him. "I don't feel the same anymore." It was on the tip of her tongue to question him about his time on the boat, yet she couldn't find the words.

Shane's eyes stayed glued to the road as he pulled into the parking lot of her residence. The building lights shone on his face, highlighting the heartache etched on his forehead and around his eyes. "Don't you think your feelings can change? I thought you felt something, too. I thought..." He parked and faced her, gesturing a hand back and forth between them, continuing, "I thought there was something between us again. If it's a trust thing, tell me what you want me to do, and I'll do it."

Trust was a small word, carrying a lot of weight. There had been a time when Shane held all her trust. A time when she never doubted his loyalty, or if he'd always be by her side. But everything changed when he had left.

Her heart broke for Shane, dealing with losing his mom in the most horrific way. But he had his life, and she had her own; he had to move on from what could have been. She wasn't in love with him anymore, and if she wanted the truth from him, she had to be honest, too.

Unbuckling her seatbelt, she sat upright, facing him. "This isn't about time passing, or healing, or getting back to some-place I was when I was sixteen. I loved you so fucking much. That's why I thought we could figure out a way to be friends. I don't want to hurt you, but—"

"You don't want me anymore," he said, sitting back against the seat, gripping the steering wheel. "I feel like I'm losing you again, only this time you're the one taking off. I don't get it, Drew. I thought you wanted us to start over." His hands dropped to his lap. "He did this to us, you know. If it weren't for his threats... if he didn't kill my mother!" His balled fist lifted and hit the steering wheel. "If it weren't for him, we wouldn't be here right now."

She'd been doing her best to suppress memories of the shooting, but Shane's words stirred up the creeping need to look over her shoulder. Panic rose, turning her stomach and chest to stone. She looked away, trying to breathe through it as she'd been taught. Gripping the door handle, she looked out the window, focusing on the cold against her skin, and slowed her breathing.

Letting go of the door handle, she pivoted in her seat to face him. She opened her mouth to tell him she would always be there for him as a friend when the phone lit up against the console. This time she grabbed it, flipping it over to hand it to him. He snatched it from her fingers, but not before she saw the name on the screen.

"Who's Leah?" she asked.

Ori's vision was real.

He clenched his jaw and turned the phone off. "No one. A friend. It doesn't matter."

"Was she the one calling before?" Heat rose to her face, surprising her. She no longer wanted a relationship with him, but the truth rising to the surface cut deeper than she expected. "Did you meet on the boat?"

His eyes widened as they locked on hers. "What? Why would you ask that?"

"Don't lie to me, Shane. No more lies." She chewed on her bottom lip to stop herself from crying. "I'm not in love with you anymore; we're over. I wanted to be honest with you, so I didn't lead you on or hurt you. Now, I want you to be honest with me and tell me who that girl is."

Snow descended faster and covered the windshield as he slowed the wiper speed. "She worked as a deckhand." He reached for her hand, but she yanked it away. "She saved me when I thought I'd die without you. There's nothing going on, I swear! I was messed up. When I was out there, I didn't think I'd ever see you again."

Her throat tightened, but she held her stance, fighting back tears. "Tell me what happened."

"You don't want to know all this. It was a long time ago."

"It wasn't that long ago, Shane. I want to know everything. Please tell me."

He rubbed his forehead and dropped his hand. "She came aboard at a port we stopped at after leaving Atlas Cliffs. Her father worked for Dominic... Ben, whatever the hell his name is. You need to understand I was ruined. Devastated. I didn't think I'd ever see home, or you, again."

She sat as close to the door as she could, ready to get out of the car, away from him, but her need to know the details held her in place. "Keep going," she said, her voice cracking.

He exhaled hard. "Keep going. Are you serious?"

"I need to know."

"Fine. One night, I was drinking, and she was just... *there*. We talked, and I told her I wanted to die. I was dead to everyone at home, to myself. I was alone and scared."

"What happened next? With Leah." Saying the name made her sick—she didn't even know the girl! She wasn't in love with Shane anymore, but she sure was back then, and while she'd been picking up the pieces, thinking he'd died, the truth was he'd turned to someone else. "Did you sleep with her?"

"Jesus, Drew. It doesn't matter! I want to forget about it, all of it."

"Don't you think I want to do the same? I thought you were *dead*, Shane! I almost died trying to find out what happened to you! Tell me the truth, I can handle it."

"What if you can't and I lose you again?"

"I'm not yours to lose! I want to know what happened on that boat while I spent months grieving."

"We spent time together, that's all," he said.

"Why is she still calling you?" Her body ached to leave the car, but she couldn't move until he said what she needed to hear.

"We kept in touch, but there's nothing between us, I swear. She knows everything that happened. Her father was involved with the whole mess, too." He tapped his fingers on the center console. "She knows about you, and how much I wanted to get back together. There's nothing going on now. You've got to believe me."

She opened the car door, and the overhead light came on. "Did you have sex with her?"

He rubbed his head with both hands and dropped them, slapping his legs. "Yes. Is that what you want to hear? She was all I had during a very, very dark time. I thought they were going to kill me!"

The pelting hail hit her as she sat with the door wide open, exhaustion setting into her bones. Tears ran down her face, burning her skin, but she didn't bother wiping her face.

Why was she so upset? She no longer wanted to be with him! She thought back to the guilt she'd felt over her feelings for Nico when she thought Shane was dead, and a strange sense of relief came over her with Shane's admission.

I can't believe I've felt guilty for all these months!

"You can trust me. I'll never lie to you again." Shane's voice shook her from her thoughts.

Trust. It was a shit word.

As she exited the car, she crushed the forgotten flowers under her feet. Petals littered the floor mat, and she resisted the urge to scoop them up—not because they were from Shane, but because Gran would never let flowers die without first fulfilling their purpose.

Sleet whipped around her, stinging her face, and soaking her hair. Shane stepped out, steadying himself on the open car door frame.

"Don't do this. Please!"

"You need to go," she called behind her as she walked toward the doors.

"Come on, this can't be it," he said, wrapping his arms around his body. "I love you."

She choked on tears and spun around. "Go home, Shane. Let me go. It's time I live my life without you." She opened the door and stepped into the residence without looking over her shoulder. The sensations of loneliness, sadness, and relief overwhelmed her, but with a sense of closure, she let go of the relationship and the memories that came with it.

46

FIVE

Drew removed her boots and shrugged off her jacket before collapsing onto her bed, sobbing into her pillow. Shane had seen her crying, and she hated herself for it. She should have kept her self-control to avoid looking heartbroken—no, heartbroken was the wrong word. She'd let herself trust Shane again, tried to be a friend to him, but should've known better. Why was she so upset?

Our relationship was a lie. He never really loved me.

A click and a groan sounded from beneath the window, and she rolled onto her back, bracing herself with her elbows. The clicking got faster, and she leaped from the bed and peeked through the tightly drawn curtains as heat streamed from the radiator. Streetlights cast a glow on the snow, blowing sideways. A gray cloud of smoke swirled close to a park bench covered in snow. The tornado cloud shifted into the Reaper, floating inches off the slushy road, sending a chill running through her body. He stared in her direction and lifted a cloaked arm like he was beckoning her.

She stood still, her heart pounding as she watched him. He angled his head downward, revealing the caved-in hood on one side. A black bird emerged from beneath the cape, landing at the top of the lamppost like a taxidermy trophy. Drew stayed motionless, scared to move or take a breath. The Reaper turned until the hood slipped, revealing his bare, gray head. Dark blood vessels ingrained all over his head stood out under the light against the snowy background as they moved and stretched across his face. His eyes had an odd glow as he stared in her direction, searching for her. She gasped and ducked away, her movements swift as she gripped the curtains together. Her ragged breaths filled the room. She could run downstairs for her car, but the slippery roads wouldn't allow her to escape fast enough. And where would she go?

She doubted outrunning him was an option. She hushed her racing mind and peered outside again.

He'd vanished.

Widening the curtains, she searched the area, but he was nowhere to be seen. He had evaporated back to whatever purgatory he'd come from. The bird—it must be a raven—stretched its wide wingspan and lifted off the lamppost. It flew through the blizzard, disappearing as it approached her window. The raven was not the Reaper; it couldn't be. It resembled the raven at Neptune Point, which had led her to the riverbank to meet Enid one night in Haven. She would never forget Enid. She missed her friend, but helping the dead never resulted in a lasting friendship. Ori would eventually go to a different soul realm, too... unless *she* ended up in the soul realm.

She sat on the bed, straining to hear any signs of the Reaper's return as she scanned the room for something to use as a weapon. Not a single thing in her possession would stop the Reaper.

She sighed and flopped down on the bed, propping a pillow under her head. Ori's arrival sent the Reaper away the night before. Maybe she needed him near her all the time. How ironic. All this time, she believed it was Ori who needed her, not the other way around. But he was right. They needed each other. If he went back to Neptune Point, perhaps he'd come back with answers.

As Neptune Point crossed her mind, her thoughts wandered home and snowballed to Nico. She missed road trips along the coastal road in the convertible he'd restored. Surfing for hours and sitting on their boards watching the sunset. Bonfires on the beach. Conversations in the garage while he worked. His ability to drop a one-liner while he was so engrossed in what was happening under the hood of a car stunned her. He never missed a word she said. But she'd broken up with him because she needed something more. Or he'd been too into her... too nice, too much, and it freaked her out.

The only way to break free of Atlas Cliffs was to leave Nico behind.

She'd wanted this new life.

The urge to call him hit her so hard, she picked up her phone and searched until his profile picture smiled back at her. One of her favorites, she'd taken the photo the previous spring. The snow had melted, and they'd ventured across the street to stroll along Jupiter Cove beach looking for sea glass. Without him knowing, she'd captured the picture while the sunset sparkled off the water. Nico was gazing out at the ocean with his hair a tousled mess and that sweet, dimpled smile on full display. At the time she hadn't thought much of it, but now, the picture melted her.

She'd tried to suppress her memories of Nico, but the emptiness of missing him lingered. She'd considered reaching out but couldn't find the courage to make the first move. The more time passed, the tougher it was to call or message. The last conversation they'd had was on prom night when she'd ended things with him. She'd seen him on the water a few times, but they only ever exchanged a wave or a nod.

She scrolled through his Instagram, glancing at a few images of cars and nights around a fire at Haven. The most recent image was with a girl she remembered from Atlas Cliffs High, Nicki—she rolled her eyes at the name similarity. How cute were they standing in his garage taking a selfie? She swiped the photo out of sight and found Piper's number instead.

Piper answered on the first ring. "What's wrong? You never call this late."

Hearing Piper's voice on the other end was the lifeline she needed. The tears returned as she told her about Shane.

"What an asshole, piece of shit..." Piper trailed off, muttering more swear words in one breath than Drew thought possible. "I cannot believe he had a girlfriend while you were risking your life to find him! My advice? Let him and all that baggage go. You don't need his friendship, and you sure as shit don't need anything else he's offering. You're fierce! You see dead people, for God's sake! It's like a superpower! You got out of town and moved to the city. Own that and walk away."

Despite the turmoil, Drew couldn't help but smile. She'd forgotten how much she missed Piper.

"Is surfer guy still hanging around?" Piper asked.

"Ori, and yes."

"You still think he's connected to your mom?"

"I'm not sure. There's some... other things going on too."

"I'm listening," Piper said.

Footsteps sounded from outside Drew's room, and she sat up, listening and waiting. She relaxed her shoulders as the sound of a door clicking shut down the hallway echoed through the silence, reminding her she wasn't as alone as she felt.

"Piper, do you believe in witches?"

"That's random. You mean like black magic and spells? Could be fun. If you see dead people, I suppose anything is possible."

"You think I might be a witch? Is that why I see ghosts?" The radiator cracked again, and Drew held the phone away from her ear as she jumped up to peek out the window. Snow piled on the park bench across the empty road. Piper's voice echoed from the phone at her side, and she held it up to her ear.

"... witch trials centuries ago."

"Witch trials?" Drew was only slightly familiar with the Salem witch trials and could remember Gran telling stories about witches in Ireland.

"Yeah. You remember the young, hot, history teacher? It was the only time I ever got excited about school back home. He walked around in his tight jeans, talking about the witch trials in Salem and Europe. A bunch of assholes accused women of partying with the devil and started hanging or burning them at the stake."

Drew remembered the class and the hot teacher, but she'd never believed the women were witches. "Witches don't really exist, Piper."

"Who's to say? You, of all people, should know there's more to life than what we see. Why are you even asking? What's going on over there in Boston? Sounds more exciting than life in New York!"

Drew laid back down on the bed. "I doubt that. Excitement finds you anywhere. New York is definitely more exciting."

"Hey, I'm only here because of my parents. I'll get my degree and then I'm leaving for somewhere sunny and warm all year round! You can come with me. We'll be roommates and relive our week in California." Piper yawned. "Seriously, why all the witch talk? What's going on?"

Until Drew uncovered the Reaper's identity, she intended to keep quiet about him. If Piper were to discover the truth, she would have more questions than Drew had the energy to answer. "Nothing, I'm just tired. Forget it." Drew shut her eyes as she cradled the phone between her cheek and shoulder.

"Me too. But hey, I have my flight booked home for winter break. We'll have a bonfire on the beach, watch movies, hang out at Maze, and eat your Gran's cooking. I miss you! And get this, Jasper sold his business and left. He's staying at my parents' house until he finds a place. I didn't think he'd actually leave California, but he got a job as executive chef at the Casting Spoon thanks to Claudia's mom. You know I don't thank Claudia for anything, but he seems happy about it."

Piper's cousin, Jasper, had lost the love of his life months ago. He'd been silent when Piper told him Drew could see the dead. Drew sensed disbelief in his voice when he questioned her about what she could see before he changed the subject. He didn't bring up the subject again for the rest of the week, and she said nothing about it. It was obvious Jasper had no intention of giving out any details, not even a name or picture. He acted like he wanted to erase that part of his life. The heartache surrounding him was palpable, and she could relate to wanting to leave a city behind. "I hope he's okay. We'll hang out soon," she said.

Piper yawned again with a dramatic sigh. "I can't wait!"

"Thanks for making me feel better," Drew said. She clung to the conversation, not wanting it to end. Piper's presence on the other end of the phone made her feel safe, no matter how false the sense of security.

"You're my sister, Drew. That's what you are to me. How many times did I call you crying after Cole left?"

"Oh, I don't know, like a hundred?" A laugh escaped, surprising her. "You can call a hundred more. How is dating life in New York, anyway? Is *that* exciting?"

"Non-existent. I'm not dating now, nor will I... at least until I graduate."

"That's a long time, Piper."

"I mean it."

"I know you do." Drew stifled a yawn. "I guess I'll see you and Jasper soon, and we'll catch up."

"Good night, Drew."

"Good night."

Her phone's light faded as the call ended. With her mind foggy and her eyelids drooping, a shiver crawled through her as she slipped beneath the covers. In her mind, she called for Ori, but he didn't appear like he usually did, and it troubled her. She pondered what to do if the Reaper showed up in the night. She struggled to stay awake and on alert, but her head sank deeper into the pillow. The silence of the room enveloped her, and she slipped into a dream world.

Walking along Jupiter Cove beach, her feet sinking into the warm sand, and a summer ocean breeze caressing her hair around her face. The clouds hid the moon and stars, but the darkness didn't matter. Not here. Warmth radiated through and around her. She was safe from all danger, as if time had frozen in place. It was a sweet haven, and she'd experienced nothing like it before. A stillness and an instinctive knowing the dead couldn't find her here. Consciousness attempted to break into the dream, wondering if she had died and this wasn't a dream at all. She kept going until she reached the gap in the water between two rocks that cut above the surface. The billowing sundress she wore wrapped around her legs and the surf crept up to the shoreline, soaking her feet in warmth. She twirled, marveling at the solitude of the beach.

This can't be the same beach across the street from my house. What is this place?

"It's peace, dear," a familiar voice said as a woman walked toward her. She was too far to see who she was, but she'd know that voice anywhere.

Drew stepped away from the water through the soft sand, approaching the woman. She recognized the nightdress covered in daisies, and the soft waves falling over her shoulders. "Gran? What are you doing here?"

Gran closed the gap between them and wrapped her arms around Drew, squeezing her tight. "Darling girl, hear me. You're going to be just fine."

Drew hugged her back before pulling away to look at Gran's face. The wrinkles had diminished, and her eyes were sparkling as radiant as Ori's and Enid's had been.

She took a step back.

Gran's whole being shimmered as she stood in the moment's tranquility. A strange instinct took over and Drew reached out, placing her hands on Gran's face. Her hands took on the same angelic glow that surrounded them both. A vision played through her mind—Gran laughing and drinking wine at a weekly dinner with friends. She'd gotten out of the car, unlocked the door, and entered the house, the door clicking shut behind her. A sharp pain coursed through Drew's chest and stopped. She could see Gran on the floor in the den. She looked like she was sleeping, only it would be a sleep she'd never wake up from. Drew's hands dropped, and she collapsed to the sand in tears.

Gran sat beside her. "I won't be far. You know that." She winked and smiled her Gran grin.

"This can't be real. I shouldn't have left you and gone away to school! I knew something was wrong. You were so thin—"

"Shh. Never say that again. I wouldn't have had it any other way." Gran lifted her hand, and a teardrop shaped black stone caught the light, glistening as it dangled from a silver chain. As Gran's light touched it, the amulet lit up with a web of lines that spread out like the roots of a tree.

Drew got up and marveled at the intricate design of the magical stone. The amulet's icy surface warmed when she touched it. "What is it?"

"For you." Gran placed the stone in her hands, and its featherlight weight settled into her palms like it belonged there. Delicate blue and white streaks glowed and intertwined deep within the amulet as heat pulsed against her skin.

Taking it from Gran, she ran her fingers over the silver chain. "I don't understand why you're giving me this. Am I dead?" She blinked back tears, her vision blurring and refocusing. "Are you?"

Gran's smile faded, and a solemn expression crossed her ghostly face as she glanced over Drew's head out to sea. "You'll understand soon, and I don't have time to explain. I'm being called away, so you need to listen to me." Gran's accent thickened the faster she spoke. "The amulet is from a friend of yours. Enid. It's for your protection."

"You saw Enid?" She scoured the beach, searching for Enid again as Gran faded away like they always did. Drew reached for her, but her hands passed right through. Gran had become one of them. She squeezed her eyes shut. "Please don't be real. Please don't be real."

"Open your eyes and look at me," Gran said.

In a rare moment, Drew did as she was told.

"You've got all you need to send him back. You hear me? Hang on to the amulet, help Ori, and remember this. What you lose will come back again. They'll see to it." Gran turned and walked away, continuing to lose luster with each step.

"Wait!" Drew yelled as she ran to catch up.

Gran paused and looked over her shoulder. "I love you, darlin'. I'm real proud of you."

"I love you too." Drew's words echoed in her head as her eyes flew open, and she bolted upright in her bed, crying and shaking. Her phone buzzed on the desk across the room, and she threw the covers off and yanked it from the charger.

"Hello?" Her voice shook as she spoke.

"Drew! I don't know how to tell you this. It's just so awful." Her father's voice cracked on the other end. "Mom... Gran is gone. She's gone! She's dead, Drew."

She gripped the desk to steady herself. "I'm coming home, Dad."

"Don't forget this," Ori's quiet voice sounded from beside her as he held up the amulet.

She took it from him, clutching it in her palm as she broke into choking sobs.

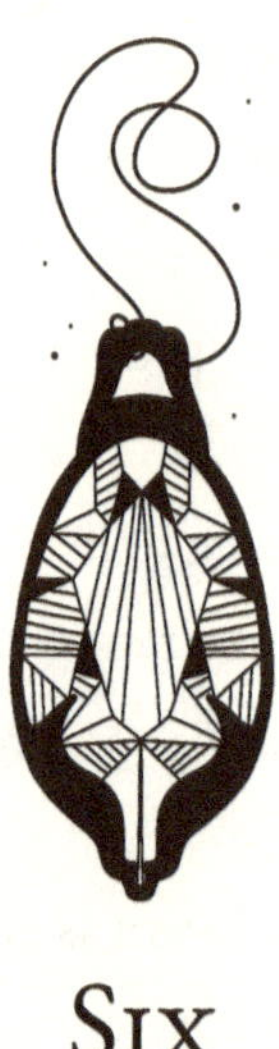

Six

With the day ending, the sky filled with deep, oppressive darkness, swallowing any hope of light.

She'd left Boston two days ago, and her lack of sleep and grief caused her to feel robotic, empty. She moved like a zombie while people close to Gran brought casseroles, desserts, and flowers—if she didn't escape the house, she might lose her mind. Her father was doing everything in his power to handle Gran's estate and helped her arrange a funeral. The full responsibility of Gran's wishes fell on Drew's shoulders. She chose lilies and orchids for the memorial service, the ladies from Gran's ballroom dance class offered to make sandwiches and platters, and Drew emailed the funeral director photos for a slideshow. But deciding on what urn should hold Gran's ashes made her nauseous.

The anguish came in waves, starting with a lump in her throat until it spread to her toes. Grief had its own way of stopping time, as if the hurt would sink so far into her body it would never leave.

Losing her only mother figure filled her with a fear she hadn't expected. Gran had shown her how to be brave and kind. She always believed Drew deserved every opportunity life offered and had pushed her to go to school and do something extraordinary with her life. Gran's death shattered her haven and the ground beneath her felt unsteady, like it was slowly crumbling away.

The streetlights flickered to life as Drew sat in her car behind the Tough Cookie. She'd searched the shadows for the Reaper, but there had been no sign of him since she'd glimpsed him through her window in Boston. She hadn't taken Gran's amulet off her neck; touching the pendant triggered a reaction, and as her fingertips brushed it, it warmed against her skin.

If Nellie hadn't asked her to meet her here, she would've avoided coming to the bakery. Revisiting Gran's business—her pride and joy—was a depressing reminder she was gone forever.

A rush of memories flooded her mind. She could almost hear Gran's laughter and smell the sweet aroma of vanilla bean oil she'd spray around the house while singing Celtic songs. She'd gone to bed too late and woke up believing it was all a bad dream, only to find out that a life without Gran was her new reality.

Taking a deep breath, she opened the car door. The snow crunched beneath her boots as she walked to the back door of Gran's beloved bakery. She tried to imagine what it must have been like when Gran opened the shop a year after Drew's grandfather had died. When she was six or seven, he was the first Wandering Soul Drew ever met. She'd been coloring at the kitchen table with Gran and told her about a man smoking a white tipped cigar that smelled of spice. The look of shock on Gran's face never left her. That night, while Gran was sobbing in her room, Drew promised herself to never speak of the dead again, and she kept that promise until she met Piper.

The motion light sprang to life, interrupting her thoughts as she fumbled with Gran's keys. She dropped them, and when she bent down to pick them up, she noticed colorful stones arranged in a row, peeking through the layer of snow. She picked up the black one matching her amulet and stared at it.

Did Gran do this?

Placing the small stone back in place, she glanced over her shoulder. A gust of wind swayed trees against the metal fence, and snow fell from the branches, hitting the ground with a thud. Shivering, she unlocked the door and stepped inside.

Familiar scents of baking bread, fresh cookies, and sugary treats greeted her, and the lump in her throat became unbearable. She'd give anything for Gran to stroll into the kitchen and hug her.

The swinging door flew open, and Nellie walked in, nearly dropping the stack of pans she was carrying. "Oh, honey," she said, putting the pans on a wire shelf before embracing her in a tight hug.

With a step back, Nellie gave her a long look through her red-framed glasses that had slipped down her nose. Sadness lined her face. "How are you guys making out?" Nellie's voice trembled as she added, "Are you sure there's nothing I can do?"

Nellie had worked with Gran for such a long time that seeing her again was a sharp reminder only one remained as the owner of the Tough Cookie. Drew wiped her eyes. "I don't think so. Thanks for keeping business going. I don't know how you're able to do it all this week."

Nellie took a few tissues from the box on the shelf and dabbed her eyes. She moved her fingers through her short hair, revealing a sleeve of intricate tattoos. The delicate floral art suited Nellie's personality. "I miss her. We all do, but she's what's keeping us going here. We're closing shop for her funeral, but I promise you, I'll be a phone call away if you need me."

"I know. Maybe I can... I don't know, help around here—"

"Are you kidding me? If I let you do that and skip school, she'd come for me dead or alive, and you know it." Nellie chuckled through tears, wiping mascara from under her eyes.

School was the furthest thing from Drew's mind. "I don't think she was happy I chose art school."

"Not true, not true at all," Nellie said as she bustled around the kitchen, tidying up and locking cabinets. "Maddie was proud of you. She said you were going to make all your dreams come true." She put her long coat on and rummaged through her massive purse.

"What did you want to talk to me about?" Drew said.

Nellie handed her a blue file folder with a rubber band around it. "The business. Maddie and I were partners, so she still owned half of this place. This is all the paperwork for my share of the business. Drew, I'm selling, and you deserve to buy it before anyone else."

She opened the folder, flipping through papers without reading a word. Her father had arranged a meeting with Gran's lawyer the morning after the funeral, but the only thing she expected was to be told of any last wishes. Business matters hadn't crossed her mind, but maybe they should have. The only thing consuming her was a deep, overwhelming grief. "You want out of the business? But why? I thought you loved it as much as she did."

"I do love this place." Nellie surveyed the kitchen, with its big ovens and large counters, and perched on a barstool. "I loved Maddie, you know I did. She was my best friend." Nellie heaved a sigh. "My daughter had a baby, and she wants me to live closer so I can help and be a part of things. It's time for me to retire, Drew. I just got an offer on my house, and I was going to tell Maddie, but..." She folded and unfolded her hands. When she looked up, her face was blotchy, and her eyes filled with tears. "I hate this. I'm here for two more months, but I know you're meeting with the lawyer, so it seemed like the right time to tell you." She hugged Drew again. "I'm so sorry, hon. Talk to the lawyer about options. You can buy my share or sell the business and I'll receive it then. I can come in and sign whatever you need, answer questions, just let me know. We'll make this as easy as possible. I can give you the name of a pastry chef across town by the culinary school who might be interested—"

Nothing about this was easy, just bad timing. "It's all right, Nellie. I'll figure it out."

"I didn't mean for it to happen this way. No one could've expected this. Whatever you need, I'm here, okay? You're not alone."

Drew closed the folder, and Nellie hugged her goodbye before walking out the back door. Somehow, she'd gone from turning her back on Atlas Cliffs and studying graphic design to returning home to handle death and business. Gran's business. Her bakery. Her home.

I can't do this.

She stood alone in the middle of the kitchen with its big ovens, empty cooling racks, and pantries full of ingredients. Every part of this place held memories she couldn't let go of. The collision of her new world with the old wedged her in the middle, leaving her unsure of what to do next.

A dull thud echoed from the front store, and she opened the drawer of pastry knives, selecting the first one her hand touched. If the Reaper attacked from the other side, a pastry knife wouldn't be of much use, but holding the heavy handle provided a sense of security. Her boots squeaked on the tiled floor as she crossed the kitchen. She pushed the swinging door open a crack. Headlights from a car passing by shone through the large picture window at the front of the bakery, illuminating the room. Chairs were pushed into cleared off tables adorned with silver napkins, and the butterfly trinkets on the corner shelf sparkled as light hit them. Tiny pot lights inside the curved glass display case under the counter cast a glow on trays of Christmas cookies.

The room was empty. She continued into the room and placed the knife on the counter.

A knock rattled the front door, causing the hair on the back of her neck to rise. She shook out her arms and took a deep breath, shaking her head. She'd felt so skittish—with everything happening, Shane, the Reaper, Gran... She was on edge.

She peered at the door and saw pink hair sticking out from beneath a skull-printed knitted hat. Piper cupped her hands around her face, trying to see inside. When she saw Drew, she waved her arms as flurries of snow twirled around her. Drew steadied her breaths and willed her heart rate to slow as she opened the door.

Piper bounded through the front door and wrapped her arms around Drew. The snow from Piper's jacket and hair melted against her warmth as she hugged Piper back. "I'm so sorry about Gran," Piper said. "I just landed two hours ago. Your dad said you were here, and I couldn't wait." Piper sat at one of the round tables and pulled her hat and mitts off.

Drew told her about Nellie leaving and the funeral plans. "I don't want to go back home yet. Dad will be gone when I get there, and it's too depressing being in that house alone." She'd insisted it was okay for him to go home at night and had spent the past two nights alone in Gran's house. A part of her dreaded going back home. *Home* as she knew it was over.

She plucked the elastic band around the folder like a guitar string. Decisions would have to be made, but she didn't know if she'd be capable of doing the right thing for Gran.

Piper snapped a piece of chewing gum, hopped off the seat, and explored the room. She ran her fingers over turquoise candles that matched the walls, and the framed artwork Drew had painted over the years. "We could just stay here. Your Gran's energy is everywhere. It's like she's right here with us." She turned around to face Drew with tears in her eyes. "But maybe it's too sad here."

Piper was right; the Tough Cookie embodied Gran's spirit. Everywhere she looked, memories seeped into her soul. The wilting flowers in a vase of water on the counter served as a reminder of what Gran left behind. She was sure Nellie resisted throwing them away.

"Everywhere I go is sad right now," she muttered.

Piper stopped roaming. "Why don't we get a pizza and bring it back to my house and hang out with Jasper? Or you can just tell me you need space, and I'll leave you alone with your thoughts."

"I've been alone with my thoughts for days. Weeks, really." The mention of pizza sent her stomach rumbling. Despite the casseroles in the fridge at home, she hadn't eaten much. "It's Monday. Maze is never busy on a Monday. Can we just go there?"

"You had me at Maze," Piper said, flinging her arms out, her mittens tumbling to the floor. "Anytime, anywhere, I'm in. You barely have to ask."

Drew picked up Piper's mittens and handed them back to her, but Piper ignored them, grasping the amulet dangling from Drew's neck. Piper's nails matched the black stone as she turned it over in her fingers, examining it. "What's this?"

"You wouldn't believe me if I told you."

"Oh yeah? Try me."

As Drew stepped away from Piper, she wrapped her hand around the amulet and her palm tingled, a pulsing glow beaming from the stone. She dropped it, letting it dangle from the silver chain around her neck.

"What's happening, Drew? I've never seen anything like that before!" Piper stared at the jewel.

Drew held her hands up to her face and scratched her palms; they were itching like mad. A faint blue light emitted from her palms, startling her, and she clapped them together. When she opened them again, peering through half-closed eyes, the light was gone.

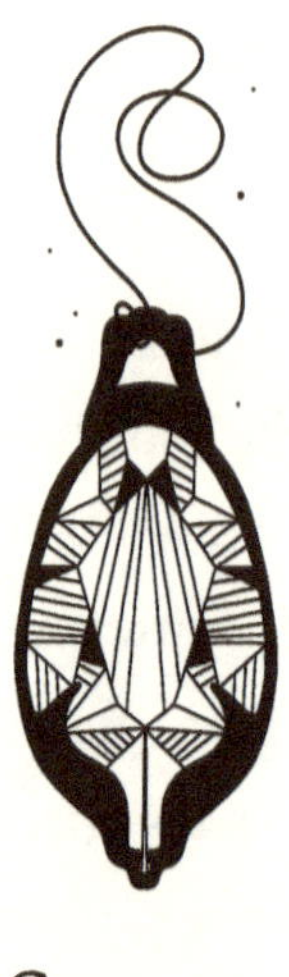

SEVEN

Returning to Maze was like traveling back in time, the echoes of the past permeating the air. A Christmas tree with rainbow decorations and silver bows stood beside the mantle. Drew's painting still hung on the wall above the fireplace. The silhouette of a girl sitting on a swing suspended from the trees was the focal point. A woman's shadow floated above, holding up the broken rope, keeping her safe. The painting had been a vision that flowed from Drew's mind to her brush one rainy Saturday night. She didn't control where the brush strokes took her, and never analyzed it before, but with Gran's death, the image held significance. The painting symbolized her hope for a mother's love and security. Gran was the closest she ever came to experiencing that relationship, and now she was gone.

Her phone vibrated with a message from her dad saying he'd left Gran's house. She pictured the door closing behind him, leaving the emptiness of a home without Gran, where the silence was too loud.

A server guided her past the fireplace, Piper trailing close behind. A handful of customers were spread out among the tables in the large space. The pizza oven behind the deli counter was bustling as an employee placed a pan in the oven and wiped his hands with a bar towel. The sweet, tangy smell of cheese and tomatoes made her stomach growl.

As she took her seat at the table next to Piper, a burst of laughter came from the big booth at the back of the room. She spotted Nico with a girl seated among the group; the girl in the Instagram post—Nicki. She had been a player on the basketball team for Atlas Cliffs High. Gran had pushed Drew to try out for the team, but she'd always lacked coordination and never had an interest in sports. Her heart raced as she hid behind the menu.

Observing her reaction, Piper glanced at the table. "I take it you don't want to go say hello?"

"Nope. Want to share a pizza?"

"Sure. You choose the toppings; I like them all." Piper flipped the menu over and set it on the table. "He's not that into her."

"Of course he is. Look at them." She peeked over the menu as Nicki draped her arm over Nico's shoulders. She used to be the one who could get close to him and put her arms around him. God, she missed him.

"I am looking at them, and I'm telling you I don't see it. He's got one picture up of the two of them, and it wasn't taken that long ago. They haven't been together long, Drew. I think he started dating her to get over you."

Feeling ridiculous for hiding, Drew lowered the menu. She was bound to run into him while she was home. She had to focus on giving Gran the memorial she deserved, being vigilant in case the Reaper showed up again, and figuring out the situation with Ori.

As if sensing her thoughts, the amulet warmed through her sweater, its heat seeping into her skin. Her hands reacted again with a burning sensation, and she rubbed them together.

What's happening to me?

Piper was staring at Drew's neck. "Why does it do that? You think Gran is controlling it or something?"

"I wish I knew. She told me it's for protection."

"Okay, so you've seen—what did you call him?"

"Reaper." Drew hugged the menu like a security blanket she couldn't let go of, providing her with a barrier as she glanced again at the group in the corner.

"You've seen him twice, right? Maybe he's like Jack—scary at first, but turns out to be cool?"

The Reaper's gray, veiny face popped into her head, and she looked around the room, almost hearing his wrathful voice.

Witch.

"He's nothing like Jack, Piper. Trust me."

"How do you get rid of him?"

"The first time Ori scared him away, but other than that... I'm working on it," she said, sighing.

Heels clacking on the tiled floor overshadowed the low hum of chatter in the room. Claudia marched between the tables in their direction. "Drew! I'm so sorry about your grandmother!" She sat in one of the empty seats and leaned into Drew, giving her a side hug. Releasing her, she unbuttoned her pink wool coat and crossed her legs, the flames from the fireplace reflecting off her shiny black boots. "I heard you were home," she continued, tilting her head to the side. Her red lips pouted, and perfectly groomed brows creased together. "I'm just so sorry."

"Thanks. It still doesn't feel real; I keep expecting her to be there when I go home." Drew pushed the menu off to the side as tears filled her eyes. She blinked fast and wiped them away as anxiety rolled through her like the ocean swells in a storm battering the cliffs.

Piper's eyes mirrored her own, and Claudia patted both of their hands the way an elderly adult would. "What can I do to help?"

"There's nothing anyone can do, really," Drew said. "I'll just figure it out as I go."

Another burst of laughter came from the group in the back, and she couldn't help stealing another look. When Nico's eyes met hers, a wave of heat rose to her cheeks and she looked away, breaking the connection. Regret settled in her empty stomach as she struggled to remember why she'd broken up with him.

I wanted to figure out what I wanted, but all that did was bring me right back to him.

Claudia leaned forward with her elbows on the table and pointed toward Nico. "They haven't been together long, a month maybe. She works with me at my mother's real estate firm, Tate Realty."

"Tate? Who is that?" Drew had never heard the name before, and Atlas Cliffs wasn't that big.

Claudia sat back in her chair, swinging her leg. "You're looking at her. Mom, my brother, and I changed our names to Mom's maiden one. We had a little party and opened a bottle of the most expensive champagne the asshole had in his cellar.

I will not walk through life with my ex-father's name." She flashed a sly smile at Drew as she nodded to where Nico and Nicki sat. "Speaking of names, that's the only thing cute about those two."

Blushing, Drew picked up the menu again and pretended to study it. "I remember her from school. I'm happy for him." The truthfulness of her words surprised her. She *wanted* him to be happy, even if seeing him with someone other than her caused her heart to sink.

Claudia crossed her arms, eyeing her. "Why did you break up with him, anyway? I mean, the two of you were inseparable for years until Shane came along. You found your way back to each other, and next thing I know, you're off to California and Nico is left behind with his heart trampled on."

"Jesus." Piper glared at Claudia. "Drew had her reasons and they're none of your business."

"I'm happy to hear you haven't lost your charm." Claudia rolled her eyes as she shot a piercing look at Piper. "She clearly still likes him, and if I can help, I will. Drew, if you want details, I've got you covered. Unlike both of you and most of our grad class, I didn't abandon this town. I'm sticking around with my mother to rebuild what my ass of a father ruined. We've got big plans."

"Thanks, Claudia, but I don't want details. Let it go," Drew shifted in her seat. Claudia had always known the town gossip, but she'd be all too willing to spread it, and the last thing Drew wanted was to be the subject of that gossip.

Piper shook her jacket off and pushed the sleeves of her black sweater up, revealing a stack of beaded bracelets. "Anything we need to know, we'll find out ourselves."

"You say that now, Piper," Claudia smirked, and stood. "I'm here to pick up a pizza, and I see it's ready."

Sitting in Maze with Piper and Claudia bickering was like old times. She'd rather sit here all night than go back to her empty home, despite enduring Nico and his new girlfriend sitting close and laughing.

A server sauntered to their table, holding a square box with steam billowing from the sides. He handed the box to Claudia, who sat back as he took their order. His golden-brown skin flushed as if he'd been running, but Drew followed his gaze and realized he was smiling at Piper. He appeared to be around the same age, but she didn't recognize him. As he shifted his stance, she spotted the name tag on the Maze logo shirt he was wearing.

Taj.

"I'm Piper. I don't think we've met." Piper's bracelets clanged on the table as she lifted a hand and twirled a strand of pink hair around her finger before releasing it. He took Piper's hand and introduced himself before walking away.

Claudia placed the pizza box on the table. "Still not interested to know what I know, Piper?"

"What, like you know him?" Piper asked.

Claudia put her gloves on, adjusting each finger of the smooth leather as she talked. "They moved to town in September. His mother opened a store downtown, Little Mysteries. Their last name is Locke, and as you can see, he's hot." She clapped her hands together and stood, plucking the pizza box off the table. She turned to Drew and said, "If you need anything, let me know. I've got to run." She threw a wave over her shoulder as she strutted toward the doors.

Drew finally understood why Claudia had stayed in Atlas Cliffs after her father went to jail. Claudia had transformed into a fierce businesswoman, aging a decade in a single year, and her confidence sure hadn't taken a beating.

They finished eating and paid the bill, Piper chattering to Taj the entire time. Drew scooted her chair back and zipped up her jacket. Taj tucked a pen behind his ear, where it peeked out from underneath his tight curls. Captivated by Piper's animated conversation, he walked with them toward the doors. She gave Drew a meaningful glance, making it clear she'd be close behind.

Drew had no desire to rush home, but she didn't want to cross paths with Nico and his girlfriend, so she hurried outside. She breathed in the night's crisp air. Lights twinkled and sparkled across the restaurants and stores, and festive wreaths decorated the doors. The tragedy of death and her inner despair were almost tangible in stark contrast.

Gran had draped the porch with lights, too. When she got home, the lights would be on, another painful reminder that she was gone. This would be the first time she would spend a holiday without Gran. The piercing ache of grief had her full stomach churning.

"I'm sorry about Gran."

Her skin prickled with electricity when she heard his voice. Nico was standing in front of her when she spun around. He'd changed since the last time she'd seen him; he was taller, and his broad frame dominated the space in front of her. Rubbing the hint of stubble on his face, he locked his compassionate eyes with hers. An overwhelming desire to grab him, hold him close and never let go hit her—but she resisted. Maybe it was guilt from hurting him, or the fact he had a girlfriend now, but she told herself she had to move on.

She stifled the longing need for his friendship and tried to speak, but the words stuck in her throat. "Thank you," she said, softer than intended.

He stepped closer, and for a split second, she thought he was going to hug her. Her breath caught as she froze, but the door swung open, and his girlfriend strode up beside him and the moment was over. Piper rushed through the doors behind her and positioned herself next to Drew.

Nicki expressed her sympathies as she talked about how much her family adored Gran's butterscotch pie. She was one of those natural, stunning-without-makeup girls, and when she glanced up at Nico, the adoration was all over her face. "Ready to go? I'm freezing," she said, tucking her hands into the sleeves of her jacket.

The doors opened, and the rest of the group from the table spilled out onto the sidewalk. Nicki joined the group, but Nico didn't budge, and neither did Drew. Piper gave Drew's hand a squeeze before she moved toward the alley, which led to the parking lot. Despite being alone, Drew could sense Nicki watching them.

"I'm coming to her memorial." Nico's gaze held hers like a magnet. A spark darted through her.

He's moved on with someone else. Let him go!

"I feel like I'll walk into the house, and she'll be singing in the kitchen or sitting in her chair. I'm on autopilot right now, with no clue what to do next."

"You're not supposed to know, and that's okay." He looked around before turning his deep brown eyes back to hers. "I'm not sure if you knew, but I was at her house the day before she died to drop off groceries. She seemed off, but when I asked if she was sick or needed a doctor, she laughed and said it was nothing a hot toddy couldn't fix." His charming dimple appeared on his cheek as he smiled, making his face light up for a moment. "If I could've made her come with me that day. Maybe she—"

"Don't do that to yourself. You know Gran. How do you think it would've gone if you tried to tell her what to do?" She looked down as tears rolled over her cheeks. She'd give anything to have Gran back, but bringing the dead back to life wasn't in her realm of ability.

He closed the gap between them, surprising her. "Jesus, Drew, come here."

He embraced her. Tight. She hugged him back, feeling the warmth of his body against hers. She breathed him in, and the scent of his cologne triggered a flood of memories from their time together. Thoughts of kissing on the beach and lounging on Gran's porch swing while he strummed on a guitar. He had stayed with her after the accident with Dominic when she couldn't stand being in her own skin. Every muscle in her body relaxed in his arms and, for the first time all week, she found comfort.

As he pulled away, the crisp, winter air replaced the smell of his subtle cologne. Her muscles tensed again as the weight of Gran's loss settled back on her shoulders.

Nicki's voice echoed down the street as she called out Nico's name, waiting by his truck.

"I'll see you soon," he said.

He walked away with his hands in his pockets, the sound of their goodbyes lingering in the air.

EIGHT

Drew pulled her hood up and raced through the alleyway next to Maze. The smell of exhaust was thick in the air as Piper waited for her by their cars—the only two cars left in the small parking lot.

"What did he say?" Piper said.

"He's sad about Gran and he's coming to her memorial." Drew unlocked her car door and climbed into the driver's seat.

Starting the engine, she grabbed a snowbrush from the back seat.

"See? He cares about you. That thing he's got going with Nicki isn't serious."

Drew got out and stomped around the car, clearing the snow away. "Piper, he's a good guy and we've known each other for years. He was just being nice, and I don't like him like that anymore. I just miss his friendship, that's all." She cleared the remaining snow from the windshield before tossing the brush inside the car. She wanted to curl up in a ball and cry but leaned against the car instead. "I'm going to get through these next few weeks, do what needs to be done, and get back to Boston."

"I call bullshit," Piper said. "This is me you're talking to. I know you aren't over him. But I've got you, okay? I'm sticking around until after the winter break. Your dad is here for you, too." Piper gave her a quick hug and stepped back. "You're not alone. Let's go home before we freeze to death and turn into one of your ghosts."

The night air stilled, feeling like a sudden deep freeze, and despite the warmth from the vents, the car windows frosted over with intricate snowflakes. The amulet warmed against her chest and the palms of her hands burned. She spun around, her eyes darting back and forth as she tried to figure out who was coming. What if the Reaper had found her?

Fog curled by the alleyway. She glanced through the shadows, expecting the Reaper to appear. "We need to leave."

"What's going on?"

She grabbed Piper's arm as Ori emerged from the mist. With each step, his human form became more defined, and his T-shirt and jeans remained unscathed from the snow and cold. She clutched the amulet, still emanating heat. The burning sensation in her hands subsided and turned into a tingling sensation. Ori's approach caused a sudden shift in the air, like the release of pressure during a plane's landing. The intricate ice-artwork on the windows disappeared, and the car engines ebbed and flowed as a fan kicked on. Piper turned hers off and held the keys in a fist as she stood beside Drew, staring in the same direction.

"Is the dead guy here?" Piper's breaths puffed into the air.

"She knows I have a name, right?" Ori said, pushing his blond hair away from his deathly pale face—the one part of him that never looked human.

The scrapes and scratches appeared brighter than usual, prompting thoughts of him lying on the pavement, broken as the life left his limp body. "Where have you been? I haven't seen you in days and thought something happened to you. I was worried."

Ori strode in front of her and smiled. "That might be the sweetest thing you've ever said to me. Tell Piper I say hello."

"Can he see me?" Piper reached forward, trying to touch what she couldn't see.

"He says hello," Drew said.

"Is he cute?"

"Seriously, Piper?"

"Dead serious. Is it weird to ask that?"

She'd never looked at Ori like that before. Death was a significant barrier, but even if he was alive, they didn't have that sort of relationship.

Ori reached for her face. "Let me show you what I've seen."

She took a step back, her stomach in knots as she feared what he was about to reveal. "I don't like this. Just tell me."

"It doesn't work that way, and you know it." He sighed, shaking his head. "This is different from last time; it won't break your heart. But it's important."

"How'd you know he'd broken my heart? Did you know him?"

He ran a pale hand through his blond hair. "I just knew you cared about that guy, and he'd hurt you. This won't be the same."

"You need to fill a person in over here." Piper waved from behind her.

"I'll explain after. Just don't freak out if you see anything weird." Drew positioned herself in front of Ori, expecting the zap of electricity that always shot through her when he put his hands on her face.

The familiar metallic taste filled her mouth, and she swallowed, her throat burning. With his hands on her face, the vision began. She ambled through the forest at Haven until she came to the clearing by the water's edge. A kaleidoscope of blues and greens whirled between the trees—like a portal to another world. She inched closer until she could place her hand inside. Icy needles ran along her arm, and she yanked it back, out of the swirling window into the unknown. A shadow moved on the other side, coming nearer and nearer. Screams resounded from a dark abyss until they penetrated her soul. Dark gray smoke circled the shadow until it crossed into the forest through the kaleidoscope where she stood. The Reaper charged at her, and she fell back away from Ori with a gasp, landing against the hard metal of her car. A murmur echoed in her head.

Death seeks you.

She crouched down, balancing on bent knees, breathing the cold air into her burning lungs.

Piper offered her a hand, and she grabbed hold of it, rising to her feet. "I'm going to need a debrief of what just happened."

Drew stumbled over her words, shivering as she tried to describe what she'd seen under Ori's hands. "It looked like... an opening into another world, but it was Haven."

Piper stood next to her car, oblivious to Ori, who was right beside her. "Maybe it's not real, Drew."

"It's real." Ori bent down and tried to pick up snow, but his human shape was fading, making it impossible.

"Was it like the place where the ghost girl, Enid, and her brother went? You never saw it, did you?" Piper said.

Enid's name evoked memories of the year before. Enid and Ezra had faded into the same invisible realm as Iris. The moment they'd crossed the unseen veil between the living and dead had been an all-consuming gentleness. It had left her breathless, like a gust of warm air in the middle of a snowstorm. Peace had covered her skin in the softness of a thousand flower petals. The life of a steady heartbeat had thrummed in her ears, drowning out the chaos in her head. The dead went to that place, and it had been the same place Gran had gone in her dream. Ori's vision was not the same at all. A sudden awareness hit her as she glanced at Ori. His time to leave would come as well. Letting go of her friendships with the dead was the most painful part.

Unless the Reaper wins, and I end up on the dead side with him.

Piper moved beside her. "You okay?"

"Whatever is at Haven is very different, Piper. It's dark and angry... and the Reaper. He's like a..."

"Demon? Devil man? Warlock? Lucifer?"

"Is your friend a Supernatural fan?" Ori asked. "It was a good show. I miss television."

"That stuff isn't real. I don't believe in devils or demons. At least I didn't." Drew shrugged. "The Reaper, he's sinister, like a vengeful spirit."

"What does he want revenge for?" Piper cupped her hands and breathed into them before stuffing them into her jacket pockets. "Can he actually hurt you? Are you in danger? What should we do?"

Ori walked around the car. "You need to get in your cars and drive before you're out of gas. That's what you should do."

Drew glanced between Ori and an oblivious Piper, wishing there was a way she could hear and see Ori. "We drive home before we run out of gas. Ori's words."

"I like those words. I'm freezing!" Piper exclaimed.

Ori held his hands up as they faded into a translucent film. "Shit, here we go again. It's your mother, Drew. Figure this out for me, will you? What's her deal? And why me?" A glow surrounded him as he spun into a mist. He cursed as he faded away, a cloud of vapor lingering in his wake.

She'd never be ready to face Joelle. *Never.* But something told her the choice wasn't going to end up hers to make.

"Did he say something? You're staring." Piper scanned the open space around her.

"He had to go. It's my mother again."

"Your mother? Is she here in Atlas Cliffs?" Piper hesitated. "Is she *dead?*"

"She's not dead." Drew opened the car door, pausing. It had never occurred to her that Joelle could be near Ori because she was dead. "That's impossible. I'd know if she was dead; Ori would know." Imagining Joelle gone forever gave her a sick feeling. Therapy helped her understand her anger toward her mother for leaving, even if letting it go was harder. She'd abandoned any hope of salvaging the relationship a long time ago, but never wished her mother would die.

Piper narrowed her eyes at Drew's neck. "Something's moving inside that stone!"

Magnetic energy tingled in her hands as Drew's fingers curled around the amulet, holding it up. A spark of light shone from the center, as fine lines curved and crawled like roots spreading into the ground. Gran had advised her to wear it for protection, but more than ever, she needed to discover the amulet's secrets.

"Look at your hands, Drew. Do you think it's... *Gran?*"

"I don't know what it is." Drew tucked the amulet under the neck of her sweater, extinguishing the light from view as she scanned the parking lot for Gran. It was empty and quiet except for the two streetlights at each side and the steady hum of the vehicle's engines. "There's no way I'm dragging you into any of this." She sat in the driver's seat, and heat enveloped her like a sauna. "Let's go home before we've got no gas left to get there."

Piper held the frame of the car door open. "Let's get something straight. You're my best friend. We're family, Drew. Got it? Because I don't think you do. When shit goes down, you better always drag me into it. *Always*. I'll see you at your house." Before Drew could respond, she shut the door and climbed into her own car. With a wave and a smile, she headed for the street.

As Drew exhaled, a weight lifted off her shoulders, and tears welled in her eyes. There was comfort in knowing that, at least for tonight, she wouldn't have to face the emptiness of her house alone.

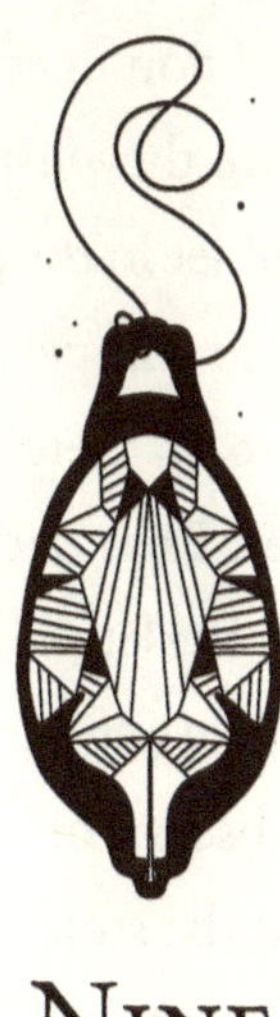

NINE

Piper followed Drew into the kitchen and wandered around, looking at Gran's trinkets and cookbooks. "It really is strange being in this house without her."

"It's brutal. I wish she'd come around and talk to me. I miss her."

Piper leaned against the swinging door leading into the den off the kitchen and peered in. Drew stood next to her. "That's where she died," Drew whispered, choking back more tears. "I've sat in there for hours talking to her, hoping she'd show up. But nothing happens. I don't get it."

"Does it take time before they visit? After someone dies, I mean?" Piper sat on the glider in the corner.

"I don't have anything to compare it to. No one I've been this close to has died before, so there's not really a time frame. It's that dream I had, Piper. That was *real*. I have this to prove it." Lifting the silver chain, she let the black stone dangle in the air. This time, the amulet held a stillness that was both calming and unsettling. Did the absence of vines and light mean she was not in danger? Or did the stoic state suggest a threat was waiting for her? "Gran gave me this necklace to protect me."

"From what? The Reaper?"

"That's what I need to find out." Drew padded around the small den. The tall oval clock against the wall was eerily still, its hands frozen in place on the weathered face at eleven minutes past eleven. The pendulum no longer swung back and forth. She couldn't remember when it had stopped working. The chimes had never worked. She tapped the glass casing and ran her hand over the smooth surface. Butterfly shaped corners complimented the vines and flowers engraved in the wooden frame. Gran loved this clock, and the more she studied it, the more she could see why. It was art.

"What is it?" Piper said.

"The clock is broken."

Piper rose from the chair and stared at the clock. "You could get it fixed or sell it."

"Sell it?" She glanced around the room. "I'll have to get rid of Gran's things, won't I? And the house! What will happen to the house?" Panic rose, clawing at her insides on its way to her throat. Without Gran to hold everything together, her home was slipping away like sand through her fingers.

Piper turned her away from the clock. "You don't have to do anything you're not ready for. It's going to work out." She glanced around her toward the cabinet on the opposite wall. "Do you like wine?"

"What?"

Piper strode up to the cabinet and opened the glass doors. She pulled out a bottle of Gran's favorite red wine and spun around. "I say we have a toast for Gran."

"I don't know how long that's been there—"

"Trust me, wine gets better with age—my mom is like a connoisseur, or something. She never notices when I take a bottle from her stash." Piper turned over the black bottle, displaying its white label and red lettering. "If Gran liked it, I'm sure it's good. Come on, Drew. What do you think?"

Gran would tell her to take a load off and have a glass after reminding her the drinking age was eighteen in Ireland. And the holidays were coming. "There's a corkscrew in the drawer."

Piper trailed her into the kitchen. Handing her a corkscrew, Piper opened the bottle in no time. They lifted their glasses with care to avoid spilling the burgundy contents.

"Cheers to Gran," Piper said. "The most loving, sweetest woman I've ever met."

"To Gran. May we meet again soon." Sipping the silky wine, Drew blinked away tears. She inhaled the sweet cherry aroma as the liquid slid down her throat, bringing with it a comforting warmth that spread through her. With every sip, her freckled cheeks grew hotter, and she still couldn't determine if she liked it or not.

"Your Gran had good taste." Piper refilled Drew's glass and topped up her own before they headed into the living room and plopped on the sofa.

Colorful lights twinkled on the porch outside, but for the first time, the corner was bare where a Christmas tree should be. "She'd have a tree up by now. It'd be the one no one else wanted, and she'd somehow feel like she'd done something good."

"We can get a tree. That's easy." Piper set her phone down on the coffee table and turned on her usual alternative rock music, keeping the volume low.

"I don't know, Piper. I don't think I'll do Christmas this year." She gulped the rest of her drink and put the empty glass on the side table. The fire had burned down to a bed of bright orange coals; the warmth from it and the wine left her sleepy.

"It sucks right now, but you are going to get through this. Just like you've gotten through all the other shit. *Not alone.* Gran wouldn't want you to be sad and lonely during the holidays, so we're going to make sure that doesn't happen." Piper pulled her fuzzy pink-and-black striped socks up over her leggings. The vibrant pink matched her hair and the cashmere sweater she wore. Gran would have loved those socks, and Drew would've made it her mission to find a pair for her stocking.

"Are you taking more time before going back to school? It might be a good idea. I can stick around a bit longer if you need me to." Piper said.

"I hadn't even thought about school. I'll just see how it goes. You don't need to stay; you'd miss too much."

"Nothing I can't catch up on. I'm not in a hurry to go back. Taj's band is playing at Maze Friday night and he's saving the table by the stage for me. I want you to come too." Piper held her hand up. "Before you say no—you've got good reasons, I know you do—I'm not letting you lock yourself away in sadness. Gran wouldn't want that for you, and you know it.

After these next few days, you'll need some Piper in your life. You've got a lot going on, Drew. I've got you."

Preparing for Gran's funeral and the upcoming meeting with the lawyer had been weighing on her, but memories of the fun and freedom of their California trip flooded her mind. "Okay. Count me in."

"Stop! That's all it took?"

"If Taj is in the band, you'll need a wing-woman," she said as Piper's face lit up with a daydream smile. "I've got you too. That's all I'm saying."

Piper swirled the wine in her glass, the smooth liquid coating the sides before sliding to the bottom. She gulped the last bit and set her glass down. "You ever feel like you're never the best at anything?"

Drew laughed. "Have we just met? All the time. Every day. What's going on?"

"My parents want me to be this big city defense lawyer. Like, wear a pantsuit and high heels and dye my hair a 'reasonable color.'" Piper's hands performed air quotes as she rolled her eyes.

"Lawyers can have pink hair and wear combat boots," Drew said, fighting a smile.

"Come on. Not that kind."

"Maybe you'll be the first. Start a trend. If I ever need a lawyer, you'd be my first call."

"Don't say that." Piper paused, then grinned. "You do live an exciting life, it might not be so far-fetched. But trust me, you wouldn't want me to defend you. I'm not that good! Probably near the bottom of my class."

"My life isn't exciting. It's chaotic."

"It's an adventure. The way life's supposed to be."

In Drew's eyes, Piper could do anything. Since they'd met, she had always been her biggest defender. Selling herself short wasn't her style. "What if your parents' opinion didn't matter and you could do anything? What would that be?"

Piper fidgeted with her tiny, heart-studded eyebrow ring. "I'd be a lawyer, but not the kind they want me to be. I'd be pro bono. Help people who need it. I hate the mentality that if you have a shit ton of money, you can buy freedom even if you're a criminal."

"You could be a big city defense lawyer for people fighting against the rich criminals."

"Maybe. But only if I can have pink hair and wear combat boots." Piper smiled.

"I like it. That's the only kind of lawyer I want in my life."

"Right?" Piper laughed.

Perhaps the alcohol was to blame, but Piper's unrestrained laughter was contagious. Drew crumbled into laughter along with her, feeling lighter than she had in days... *weeks*.

Why didn't she have more fun? She was almost nineteen, not ninety. Not that ninety-year-olds didn't have any fun; Gran would've had a blast if she lived until one hundred and nineteen. Guilt for letting herself have a moment of happiness when she should be grieving hit her, and she reached for the amulet. It warmed against her skin, sending the prickling sensation through her palms again. She rubbed her hands together, scratching her palms.

"Are you allergic to something?" Piper said. "My mom might have a cream for that."

"Not that I know of." She held her hands, revealing a faint blue light emitting from them. "Does this look like an allergic reaction?"

Piper's face beamed, and she grabbed Drew's hands. "Sure doesn't! This is just cool!"

"It's not cool at all. It's been happening ever since Gran gave me the amulet."

Piper turned off the music. She pushed her sleeves up and sat cross-legged on the sofa, bracelets clanging as she did so. "Turn around and face me."

Piper was relentless when determination took over, so Drew did as she asked. Her curiosity got the better of her, too. "What are you going to do?"

Piper took Drew's hands, turning them so her palms faced upward. "Yoga."

"Yoga? Piper, I've never done yoga in my life." This might be a little out there, even for Piper.

"Mom goes to yoga classes, and I went with her twice before I realized yoga and I just don't mix. I can't stop thinking about everything and anything else. There's just no shutting down my brain." Piper tucked her hair behind her ears and made animated hand gestures as she spoke. "We did this thing where we put our hands together like this." She put her palms and fingers together. "It's supposed to, I don't know, channel your energy or something."

Drew glanced at her hands and back to Piper. "Energy. Got it." She mirrored Piper and placed her hands together. "Now what?"

"Close your eyes, and wait, I guess."

Seconds felt like minutes as they sat in silence. Nothing happened. A sneeze was on the verge of erupting as her nose itched. Her arms grew heavy. A ticking resounded from the other room, and she dropped her hands.

"Did anything happen?" Letting her hands fall to her lap, Piper opened her eyes.

Drew rose from the sofa. "Nothing happened, but do you hear that?"

"Hear what?"

Drew burst into the den and flipped the light on. She stared into the face of the grandfather clock. The second hand was moving. "Piper, what time is it?"

"Eleven-eleven, to the minute. Why?" Piper called out from the living room.

The time on Gran's antique clock had stopped and started again at the same time. Her hands tingled, and she held them up to the clock. The hands inside changed from gold to bright blue.

"Gran? Are you around?" Drew whispered into the air, but there was no reply.

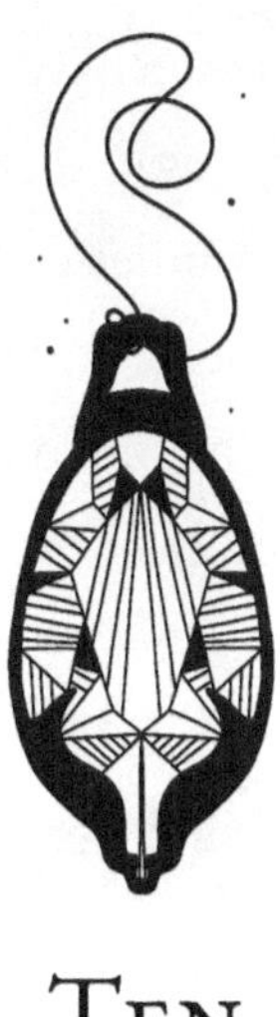

TEN

Drew sat in the front seat of her father's truck as they led the slow procession of cars to her house. The funeral director followed them to deliver a last goodbye before they released Gran's ashes to the sea—her wishes as written in her will. She still hadn't spoken to the lawyer about the rest of Gran's estate; that would come next. She dreaded it all. The sadness was a deep break she couldn't mend, and she didn't think she'd be able to get through the day without falling apart. She was defenseless against grief's power to knock her down whenever it wanted. She would have given anything for another minute with Gran and was desperate to see her again. Her fingers moved across the amulet concealed below her shirt's neckline. Tears burned her eyes and ran over her cheeks when she squeezed them tight. She rested her head against the window, hating how bright and clear the sky was today, of all days.

Where are you, Gran?

She stood beside Nellie and her father on the cliffs across the street overlooking Jupiter Cove, the chill of the winter air biting at her cheeks. The offshore wind collided with the ocean's breeze and filtered through her wool coat to her skin. A small group of Gran's friends sniffled as they dabbed their eyes and noses with tissues. Locals who had known Gran through the Tough Cookie arrived to pay their respects. Claudia and her mother stood together with matching leopard print scarves and long black coats. Shipyard staff and fishers passed by her dad, patting him on the back to offer condolences. Piper broke away from the group and ran across the sand to Drew's side.

As they made their way down to the beach, Drew glimpsed Nico. The entire time she'd known him, the only time she ever saw him dressed up was for prom. He appeared to be oblivious to her staring at him, so she kept her gaze fixed on him, a comforting sight warring with her inner turmoil. The knot of his tie was visible from under his casual jacket and his dress shoes left deep footprints, kicking sand up as he proceeded down the beach with the others. She knew it would take every ounce of willpower for him to leave his shoes on and not walk in his bare feet; she knew him better than she knew herself in some ways. It took everything in her to not run and hug him.

The funeral director waited for everyone to gather, while his attendant stood next to him, holding Gran's ashes in a cylinder-shaped scattering tube. With his glasses at the tip of his nose, the director looked down at a piece of paper in his hands, and recited, "I am the shadow that dances on the edge of your vision..." His voice carried over the loud surf as he kept reading until the end. When he was done, he removed his shoes and socks, and moved closer to the water. "Maddie will forever be in the sunshine, the wind, the stars, and now she will be part of the earth." He nodded to Drew—the cue to join him.

With her stomach in knots and her eyes and nose running, she followed her dad to where the waves lapped the cold sand. If she was going to do this, she'd do it right. She unzipped her boots, stuffing her socks inside them, and pulled the legs of her pants up to her knees. Her father hugged her before she took the urn from the director's gloved hands. She turned it over, admiring the garden of flowers and butterflies painted on the tube. Gran had arranged for her death down to the last detail.

She used to talk about returning to the earth when she passed away. Drew had laughed at her words, never thinking they'd come back to haunt her.

As her last goodbye, with hot tears trickling over her cheeks, she brushed her fingers over the tube and hugged it to her chest, her legs quivering as she stepped into the icy water. Her feet numbed to her ankles as the waves tugged at her, trying to pull her into the ocean depths. The sky transitioned from blue to pink as twilight descended, and she shivered, walking deeper into the frigid water. Facing the endless ocean, she glanced at her father, who gave a nod to let her know he was ready. It was at that moment she locked eyes with Nico standing on the beach where she'd left her boots. He was the eye of the hurricane. He held her with his gaze, bringing the familiar, comforting calmness like a superpower only he possessed. She ventured further into the icy water until it almost reached her hips.

Gran was gone. She ignored the pain of losing the woman who had raised her and focused on holding the tube at waist height, noting the wind's direction. A burst of mist swirled through her hair, spinning like a funnel cloud. She tilted the urn and let the tornado-like mist carry Gran's essence out to sea.

"You've got wings now, Gran. Don't forget about me." The warmth of the amulet soothed her chilled skin. If Gran had crossed over to the other side, like Enid and Ezra, she might never see or talk to her again. The dream might have been her last goodbye.

Trembling, she cradled the empty urn and stumbled back to shore, where Piper greeted her with a blanket and an embrace that could cure depression. "I love you, girl," she said.

People hugged her father and expressed their sympathies as they headed up the steps toward the road. She handed him the urn as he invited the small group left to join him at Gran's house. With shaking hands, she buttoned her jacket and pushed her wet pant legs down to her ankles as Nico approached, carrying her boots.

Piper raised squeezed her arm as she stepped away. "I'll be up at the house."

Nico held onto her boots as he stood in front of her. "If there's something I can do to keep you from falling apart, will you tell me what it is? Because I know you're having a tough time, but I don't know how to help like I used to. It's been a while, and things have... changed." He shifted his gaze from the ocean and back to her. His brown eyes glistened under his thick lashes.

He could connect with her soul like nobody else, something she had forgotten. She could chalk it up to kindness, but they had a long enough history for her to know better. "Just being here helps. It means a lot to me you came." As she took the boots from him, their fingers touched. She hesitated, letting her skin hold contact with his as goosebumps ran along her cold skin. This time, the tingling sensation had nothing to do with the amulet or her hands, and everything to do with Nico.

He put his hands in his pockets. "I had to be here for you. Maddie was the best. I can't believe she's gone."

"You and me both." She tried to balance on one foot to put her socks on and tripped, but Nico caught her before she hit the sand. Her heart thumped erratically, like a pinball bouncing around a machine, and her cheeks flushed with a sudden warmth. "You're soaked and freezing. Here," he said, holding her steady, "put your boots on and I'll walk you up."

She broke out in a sweat under her layers, not feeling the cold anymore. Nico held her steady with his warm hands as she struggled to pull on her socks and boots. Part of her yearned to turn around and kiss him, and the other wanted to run away to escape the overwhelming emotions. God, she missed him more than she thought possible. How could she have let him go?

"Do you want to come to the house with me? Gran's friends brought food, and Dad invited people... You don't have to, though."

"I'm supposed to..." He looked at his phone and tucked it in his back pocket. "Sure. I'll come in for a bit."

She didn't know who was on the other end of his phone, but she was grateful he stayed by her side. It brought her comfort, even though it probably didn't mean anything. As she climbed the stairs up the cliffside to the road, his steady footsteps followed close behind, matching her own rhythm. They'd been apart for so long. Being with him again ignited a spark of passion and nostalgia that sank into her bones.

Eleven

A row of vehicles lined the road to her house. Snow blanketed the yard, and smoke curled out of the chimney. Gran had taken care to wrap the cedars in their usual burlap slumber for the winter. The sight of the burlap caused the finality to hit her. Gran wouldn't be around to care for her garden again. Ever. Another wave of gut-wrenching sadness swept over her as she surveyed the rest of the front yard. The porch swing sat still and unused, with paint flaking off the wooden railing. This weathered Cape Cod house had been her haven since childhood. She couldn't imagine a time this wouldn't be home anymore.

Saying goodbye to Gran and the life she had here in Atlas Cliffs was going to be the most difficult thing she'd ever do, but with Gran gone, there were no other options.

As if he sensed her heartbreak, Nico stopped walking as they headed up the driveway. "Do you need a minute before you go in?"

"Can we turn around and hang out on the beach until everyone leaves?"

"Want to go for a winter surf?" He glanced toward the beach. "It's been a while, hasn't it?"

"Sure has." She sighed hard as she glanced toward the beach, wanting nothing more than to suit up and go in the water with Nico. "But it's expected of me to go in there and see people, so I've been told."

"I think you got the wrong advice." He smiled at her. "But we can go in together. Let's do this." He stepped up to the porch and waited for her to open the door.

He hadn't lost the calming effect he had on her, but all it did was make her want him more.

The daisy-covered welcome mat lay crooked on the porch, revealing something gleaming from underneath. She crouched and lifted the mat. Colorful stones were arranged in a line, resembling those at the Tough Cookie. The nagging feeling that Gran knew something returned, making her uneasy. Who else would've placed stones in a row? She couldn't make sense of it.

"What is it?" Nico asked.

She replaced the mat, straightening it back in place. "Nothing. Let's go inside."

As she entered the front door into the foyer, the sound of hushed conversations filled the air. Warmth from the fireplace drifted from the living room. Her gaze lingered on the empty space at the top of the stairs, and a dull ache settled inside her. She took a deep breath, bracing herself for the unknown challenges in the days ahead.

Her head was spinning from the endless rounds of condolences. Losing Nico in the crowded room, she spotted Piper carrying several mugs of hot coffee and tea. Overwhelm crept through her body as a headache throbbed and sweat beaded along her hairline, her mouth going dry.

"Do you want to go sit somewhere?" Nico appeared at her side with a glass of something pink filled with ice cubes. "Punch? There might be alcohol in it," he said, sniffing the contents of the glass.

Taking the glass from him, she devoured the cool drink, relief coursing through her as it soothed her parched throat.

The sweetness of strawberry and lemonade mixed with a bitter taste. "Definitely alcohol in it. Maybe it'll keep the anxiety away until everyone leaves."

"The den is empty. Your dad closed the door so no one would go in," he said.

She placed the empty glass on a nearby shelf. Her own living room had become suffocating. "Let's go."

Weaving between clusters of people, she followed Nico to the kitchen. She passed her father in conversation with the older couple who owned the local recreation center. Lines deepened between his eyebrows as he stood with his arms folded. He despised socializing and witnessing him hold the room so well made her appreciate him even more. They'd come a long way over the past year; she wouldn't have gotten through this week without him.

Gran's friends dabbed their eyes and reached for her, a barrage of questions thrown at her as they talked over each other, their brows furrowed with pity.

What will you do with the house?

The bakery?

Did you know Nellie is leaving town?

You poor dear...

The well-meaning words caged around her like a prison.

Piper marched into the room holding a tray of sandwiches, her short, pink ponytail bouncing with every step. "Question period is over. I think it's time to give Drew some space and eat a sandwich. Who made these cucumber delicacies?" She kissed her pinched fingers and thumb before tossing her hand away in a dramatic gesture as she placed the tray on the coffee table. On her way back to the kitchen, she took Drew with her. Nico tried to hide his smile of approval with his hand over his mouth as he followed behind them. Her father must've noticed too, because he stepped forward and took over the conversation, nodding to her as she walked away.

Piper pointed to the closed swinging door leading to the den. "Go ahead, both of you. Your dad's back there and I'm here. It's under control. I'll help him get everyone out of here soon."

Drew hugged her friend. "Thank you. Seriously, thank you."

The only source of light in the den was Gran's stained-glass butterfly lamp. The antique clock stood motionless, holding the time at eleven-eleven. She ran her hand over the varnished wood, thinking. The clock had been working when she'd checked first thing in the morning, but that was before eleven. What did it mean?

She shivered, her still-damp pants sticking to her legs. Taking a seat in the swivel rocking chair, she wrapped the quilt around her and ran her hands along the faded upholstery. Nico leaned against the doorframe, letting the door swing closed.

His stature filled the space more than it ever had before. He somehow made a wrinkled dress shirt, crooked tie, and messy hair look good.

Too good. Stop looking at him like that!

As heat rushed to her face and her heart raced, she fluffed her hair and pulled it forward to conceal her reddening skin. "Do you want to sit?" she asked.

He slid past the ottoman and settled on the cushioned bench seat against the window beside her. Leaning forward, he rested his elbows on his knees, so close she could touch him. Months earlier, she wouldn't have thought anything of it, but everything had changed. Everything except her longing for his arms around her again. And that wasn't a good thing to crave. Not anymore.

She shifted her weight in the chair, bringing one leg up and tucking her foot underneath herself. Piper's melodic voice rang out in the other room as she offered coats, encouraging those lingering to head home.

"She said she'd take care of it." Nico laughed.

"Taking care of stuff is one of her best qualities."

"It's one of yours, too." His brown eyes appeared golden as the lamplight reflected off them.

Her hands begged to touch his face, but she'd been good at resisting Nico in the short time she'd been home. "I'm not so sure about that."

"What will you do now? If it's too soon to ask, just say so. I just wondered if you'd be going back to Boston or sticking around after the holidays."

"Dad and I are going to meet with Gran's lawyer this week to sort things out. I don't know what to expect, you know? I'll figure it out."

He smiled at her, exposing his dimples, oblivious to his undeniable charm. "See? You take care of stuff. You'll have some decisions to make, but you've got this."

"I don't always get it right, Nico."

"Neither do I." He shifted in his seat, loosened his tie, and unfastened the top button of his shirt before taking a deep breath. "Never been a suit kind of guy."

"I know." She couldn't tear her gaze from his broad chest, remembering how he used to hold her.

Pull yourself together. He's with someone else now.

"It'll be about the house, and the bakery, money stuff," he said, his voice cutting into her thoughts. "What to expect at the lawyer's office, I mean. You'll have to decide what you want to do about Gran's estate. I remember Mom going through this when my grandfather died."

"That's what I'm worried about. Her entire life revolved around this house and the bakery. How do I know what the right thing to do is?"

"Okay, think about it this way. What's the worst that can happen?"

"That's easy. Selling this house means I'll be homeless." Drew's leg went numb, and she straightened it out in front of her. Lack of sleep from the past few days had caught up with her, and her body ached from exhaustion.

"Don't say that. Your dad won't let that happen. *You* won't let that happen."

"I don't know. He might have no choice. He's at sea most of the time, and I'm in school. And there's the Tough Cookie and Nellie's leaving and—"

"And you have options." He reached out and held her hand. The warmth from his hand coursed through her, and she closed her fingers around his. "Just do me a favor and don't decide anything too fast," he continued. "Really think about what you want. Promise me that. You can still go to school and keep your home." As if the sudden realization they were holding hands hit him, he pulled away. "Have you... *seen* her? Gran? Don't answer that. I shouldn't have asked. It was insensitive."

"Only the night she died. I had a dream about her. I knew she was gone before the phone call."

"That must've been awful. I'm so sorry, Drew."

She gripped the amulet, and intense heat caressed her palm. "I'm just glad I got to say goodbye."

"If there's anything I can do, or if you want to talk, I'm not far."

"Are you still at home? Or do you... have your own place now?" The idea of him living with Nicki made her cringe, but if they were going to be friends again, she needed to let go of these feelings.

Can I be his friend and nothing more?

"I'm still down the road, but I'm in the apartment above the garage instead of in the house. I get to be on my own, but the kitchen is just a few steps away."

"I miss your mom's cooking!" She could almost taste his mother's homemade spaghetti sauce. Family dinners at Nico's were like something out of a holiday movie. The massive dining room table engulfed the room, but no one gave it a second thought. His parents had welcomed Drew like a member of the family.

"Maybe you can come by for supper sometime."

Maybe we can be just friends.

"Maybe."

"It's been good seeing you again, Drew. I just wish it was for a different reason."

"Me too." Talking with him solidified how much she had missed his friendship, but if they were going to do this, she'd have to be okay with him seeing someone. "How long have you been seeing Nicki?"

His gaze darted away from her to his hands. "Um, just a couple of months."

The thought of Nico with someone else made her feel sick, but she'd been the one who had broken up with him, so she had to accept it. She *did* accept it. She *was* okay with it. She took a deep breath, repeating the phrase in her mind. It didn't help.

"I remember her from school." She didn't know what else to say.

He clasped his fingers together, fidgeting as he looked up at her. "She's been texting me all day. She knows I'm here with you."

"Does she know we're... friends? I mean, I think we're still friends." She weighed every word, trying to sound casual while her palms and the back of her neck were slick with sweat. The small den was so still, the fire's crackling echoed from the other room. The voices in the living room had gone quiet; Piper must've succeeded in clearing out the house.

Nico's Adam's apple moved as he swallowed before he spoke. "Honestly? She doesn't like it, but I had to be here for you. So, yeah, I guess that means we're still friends."

"Nico, you don't have to be here. I don't want to come between you and Nicki." She kept her tone neutral.

"I'm here because I want to be. Look, we haven't talked since last June? And I wasn't going to bring it up, especially today, but you *broke* me. It took a while to get over you, and seeing you again..." Looking down, he ran a hand through his dark hair. "Fuck. I still care about you. But I can't... I just can't get hurt again. And I know you've been hanging out with Shane. I'm surprised he didn't show up today—"

"Shane won't be coming to visit me, and I won't be seeing him ever again if I can help it." The days of messages and calls from Shane had stopped, and she hoped he'd given up. No amount of regret and begging would make her forgive him.

Nico's head snapped up, his intense eyes sparkling in the dim light. "What happened? I heard you two were back together."

"We were never back together. We were hanging out as friends, or so I thought."

"Claudia told me you were with him all the time, I just assumed—"

"Nothing happened with Shane. We aren't friends, acquaintances... we are nothing." She sat up in her seat, her body tense. The last thing she wanted was for Nico to think she was still in love with Shane. She had no interest in getting back together with Shane, even if he hadn't been with someone else while she was mourning his death.

"Sounds serious. What'd he do?"

"It doesn't matter. I was stupid and wrong about him. I don't want to talk about him anymore." Her gaze fell on his calloused hands as she leaned forward. She resisted the urge to hold them. He still cared about her...

His remark about not wanting to be hurt again cut deep; even though she'd broken up with him, she missed him so much, but he was with someone else. It was almost funny. Her emotions were a jumbled mess. "I'm sorry I hurt you. I didn't know what I wanted at the time and... I just want you to be happy. Thanks for coming today, having you here really helped."

His eyes lingered on hers, their faces close for a moment, until he pulled away. Her shoulders slumped as he rose from the bench. "I should go," he said, clearing his throat. "Let me know if you need anything. And remember what I said about the lawyer; don't decide anything until you're sure."

"I won't."

The ache in her chest returned. As he left through the swinging door, Ori walked through him into the den, his frame much smaller than Nico's. "You've got a thing for that guy, don't you?"

"How long have you been here?" she said.

"Long enough to know you like him. But that's not why I'm here."

She stood and folded the blanket, placing it over the back of the chair. In a hushed tone, she fired off a series of questions, never knowing when Ori would disappear again. "Where've you been? Neptune Point? Was the Reaper there? If you were with my mother again, I still don't have answers."

Ori pushed a loose strand of blond hair away from his face and folded his arms across his chest. "Yes. Yes. And a resounding let's forget about your mother for just a minute."

"This must be good if we're leaving Joelle off the table."

"For a minute, yes." Shifting to human form, he paused in front of Gran's clock and tapped the glass. "The clock is broken."

"It stops and starts. This is the stopping portion of the day… I haven't figured it out yet. What did you find out?"

The door swung open, and Piper peered in. "Who are you talking to? Am I missing something?"

Drew and Ori exchanged glances, and he shrugged. "If only they could see me too," he said. "I like her. She's cool."

"Is my dad still here?" Drew asked.

"He's outside getting wood for the fireplace before he leaves. I think he's talking to Nico. How'd that go?"

"It was fine." At least she had his friendship back. "Just like old times."

"Yeah right, it was. I want details."

"There are no details. He came to support me, his friend, today, and he's living a happy life with his new girlfriend."

Ori raised his eyebrows. "That's what you got out of your conversation with Nico? Oh my God, Drew. Really?"

"Yes, there was nothing said."

Piper chuckled and plopped down in the chair. "Ori here?"

"He's got news."

Piper rubbed her hands together. "I'm here for it."

"Do you believe in witches?" Ori said.

Drew exhaled sharply and relayed his words to Piper. This wasn't news. "The Reaper called me a witch, but that doesn't mean they exist."

"What if they did?" Piper stared with curiosity at the direction where Ori was standing. "You keep looking over there, but I see nothing. A dead guy is standing a few feet away from me, and I'd be oblivious if it wasn't for you."

Her ability to see dead people had been a constant mystery, but she'd given up trying to understand how she saw the world differently than others and accept it as part of her normal.

"She has a point," Ori said.

"What point? You think what the Reaper called me is *true*? That's impossible."

"So is seeing dead people," Piper said. "Impossible, but not for you. Aren't you curious?"

"Of course, I've always been curious, but it just doesn't seem to matter anymore. It's a part of me I can't change."

Piper got up from the chair and placed her hands on Drew's shoulders. "It's a badass, amazing part of you! When I think of the word *witch*, I think of magic and cool shit."

"That's a good way to look at this." Ori moved beside her. A faint glow surrounded him as he shifted into a ghost. "Because, my living friend, our pal Reaper thinks you're a literal witch, and he wants you dead."

"I haven't seen him since I left—"

"He's watching you and the house. I'm not so sure I can keep him away. It's like he's hunting you, biding his time for the perfect opportunity to strike."

"Hunting me?"

"Who is hunting you?" Piper dropped her hands and eyed Ori without realizing.

As she repeated his words, the amulet's light swirled deep inside, illuminating the vines as they burrowed their way through the stone.

"Your gran gave you that to you for a reason," Ori said. "Want my opinion?"

"No, but you're going to give it, anyway." She smiled through tears as she said the words. Her emotions were all over the damn place, and Ori's connection to the soul realm was her lifeline to solving this mystery.

"Start digging into where Gran found that glorious gem, and you'll figure out who you are and how to stop the Reaper. Just my opinion. What do I know?" He smiled at her with his hands held up in

"At the moment, more than I do," she whispered as he swirled into a mist and disappeared.

A soft whisper came from the window, and she spun around and pushed the curtains aside. Along the ledge was a row of stones, all the same colors as the ones at the front door and at the Tough Cookie.

What did you keep from me, Gran?

TWELVE

Despite the spectacular view of the harbor through the floor to ceiling windows in the lawyer's office, Drew couldn't take her eyes off the warehouse in the shipyard across the street—the same one where she'd been shot the year before. Pins and needles crawled over her scarred leg at the memory, and she ran a hand over the stretchy fabric of her black jeans. She pulled her loose-knit sweater over her thighs and crossed her legs, tucking her hands in her lap to keep from fidgeting.

It was hard to focus on anything but Ori's words; the Reaper believed she was a witch and wanted her dead. The amulet warmed against her skin, as if sensing her thoughts. If Ori was right and the Reaper was hunting her, she'd have to find a way to get rid of him, and quick.

He's hunting me.

He's hunting... witches.

She wanted to pull out her phone and start searching for any history on the subject, if such a thing existed.

"As far as Madeline Harlow's estate, it's clear that it all belongs to you, Drew." The lawyer's deep voice didn't match her delicate features, and it snapped Drew out of her thoughts, commanding attention. "She was smart about it, transferring the property to a trust before she died. She took care of everything. The house, and her share of the Tough Cookie—it's all yours. Nellie Quinn has signed the agreement to sell her shares for the purchase price. I can help you with your end of the paperwork for purchase. She doesn't want anything more."

"What does that mean?" she said, turning to her father. "Dad? Did you know anything about this? Why would she do that before she died? Was she sick?"

"No, not that I know of. I didn't know any of this. I mean, I figured she'd leave you whatever she had, but no." Her father rubbed at his bearded face, the gray hairs standing out among the red. The suede elbow patches of his suit jacket appeared worn, and threads frayed along the cuffs. It was the same jacket he'd worn to Gran's funeral, and probably the only one he owned. He tapped his foot against the dark wooden floor as he looked across the mahogany desk at the lawyer. She put on a pair of dark-framed glasses and started reading. Drew listened, trying to drown out her swirling thoughts, but her overthinking mind was winning the battle.

The lawyer removed her glasses and crossed her hands on the desk. "It means that your grandmother wanted you to be taken care of. She handled everything so you wouldn't have to." She picked up the papers again. "Her savings, belongings within the home, and her vehicle, a Buick—"

"What am I supposed to do with all of it? Do I sell the house and the Tough Cookie?"

The lawyer smiled at her, cracking her pink lipstick. "Like most people in this town, I knew Maddie, and it wasn't a secret that she loved her granddaughter." She opened a drawer and handed Drew a business card. "I recommend Anna Tate if you decide to sell. She's the best in town. She'll get you a good deal on both the house and the business. You probably know her daughter, Claudia."

Drew turned to her father. "Do you think I should sell everything?"

He reached over to squeeze her hand and leaned back in the chair. "You're gonna be nineteen in a couple weeks. You're an adult now. What you do with the house, the Tough Cookie... that decision is yours to make, not mine. Just tell me what you want to do, and I'll help with whatever you need."

Gran gave her their house. The *business*. She couldn't run a business! She had to go back to school. She had expected Gran to leave the big stuff to her dad, not her.

She signed the documents before leaving the office with trembling hands and a chaotic mind. They descended the elevator in silence and headed for the truck. Her dad drove through town toward home, tapping his thumbs in time to the beat of the music playing on the radio. Drew stared out the window, passing by familiar stores and cafes, until the truck stopped at a red light by Portal Park. A sign danced in the wind at the entrance of a shop with bells dangling from wreaths woven from twigs inside the window.

Little Mysteries.

Claudia's voice echoed in her head, *Taj... moved to town in September... his mother opened a store... Little Mysteries.*

A small wooden sign pressed against the window. Drew rolled down the window, the icy breeze from outside clashing with the heat from the car, taking her breath away as she tried to decipher the ornate writing.

We are the granddaughters of the witches you could not burn.

Her father sped away as the light turned green. "Roll the window up, Drew, it's freezing."

You are a witch. The words tumbled through her mind again. This time, she knew where to go for answers.

Her dad followed her into Gran's house. She placed leftover sandwiches on plates, as he grabbed a beer from the fridge and sat at the kitchen table. "You'll have enough money for a place in Boston if you sell everything. There'd be lots more opportunities."

She sat across from him. "Would you be sad if I sold the house? If this place was no longer... home?" she said between bites.

He rubbed his beard. "I'll be sad. But I get it. You've got school and a life now. I'm away a lot. I mean, it's better than it used to be, but still."

"You think I'll find a buyer for the Tough Cookie?"

"Someone will buy the space," he said, before taking a drink of his beer.

Space. The Tough Cookie would be nothing more than space to a buyer. The thought hadn't dawned on her before. Gran's business would be gone. Bread from the sandwich stuck in her throat and she got up, poured water in a glass, and gulped it down. "I can't run a business, Dad, I'm in school."

She shook her head. "It'll all be gone, won't it? It'll be like she never lived here."

"This place will always be where you grew up and where she lived. Nothing will change that." He peeled the beer label. "All I care about is you. I'm leaving after Christmas for ten days at sea. It'll pay a bonus, and I'll pay for your next semester."

"No. I told you—"

"I don't wanna hear it. It's done. Mom... Gran wanted you to have the best. Take it and don't look back. I'll come see you wherever you go. Leaving Atlas Cliffs for good might be the best thing you do for yourself. What does this town have to offer?"

She found solace at Jupiter Cove Beach across the street. Not to mention Nico, but she didn't have him, not anymore. She looked around the kitchen, the sage cabinets Gran had painted catching her eye. She'd taken the time to create beautiful flower stencils on the doors.

Home.

This was her home, her haven, but maybe it was time to find another place to belong.

"Maybe I should sell the house, unless you want it. Would you live here?"

He placed his beer on the antique kitchen table with a clink, the varnished wood gleaming in the light. Drew grabbed a coaster from the spinning wheel in the center and slid it beneath the cold bottle. It's what Gran would've done. She eyed the teapot on the counter. Gran would've been the last one to touch that. Her bedroom would have to be cleaned out, her clothes... Her heart clenched, clamping down inside her chest. Grief. The uninvited guest who showed up and never left.

Her dad sat back in his chair. "I'm a drifter. Home is wherever I am at the moment. Right now, it's here with you. My downtown apartment is home enough too. It keeps it simple. When I'm at sea, the boat is home. What I'm trying to say is wherever you choose to live will be home. I grew up in this house too, and it has memories. It's just... it's been a long time. So, like I said, if you need help, I'll be here. I'll clear out stuff, pack up boxes, whatever it is, but you have to decide. I can't do that for you. I won't. It's not how she wanted it."

For the past year, he'd come through on every promise, proving to be the dad she'd needed in her life. And she'd always been comfortable at home alone before, but not anymore. She cleared the plates and put them in the dishwasher. "Are you sticking around for a while?"

"If you want me to, I'll stay as long as you like."

Despite her fear of being home alone while the Reaper wanted her dead, she forced a brave face, not wanting him to see it. She couldn't talk about the ghosts she saw. He'd never said much when she described Jack and Iris at Neptune Point, and how she knew where Iris's body had been hidden. She accepted that there would be people, her father included, who wouldn't believe her, and she'd have to be okay with that. There'd be no way she could keep Gran's—*her* home and run a business. She wiped her eyes and sniffed back tears before facing him. "You can go home. I'll be fine here. I'll meet with the real estate agent and see what my options are."

"Do you want me to come with you?"

"No, I'm going to handle this like she wanted."

"She'd be really proud of you. I know I sure am." His voice cracked as he spoke, and he stood, gripping the edge of the counter. Dropping the dishcloth, she hugged him tight, grateful to have her father and his love in her life. He wrapped his arms around her like she was a child, and she broke down, letting go of trying. Trying to hold back and keep it together. They both did.

As her father pulled out of the driveway, a cloud of charcoal smoke blew over the cliff across the road in front of the truck. A sudden gust of snow transpired into a full-blown blizzard. Screeching tires filled the air as the truck fishtailed, spinning out of control. Leaving the door open behind her, she bolted from the house. She ran to the end of the driveway in socked feet, screaming until her throat hurt, her heart pounding in her chest.

"Dad!"

Tall boots materialized from the cloud, and as it whirled upward, a cloak billowed around them. The Reaper threw his head back and released the most menacing, unhinged laughter she'd ever heard. He embodied death.

The truck came to a dead stop off the road, too close to the cliffs. She tore through the snow until she reached the driver's side door. Fumbling with the handle, she pounded on the window, yelling for her father.

As the door opened, he stumbled out and held onto the truck for support. Flurries whipped around them as she threw her arms around him.

"Are you hurt?" she cried out through tears.

His arm wrapped around her. "No. No, I'm fine. I must've hit black ice. It came out of nowhere. What the fuck!"

She pulled away and surveyed him for blood. "Should I call an ambulance?"

"God, no. I'm okay, Drew. It's winter roads, that's all." He walked around the truck. "There's no damage. I just spun out."

She glared at the Reaper hovering over the cliff side. As his blackened eyes stared back at her, the amulet vibrated over her neck, and her hands ached and tingled. A shot of electricity tore through her body, and she stomped toward the cloaked terror. If blood ran through his dead veins, she was ready to spill it over the road. The "how" wasn't important. He'd launched an attack on her family!

"What are you doing?" her dad called out to her. "You're wearing socks and a T-shirt. Go inside! I'm fine."

Fading in and out, the Reaper hovered over the seagrass. As he disappeared, a sleek raven soared over her head into the dissipating blizzard.

She hugged her father goodbye before he hopped into his truck and drove away. With soaking wet feet and hair, and her entire body shivering from cold, she shut the door and locked the deadbolt. That asshole was playing with her. Taunting and testing her. She could feel it, and she'd be damned if she was going to let him win.

THIRTEEN

For centuries, the old brick building had been in the center of Atlas Cliffs next to Portal Park. Drew had never set foot in the place before, but it was time for her to make her debut with Anna Tate, Claudia's mom. Holiday decorations surrounded her, and she wished she could fast forward time and bypass the season, hiding away inside until it was all over.

All she'd wanted was to leave Atlas Cliffs and shake off her hometown like an itchy wool sweater. Somehow, this town kept pulling her back, this time in a world without Gran and instead with a specter from hell, the Reaper.

She hurried through the parking lot toward the entrance of Tate Realty, casting a glance at Little Mysteries on the corner. Her next stop. Witches weren't a part of her reality, but that didn't stop people from believing in them. If the Reaper wanted to kill her because he assumed she was a witch, she'd need to find out how to stop him.

She caught her reflection in the glass door and smoothed out her unruly hair before pushing down the handle and stepping inside. She knocked the snow off her ankle boots on the welcome mat. They were impractical, but she wanted to appear as professional as possible. When she'd gathered herself and stopped fidgeting, Nicki looked up from a phone call and narrowed an unfriendly gaze toward Drew. She spun her chair around and stuck a pen through her bangs.

Drew forgot Nicki worked here, and it was clear Nicki wasn't expecting to see her either. She picked at the buttons on her coat and shuffled from side to side.

Nicki's honey-filled voice chimed as she hung up the phone and turned back around to face Drew. "Ms. Tate will be with you in just a moment." She eyed Drew from top to bottom and stood with a sigh. "I can take your coat."

Drew shimmied it off her shoulders and handed it to Nicki. "Thanks."

"No problem." Nicki hung it on a fancy coat rack and headed back to her seat, running her hands over her black skirt as she sat. "Have a seat, if you want." She pointed to two plush chairs, and Drew sat in the one furthest away.

Nicki typed on a laptop. "Will you be moving back to Boston for good?"

Drew could only think of one reason this girl cared so much, and that reason was Nico.

"I guess so."

"Are you staying for the holidays?"

It's none of your business and I couldn't steal your boyfriend away if I tried.

"Does Ms. Tate know I'm here?" she asked instead.

Nicki stopped typing. "She'll be out in a minute."

Drew peered around the room, noting the large office off to the side. Blinds flew up the glass walls, revealing Claudia and her mother. Anna Tate opened the door, locking eyes with Drew, and flashed a bright smile. Now she knew where Claudia got her ability to turn on the charm from.

Nicki gave her a side-eyed glance as Anna Tate sashayed across the room to greet her.

"Drew Harlow, I'm Anna. I believe we've met before." Glittering gold bracelets and diamond rings shimmered under the ceiling light as she stretched out her arm.

Drew stood and gave her hand a firm shake before letting it go. A heavy scent of perfume filled the air between them as Anna led them to her office and took a seat. Claudia winked at her as she walked out with a stack of papers, closing the door behind her.

Anna slid papers across the desk for Drew to look at as she discussed the housing market. She used words like list price, offers, closing, and a bunch more details Drew tried to sort through.

"Your grandmother's house is in a prime oceanfront location. The holidays haven't slowed business and I predict we could sell rather quickly." She crossed her hands and sat with impeccable posture in her chair, just like Claudia. She'd flicked her black eyeliner out to the sides, blending with her dark mauve eyeshadow. Her platinum bob and white blazer made her look magazine worthy.

Drew straightened her back and resisted the urge to chew the inside of her cheek. "And Gran's business? What about the Tough Cookie?"

"It's close to the waterfront, well maintained, and equipped with a full kitchen; the space has so much potential. Don't worry, Drew. It will sell for a fair price."

Although she'd decided in her mind to sell Gran's house and the Tough Cookie, putting that decision into action overwhelmed her. She'd made a list of all the reasons to sell and ran them through her mind as she looked from Anna to the paperwork she'd drawn up.

She left everything to me. I'm doing the right thing. I can't take care of a house and run a business and go away to school.

"Okay. Let's do this." She scribbled her signature on the papers, desperate to keep her composure. There was nothing for her left in Atlas Cliffs and there never would be.

Anna finished explaining the process and ended with a sudden pause. "Business aside, I want to express my deepest condolences for your grandmother. She will be missed in this community."

"Thank you." Drew stood to leave.

"I'm not finished," Anna continued. "Please sit. Please."

Drew perched on the edge of the chair. Dominic Sloan had been this woman's husband. A monster who ruined lives, including those of his own kids. She had no idea what Anna wanted to discuss with her, and she wasn't sure if she wanted to hear it, but she couldn't bring herself to walk away.

"I'd be remiss..." Anna sat back in her chair, her perfect posture faltering, if only a little. "My *ex*-husband is dead to me. What he has done is despicable, and I remain in complete disgust at his actions. If you require anything, now or in the future, I request that you come to see me."

Drew teetered on the edge of the chair, speechless. She opened her mouth, hoping words would fall out, but Anna continued.

"I am not in anyone's debt for anything. I've never owed a soul before, but somehow, here I am, sitting across from the only person I owe my life, and my children's lives, to."

"Oh, no. No, you don't owe—"

"I need you to promise me that if ever you need assistance, come to me first. You saved me from a monster."

"Yes, but—"

"Please. I should have said this a long time ago. Let's not make it awkward." Anna snapped the smile back on and stood, once again reaching her hand out to Drew. "Ms. Harlow, it's going to be a pleasure to do business with you. I'll be in touch, and you have my number. Call if you need anything."

Drew shook her hand, her heart racing as she walked away from the glass box of an office toward the coat rack. She ignored Nicki's intense glare as she stuffed her arms in the sleeves and gripped the chair for balance, desperate for fresh air.

She expected walking out of there would lighten her burden, but she felt a sense of dread, as if she had just signed her life away. Perhaps she had.

She rushed outside and breathed in the crisp winter air as her phone buzzed in the canvas cross-body purse she wore and read Piper's text.

I'm downtown. Are you still at Tate's?

She eyed the store on the corner with its witch sign in the window and messaged Piper back.

Meet me on the corner. Little Mysteries.

The shop had a unique charm, from its wrought iron planters to the purple trim on the windows. A blue moth-like butterfly over the words "Little Mysteries" appeared as if it was about to fly away. She wanted to reach up and touch it, but the sign was too high, swaying from the fancy metal holder. She cupped her face in her hands and peered inside, the chill of the frost on the windows causing her breath to fog the glass.

"How'd it go?" Piper's voice sounded from behind her, and she jumped.

"Good, I guess. I signed papers to sell."

"Shit, really? That fast?"

"I'm back at school soon, so the faster the better, right?"

Piper had a lid-covered paper cup in both hands. Her mittens were so thick that they completely enveloped it as she took a drink. "Why don't you give it some time? This is your home we're talking about."

She refused to let herself feel the pain of the word home, and how she'd be leaving the only one she had ever known. She locked those feelings in a box inside her soul. Staying in Atlas Cliffs wasn't an option if she wanted to accomplish a career—a life for herself. Staying was *never* an option. "I made my decision. It's done. I'll find a new home. I have to." She turned away and faced the store.

Piper walked along the slush-covered sidewalk and pointed to a chalkboard sign. She read out loud. "The lawn is pressed with unseen feet, and ghosts return. Gently at twilight, gently go at dawn, the sad intangible that grieve and yearn. T.S Eliot. Creepy." She shook her cup and tossed it in a trash can and bent to tie her combat boot. "So, tell me. Why are we at Taj's mom's store?" She snapped upright and glanced at the sign in the window. "Witch. You're embracing it now? Is that why we're here?"

"I saw him again, the Reaper. He tried to hurt my dad."

"Are you serious? What happened and why didn't you tell me earlier?"

"The night we went to see the lawyer. He tried to crash Dad's truck."

"Is he okay?"

She remembered the Reaper's disgusting face and sinister laugh, and a surge of anger coursed through her. "He's fine, but it could've been worse. What if he goes after someone else I love? I need to figure out a way to get rid of him, Piper."

"I bet a witch could handle that."

"I'm not a witch."

"You sure about that?"

She wasn't sure about anything.

Fourteen

Drew opened the door, setting off a chorus of wind chimes over her head. The smoky smell of patchouli filled the room as the incense burned on the counter. Piper trailed her into the store, the door clanging shut behind them. A mellow soundtrack emanated from the next room. The rich tone of a saxophone played as a piano caught up in rhythm. Glazed pottery with intricate symbols of moons, and hands with an eye in the middle, sat on a yellow shelf. An assortment of candles and holders of different sizes rested on the big shelf against the wall. Display cabinets along the counter contained oddly shaped pendants and stones. She ducked underneath dragonflies and birds suspended from the ceiling as she held the stone around her neck.

"Hello?" Drew called out.

"What do you think this is for?" Piper said as she picked up a chicken foot key chain.

Drew touched the acorn hanging from the chicken's foot and pointed at the sign. "It's for protection against dangerous energy. I'm going to need the entire basket."

Piper made a face and let it drop back into the basket with the others. "Do you believe in all this? Is this the witchy stuff we've got to embrace? It's weird, but I'm here for it."

"I don't know what I believe in these days, Piper." Drew followed the music toward the back room. She parted the beaded curtains and peered inside. A woman moved in perfect sync with the song, the sleeves of her emerald silk blouse dancing along. The words she sang didn't quite line up with the baritone voice of the man singing, but still sounded beautiful. A matching scarf held her hair off her face, although a few black coils sprung loose around her temples.

Drew cleared her throat. But instead of startling the woman, she continued stocking books on a shelf without turning around. "Can I help you?"

"I hope so." Drew hesitated, trying to think of how to say what she wanted to say.

What do you know about witches? Because a terrifying dead guy thinks I am one and wants to kill me.

The woman diverted her attention from the box she was emptying and looked up. She bore a striking resemblance to her son. They had similar brown skin and dark hair, but Celeste's eyes held a different sparkle. Like she knew something others didn't.

"Cat got your tongue?" The woman's voice was gentle. Calming.

"I saw the sign in your window. Um... what can you tell me about—"

"I don't practice dark magic or voodoo, or whatever you think might get someone to love you."

"What? No. I want to know about witches."

Hands on her hips, the woman scrutinized Drew. "What would you like to know?"

Drew moved further into the room, closing the gap between them—careful not to trip on the boxes spread across the floor. "How do you know if you are one? I mean, if witches were real. I know they're not, but if they existed."

The woman removed her glasses, letting them dangle from a chain around her neck. "What's your name?"

"Drew. What's yours?"

"Celeste. You've lived here your whole life, haven't you?"

It wasn't a question, but a *knowing*, and Drew couldn't hide her surprise. "Is it that obvious?"

"To me, yes," Celeste said, turning back to her box and adding to the wall of books.

Drew glimpsed a few titles. Spells. Moon Phases. Shadow People. The Sisterhood of Salem. Sixteenth-Century Witches.

She wandered around the room. On the other side of the beaded curtains, Piper flipped through a book.

"This store wasn't here last summer. When did you open it?" she asked.

"Life is a series of coincidences, Drew. And those just happened to guide me back here, to the town where I was born."

"Did you grow up here?"

"Just until I was sixteen. But I'm back now. I think I'll stay for a while." Celeste winked, her small beauty mark moving as her smile widened.

The beads in the doorway jangled, and Piper sauntered toward Drew, extending her hand to Celeste. "Hi! I'm Piper. I'm friends with Taj." She beamed.

Celeste raised an eyebrow and shook Piper's hand. "So I've heard."

Taj's appeal to Piper was clear to Drew. He was good-looking, and like his mother, surrounded by a charismatic charm.

Piper picked up a jar filled with what looked like dried parsley. "Herbal magic," she read out loud and looked up at Celeste. "Well, riddle me intrigued."

Celeste's focus shifted away from Piper and to Drew's neck. "Maddie give that to you?"

Drew gripped the amulet, and its warmth spread through her fingers, a bright glow emanating from it. "You knew my gran?"

"I did. Keep the crystals where she left them. She used a Safe Haven spell if I'm not mistaken."

Piper glanced at Drew, giving her a wide-eyed look that begged the question, 'Who the hell is this woman?'

"How did you know?" Drew asked.

Celeste handed her a book with no title and a hand on the cover with an eye in its palm. "Take this. And do not remove that necklace from your body. She gave that to you for a reason."

Drew took the book from her hands and opened it to the first page without reading. Her mouth went dry, and her thoughts scrambled as she attempted to unravel the cryptic message in Celeste's words. Piper stood in silence beside her.

"What reason? How do you know my grandmother exactly?" Drew looked around the apothecary of a room, the shelves full of unique items, old books, and trinkets that had an air of... *magic*.

Celeste moved closer to Drew until they were face to face. Her silk sleeves rustled as she put her hands on Drew's shoulders and looked so deep into her eyes, Drew glanced away. Was she casting a spell? It was like this store was a portal that had sucked her away from reality.

Celeste let her arms fall to her sides as the seconds dragged on. "You saw her. You know she's watching. Light and dark coexist. But you... you are light. And you're not alone."

As if on cue, a sharp dip in temperature swept around her as a swirling mist moved through the beaded door frame. Celeste went back to tidying up the bookshelves. "See? Not alone."

"What's happening," Piper whispered.

"Ori's here, and somehow, she knows."

"Shit just got real," Piper said.

Ori stepped in front of Celeste. "Can she see me?"

Drew stood beside Ori. Celeste appeared unphased, and didn't glance in Ori's direction. Maybe she couldn't see him. "Tell me what you know. Please. Could Gran see things, too? Was my grandmother... am I... a... a—"

Celeste chuckled. "How is it I know what you're going to say? If you've come in here today to ask me if you're a witch, I wish it were that easy, but this is a journey of discovery for you, and only you." She stopped cleaning and adjusted the scarf around her temples. "Atlas Cliffs has secrets and they're older than you and me, and your grandmother. You've got friends in special places. Listen to them." Celeste gestured toward where Ori stood. "He's got a story too, by the way."

Ori paced back and forth; his hands animated in full ghost silhouette. "Drew, ask her who killed me! She knows!"

"Do you know who killed him?" She adjusted the book before it slipped from her hand, placing it under her arm.

"I can't help you there. That's not my area of expertise," Celeste said.

Piper looked from Drew to Celeste to what must look like empty space by the door frame. "Drew... talk to me. What's going on?"

"Can you see him?" Drew asked.

Celeste smiled, and its warmth could envelop the iciest soul. "No, darlin'. I just feel the shift. So did she, your grandmother. Her thing was plants. Gardens. She talked to them, and they bloomed. Prettiest thing I've ever witnessed."

Drew's head was spinning as she looked from Celeste to Ori. "Gran was a witch, too," he said.

There's no such thing as witches!

She wanted to say it out loud to anchor herself back to her life before the Reaper had showed up. Back to normalcy, whatever that was. "Gran knew about the ghosts?"

"I met Maddie at the Tough Cookie before I opened this place. She was one of my best customers. One day we started talking, and she told me she'd raised her granddaughter. She worried about you and wanted to keep you safe. Didn't want you to be a part of all... *this*. She mentioned she'd thought your ability disappeared with childhood until an incident last year."

Gran had believed her when she spoke about Iris, Enid, and Ezra after Ben Morana's arrest, but the conversation had ended with Gran's enthusiastic approval of her decision to leave Atlas Cliffs.

"Why didn't she ever say anything to me?"

"We didn't get into details, and I'm not one for prying into someone's personal business, but from what I gathered, she wanted to keep you safe."

"From what, though? Did she tell you what this is for?" Drew yanked the necklace over her head and held it out to Celeste, whose smile faded, her amber eyes turning serious.

Celeste touched the stone, picking it up in her fingers. The light inside glowed stronger. "It's for protection. Does it always light up like that?"

"It reacts to things." If Gran trusted Celeste, she could too. "I'm having a little problem with a dead guy."

Celeste let go of the amulet. "I see." She turned to the stack of books again. "What sort of problem?"

"He tried to run my dad off the road last night, and he's stalking me. I want him gone. Do you have a…" She searched the room for a mystic weapon. "Is there anything in here to get rid of a sinister ghost?"

Placing the books on the shelf, Celeste faced Drew. "For starters, put that jewel around your neck and don't take it off."

Drew clutched the amulet, and it pulsated in her hand. "What's next? You said, for starters. My dad almost crashed his truck over a cliff last night! The amulet didn't stop the Reaper. I need more."

"The Reaper?" Celeste knitted her brows.

"He called her a witch." Piper shifted to stand beside Drew.

"Witch is a label, a word that means a lot more than potions and magic. It sure isn't *evil*. One of the biggest misconceptions." Celeste clicked her tongue and pointed at the book in Drew's hand. "Your Gran had it last. The first part will hold her discovery. The rest is for you."

Drew put the necklace over her head and ran a hand over the book's cover. The amulet nestled against her neck. "Why did Gran have this book?"

Celeste exhaled a sigh and twisted the chain her glasses hung from around her fingers. She narrowed her eyes at Drew. "Get a feel for the book. When you're ready, I'll be here."

The chimes rang out from the front of the store, startling Drew and sending Ori into a fine mist.

"I've got customers." Celeste glided through the beads, her silk dress swishing with each step. Drew and Piper looked at each other in confusion as Celeste stuck her head back through the beaded curtain. "You know someone named... Jo, Joey, Joel..." She snapped her fingers as she said each name.

Drew racked her brain until the lightbulb clicked on. "Joelle?"

Celeste clapped her hands. "Bingo! They're connected to your ghost friend who was just here. It's dark. Very dark. Decisions will have to be made, I'm afraid." The beads clanged together as she moved through them, back to the storefront.

FIFTEEN

Taj and his band's vibrant, edgy rock music filled Maze with an electric energy. Next of Kin was written in black letters on the front of Taj's drum set. He exuded passion as he controlled the beat of every song. After twenty minutes with no sign of Nico and Nicki, Drew let her guard down and stopped looking over her shoulder. Using her straw, she twirled the ice cubes in her glass of soda. The round table near the stage was bustling with Claudia and her friends, and acquaintances of Piper and Taj's bandmates. Jasper had gone up by the stage, but left his jacket slung over the back of a chair. Drew recognized a few people from high school and engaged in small talk. She accepted kind words of condolences about Gran and answered the standard "where are you now?" questions. It didn't surprise her how many already knew the house and business were for sale, but hearing it said aloud left her with a pit in her stomach.

Piper moved in her seat to the music. "Isn't he amazing? Have you noticed his arms? Like, damn."

"When a drummer can play like that while being completely distracted, it's a sure sign of talent. He's barely taken his eyes off you, for God's sake." Claudia leaned forward and raised her voice over the music.

"You're actually not pissing me off tonight, Claudia," Piper said.

Claudia rolled her eyes and flashed a smile. Her red lips made her teeth look extra bright. "He's single, you know. My advice, just have fun while you're home and cut ties when you're done. Long-distance relationships never work."

In an instant, Piper's face reddened, her pink hair paling in comparison, and their truce dissolved. Drew pushed her glass aside and clasped her hands together to stop herself from fidgeting. "I don't think Piper needs relationship advice. She's got this."

Piper linked Drew's arm in hers. "Thanks for being my wing-woman. I hope you can have a little fun tonight. Just get your mind off stuff, you know?"

Even the loud music couldn't distract her from her racing thoughts. "I'm glad you dragged me out tonight. It's better than being home alone."

"Exactly. You need this. Look how festive everything is! They even have lights around your painting." Piper pointed toward the fireplace lined with tree garland and rainbow lights.

"I'm going to buy that painting," Claudia said.

Drew snapped her head toward her. "You're what?"

"I'm going to buy it from you. I have a plan that's better than having it hanging on a wall in Maze. It's good, Drew. I'll be in touch soon with numbers and a plan."

Claudia had something up her sleeve, but Drew wasn't interested in finding out what it was. "It's not for sale."

"Oh, please, everything is for sale at the right price. You're going to benefit from this. Trust me."

There was that word again. Trust. "Just leave the painting alone. It's fine here. I'm not looking to make money off it—"

Claudia grabbed Drew's arm. Her matching red nails dug into the soft green sweater Drew wore. "You're in art school, you're talented, and you've got the potential to turn something you love into a money-making career. Let *me* help *you*." She let go and flipped her blond hair to the side as she waved to a young man in a suit making his way to the table. "I'll fill you in later." She pushed her chair back and threw her arms around the clean-cut man, who seemed to be in his mid to late twenties. It was clear from the way they held onto each other that their relationship was more than just friendship or coworkers.

"Claudia's seeing Grant Salinger?" Piper asked.

"That's Grant Salinger?" Years ago, his family's brick laying company had gone under following the tragic death of their daughter in a car accident. Gran rallied the community to help raise money for the family. Drew was around eleven when Grant had graduated and left for school, leaving the family devastated.

Drew had a different perspective on Claudia. One that continued to exist behind the perfect façade. Claudia was determined to break free from her father's shadow and monstrous reputation. Ambition and determination fueled her. The bond created between them after Claudia had showed up the night of the shooting would forever be unbreakable.

Jasper pushed through the crowd toward the table, sweat beading on his forehead. His damp head of waves curled as he plopped down across from Drew with a drink in his hand.

Adjusting the buttons on his paisley shirt, he settled back in his seat. Jasper had the same adventurous spirit as Piper, and Drew had easily clicked with him in San Francisco. He had a way of filling the room with his unique, charismatic energy. His laid-back, modern-day hippie persona had a touch of modern coolness that reminded her of a younger version of Gran.

"Where have you been?" she asked.

"Dancing by the stage. It was glorious. You should've joined me! It'd be like our San Francisco party days." With a wink, he downed the drink garnished with a lime wedge.

It would take a large dose of California confidence and alcohol to get her up dancing tonight. But the mention of the trip brought a smile to her lips.

The band finished their set, and a DJ took over. Piper rose from her seat as Taj waved to her over the crowd. "I didn't think Grant would ever come back here. For someone who talks about everyone else, Claudia sure keeps her private life a secret. Come with me." Piper gestured to Drew, and she got up to stand with her as Taj and his band mates arrived.

"Hey, Drew. Thanks for coming out." Excitement filled Taj's voice as he introduced his friends. He pushed his shirt-sleeves up to his elbows and loosened the buttons on his black-and-white checkered vest. Piper's eyes wandered over him as he brushed a strand of pink hair from her eyes.

Their playful dynamic made her long for what she had with Nico. It was fun and easy. Comfortable, but not too comfortable. They could talk for hours or sit in silence without awkwardness while he strummed a guitar on Gran's front porch.

"Nico! Did you bring your guitar?" Taj asked out of nowhere.

"No, man. I'm just here for you guys."

Drew's eyes widened at the recognition of Nico's voice. She spun around, and her eyes locked onto Nico as he sauntered up for a guy handshake with Taj. His black T-shirt hugged his broad chest, and his dimpled smile could captivate the coldest heart. He looked down at her, his dark lashes framing his intense gaze.

She struggled to maintain the air of friendship when all she could think about was kissing him.

"I didn't think you'd be here." he said.

"Blame Piper." Her cheeks hurt from the foolish grin plastered across her face.

Get a hold of yourself. He's got a girlfriend!

He nodded toward Piper, who sat next to Taj. "I'll happily blame Piper for bringing you out tonight. Can I sit with you?"

A server arrived and took orders for the table. She couldn't tell if the thumping in her ears was from the speakers' bass or her racing heart. Sweat gathered at the back of her neck, confirmation of the latter. "Okay... I mean, sure."

Nico held out her chair before sitting next to her. It was the same swoon worthy Nico she'd grown accustomed to in the past—stark contrast to Shane's behavior.

She sat and scooted her chair close to the table. "Do you play with them, too? I didn't realize you and Taj were friends."

"I fixed his mom's car when they first moved here, and we hang out on the weekends when he's home from school. I've jammed with them a few times, but I just don't have the time. He keeps asking, so maybe some time."

She always admired him when he played the acoustic guitar. His wanting to play with a band had never occurred to her as something he wanted to do.

He leaned forward with his elbows on the table, so he was closer to her.

They used to be friends. Just friends. She could do it again.

"I saw the sign on the house," he said. "You're doing it. Selling?"

"It's the best option for me."

"Are you sure? It's not the only option, and it isn't too late. It's your home."

Their heads angled close as they talked, getting lost in each other's eyes. The surrounding chatter faded away. His expression was desperate, silently pleading with her to change her mind about selling everything. She could still read him so well.

"Nothing's here for me anymore, Nico."

"Yeah, there is!" He glanced around the table. Jasper talked with animated hands with one of the band members, Piper and Taj laughed, Claudia returned with her well-dressed beau. "Everything is here for you. Your friends. Family. *Me.*"

The thumping in her ears was definitely not the base. She bit her bottom lip, pondering on her response. She didn't have him anymore, and friendships weren't enough to keep her in Atlas Cliffs.

"Say what you want to say without overthinking." He smiled. "It's just me, Drew."

He was mistaken. He wasn't just Nico anymore in her eyes. She resisted the temptation to confess how much he mattered to her, and how often she thought about him. No matter how hard she tried to envision a different outcome, she couldn't escape the reality that he had moved on, and when the house sold, she'd do the same. "I'm not overthinking anything."

"You're biting your lip. You do that when you overthink."

Shit. He could still read her, too.

"It's just..."

"It's just what?"

"You've moved on, and so has everyone here. Piper goes to school in New York. My dad spends more time at sea than at home. Claudia is Claudia. Gran's gone." She swallowed back tears, and said through a thick voice, "And you..."

"You already mentioned me."

"You've got a new life and a girlfriend. I'm not part of that anymore."

"Do you want to be?" His sincere eyes penetrated her soul, melting her resolve.

Is he serious?

A tapping on her arm tore through the moment.

"Drew Harlow?" The male voice sounded close, calling for her attention. She wanted to curse at him for ending the conversation with Nico.

"Sorry to interrupt. I'm heading out and wanted to talk to you. Do you remember me? Grant Salinger." He'd taken his suit jacket off and sat with perfect posture in a chair he'd pulled up beside her. His worried expression and her piqued curiosity softened her.

"I was young, but I remember your parents." She paused, avoiding the mention of his sister's accident.

Glancing her way, Piper and Taj pulled Nico in their conversation. Claudia stood behind Grant with her coat on. Her eyes darted from Grant to Drew before scrolling on her phone. What on earth did this guy want to talk to her about? She turned her attention back to Grant. "I'm sorry. What did you want to talk to me about?"

"Claudia wanted me to tell you... We can go outside if you prefer." He looked up at Claudia, but she said nothing as she patted his shoulder.

She couldn't imagine what he had to say that would make her need to stand out in the cold. "Here's fine. What is it?"

He leaned in with his elbows on the table and downed the amber liquid from a small glass. "A woman was in the office today. If you aren't already familiar, my office is on the same floor as Anna Tate, and Claudia, of course."

"Of course." Pivoting in her seat, she shot a glance at Claudia, who knitted her brows together so tight, little lines formed between them.

"I worked late yesterday, and Anna Tate's office was closed. This woman, she asked questions about your grandmother's house for sale. I'm sorry for your loss, Drew. Maddie was a treasure."

The longer they chatted, the more apparent it was that he and Claudia were a match. They both gave off an air of confidence and authority, like a power couple. "Thank you. But I don't understand. If someone is interested in buying Gran's house, they can just talk to Tate Realty."

"I think it's your mother, Drew." Claudia moved her hand from Grant's shoulder to Drew's.

"What? How do you know?"

Nico observed Drew with deep concern in his eyes as he mouthed, *you okay?* She didn't respond.

I'm not okay.

"I'm good," she said, holding herself together.

"She said her name was Joelle Marisol," Grant said. "I left a note this morning for Claudia, and she thought it best if I was the one to tell you about the encounter."

Claudia crouched between them. "When I told him she wasn't in your life anymore, he found her questions odd. Tell her, Grant."

"She asked a lot of questions about you. Why you were selling the house, a cell number, if you were still living in the house... She sounded desperate. I gave her the number for Tate Realty and advised her to direct anything about the house to them. I did not divulge any information, not that I had it to begin with."

"I don't know where your relationship stands now, but if you need help, I've got connections." The conviction in Claudia's voice reminded her of how Dominic Sloan used to speak when he uttered threats. But Claudia wanted to help, not hurt her. She was not like her father.

Grant stood and pushed his chair in as Claudia rose. She gave Drew's arm a gentle squeeze before saying goodbye to everyone at the table.

A high-pitched buzzing rang in her ears, drowning out the sounds in the room. She focused on steadying her breathing as she gripped the table.

Joelle was in Atlas Cliffs.

Ori warned her this would happen; if she was going to help Ori, she'd have to see Joelle.

Nico draped an arm over the back of her chair. It took everything in her to not let herself fall against him. "What was that all about?"

Their eyes met. His face was etched with concern. "My mother is in town."

"Shit. Do you want to get out of here? Talk? I can drive you home."

"No, you don't have to do that. I'll be fine once the shock wears off."

Nico took his jacket from the back of the chair and slid his arms in. "I can't stay long, anyway. I'll take you home."

Piper slid into the empty chair on the other side. "What in the hell did they say to you? I'll go take care of it right now."

"Joelle is here, Piper."

Piper's mouth hung open on her last word and her fists unclenched. "Are you serious? Where is she?"

"I don't know, but I'm going to find out. I'm heading home. You stay and have fun. Nico will give me a lift." Drew stood and fumbled with the zipper on her jacket. Piper moved her hands aside and zipped it for her.

"You call me as soon as you find out anything."

Drew waved goodbye before following Nico outside to his truck. His presence gave her a sense of security and comfort.

But allowing herself to rely on him or be vulnerable with him scared her. Her relationship with him had gone from best friend to boyfriend and back to friend again. This time around, it wouldn't be his heart breaking, but her own.

SIXTEEN

They pulled up the driveway, and Nico walked her to the front door. The light from the porch Christmas lights glimmered through the newly fallen snow.

"I can ask around and help you find her." Picking up the shovel leaning against the house, Nico cleared snow from the porch and steps. Her heart wanted him to stay, but her mind warned her to break free from him. The more time she spent in his company, the harder it was to remain just friends.

"Thanks, but I have a feeling she's going to find me first." He continued with the shovel over the walkway.

"You don't have to do that. I can take care of it," she said.

"I don't mind." He finished and placed the shovel back against the house. "The ghost who wanted you to go to California and find your mother last summer, Ori?"

"Yeah." Nico didn't forget anything. The mention of Ori's name sent icy air through her hair, and she examined the yard for any trace of him or the Reaper.

"Is he still around? Did you ever find out how he's connected to Joelle?" He slid his hands into his pockets. The temptation to invite him inside lingered on her tongue, but she resisted. She needed to check herself, and the last thing she wanted was to drag him into her chaos again. Another gust of wind swept over the yard, and the For Sale sign creaked as it swayed in protest.

"I hate that sign," he said. "I'm sorry, I know it isn't my business, but I think it's happening too fast. Don't you?"

The sign shattered her heart, but running a business to maintain a home she couldn't live in while attending school was too much. There were no other options. Shivering, she stepped up to the door and pulled the keys from her pocket. "It's definitely happening way too fast. But I'm not sure what else to do. And Ori's still around. I'm hoping Joelle can give me information so I can help him. I think she might've witnessed the accident or something. It's the only thing that makes sense. Once I talk to her and find out, he can move on." She opened the front door and warmth from inside collided with the cold air. "And so can I."

Nico stepped up to the door as she entered the house. "If I can do anything to help, you know where to find me."

With the door ajar, she hesitated for a moment, considering whether to invite him in, but ended her inner debate. She had to keep Nico at arms length; he was in a relationship with someone else and she had to protect herself from getting hurt. But she was torn between her feelings and the fear of ruining their friendship.

She had to clear her mind to figure out what to do next. If he didn't look so good and wasn't so eager to help, it would be easier to resist him. She longed to ask him about his cryptic question from earlier but didn't pursue it. She had been friends with him for as long as she could remember and believed friendship was all he meant. Friendship was better than not having Nico at all. "I'm here for you, too, Nico. Going six months without a word... I don't want us to do that again."

"We won't. I won't let that happen."

"Me neither. Hey, thanks for driving me home."

"Anytime, Drew. Good night." His smile faded as he turned to leave. She stood with the door open as he hopped into the truck and the engine rumbled to life.

The weight of their unspoken words hung in the air. But she refused to make the first move beyond friendship while he was with someone else, and he'd told her he was afraid of getting hurt again. Shutting the door, she threw the deadbolt.

"I've said it before, and I'll say it again. That guy is in love with you."

As she jumped back, the coat hooks on the wall jabbed her. Her chest heaved as her heart pounded. Ori was sitting in Gran's chair with Celeste's book in his lap. Despite his deathly pale skin and angel-like eyes, he appeared as human as his body allowed.

"Jesus, Ori! What the hell? You've got to warn someone… I'm having a heart attack."

"No, you're not."

"I might be."

"You're not! Joelle's in town."

She kicked her boots off and hung her jacket on the hook. "I know."

"Has the Reaper been back for a visit?"

"He tried to run my dad off the road, but I haven't seen him again since. Why?" With a flick of the switch, the side lamps bathed the room in a warm glow. She settled onto the sofa nearest to him. "What are you doing with that book?"

"Have you looked through it?"

"It's empty. There's nothing but blank pages."

"I see that," he said, flipping through the yellowed pages. "Where were you?"

"Out with friends. There was a band. It was all festive... people were there."

Ori beamed and tilted his head like an excited puppy. "By people I assume that includes who dropped you off."

Nico's smile and his intense brown eyes popped into her mind, leaving her breathless. They were friends. Nothing more. Shake him off like sand on a towel. "He's a friend who was there, yes. Someone told me Joelle's in town asking about me."

"That's how you know." Strands of Ori's hair fell across his forehead, but he didn't brush them away. Maybe he couldn't feel it the way she would have.

"How do you know she's here?" she asked.

"I was with her, downtown. That woman has me in a chokehold. She's got no clue. Neither do I. She must've been there that night or something, I don't know. I don't get to leave when I want, as you know."

"You'll be missing me soon enough, Ori." The months spent together were going to end. She couldn't imagine life without him nagging her or appearing unannounced. She'd miss him, too.

"Me? Miss you? Nah. The bigger question is, what will *you* do without me? You're going to need someone to point out when a guy at your front door is in love with you."

If Nico was still in love with her, she'd know it. He couldn't be in a relationship with someone else and be in love with her. "He's got a girlfriend. Have you had any more memories of what happened? If I knew your full name, I could look you up online."

"My name is an echo in my head, nothing more."

"Enid used to say that too, but she remembered. Once the pieces fit together, I guess." If Enid were still alive, they would have been friends. Why did fate allow good people to die and let the bad ones keep living?

Ori placed the open book on the coffee table. "The book needs a little help from a witch. That's what I think."

"I'm not a witch, Ori." He didn't know what he was talking about. She was a simple young woman... who could see dead people and possessed an amulet with a mind of its own. But she was not a *witch*. The idea of their existence was nothing more than a fantasy. She couldn't believe it to be true. How would her life change if she were a witch? Rumors about her locked up in Gran's house, practicing dark magic, evil spells, and sacrificing innocent creatures would spread like wildfire.

"I beg to differ. My living friend, the sooner you accept who and what you are, the faster we get rid of the Reaper, and I can get my ticket to paradise. Look at this. Go find some candles and get to work." He sat on the edge of the seat.

"Are you serious?"

"I'm, welcome to the school of magic, serious. Light some candles and let's do this."

"Are you suddenly an expert?"

"No, but did you see that witchy store? There were candles everywhere. I say you light some. Set the Reaper hunting mood."

Gran's hands held this book before she died. She knew something. Maybe she was magic. Maybe she'd been a... *witch*.

She got up and headed toward the kitchen. "What have I got to lose?" She searched the cupboards for candles, but only an extinguisher sat in the corner of the highest cupboard. Gran kept them in a closet throughout the house. "Always be prepared for anything, Drew," she used to say. The last time the power had gone out, Gran had retrieved the candles from the den. She pushed the swinging door to enter the den and opened the cabinet behind the desk.

As she gathered pillar candles of different sizes, the sudden ticking of the clock echoed through the room, and she froze. Spinning around, she approached the clock. Eleven-eleven. The amulet fluttered against her skin, casting a glow that reflected on the clock's glass face. The timing was a strange coincidence, or something else.

"Gran?" Eerie silence and the steady ticking of the clock answered her whisper.

She glanced at the crystal stones lining the windowsill before heading back to the living room. As she arranged the candles around the book on the coffee table, her palms tingled and burned.

"Your talisman is glowing," Ori said.

"My what?" She grasped the amulet as its light flickered and warmth tickled her neck.

"Talisman. Amulet. Your grandmother gave that to you after she died. It's obviously magic; look at it. Have you seen anything like that before? Because I sure haven't. You can see dead people. I think you're ignoring what's right in front of you. What I don't understand is why. You're gifted. Step into your power."

She lit each candle with a long match from the festive tube by the fireplace, filling the room with soft light. When describing herself, the words gifted and magic never came to mind.

"Piper and I tried to do this the other night, and nothing happened."

"Did you use candles?"

"No."

"Was the book out?"

"It was before I got the book."

"Bingo. Okay, turn the pages and see if something happens."

The heat in her hands intensified, and the amulet thrummed against her neck. She reached for the pages, but they fluttered like butterfly wings before her fingers could make contact. She pressed her palms on each side to hold the pages still. What did Gran want with a book without words? A pulsing in her veins picked up speed as she held her hands on the book, and she yanked them back.

"What was that?" Ori asked from his perch on Gran's chair.

An idea hit her. Maybe Gran had sat in her favorite chair with the book. "Trade places," Drew said, jumping up. In a quick fluid motion no living soul could mimic, Ori moved from the chair to the sofa. Settling on Gran's beloved television-watching-and-wine-drinking chair, she leaned forward, exhaling hard.

"Come on, Gran. I know you're not far. What's the book for? I need your help, and you know I don't ask for help often."

She turned the book around, so its empty pages faced her. Taking a deep breath, she closed her eyes and let her hands hover over the book. She didn't know what she was doing and as the minutes passed, almost gave up.

"You've got this, Drew."

Ori's voice was a whisper. Restless energy under the surface of her skin pricked like sparks igniting, desperate to break free like a burst of fireworks. A twist of the magical key was all it would take to unlock it.

Gifted. Magic.

Gran's silhouette appeared beside her in her mind, and she opened her eyes. A hand rested on her shoulder. The gentle touch spread warmth across her chest and down her legs. She tilted her head up to the side. Gran smiled down at her, holding her eyes fixed on the book. Drew gasped, unable to hold back tears.

"You're here. You didn't leave me."

"Oh, no, dear. I'd never leave you, but I can't stay now. He'll know."

"What do I do? There are no words."

"Aye. You're wrong. The words live inside you, as they did me. You just gotta make them dance. Look."

"Drew, the book!" Ori shifted into a silhouette like Gran as he bolted from the sofa, clasping his hands together in a silent clap.

Sparks erupted from her hands over the book, raining down like confetti. Gold letters danced across the page, their movements fluid and graceful. When the words reached the edge of the paper, she raised her hand and the page turned. Gold light beamed from her hand, trickling onto the next page, and the next. How was she able to do this? The world of seeing the dead was transforming into something beyond her understanding. Another worldly energy surrounded her in something magical, as though seeing the dead her entire life had been preparing her for this journey.

Ori crouched close to her and read out loud. "'The talisman is a rare amulet. This powerful object contains source magic, gifted only to those with the strongest connection to the soul realm, usually by a spirit who was close to them in life.'"

Gran winked at her. "You did it. Now use it to send Hathorne back."

"Don't go, Gran! I need you!"

Drew leaped from the chair. She threw her arms around Gran, but as she did so, Gran vanished, leaving her stumbling forward.

Collapsing to the floor against Gran's chair, she covered her face, crying. Gran was still around, but the pain of not being able to keep her on the side of the living was like a knife in her stomach. Ori sat beside her. "I'd hug you if I could."

Wiping her eyes, she dropped her hands as Ori stared at his own translucent shape. "Hathorne," she said.

Ori's eyes met hers. "Reaper's got a name."

They both raised themselves to their knees to better see the book. She placed a finger on the page where he left off and read the fancy lettering out loud, her voice shaking. "'The talisman is the key to unlocking the moon gate and vanquishing a malevolent specter.' Moon gate?"

She sniffed and dabbed at her nose.

What's a moon gate?

The vision of swirling colors Ori had shown her in the parking lot came to her mind like a vivid dream. "I know where the moon gate is! It's at Neptune Point—Haven."

"Yup." Ori's voice was quiet. "Keep reading, Drew."

Her head swimming with other realms and moon gates, she cleared her throat and continued. "'If the moon gate unlocks to the shadow realm, the strongest of the banished can cross over to walk among the living. The harmful intentions they once held as a living soul transcend into power as one of the wandering.'" The Reaper... Hathorne's intentions in life empowered him in death. The gold lettering glimmered, beckoning her to read its message. "'Under the guidance of a mystic, the talisman harnessed with light seals the moon gate, trapping the malevolent soul in the shadow realm.'"

Ori tilted his head and picked up where she left off. "'Witch hunter banishing spell.'" He trailed off. "The words stop there."

Hathorne wanted her dead because he believed her to be a witch. Her thoughts trickled from her mind out loud. "If his intention as a human was to kill witches, what would that make him?"

Ori snapped his fingers and smiled. "That'd make him a witch killer." He rubbed his hands together. "You need to do what you just did to finish the spell and get rid of his sorry ass."

She bit her bottom lip.

Do what I just did.

Holding her hands over the book, she directed her thoughts to the pages and Gran. She took a deep breath and closed her eyes. "I don't feel anything, Ori. Is anything happening on the page?"

"Nothing. Maybe picture the words in your mind. You can do this."

Blowing a stream of air between her lips, she squeezed the amulet before holding her hands close to the book again, begging words to appear. Burning seared through her palms, sharp and quick, and she opened her eyes as red lettering scrolled across in one sentence. The words jumped off the page as she deciphered them.

Ori glanced at the book before raising his head to face her. For a moment, they held each other's gaze. Sadness clouded his normally clear blue eyes.

"If I close the gate with this"—she held up the amulet, and it glowed from the inside out, the vines creeping around the black stone—"I won't be able to see them any-more. My gift... my magic. It'll be gone."

Her unique ability to bridge the gap between the living and the dead defined her identity. She sometimes cursed seeing the dead but losing her view through the veil to the other side, and her ability to help them cross over, would be like removing a piece of her soul. There had to be another way.

SEVENTEEN

Drew parked near Little Mysteries to visit Celeste and show off her newfound magic skills, but her excitement faded when the closed sign greeted her. She peered inside the large front window, but darkness engulfed the interior. It wasn't yet four o'clock on a Saturday, and she could've sworn Celeste kept her store open until six.

She'd spent the night searching online for anything about witches or witch hunters. Movie characters weren't going to cut it, and she needed more than historical articles on the witch trials.

The straps of her crossbody bag dug into her shoulder from the weight of Celeste's book. She adjusted the leather satchel against her hip, her hopes of talking with the mysterious woman gone. Her questions would have to wait. Onto bright idea number two, the Atlas Cliffs Library.

She hopped down from the steps and trudged through slush along the bustling streets of downtown Atlas Cliffs. She pushed her way through the crowds of people, their festive shopping bags brushing against her, as the sound of car horns and chatter filled the air.

She sprinted up the cement steps, her heart racing as she flung open the black painted door and stepped inside the stone building. Vaulted ceilings made the space appear larger than it was. Rows of tall shelves with narrow aisles stood beyond large wooden tables illuminated with green hooded desk lights. The door shut on its own with a force that pushed her forward before slamming behind her.

A young man wearing a collared shirt behind the information desk glanced up from his stack of books. His creased forehead matched his wrinkled pants as he glared at her with disapproval. A faint burst of laughter erupted from the corner as a man sat in a too-small chair flanked by two children with a book in his hands. Two women sat side by side peering over books. One of them wrote in a notebook while the other read to her in a whispered voice. Growing up, all she'd ever wanted was a life without seeing the dead. She used to look at people with envy as they lived their lives in blissful innocence, unsuspecting of what lurked on the other side. She could have that life when she figured out how to send Hathorne back to where he came from. Why did the thought of her lifelong desire coming true spike her anxiety, giving her an ache in her chest?

As she made her way to the history section at the back of the room, a wave of silence surrounded her among the tall bookshelves. The scent of must and vanilla combined, taking her back to Atlas Cliffs High as the books enveloped her. Piper had dragged her here for a study group so she could hang out with Cole. He'd been the nice guy who ended up breaking Piper's heart and causing her to swear off dating. The thought of Cole reminded her of his mother and Enid. The day Enid and Ezra crossed over at Neptune Point was the last time she had seen her ghostly friend. Goodbyes had become a natural part of her gift, but nothing prepared her for how often she'd had to say goodbye to people in her life, too.

She shifted her attention to the rows of books, tracing her fingers along the various spines. With fierce determination, she set out to uncover any information about witches or the existence of Hathorne as a real person. The library was a long shot, but she had to try.

"Can I help you find something?" The young man from the information desk looked through the shelves on the other side of the aisle, startling her.

"No. Yes. I don't know."

He stacked books, blocking her view of him, and soft footsteps padded around the corner to where she stood. "History? What do you need? Are you working on an essay or thesis? I'm in my third year—"

"Witches. Any books on witches?"

He laughed. "Have you been to the new store in town? It's great if you're looking for a good gag gift." He snorted and stopped laughing when he looked at Drew. "Not into gag gifts, I see."

Piper would pluck a strand of hair from his head and thank him for his contribution to the spells they'd been working on turning humans into toads. She wished she had the audacity to be so bold. "I would appreciate any gift from that store. It'd be quite useful in certain situations. About the books? I don't see a section specific to witch history."

"We don't have anything like that here." He hesitated. "I'll look in the system to be sure. Follow me." He took her to a small desk in the back corner, where a computer hummed and flickered to life. She stood over him, observing as he typed in a standard username. "Do you mind?" He placed his hand over the keyboard as the cursor blinked in the password space.

Stealing his password hadn't crossed her mind until he made a big deal about it. What could be so secretive in the Atlas Cliffs Library? He gestured for her to turn around, but she held her ground, folding her arms. She didn't know what his deal was, but he'd have to accept her averting her eyes instead. "I'm not watching," she said.

"Fine." Typing and clicking followed. "I am correct. We do not carry such books in this library."

She leaned forward to get a better view of the screen as he scrolled through book titles in alphabetical order. As he scrolled the opposite way, she caught the words *Neptune Point.* "Stop. What's that?"

"What's what?" His voice hinted at irritation.

"Neptune Point. There are three books under Neptune Point. Where are those?"

He clicked on a box beside the title and pointed to a small hallway beside the desk. "Those are in storage in the back. The owners of the keeper's house donated them years ago, before they boarded up the tragic place. Especially after everything came to light about Dominic Sloan last year." He turned around in his seat and glanced up at her. His face lit up like a lightbulb switched on in his mind. "That's who you are! Drew

Harlow. I knew you looked familiar. What a wild ride that must have been. He shot you, right?"

She longed for the anonymity of Boston, where no one knew her back story. She swallowed the rising panic at the mention of Dominic's name. The high ceilings did little to ease the feeling of being trapped as the walls closed in on her. She leaned against the closest bookshelf and fiddled with the metal closure on her leather bag. As if sensing her distress, the amulet tickled her neck before warmth spread across her skin. "Can you just get me those books so I can get out of here?"

Logging off the computer, he rose from the chair. "No can do. They're not available for the public."

"Why not? This is a library."

"I don't make the rules," he said.

She followed him as he headed for the front desk. *This is ridiculous!* "Just let me look at the books. I won't take them out of here."

He stormed behind his desk and shut a half door, blocking her out. "No can do," he repeated. "I think they'll eventually end up in a lighthouse museum somewhere. Nonsensical books about a cursed lighthouse or witch history aren't the best use of your reading time. Just my opinion."

With her hands on her hips, she glared at him. Her anger was a shield against the panic threatening to overwhelm her. Who did he think he was? Maybe those books were nothing more than old photos or lighthouse history, but she wasn't leaving without knowing for sure. "I'm not interested in your opinion. I am interested in those books."

The man with the two kids gathered their jackets and readied them to leave. The two women glanced up from their books.

The frustrating librarian lowered his voice. "I'm not authorized to give you those books. If there is nothing more you need help with, please let me get back to work."

Spinning around, she marched to the back of the library. Leaving without those books wasn't an option. She was going into that back room.

Slowing her pace, she wandered through the aisles, plucking a book from the shelf within the librarian's sight. When he looked up from his stack of books and glanced her way, she pretended to be engrossed in the book. As soon as he turned his gaze away, she returned the book to the shelf and hurried down the aisle to the back hallway.

Restrooms were on both sides, with a closed door at the end. Stepping as quietly as her winter boots allowed on the tiled hallway, she turned the knob and opened the door a crack. The hinges creaked and her heart raced. She glanced over her shoulder before opening the door wider. A blast of cold air hit her as she stepped into the storage closet, and a shiver curled over her skin. Floor-to-ceiling shelves covered the walls, with two additional rows in the middle, leaving a narrow passageway. Not wanting to draw attention to the room, she avoided turning on the light and resorted to the flashlight on her phone. With a deep breath, she closed the door behind her and scanned boxes and old books in search of anything titled Neptune Point. The smell of mold and mildew invaded her senses, and her eyes watered as she stifled a sneeze.

Binders, encyclopedias, and books missing covers crowded every shelf, but she couldn't find any books mentioning Neptune Point. She had seen the books on the computer screen; they had to be in here... unless someone had already taken them.

Yanking boxes from shelves, she opened the lids and rummaged inside before placing them back. Her nose itched, and she covered her face with her sleeve, muffling the sound as she sneezed. Voices echoed from the hallway, and she froze. A burst of laughter rang out, sounding close. She surveyed the closet of a room. All this for a few books?

What am I doing?

"Wrong shelf, dear."

"Gran?" She whirled around, but no one was there.

"Help her," Gran's voice whispered.

Who is she talking to?

The amulet's heat intensified as it vibrated underneath her sweater. She grabbed the chain and held the radiant black stone up to her face. The vines twisted, gaining momentum until a flash shot toward the bottom shelf on the opposite side of the room. For a moment, the amulet's magic surrounded her with a sense of safety. Hathorne terrified her. A few encounters with him introduced her to a new level of the dead's capabilities. The amulet radiated energy like nothing she'd ever experienced before, giving her a glimmer of hope. Harnessing the stone's magic was the key to her gaining the upper hand with Hathorne.

She kneeled and cleared a path through a pile of boxes to uncover a package wrapped in brown paper. She wiped off dirt smudges and dust, revealing words written in black marker.

NEPTUNE POINT

Boots stomped on the tiled floor outside the storage room, and she shoved the package into the bag draped at her side with Celeste's book. She'd stolen once in her life; she'd taken a pack of watercolor paints off the shelf on a shopping trip with Gran when she was eight. Gran had marched her back into the store to apologize and beg for forgiveness.

She wasn't leaving without the package. It might be nothing more than photos or the history of Aurora, but she had to know for sure.

Cracking the door open, she peeked down the hallway, shutting it again as the librarian passed by. She waited and listened. Opening the door again, she stepped into the vacant hallway as the librarian's head popped around the corner, giving her a startled look. She strolled by him, a grin spreading across her face. "Happy holidays!" She waved over her shoulder as she hurried outside through the front door.

The sun set and a blast of flurries transformed the downtown core into a snow globe. Drew shivered as she pulled up her hood and dug into her pocket for her gloves. Gran would've loved shopping in this weather. She'd dance in the snow, laughing, unconcerned with who stared as she sang along to the Christmas carols filling every shop along the street. Grief's ache squeezed her insides and tears burned behind her eyelids. Christmas would never be the same again.

Slush sprayed as she ran toward her car. As she reached for the door handle, a sudden burst of dark smoke churned up from the snowy ground beside Little Mysteries. The frigid evening air changed, shrouding her in a deep freeze. Frost crept along the car window and snaked over the metal handle until it numbed her hand, forcing her to pull away. She rubbed her frozen gloved fingers and scanned both sides of the street. "I'll Be Home For Christmas" played over the chimes as people filed out of a store beside Little Mysteries, sounding more sinister than festive. The song filled her mind in slow motion like a broken record cracking with static. She bit her lip raw as she blinked snow from her eyes, her panting breaths visible in front of her.

Hathorne's cloaked shadow loomed under the flickering streetlights. She gripped her keys, glancing from the car to Hathorne. Driving away was looking like a good option, but if he wanted her dead, he would've killed her by now. Shoving the keys in her pocket, she moved closer. Gran had given her the amulet, a talisman, for protection. Time to put the strange jewel to the test.

He dragged his long nails against the building. The sound of metal blades on brick echoed through the air. The music stopped, traffic slowed, and the street emptied of people. Stores downtown closed early on weekends, and no one would be around to hear her scream. She couldn't call anyone for help, and wouldn't, anyway. Hathorne was her problem to solve.

The hood covered his head, and he didn't look in her direction, but she sensed his awareness in the way her skin pricked like needles scraping under the surface. His presence wasn't like the others. The tortured emotions oozing from this spirit penetrated her soul, shattering her heart into a thousand pieces. He'd done terrible things.

As she approached the stairway, her foot sank into a puddle of slush, soaking through to her socks. She tripped, grabbing the railing to stop her fall. In a swift movement, Hathorne appeared before her on the landing entrance to Celeste's store. Heavy footsteps thudded down the cement steps as boots materialized before a man appeared, not quite human-looking, and of bone crushing stature. She backed up onto the sidewalk, but he continued to move closer. The cloak slipped from his gray head, revealing pulsing veins, and his eyes narrowed to slits as he locked his unblinking gaze on her.

She pulled the amulet from beneath her sweater and held up the silver chain. Light spun and danced from deep inside and vines multiplied as they wrapped around the obsidian jewel. The prickling sensation changed to a thousand sparkler candles igniting at once. She darted a quick glance around the street to see if anyone was watching, but visibility had diminished as the snowfall advanced into a blizzard.

"Why are you here?" Her voice wavered as she spoke, her body wracked with shivers.

He leaned down until he was inches from her face and tapped the amulet with his clawed finger.

"That is mine, witch," he seethed, spreading a vile breath into her face, and she held her breath to suppress the nausea threatening to erupt.

He wants the amulet.

She snatched the vibrant stone from his reach. "You're wrong, asshole. It belongs to me. A witch. You need to leave."

A bright, melodic laugh burst out, and a little girl emerged through the snow, holding a man's hand as she skipped along the sidewalk. Holding his hood with one hand, the man smiled at the girl, who was trying to catch snowflakes on her tongue.

"I got a whole bunch, Daddy!" her small voice chimed. She let go of her father's hand and clapped at the snowflakes with her little mittens.

"Stay close. I don't want to lose you! In the car, Maddie!" The man opened the door of the car parked across the street from Drew's and started the engine. He wiped snow from the windshield as the little girl danced on the sidewalk and jumped with both feet on the street toward the back seat of the vehicle.

Maddie was Gran's name.

Her body tensed as she glanced back and forth between the pair and the Reaper of Death in front of her. Hathorne's grotesque head tilted to the side as he stared at the little girl. He wouldn't hurt an innocent child! It was witches he wanted dead! Childhood memories of her father patching up bloody knees and goodnight forehead kisses rushed through her mind. She would die before allowing any harm to come to a single hair on that child's head!

Stepping onto the road, she positioned herself to protect the girl, keeping her eyes on Hathorne. The pulsing amulet synced with her heartbeat, and her hands burned like they'd start a fire. A dark film covered Hathorne's eyes with each slow blink. He emitted a clicking sound and advanced toward the child. Drew grabbed at him, but he was too fast.

She dashed across the street, throwing herself between him and the girl, almost knocking the child over. Blinding snow whipped around them, and the man's frantic voice called out to his child.

Drew pivoted the girl back on the sidewalk and shoved Hathorne. As she reached out, the amulet sent a shock through her body and out of her hands, surrounding him in smoke. She stood gasping as the man ran toward her, shielding his eyes as he tried to see through the flurry of snow. "Lightening in December? What the—"

"Daddy, it was so pretty." The girl pulled at his hand, and he picked her up, glaring at Drew. "I didn't see a car coming. Why did you run after her?"

"Umm." A snowplow spreading salt over the road made its way toward them. "I heard the snowplow coming, and she was in the street... I just panicked. I'm sorry if I freaked you out. It was my mistake."

"Don't worry about it... Thanks for looking out for her. I was rushing and not paying attention. Happy Holidays." Placing the girl on the ground, he opened the door to the backseat.

The little girl pointed up at Drew. "Magic," she said, as her father lifted her and put her in the car. She covered her mouth and giggled.

Drew stood in the middle of the road and watched them drive away. Snow blew sideways under the streetlights and Christmas lights twinkled along the storefronts. Snow accumulated in her hair, clinging to her eyelashes, and she wiped her face. The cold seeped into her bones, and her feet squished with every step closer to her car. She pulled the heavy bag filled with books off her shoulder and threw it in the passenger seat, rubbing her aching neck. Sitting behind the wheel, she turned her wipers on, letting the window defrost.

Hathorne's intention was to hurt Maddie, an innocent little girl. Message received, but why play games? He could've killed Drew if he wanted to. She grasped the amulet as it warmed her skin. He wanted the amulet, and she wasn't going to let him have it.

A churning funnel of black smoke emerged from the shadows and blew across the hood of her car before disappearing. The raven swooped through the flurry of snow, dipping its wing along her windshield. The sleek bird landed on the Little Mysteries sign, tilting its head from side to side before flying away.

She patted the damp leather bag beside her. There must be information in the books; the amulet had led her right to them! Maybe they'd help her understand her newfound power. That's what it was, wasn't it? Power? Magic? The little girl had seen the magic and it had delighted her. Why was Drew so scared of finding out the truth? She set her eyes on the road and flicked her wipers. She was done being afraid.

Eighteen

With the wrapped Neptune Point books perched in her lap, Drew sank into the soft cushions of Gran's chair. She'd changed out of her wet clothes, but still couldn't get warm. She pulled a blanket from the chair and wrapped herself in it before tearing into the brown paper. A small book of poetry lay on the top of the pile. Worn and weathered, she opened the faded cover to the dedication on the first page.

"To my darling, Aurora." She ran her fingers over the faded handwritten ink.

A series of love letters and poems followed, ending in the lighthouse's dedication, named Aurora in memory of the writer's love. She paused at the last sentence; *thy magic mingled with fire. Forevermore, my heart will break. Forevermore, I will love thee.*

Magic?

Sitting upright in the chair, the blanket slipped to the floor. The next book was larger, with a hard cover. Red print across the top stated Neptune Point History. The curled pages crinkled, and the spine cracked as she skimmed through description and grayed-out images of the lighthouse's construction and automation. Interesting, but not what she was looking for.

The third book, which had no title, was bound by a frayed rope. She bit her bottom lip as the librarian's words about the books going to a museum lingered in her mind. They'd been sitting on that shelf for years, and not going anywhere anytime soon. She'd be doing a disservice by ignoring the contents inside. As she pulled the tie to release the knot, the rope disintegrated in her fingers.

The thin pages crumpled as she touched them. She struggled to read the fancy, hard-to-read handwritten entries dating back to the 1800s. Flicking the side table light on, she held the book up, straining to read.

It's a journal.

Taking care to preserve the pages, she turned to the end of the small notebook. On the last page, a simple but bold sentence sent chills along her skin.

A fire shall come with his death. And mine.

Love, Aurora

This book was Aurora's journal!

With her heart racing, she sat on the edge of the chair and started at the beginning. Aurora wrote stories of hauntings in the keeper's house, professing her terror of death in every entry. She wrote about a beautiful necklace she found in the attic and the strange light emitting from it when whatever was haunting her was around.

The amulet.

Drew tried to swallow, but her throat was so dry. Could it be? Had Aurora seen Hathorne, too? Each entry turned more and more frantic, the writing choppy, as though the woman wrote with shaking hands. She feared for her life and the lives of her husband and children, begging them to leave Neptune Point. Drew neared the end of the thin journal and there it was. A name, scribbled on the page before the *fire shall come* pronouncement.

She whispered the words as she read them. "'He speaks his name in my ear. A hunter of mystics. Hathorne. Claws of death wrap around my throat. He utters a word, promising to end my life. Witch. I shall sacrifice my own to end his. I shall preserve future legacies.'"

Light twirled from the center of the amulet. She lifted the chain as it dangled in front of her eyes. What secrets did the jewel hold, and how had it come to be in Gran's possession?

Hathorne, hunter of mystics. Hell, he was a hunter of anyone in his path. She had to stop him before he hurt someone, or worse. He'd gotten too close to her father and that innocent little girl.

The questions piled up with no obvious answers, and she shivered uncontrollably. The fire had burned down to ash, and she hadn't turned the heat on. Gran always preferred a roaring fire to electric heat. Placing the book on the side table, she forced herself up to tend to the stubborn fire. Taking pieces of kindling from the metal basket, she crossed them together, stuffing crumpled pages of newspaper in the cracks. She plucked a long match from the tube and lifted it to the sandpaper striker surface. But before she connected the match, a flame ignited from the red match head.

The match had to have struck the surface. With the flame swaying, she held the match up to her eyes. As she examined her hands for a sign or a spark, the flame crawled down the wooden matchstick, burning her fingers.

"Ouch!"

She dropped the flame on the paper and added a log as the flames consumed the kindling. The white bark cracked and burned, and she returned the metal mesh to prevent sparks from flying.

Rubbing her sore fingers, she plopped back on the edge of the chair. Exhaustion was playing mind games. Magic or not, she couldn't start a fire with her hands. Matches didn't self-ignite. The amulet's warmth intensified, tingling the skin along her neck. She still hadn't deciphered the jewel's signals, but if Hathorne returned, she needed to know.

Rising on her knees in the chair, she pushed the drapes aside to peek out into the darkness. Shadows cast over the driveway as the wind blew through the barren trees. It took every ounce of willpower to not tear down the For Sale sign whipping back and forth in the front yard. Maybe the wind would be victorious and carry the sign away. A sudden snap rattled the wood in the fireplace, distracting her from the view outside the window.

She took a mental inventory of pictures on the walls, all Gran's trinkets, the furniture, and a lifetime of items she'd have to sell, discard, or pack. Selling the house and the Tough Cookie was what she wanted. Waiting only delayed the inevitable. She vowed to repeat those words to herself until she drowned out the doubts.

Tilting her head from side to side, she rubbed the knots in her neck. The ache returned, spreading from her stomach to her chest as the silence of the house settled around her. Sinking back into the seat, she picked up Celeste's book of magic. Celeste had known her mother's name, and said she couldn't see the dead, but she felt their presence. Was she a witch too?

I'm calling myself a witch now. I've officially crossed a line I never knew existed.

But the signs were pointing to an invisible world surrounding her, waiting to be discovered. Celeste had put together a link between Joelle and Ori, turning the connection ominous. Both Ori and her mother's letters had originated in California, and Ori was still here, desperate to uncover the identity of the driver who hit him.

A sudden vision invaded the clutter in her mind of her mother speeding away, leaving Ori motionless on the pavement. No. No, that couldn't be right. Perhaps her mother had been a witness to the accident, and if she found her mother, she'd find out who hit Ori. Now, to find where Joelle was hiding in town. A resort hotel was situated along the boardwalk, with a few older motels on the outskirts of town and countless Bed and Breakfasts. Joelle wouldn't leave until she found Drew; she had come a long way and wouldn't be questioning strangers if she was not desperate to locate her.

The inside cover of Celeste's book displayed a sketch of a dense forest with a shadowed figure among the trees and a fire burning in the background. That image hadn't been there before. She shuddered. She knew that forest.

Haven.

A sharp, icy feeling gripped her chest, and she flipped to the gold words spread across the pages. The electric sensation in her hands had subsided, but she held them over the book and closed her eyes. "Ori? You around?"

Nothing happened.

She breathed in through her nose and released the air from her mouth as Piper had shown her.

Come on, do something!

She opened one eye, but this time, no flash of light or fireworks flew from her hands. Candles. She didn't have candles lit!

As she stood from the chair, headlights illuminated the living room. A car engine rumbled outside. She wasn't expecting anyone, and Gran's friends had stopped checking in on her. A car door slammed shut. And another. Her heart raced as she rushed to the front door.

Her father was at his apartment downtown; they'd spoken earlier. Could it be... Joelle?

She peered through the blinds over the glass window. A green Volkswagen bus parked as close to the house as possible.

Jasper's vehicle. The sight of his beloved hippie van in her driveway brought back memories of carefree days spent driving along the California coast.

She opened the door as Piper bounded up the porch steps with Jasper behind her, carrying a small tree.

"You didn't message me back, so I came with help to spread Christmas cheer in this sad house." Piper made a grand gesture, and Jasper followed her lead by standing the tree upright.

She didn't want to say anything against Christmas and decorating after they'd driven in a snowstorm to see her. "I see that."

"It was my idea. I needed something fun to do." Jasper carried the tree through the door. "I don't know what I was thinking, leaving California weather to come here." He set the tree against the wall. "I wanted to apologize last night, before we went to Maze."

"Apologize?" She shut the door behind them and secured the deadbolt. She couldn't imagine what he had to apologize for.

"I'm sorry I didn't come to the funeral. I should have, but I... I just couldn't do it. It brought back too much pain, and—"

"Jasper, don't apologize. You don't have to explain. I get it."

He looked more like Piper's brother than her cousin. Their eyes held the same warmth, except for the grief palpable in his own. He needed friendship as much as she did, even if she didn't want to admit she needed anyone. She might not have a big family—hers was non-existent except for her father—but a lesson was becoming more and more clear... Family wasn't always those related by blood.

Jasper shook off his winter coat and gloves. He pulled at his paisley shirt, the static cling visible as it cracked and stuck to him. "I won't get used to this," he said.

"Sure you will. You'll be ice skating and skiing before you know it." Drew's mood lifted, like it had the night before at Maze. Having them in the empty house with their chatter and the sweet, refreshing aroma of winter mixed with the pine tree eased some of her loneliness.

Piper kicked her boots off with a laugh. "Yeah, right, he will. He's already complaining he had to buy all new clothes. He hates long sleeves."

His hair rose as he took his hat off, and he combed his fingers through his wavy hair. "See? Look at me. I'm a hot mess."

She gave him a hug. "Welcome to the hot mess club."

They gathered around the living room, each with a glass of Gran's red wine—Piper's suggestion to create a festive atmosphere. Drew dug out Gran's tree stand and a box of decorations. Jasper rolled up his shirt sleeves and helped her set it up. She hung antique ornaments, glass snowflakes, green shamrocks, and red velvet bows. She paused at the wooden stockings and wreaths she'd painted as a kid. Gran kept the special ones. Balancing on the chair, she placed Gran's star on the tree's peak. She'd always found the star tacky with the silver garland and colored lights, but it had a new meaning now. Her throat tightened with emotion and her eyes watered.

Piper plugged in the ceramic village along the mantel and clapped her hands together. "Mission accomplished. Christmas has officially thrown up in your living room, and it looks beautiful!"

Drew added another log to the fire, sending the flames higher and brighter in the fireplace. Gran's essence filled the room like she was right there with her. "It looks good in here. Thanks for doing this. I wasn't going to bother with any of it."

Piper hugged her. "Gran would've kicked your ass if you let her decorations sit in a box and you know it."

Drew expected Gran to burst into the room nodding her head with an exasperated, "Hell, yes!", but she never came.

Jasper picked up the magic book from the coffee table and sat on the sofa. He swirled his glass of wine, holding it by the stem with a pinky finger extended, before taking a sip and placing it down. Gran would have adored Jasper, talking business, baking, and cooking. Drew wished she could've met him.

"There's no title," he said. "What's the symbol mean?" He held his hand up to mirror the cover. "Is this a ghost girl thing?

Hey, did you find your mother? After all that distance you traveled searching for her, and she's here. How wild is that?"

"Not yet." Her stomach pinched at the mention of her mother. Ori would be around soon enough, with a new revelation or asking the same questions. Piper picked up the small journal on the side table, and Drew sat on the sofa. "Careful with that one! It's ready to fall apart."

"It's an old diary. Have you read this, Drew? Aurora, what in the... like Aurora who the lighthouse is named after?"

"The same one. She knew him, Piper. Reaper has a name... Hathorne."

"Heath Hathorne? The crusty judge who murdered people accused of witchcraft?" Jasper turned the pages in the magic book with care.

Both Drew and Piper snapped their heads toward Jasper.

"Who?" Drew asked. Jasper was a chef, not a history major. "How do you know that?"

"I studied business in London for a semester before coming back to the states to become a chef. I fell in love and lost everything. The rest is history... literally, in this case. I'm a pro at making excellent decisions." Jasper wiped his eyes. "I'm sorry. I keep waiting for time to heal me like everyone says, but it's not getting better. It just hurts more." He looked at Drew. "You, of all people, must get it. You can see ghosts! How do you let go? It's too hard, I can't do it. I'm losing my mind."

Drew was no stranger to letting go. She set aside her burning history questions as her own grief coursed through her, bubbling over in a frenzy. "It's so fucking hard. I get it. Gran is gone. The only home I've ever known is for sale. The Tough Cookie is about to be gone forever. I'm stuck with a ghost who can't find peace until I help him. My mother's probably going to show up at my door any day. And on top of everything, turns out I'm a witch with a witch hunter stalking me. Does this seem like I've let go?" She flopped her head back against the sofa. "I'm sorry. I couldn't stop."

"You'll burst if you hold all that inside," Piper said.

Jasper crossed his legs, his bell-bottom jeans hanging over candy cane socks. "A witch, you say. Interesting." He reached for his wine and took a long sip. "Chaos burns a person right the fuck out. Take it from a twenty-four-year-old bistro owner who couldn't do it anymore. Who's the ghost, by the way? You've piqued my curiosity in this welcome distraction."

"It's the surfer guy," Piper said.

"He was a surfer?" Jasper placed his glass on a coaster.

The situation would be perfect if Ori could sense the conversation within the realm of his ghostly possibilities and appear in the room, but there was no sign of him. "He was a surfer from California, but that's not how he died."

"Really?" Jasper looked down at his hands, fiddling with a silver ring around his index finger. "I knew some surfers in my time in California... I don't want to talk about it though." He raised his head and met Drew's eyes. "Can we do like a séance or something? Can you choose the ghosts you want to see?"

"Unfortunately, no. Not yet, anyway." She wanted to steer the conversation back to what Jasper knew about Heath Hathorne, and if he could be the same tortured spirit haunting her.

Jasper picked up the wineglass again, swirling the last of the red contents. "Is there any way you could... call on him? I can't believe I'm saying this."

"It doesn't work like a cell phone, J." Piper opened the book again and turned the pages. Her eyebrows knitted together as she strained to read under the table lamp. "Just tell her about him. She might be able to help."

Jasper threw back the last gulp of wine in his glass and stared at the tree. "I don't want to talk about it."

"If you change your mind, I'll be here," Drew said. "Can you tell me more about the witch history? Who is Heath Hathorne?"

"That, I can do. He was a judge in the 1600s who took pleasure in murdering women he believed to be witches. I'm surprised you haven't heard about him being a witch yourself." The words fell out as matter of fact and without judgement. Typical Jasper style. "He was from Atlas Cliffs before moving to Salem, but there were others in Europe. They either burned or hanged the women. Horrific reign of power. He deserved what happened to him."

She'd never heard of him before. Gran had lived in Atlas Cliffs since her twenties, and never spoke of anything paranormal in her life. But the more she uncovered, the less far-fetched her grandmother's witch status appeared. "What happened to him?"

"The legend says a group of women slated for death row set fire to the prison and he burned to death."

"They all died?" Piper asked, looking up from the book.

"A sacrifice to save others after them. They were heroes. It was the late seventeenth century and the end of the witch trials. That's really all I remember. The name stuck the most. Not sure if it helps at all."

"It helps a lot." The amulet suddenly reacted with an intense vibration underneath her sweater, and she placed her hand over her chest. Aurora had discovered the necklace in the attic of the keeper's house, and Gran had found the amulet along the way, before giving it to Drew after she'd died. She didn't know why Gran had kept her secrets hidden, especially knowing Drew could see the dead. Her best and only guess was that she did it to protect her, keeping her safe.

But Hathorne had returned to Atlas Cliffs from the grave with a deathly fixation on Drew. Aurora had seemingly sent

Hathorne away once, and now she'd have to figure out a way
to do it again.

NINETEEN

Jasper had left after midnight. As the credits for The Nightmare Before Christmas scrolled down the screen, Drew turned off the television and stretched.

Piper's attention turned back to Aurora and witches. Drew finished telling Piper about the book's words coming to life under her hands the night with Ori and how Hathorne had tried to harm the little girl, Maddie. Piper read through the magic book twice, trying to help her decipher the messages. They sat beside each other on the sofa, staring at the tree's twinkling lights.

"Have you tried to do it again? Recreate the moment? Maybe instructions on how to get rid of him will appear," Piper said.

"Right before you and Jasper showed up I was trying, but nothing was working. I went to see Celeste again. Her store was closed, but I'm going back. She's the only one I can think of who might be able to help."

"Can I come?" Piper asked.

"Can I stop you?" Drew fiddled with the fringe on the blanket. "I'm scared something bad will happen to you, like Dad or the little girl."

"But it didn't."

"Yeah, because I was there, and this protected them." Drew held up the silver chain and the obsidian stone dangled, quiet and shrouded in darkness—for the time being.

"As long as you or Ori are around, we'll be fine, right?"

"I'm not sure it works that way. What if Hathorne could've hurt them but stopped for another reason? Like he wants to drag this out and make me suffer? It's working, by the way."

"If I was a tortured asshole with powers from the underworld... I suppose that's possible."

"That's why I need to see Celeste and learn how to be all witchy with magic and stuff."

"It's like a fairy tale!"

"A twisted fairy tale."

"How about we get up early and go see Celeste tomorrow?" Mascara smudged under Piper's eyes as she rubbed them.

"I like that plan. Then I'm taking a drive out to Neptune Point." Ori hadn't come back, but Haven was a must if Drew was going to find any signs of a moon gate's existence, and how it related to Hathorne.

Piper's yawn stretched into a grin. "You read my mind. Makes sense when you read all this; Hathorne has a history with the place." She thumbed through Celeste's book. "All these blank pages. Do you think Gran had filled them, but it all magically disappeared?"

"I wish I knew. Maybe I brought back the words she already created?" A longing to talk to Gran returned. Its intensity was so intense her throat tightened, and her eyes filled with tears. "Thanks for staying, Piper."

"No problem. I'm worried about you. Where's your head? I mean, with selling the house. Do what you've got to do, but it feels too soon if you ask me."

"I can't run a business and maintain this place. It's too much. But if I stop and let myself think about never coming back here, I won't be able to do it." Choking panic crept back into her chest. "It's so hard to think of other people living here, sitting around the fire, cooking, and celebrating birthdays and stuff. Gran's flowers will come up in the spring. They could dig them up and throw them away. I'll miss the beach, the bakery..."

Nico.

She didn't say his name out loud. If she did, she'd have to admit her feelings for him were more than just friends. "I'll miss people," she continued, "but I can't keep letting myself go there, or I'll never sell this place."

"There's your sign. Wait. What people, Drew?" Piper folded her arms across her chest and stared at her with a smile.

Drew knew what she was doing, but didn't give in. "My friends, like you, Dad, no one in particular. You know... people."

"Stop. It's me you're talking to! It's okay to say it. Nico. You still like him. Of course you do! He's a good guy, he's cute, and he cares about you."

Being vulnerable to anyone wasn't easy, but Piper was like her sister. She trusted her with deeper secrets than love lingering for Nico.

Love. Dammit.

"You're right, I still like him. And I feel shitty for breaking up with him, even though it was the right thing to do at the time. I'm just sad I lost him." She exhaled. "There, I said it."

"I'm proud of you. Was that so hard? Now go tell him that." Piper's hands dropped to her lap.

"I can't. And don't you dare tell him, Piper. Please."

"Oh my God, I wouldn't. But I do think you need to talk to him. What's the worst that could happen?"

"Let's see, where do I start? He'll say he's happy and in love with Nicki, but he wants to hang onto our friendship, and I'll be left broken-hearted and feeling like a fool. I've got too much going on right now to lose focus, and I'm not staying in Atlas Cliffs, anyway. Nico and I would be right back where we were last summer."

"People can have long-distance relationships, and Boston isn't far," Piper said. "I'd be open to it with Taj. We're still getting to know each other, but what I'm saying is, for the right guy? Anything is possible."

"Nico and I made nice memories, and he was there for me when I needed him, but it's over, and I have to be okay with that."

"It's not over, Drew, but I'll drop it." Piper picked up the book again. "What if it's true, and the only way to stop Hathorne from hurting you is to give up seeing the dead? Will you do it?"

She was going to lose Ori, but she'd never see Gran again. Losing them once they crossed over was the lonely, tough part of the deal. The weight of responsibility would lift off her shoulders if she no longer could see the dead.

But what if seeing the dead was the one gift that made her special? The amulet gifted her magic—for how long, she didn't know, but she could do what no one else could. Without ghosts needing her help, the silence would be too loud. She'd discovered and accepted the part of her that was unique, with purpose... She held magic. She never wanted to feel lost again. There had to be another way.

"If it means keeping people safe, I'll have to give it up. But it scares me, Piper. I always cursed it, always. If it happens, and I lose it all... I wouldn't feel like me anymore."

Piper turned to face her. "You will always be you. My best friend, my sister. That part that we all have inside us never goes away. No one and nothing can take it from you. No matter what happens, I'll be in your corner."

Drew hugged her. "Same, Piper. Same." Their friendship, a sisterhood, would keep them connected for life, no matter where they went.

They talked for hours into the night before Piper crashed on the bed beside her. Drew tossed and turned, flopping onto her back, aching with fatigue. Sleep was an elusive beast. Getting up, she grabbed her phone and went downstairs to curl up on Gran's chair. She clicked on her music playlist, but her curiosity overpowered her will to resist, and she checked Nico's social media page again. She had to know if he'd posted anything new with his girlfriend, but the same photo of him and Nicki smiled back at her. Drew rolled her eyes, frustrated with herself for being drawn to him again. She might as well use her time for research. Opening an internet browser, she searched for witch trials, witch hunter, witch *anything*. With the fire nothing more than coals, a chill filled the room, and she pulled the thick, crocheted throw over herself. The scent of Gran's shampoo and lilac body spray still lingered, ramping up the grieving ache in her chest.

She switched off the music and nestled as deep into the chair cushions as they'd allow. As her eyes drifted closed, a ticking sound pinged her brain. She bolted upright and listened. The clicking of the hands echoed from the den. The time on her phone showed two in the morning. She'd been so engrossed in her music and hadn't noticed when the clock started working again. Throwing the blanket off her legs, she got up and crept from her chair through the darkness. She plodded along the light-spun path coming from one of Gran's decorative night-lights. As she stepped into the den through the swinging door, she braced herself for what, or who, she'd find, wishing it was Gran.

The only sound penetrating the empty room was the clock keeping steady time until a whisper buzzed in her ear.

Burn, witch.

The raspy hiss belonged to Hathorne. She spun around, the sensation of someone's breath on the back of her neck, but no one was there. Her heart raced and sweat trickled down her back underneath her hoodie. She pulled the amulet's chain, letting it dangle over the sweater, begging it to back her up when she was ready. Scouring the main floor, she flipped lights on and opened closets, finding nothing.

Was he upstairs with Piper? She took the stairs two at a time, almost tripping as she slipped on the hardwood floors. Breathless at the top of the stairs, she gripped the railing, but the hallway was empty and dark except for the small Tiffany lamp set to the dimmest setting. Piper was still asleep in her room with the door ajar. The spare room had remained an untouched mess since her father had stayed the night she'd arrived home. Holding onto the handle of Gran's bedroom door, she took a deep breath, willing the amulet's magic to shield her from harm if Hathorne was on the other side. Turning the knob, she pushed the door open, clutching the cold amulet. She flipped the light switch, but she stood alone in the room, catching her reflection in the mirror on Gran's dresser. A layer of dust had gathered on top of the armoire where a set of sponge curlers rested, and the curtains remained drawn tight.

Hathorne's threat was a constant presence in her life, its beat pulsing with every breath she took, and his voice burned into her mind. Fatigue wracked her body and her head ached. The numbness on her leg intensified with the exertion, and she rubbed the top of her thigh to create blood flow. Sleep enticed her, but downstairs was the best spot for her to keep watch. She balanced the weight from her numb leg to her uninjured one and headed down the steps to curl up in Gran's chair. Settling in with the blanket again, she rubbed its rough yarn against her cheek, trying to stay alert, watching the shadows. Watching for Hathorne's wrath. But her eyes had other plans.

She walked along the path covered in snow, the same path she used to dream about every night after Shane's accident. The trees closed in on her, their branches moving, weaving, and linking. They moved the same way the vines did on the amulet, forming a canopy over her head as she stepped deeper into the forest. Dark gray smoke floated toward her, wafting into her lungs with every breath. Coughing, she moved through the tree-lined tunnel until the heat from a blazing light warmed her hands and face.

Ori's voice screamed from somewhere unseen. "Wake up, Drew!"

A high-pitched beeping pierced her ears, and a knocking sounded, getting louder and more forceful, jolting her awake. She sat up and wiped the drool off her mouth while trying to focus. Smoke drifted down the stairs into the living room. Piper's stifled screams came from upstairs. She leaped from the chair, tossing the blanket aside, and stumbled up the stairs.

Smoke filled the hallway, and she choked and coughed as she ran into her bedroom. Piper was gone. Loud, frantic knocking thudded in her ears, and she felt her way along the wall toward the sound.

"Piper!" she yelled between coughs.

Piper shrieked and banged on Gran's closed door as smoke slithered out from the gap underneath. Drew grabbed the doorknob—heat warmed its metal, but it wouldn't turn. She shook it, kicking the door as hard as she could.

Ori appeared beside her. "I've got her." His voice was muffled as he crossed through the door in his ghost form.

The door flew open, and Piper fell out of the room to the floor, choking. Flames snaked along the curtains, licking the ceiling, and Drew seized an extinguisher from the hall closet. She pulled the trigger, soaking the wall and cutting the flames off from their tirade.

Sirens screamed, growing louder.

"I called 9-1-1," Piper coughed from the hallway, sitting against the wall with her knees bent, her phone in hand.

Drew's face burned and sparks landed on the ends of her hair, turning the red to a bright orange. She snuffed them out with her hands before they could ignite her hair into flames.

The wall around the window burned to charcoal, and the metal rod that once held the curtains was the only thing left hanging. A dusting of black ash covered the hardwood floor, but it still looked sturdy. Gran's armoire had burned, her clothes disintegrated, leaving part of the frame behind. Remnants of melted plastic from the curlers had fallen to the floor. She wrapped a blanket around her hand and used it to turn the crank and open the window, letting cold air rush into the room.

"I saw him," Ori said. "I saw him, and I tried to stop him. You were sleeping... he was going to kill her."

Piper.

Drew ran to her friend's side as the doorbell rang.

A loud thud sounded on the front door, and someone yelled, "Fire department!"

Piper sat in a heap on the floor, shivering. "I heard a loud noise from Gran's room and thought it was you. The door slammed shut. It was pitch black, and I smelled smoke. The curtains burst into flames, but I couldn't open the door, and I heard laughing, Drew. *Laughing.*"

Piper shook with sobs as Drew hugged her. Ori sat beside her as boots thumped up the stairs and sirens blared from outside. Voices yelled orders.

Drew stared into Gran's room as firefighters attended the scene.

Someone was going to die if she didn't stop him.

TWENTY

Firefighters inspected Gran's bedroom, asking about electrical issues unknown to Drew and assessing the extent of the damage. She and Piper both gave statements, avoiding mention of the dead witch hunter. Telling them would grant her a psych assessment and put more people in danger.

She followed Piper outside to the waiting ambulance to be checked over as a precaution. The snow had subsided, but the frigid sea wind bit hard and she shivered, tightening a blanket around her shoulders. Her breath rolled upward in the frigid air. Dark clouds dominated the night sky, snuffing out any hope of starlight.

Hathorne was a cobra taking pleasure in playing with his prey, striking over and over again until he decided to kill it. She struggled to look at Piper, whose breathing had stabilized after she'd received oxygen. She wanted to run screaming into the ocean and let hypothermia numb her entire being.

Piper's parents arrived in their big SUV, her mother leaping from the front seat before it came to a full stop.

"Piper!" she screeched as she ran past the trucks with their flashing lights, her coat swinging open, revealing a matching flannel pajama set.

"I'm fine, Mom," Piper said as her mother fawned over her like a child.

Mayhem surrounded them as Drew rehashed the events of the evening.

Piper's mother turned her attention to the medic, and Piper hopped off the back of the ambulance, pushing her oxygen mask to the side. "You came in time. It could've been worse. Don't beat yourself up about this."

"Piper, he tried..." Drew lowered her voice to a whisper, "He tried to kill you. I'm going to fix this."

"Wait for me. I want to come with you. They're making me go to the hospital and get checked out." She patted herself down and rolled her eyes. "Look at me, I'm fine. I'll come as soon as I get out."

Piper's mother faced Drew; concern spreading through her eyes and forehead as she placed her hands on Drew's shoulders. "They said you were okay? Why don't you let me take you to the hospital, too?"

"I'm okay. I don't need a hospital." Tears burned Drew's eyes, and she looked away from Piper's mom. She envied her friend's close relationship with her mother, wishing she had the same bond with her own. Gran had done everything in her power to make up for Drew missing her own mom; her unconditional love was a lifeline that had rescued her in ways she might not ever understand. But it was still a different type of love than a mother's love.

Piper's mother released her hands from Drew and zipped her coat. "Pack a bag and come with us, anyway. I'm taking Piper to the hospital. She's not riding in the back of an ambulance on my watch. You can stay with us."

It wasn't a question, but Drew wasn't going. "Thank you, Mrs. Arlott, but I'm needed here. They might have questions."

Standing with her arms folded, Mrs. Arlott's posture mirrored her daughter's strong-willed demeanor. She was a lawyer, and Drew could see why she was so successful. "Drew, you cannot stay in a house where a fire has caused damage. I cannot in good conscience leave you here alone—"

"I can go stay with my dad. I'll call him right now. Thank you for offering; I appreciate it." Drew refused to leave her home, but she needed Piper to leave and be safe. "Go get her checked out, make sure she's okay. I'm good. Promise." The lie slipped off the tongue without a second thought as Piper hugged her goodbye.

As the SUV drove away, the streetlight across the road cast an eerie glow on the dense mounds of beach grass poking through the snow. Drew left the fire trucks behind and made her way to the end of the driveway as boot prints cast impressions in the snow under the light.

He's still here!

Anger burned hotter than the fire, threatening to burst free. She wanted to kill him like she'd wanted to kill Dominic.

Hathorne lurked in the shadows on the other side of the road as dark smoke circled around his feet, exposing his tall boots and the bottom of his cloak. The smoke and mist continued to swirl skyward, revealing the hood on his cloak hanging down his back. His veiny, sunken head was exposed as he stared at her with piercing eyes. His mouth curved like a cruel beast about to attack, and he turned away from her, walking toward the cliff.

She glanced back at the house. The For Sale sign swung, and light beamed from the upstairs windows. Firefighters were inside trying to figure out an unsolvable mystery. Hathorne, an ancient spirit from the pits of an unknown world, had tried to burn her house down.

He had tried to kill Piper.

She was in an impossible situation, with no one to help her. Gran was gone, leaving her lost and alone to sell the house and the bakery, with an amulet encased in magic she didn't know how to use. Ori needed her help to find peace, and she had to come face to face with her mother for the first time since she was a child. As she struggled to make the right choices, a sense of desperation crept in as she tried to hold the pieces together. If she ran away and left Atlas Cliffs, she wasn't convinced Hathorne would follow; Aurora's journal made it clear Neptune Point had tethered him here. Any attempt to escape him would lead to more threats and danger. The home—her haven—she had grown to love was slipping away from her.

The danger surrounding her extended to anyone in her proximity, most importantly her loved ones.

Her thoughts spiraled out of control, and she'd be useless if she didn't break the cycle. She wasn't alone anymore. She had her father, who'd be there for her when she needed him. He had proven it more in the last year than he had in her entire life. Piper wasn't just her friend, she was family. If Hathorne had killed her, Drew would never forgive herself. Nico may have moved on, but he was still there for her when she needed him, even if she didn't want to need him.

I'm not alone anymore.

She stepped closer to the road as Hathorne's cloak swung over the cliff side. She tore after him toward the edge of the cliff, the blanket slipping off her shoulders. As she ran, her untied boots slapped against her heels. The surf pounded the shore, but he walked through the water unscathed. She scaled down the stone steps until she reached the bottom, gasping for breath. The wind whipped her hair in her face and sea mist soaked her sweater as she ran after him.

He'd gone too far, and she was too far gone to stop now.

"What do you want from me?" she yelled over the crashing waves.

He stopped and raised his hands. The beach lights above reflected off the water, lighting up his curled fingers. Veins crawled along his head like worms trying to escape, making her stomach churn like she'd throw up.

Gran, Ori, please help me.

As if on cue, her skin burned along her neckline, and she covered the amulet with her hand to hide its light.

Not yet.

Hathorne contorted his body until he was facing her and inched closer. As the gap closed between them, a sharp pain shot through her head, and she dropped the amulet, gripping the sides of her face.

"I warned you. Death seeks you, and anyone near you," he seethed between yellowed teeth.

She forced herself to look at his face. The veins rippled beneath his gray, ulcered skin. "Like it did for Aurora? Or the women you murdered?"

In one swift motion, he raised his hands over her, and her chest tightened as she gasped for breath. He dripped with cruelty and punishment, and she was powerless to break free. "You know my name, witch. I laid claim to her power, and I will take yours before I watch you burn."

As he wrapped a clawed hand around the glowing stone, Gran's voice echoed in her ears.

You've got all you need to send him back... What you lose will come back again.

The stone radiated light through the dark. A warm sensation cascaded from the top of her head and down her body. The sound of a hundred hummingbirds buzzed around her and an aroma tickled her nose like blowing out a sweet-scented candle. Oxygen flooded her lungs, and she sucked in the sweet air as she snatched the amulet from his reaching fingers and held it out toward him.

Who did he steal power from? Aurora sent him back before... Was it her magic he took?

His eyes bore into her, holding her captive. Her eyes burned, but his power made it impossible to break free from his intense stare. He wanted her to see, and like Ori, he knew how to show her. Through his eyes, she glimpsed his rage-filled soul as he murdered women, chanting the same word over and over as the fires burned.

Witch.

Witch.

Witch.

He saw her as one of many *evil* women and was on a mission to ensure she met the same fate, even if it meant harming innocent people around her. He'd been a person unwilling to see any other way in life. In death, he continued with his duty to cleanse the realms of witchcraft fueled by the stolen power of those he killed.

Eradicating him was the only way to save herself. Taking deep breaths, she held the amulet in front of her and stepped through the sand. He grabbed for the sparkling stone, but she persisted forward, keeping it out of his hands. Its light bathed her in heat, and with a flash of light, he cowered away before bursting into a single flame extinguished by the sea. The raven charged past her face before it flew over the cliffs.

She steadied her trembling legs. The magic inside the amulet swirled into a ribbon of light before vanishing in a blink. He craved the power around her neck. Somehow, she knew if she didn't send him back to where he came from before he stole it from her, his promise of death would come true.

Ori appeared beside her. "You got rid of him!"

"For now. He won't stop, Ori. I need to do something; something big. Permanent." Frozen through her skin to her bones, she headed for the stone steps to the top of the cliff.

"What are you going to do?" Ori said, following her.

"I'm going to ask for Celeste's help. I'll beg if I have to. I'm going to Haven to find the portal, or moon gate... whatever it's called."

"I'm coming with you! You can't do this alone!" Ori called from behind her as she picked up the blanket from the road and headed back to the house. One truck remained, and two firefighters stood outside the house. She needed a hot bath to thaw her numb feet.

"Are you all done? Can I go back inside?" she asked.

"I'm sorry, Drew. I thought you'd left with your friend. We were going to lock up." The shorter of the two peered behind her. "Where'd you go?"

Telling them she was chasing a dead killer wouldn't work.

"I needed fresh air. The ocean is the best, you know... it calms me."

He peered behind her with a puzzled expression. "Right. Look. We don't recommend you stay in the house until it's been cleaned by a professional for smoke damage. You were smart, thinking on your feet the way you did. The structure is intact, but you're gonna need repairs to that side of the house. Like I said, chemicals from smoke damage can make you sick if you breathe it in. You have to get it properly taken care of."

Repairs and a professional smoke cleaner. Two more to add to her endless list of things to get done she knew nothing about. She bit her lip to keep from a full-on meltdown in front of the firefighters. Draping the wet blanket over her arm, she faced them. "So, don't stay in my house. Got it. For how long?"

He handed her a card. "Here. Ask for Sue and tell her I sent you. She knew your grandmother and will get this taken care of right away." He nodded to the For Sale sign. "Especially with the house for sale."

"No one will want to buy it now," she muttered, trying to figure out where she should go. Piper's house was always an option, but putting Piper in more danger was the last thing she wanted to do. Her father would be distressed if she didn't reach out to him. And of course, Nellie was an option... or the floor of the bakery. Or Nico's.

I can't drag Nico into any of this.

"Do you have a place to stay? Do you need a drive?" The firefighter's voice interrupted her jumbled thoughts.

"I'm good, thank you. I'm going to stay with my dad. Can I get anything out of the house?" She gestured over herself, shivering in her sweatshirt and pajama bottoms.

He handed her a mask from his truck. "Put this on and go get what you need. We'll wait until you've left safely."

Trudging up the stairs to her bedroom, she dug out a small suitcase from her closet, throwing in clothes and a makeup bag, still packed from school. She stacked the books and secured them in one of Gran's grocery bags before zipping them inside the suitcase.

Setting the suitcase down in the hallway, she stepped into Gran's room, turning the light on. As she moved closer to the window, rubble crunched under her feet, and an acrid smell burned her throat through the mask. She ran a hand along the warm charcoal wall and rubbed the black soot from her fingers.

This place, with its gardens and love still beating within its walls, beckoned her to stay. It clung to her like a small child would their mother, not wanting to let go. She couldn't shake the feeling of belonging in this house.

For as long as she still owned it, this was her home. She'd do whatever it took to defend it.

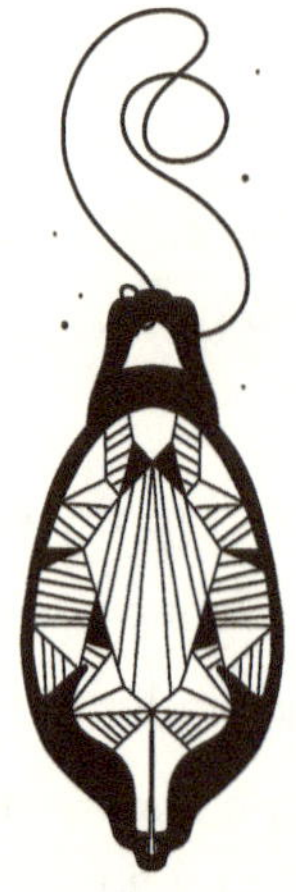

TWENTY-ONE

The window of Little Mysteries displayed a black and white sign that said *Closed*, but the sound of drums and a low saxophone sounded from inside. Celeste had to be in there! Drew grasped the handle and shook it, setting off the chimes. She knocked at the door. Nothing. Plan B—find a window and get Celeste's attention. Celeste was her last hope to take control of the amulet's magic. She might also be a witch, and if Hathorne didn't know it now, he'd find out. No one was safe.

Drew hopped down the stairs to the sidewalk as pedestrians hurried along with shopping bags weighing them down and eyes glued to cellphones. Cars whizzed by, sending up a spray of slush, and she scrambled back to avoid getting drenched. She walked around the side of the building and peered into a window. The beat of the music continued thumping from inside.

"What are you doing out here?" Celeste stood at the corner of the building with her hands on her hips. She wore an elaborate black coat with a fur-trimmed hat.

"Why are you closed? It's not five o'clock yet." Drew's voice raised an octave, sounding as desperate as she felt. "I heard music inside—"

"Last I checked, I didn't need to clear my store hours with you."

Drew bit her lip to tame her demanding attitude. She dug in her cross-body bag for the books and held them up. "I found more. And I used magic—there are words now—but it's not enough. I need help." She took a breath and plowed on. "And how did you know about Joelle? You gave me the name, but how? She's my mother!"

"The woman with your ghost is your mother?" Celeste appeared thoughtful as one eyebrow raised.

"That's right. You said she's involved with my friend, but I need to know how." Drew held up the book again. "I know I'm rambling, but I have nowhere else to go. I've got a bigger problem than I thought."

"I can't help you any more than I already have. It's not safe to dabble too much."

"You gave me this book. Gran had it last, and I think I know why. Please help me. I need to get rid of a witch hunter. If you're one too, he'll find out."

Celeste glanced around, smiling and nodding at a few locals as they walked by, staring at Drew. "Lower your voice. You can't talk like that out here—"

"He tried to burn my house down last night! It needs to end now, before he comes back. If I do this alone... I don't want to do this alone. Please." She chewed her lip, flinching at the raw skin. She'd laid it all on the line, begging Celeste with her words and her eyes.

Celeste turned around and shook her keys. "I didn't realize it had gotten this bad. I thought she'd taken care of him. Come with me."

She followed Celeste inside, who kept the closed sign up and locked the door behind them. "We have work to do. Lay the book on the counter."

Drew put the book on the counter, grateful Celeste hadn't turned her away. Shaking off her jacket, she slung it over a stool and opened the book to where she'd left off. "If I can lure him back to Haven and find a moon gate, do you know what that is and how to close it? He needs to go before he kills someone I care about."

Celeste hung her coat on a coat rack with knobs shaped like crystal balls and put her hat on the shelf above it. She took a headband that was wrapped around her wrist and put it over her head to hold back her black curls. She placed different colored crystals on the counter and lit a row of candles. When she was done, she ran her hand over them with her eyes closed. "You need a spell. I assumed she'd completed the book, and you had what you needed."

"You mean Gran, right? I saw her. And I found this journal. It belonged to Aurora; the woman the lighthouse is named after." Drew held up the small book.

Celeste opened her eyes, taking the book from her hands. "Where'd you find this?"

"The library. They don't know I have it." Drew struggled to decipher the shocked look on Celeste's face. "Are you a witch? Is that what we are, what Gran was? I see dead people, Celeste. And isn't that... magic? So anything is possible, right?"

"This was in the library?" Celeste sat down on a chair, turning the pages, ignoring Drew's questions. She covered her mouth as she read. "I thought this was destroyed."

"You've seen it before? How?" It was clear Celeste knew more about this town than Drew thought, but she couldn't fit the puzzle pieces together.

"Maddie tried to warn me about this. She said she'd take care of him, and I assumed she'd done just that." Celeste rose from the chair and handed Drew the book. "Keep this safe. The legend is Aurora was the last witch to close the gate. It was your grandmother who said change was coming, but I didn't believe it to be true. She wouldn't tell me more. Said it was to keep us all safe." Celeste tilted her head to the side, candlelight sparkling in her amber eyes. "To answer your questions, we're part of something bigger. Connected to a sisterhood spanning centuries."

"Witches?" The word had meaning, now. It wasn't something out of a fairy tale. This was her reality. "Gran told me his name is—"

"Hathorne. I know the history he has in this town. Centuries go by without a sign. You think it's the end, but I should've known. That lighthouse curse won't end until it's burned to the ground."

"Burned? Like he did to all those innocent women?"

Celeste waved a hand over the candles, and they flickered, growing taller. "Witches, mystics... they're just labels. Don't forget that. People like labels, but they don't mean a thing.

What you are, what we all are, is light. Our eyes aren't covered, letting us see. It's part of the magic."

"The amulet has the magic, Celeste, not me."

A gentle laugh escaped her lips, and she placed her hands on Drew's. "The magic is inside you now. It runs deeper than that beautiful obsidian jewel, honey."

Energy spun through her hands, up her arms like she'd touched an electric socket and didn't pull away. Celeste's calmness surrounded her, keeping panic and fear away. Releasing Drew's hands, she stood. "We've got work to do. You're not alone. Remember that."

"If you're a witch, too, why hasn't he come for you? Why only me?"

"He doesn't know I exist yet. Witch's magic isn't the same for everyone. He can't get in this place—he can't see it for what it is." Celeste winked. "Your grandmother, bless her, led him to you when she tried to send him back. She gave you what she took back from him." Celeste pointed to the amulet. "Never belonged to him, but he'll come for it, anyway. Everything your grandmother did was to keep you safe."

Grief's clenching ache returned, and Drew swallowed to keep it from taking control. Gran had kept her secrets guarded her entire life to keep Drew safe and out of this mysterious world. She never approved of Drew going to Neptune Point, and now she understood the reason. Gran had only nodded after the Dominic Sloan incident when Drew told her she could see the dead, never acknowledging her gift beyond those words. Drew knew her grandmother was afraid of what that meant for her life. No wonder she had been so determined for Drew to leave Atlas Cliffs; maybe she believed leaving would take away the magic.

"I'm ready, Celeste. What do I have to do?"

Celeste stood still and closed her eyes. "Let me make space. Breathe." She exhaled a heavy breath.

Drew clung to the counter's edge and tapped her fingers along to the melody playing in the back room. It was an absentminded effort to relieve her frazzled nerves more than anything else.

Celeste opened one eye. "I said, breathe, Drew."

"I am breathing."

Celeste opened her eyes and ambled over until they were face to face. "May I put my hands on your face?"

Everyone else does.

Did Celeste have the power to show her things as the dead could? Drew decided it didn't matter. She was in it now, nothing to lose. There was no turning back.

"Sure, why not?" She did as Celeste told her and breathed as the woman cupped her cheeks. The amulet pulled against her skin like a magnet as it glowed warmly on her chest. Celeste's hands produced a current along her face and a crackling exploded in her mouth. It popped and fizzed, tasting sweet, reminding her of the pop rock candies she used to eat on Halloween night after trick or treating when she was a kid. She knew in her heart she was tasting magic.

Through her mind's eye, she could see Haven. A circular, blurred veil among the trees swirled near the edge of the Coda River, though it was not as clear as Ori had shown her. Heath Hathorne hovered between the trees, his presence looming in the darkness. The full moon shimmered, its light bouncing off the surface of the torrential river as it coursed through the forest, flaunting its power.

A strange energy radiated through the night air. Ori appeared with his hand extended toward her, and she accepted it. Shadows surrounded her—other souls, but she couldn't make out their faces. The scene in her mind blurred and dissipated, and Heath Hathorne faded into a mist on the other side as the swirling gate narrowed to a pinpoint before vanishing. The raven soared toward her face as the image collapsed.

Celeste released her and stepped back against the counter, taking purposeful deep breaths. "I've given you a glimpse. I'm afraid there isn't much more I can show you."

Drew tried to swallow, but her mouth was too dry. "How'd you do that?"

"You can do it, too. Focus and intention." Celeste rubbed her hands together and placed them on the counter as she wavered from side to side. "I'm out of practice."

Drew held her hands out. What else hid beneath the surface? "I'll be the bait. Get Hathorne to the gate, and Ori and I will send him through and lock it up. The how part is where I'm lost."

"The amulet, that's how. It's for your protection until it's the key. It'll keep him there and you... here." Celeste drank from a water bottle and wiped her forehead. "It has to be done on a full moon."

"A full moon? Is he a werewolf or something?"

"Don't be silly, there's no such thing." Celeste smiled. The flames from the candles flickered and reached for her. She waved a hand over them, sending them back to a gentle rhythm.

"So, no werewolves, but yes to witches. All right. Is that why I see dead people?"

"Be careful with the labels." Celeste made a face. "If aligning yourself with nature's energy and walking through life with your eyes open to what the universe holds makes you a witch, so be it. It doesn't make one bit of difference who believes you or what they think. You are light, and you know what you're capable of, what you are. What you must do is be honest with yourself and accept your truth. Focus and intention. That's it."

Drew placed her hands on the counter on either side of the row of candles. Embrace who she really is. She had reached a level of honesty with herself in the last few days than she'd ever experienced before. Desperation and grief did that to a person. Everything had changed when Dominic Sloan shot her, and the Morana family tree came to light. She stopped hiding, being honest with Gran about her... talents. She wasn't afraid anymore.

Drew raised her hands off the counter, and two of the flames followed, reaching for her palms. She froze, hovering over the flickering lights.

Celeste pushed loose curls from her forehead and crossed her arms. "Lesson one. Focus and intention. Try to make it dance."

"I can't do that. It's the amulet, not me. I'm sure of it."

"Try," Celeste said.

Drew lifted her palms over the flames, stopping over each candle. "Nothing is happening."

"Focus and intention." Celeste held her hand over the candle, and the flame stretched, reaching for her hand. She dropped her hand back down to her side.

"How?" Drew held her hand over the dancing flames again. One of the tiny flames doused into a thread of smoke. "It burned out. That's not good, is it?" Panic rose from her stomach to her throat. "What if I can't do this?"

Celeste's eyebrow lifted as she smiled. "The universe is too vast for anyone to determine what's possible. And you can and will do this, I promise. I like to spell magic with a *k* at the end. M-a-g-i-c-k. It's the eleventh letter of the alphabet. Eleven is a sign you're connected to the soul realm. Open your eyes, child. The signs are there. Now, try it with the book."

Drew focused on the pages of the book and visualized Gran using the book to protect her. A faint buzzing prickled her hands, and she lowered them closer to the pages, but no gold letters appeared to form words into sentences. "It isn't working. I don't get it. The other night with Ori, the words flew over the pages. Why not now?"

"Try again." Celeste leaned over the book as Drew continued to focus and bring the pages to life, with no success.

Closing the book, Celeste handed it to her. "Take this home and keep practicing. Don't give up. You need a spell to use on the next full moon to send his decrepit, evil soul back. It's close, I can feel it. Find the balance of pushing and pulling back. You can do this, Drew."

"But I don't want to leave until I figure this out, even if it takes all night." Her home was upside down until she could live there again. Hathorne had her trapped in a deadly chess game where he had all the moves and she was a helpless pawn.

"You need the full moon, Drew, and you have time. Keep the amulet on your body and practice. Get ready and come see me again soon."

Seeing the dead was one thing, but witches, spells, and portals to another realm were growing into something else entirely. Something unbelievable, but true. Her truth. She rubbed her face and spotted a stack of photos on a table by Celeste's coat. Photos of the keeper's house at Neptune Point. She stepped closer and picked the glossy images up, flipping through them. "Why do you have these? Is this where you were today?"

"Yes. I was there. I've been there quite a lot lately."

"Why? Are you a photographer or something?"

"Or something." Celeste tucked the photos in a briefcase on the floor. "I'm buying the place."

Drew stepped back, her legs almost giving out. Celeste couldn't buy the house at Aurora. The last she'd heard, Dominic Sloan owned it. "Why would you want to buy that moldy rundown place?"

"For the same reason you want nothing to do with it."

She'd been avoiding Neptune Point and Haven, vowing to never enter the house of pain again. "I want nothing to do with it because of what happened there. That house represents nothing but death and sadness. Why do you want to buy it?

Will you live there? I didn't realize the house on the property was for sale."

"It wasn't. But the man who owns it is despicable, and his ex-wife wants to rid herself of everything connected to him." Celeste gestured a hand over herself. "I just happened to answer the call."

"What call?"

Celeste hesitated. "The only reason I'm going to tell you this is because of what he did to you."

Drew had relived the night in the warehouse too many times, and still looked over her shoulder throughout the day, ready to run or defend herself. If it was possible to burn out your fight-or-flight response, hers was about to sizzle.

Celeste went to the back room and came back with a purse sized album adorned with butterfly stickers. She gave it to Drew. "We were best friends... sisters, really. Maybe you can relate."

Piper's face flashed in her mind. "I have a friend like that, but what does this have to do with buying Aurora?"

"She lived there." Celeste reached for a pink crystal stone on the counter and held it, closing her eyes. "She died there. He killed her. I plan to avenge her death." The remaining lit candles flickered, and one of the small flames extinguished. Smoke curled up from the glass holder in the shape of a butterfly. Drew's skin crawled as she opened the picture album.

Enid.

Twenty-Two

Dusk had fallen by the time Drew left Little Mysteries and got into her car. Soothing her impatience was going to take more work and practice. The amulet didn't grant her an instant knowledge of how to do any of this. The gem had imperfections, and so did she. They were perfect together.

Focus and intention.

Push and pull.

She could do this.

She had to do this.

Sitting in the driver's seat with the engine rumbling and heat blasting from the vents, she replayed the conversation with Celeste. Enid and Celeste had grown up together and been best friends. How did buying the keeper's house at Neptune Point factor into Celeste's plan to avenge Enid's death? Unless Celeste planned to tear it down.

There was a part of her that selfishly longed for Enid's return. She missed the friendship she'd developed with Enid in the short time she'd known her. Knowing Ori so much longer meant the sting of the inevitable goodbye would hurt even more when his time to cross over arrived. But Ori knew the moon gate's location, and his presence was like a repellent to Hathorne. She didn't know why or how, but his appearance had saved her more than once. She needed Celeste's guidance, but Ori's help was integral to defeating Hathorne. He was her connection to the other side.

When is the full moon?

A quick search on her phone showed the next full moon was December 27, eight days away. One week too long. She had time to do what Celeste told her and practice. Unless Hathorne attacked and won his deadly game before the full moon's arrival. If she took a trip to Haven to see the gate for herself, maybe she'd know what to do. She gripped the amulet, reminding herself it would keep her here, in the world of the living, and send him back there. To the shadow realm.

A voice message notification flashed on her phone. Anna Tate's enthusiastic voice expressed compassion about the fire and gave her a number for a contractor. She ended the message by telling her about an interested couple ready to see the house, fire damage and all.

The message should have triggered excitement in her but instead brought on nausea, and without thinking, she deleted it.

Driving away from the downtown core, she stopped at an intersection. She was the only car waiting at the red light. Her signal light clicked as the right remained red. The seconds dragged on as she waited for it to turn green.

She couldn't go home.

The cleaning service promised she'd be back in the house by next week, but for now, she was in limbo. The next time she visited Atlas Cliffs, without a house to call home, this is what it was going to feel like. A restlessness crept up on her, making her doubt all the decisions she'd made since Gran died.

She could go back to her dad's; he'd opened his home to her, ecstatic to help his daughter and be the support she'd needed for so long. But he had been right when he said she was almost nineteen and had to decide what was best for herself. Selling the house didn't mean she'd never have a home again. It would be different, but she'd find a place of safety and love. Selling the house and the business would give her freedom to move on. But the doubts in her head grew louder and more persistent.

If selling the house is what I want, why does it feel so wrong?

Rain spattered over the windshield, and the traffic light swung as the wind picked up. Turn right toward her father's apartment, or go straight, toward home. Toward Neptune Point to see if the moon gate even existed. Her internal compass spun, waiting for her decision.

The light turned green, and she went straight. She traveled along Adam's Ale Road toward her house. Toward home. But tonight, she wouldn't stop.

Flying by the seat of her pants and accepting the unknown with grace would do her good. Trying to control everything in her life hadn't gotten her far. If a portal to a soul realm existed, she wanted to witness it, and she wouldn't wait until a full moon to find it.

Rain streamed like a waterfall down the window, turning the snow on the road into slush. She flicked the wipers on and slowed down as her dark, lonely house came into view, locked up without a light on inside.

A shadow moved on the porch.

She rolled the passenger window down for a better look. The only car in the driveway was Gran's Buick.

Hathorne.

The cloaked silhouette churned, spinning like a tornado reaching for the sky. It charged down the driveway, gaining speed as it plummeted toward her car. The tires squealed as she fought to hold on to control of the steering wheel, the back end of the small car wavering from side to side through the wet slush. Vivid memories of her car accident a year ago flashed through her mind. The sound of metal grinding against the pavement screamed in her head.

The car careened over the shoulder of the road, and she slammed on the brakes, bringing it to a screeching stop. Her hands trembled as she fumbled with the gearshift before putting the car in park. Hathorne hovered on the other side, flashing a sinister grin before his shifting cloud swept over the cliffs to Jupiter Cove Beach below.

One more week of putting up with this asshole's messed up game of cat and mouse. She refused to let him win.

She turned the engine off and stepped outside. Rain blew sideways, obstructing her view as it soaked into her hair and ran down her face. Anger pumped through her veins, keeping the cold out as she ran across the street to the stone steps leading down to the beach. Waves rolled over the sand and crashed between boulders on the beach below. The row of streetlights above shone down, casting shadows over the water. One shadow wore a long cloak that whipped in the raging wind blowing off the ocean.

She stood overlooking the beach, not taking her eyes off the witch hunter as he stared up at her. Waiting to strike. Unzipping her jacket, she reached for the amulet, letting it hang over her chest.

Do something! Throw lightning, fire... Anything!

"Don't do this," Ori's voice said in her ear as he materialized beside her.

"If he thinks I'm scared, he wins."

"Aren't you?" Ori's silhouette shifted into his human form—untouched by the rain like a shield surrounding him. He gripped her arm. "I crossed the barrier into his world and almost didn't make it back. If that's where I end up? I'd rather just stay here forever." His hand dropped and his gaze drifted to Heath Hathorne, who didn't move.

They stood beside each other, watching. Waiting. The cold broke through the anger, turning her into a trembling, drenched mess, but she didn't back down. Nothing was going to make her step away from him.

"You were in his world? How?"

"Turns out I'm capable of a few things, too."

She hated admitting it, because he deserved to cross over, but Ori was part of the key to unlocking the other side. The guilt of asking him to wait for her again weighed on her; he'd been in limbo for so long. "I'm sending him back, Ori, but I'll need your help."

"You know what to do?"

She pushed her wet hair off her face and folded her arms across her chest, letting the amulet dangle. Loose threads twirled inside, illuminated by a faint light. The amulet was the key, and she'd become the locksmith. "The next full moon is one week away. I'll find the moon gate, learn a spell, and master these magic powers I never knew I had. We just have to survive until then."

"Speak for yourself!" Ori gestured his hands over his translucent ghost-like frame.

"Right. Sorry." She blinked through the rain as she darted her eyes between Ori and Hathorne's motionless figure as he stared in her direction. "I know you want out of here, and you have my word I'm going to help you get to your paradise."

"But you need me. I get it. I've been stuck with you for months. What's a little longer in the span of eternity?"

"I owe you—"

Ori put a hand up. "Let's not do that. Debate on who owes who what. We're friends, right? On opposite sides of life, but still. I'm in. Hey, it's either I help you, or you end up on the wrong side with me. Then what? It's the only option, Drew, and you know it."

Hathorne maintained his soulless stance as the surf pummeled around him without touching him. Centuries ago, he thought his duty was to get rid of evil; misguided as hell, but in his warped mind, he was doing a service. Maybe he loved someone or had children. A family.

"He was a regular person with a life before he turned into this... this monster," Drew said. "Think he remembers it? If I could find a weakness and talk to him, like I can with you or Enid, and make him see that I'm not bad or evil, maybe he'd stop."

Ori's eyebrows raised and his mouth gaped open. "Yeah, just a regular person who murdered women he thought were witches. What are you even saying right now? He's not talking to you or anyone. He strikes me as more of an introvert."

"I'm not being funny," she said, huffing.

"Neither am I."

She marched down the steps and across the sand. Enough of the taunting threats! He was dead, for God's sake! She'd follow him as deep into the water as he wanted to go.

"Do you have a death wish? Come back!" The wind and pounding waves drowned out Ori's calls.

She persisted toward Hathorne over the wet sand and waded into the water. The light from the stairs receded with each step she took, and darkness enveloped her. Numb with cold and fear, her shallow breaths turned to mist bellowing in the air. He might attack and kill her this time. She shouldn't be doing this, but the anger inside fueled away from common sense. "Back so soon?" she hollered.

His head contorted to the side, and his hood fell back, but the murky water around him and the black night shrouded his features. "The time has yet to come. Give me back my jewel."

She clutched the amulet; the heat pulsing from it burned her icy hand. "This? It's mine. Not yours."

In a blur of movement, he was standing in front of her, a firm grip on her wrist. She gasped, her heartbeat thumping in her ears. She couldn't break free or run and Ori had disappeared. The world of the wandering souls as she'd known it was over. Telling herself for years that they couldn't hurt her had been a lie.

At least if he ended her life, Ori would be waiting on the other side.

"Trust, Drew. You're not alone." Everything else went silent except for Gran whispering in her ear.

The amulet was the key. The magic inside of the black stone would protect her.

Underestimating his strength, she swung her hand back to break free of his death grip, but he held on tighter, unflinching.

Focus and intention.

She steadied her breathing and ordered every ounce of energy inside her to awaken the amulet's power. Her hands tingled and burned. A sizzling sound buzzed, and he released his grip on her wrist. She leaned closer so she could stare into his wretched face. "Burn, asshole."

Hathorne's cloak burst into a cloud of smoke over the water, his face still visible as he stared over her shoulder.

"Drew! What are you doing?" Headlights lit up the top of the cliff where Nico stood. He ran down the stone steps.

Hathorne's mouth twisted into a disgusted smirk. He hissed in her ear. "He's next." The smoke swallowed him, and he vanished.

Nico stopped at the edge of the surf. Rain and sleet obscured his face in the darkness. "What are you doing out here? Are you alone?"

Shivering and cursing Hathorne under her breath, she waded out of the water to shore. Her boots squished with icy water.

He's next. Over my dead body!

"It's not a good time, Nico. You should leave." Hot tears stung her frozen cheeks.

Nico followed her up the cliff side steps. "I'm not letting you push me away. You used to trust me enough to talk to me. What the hell happened?"

Storming to her car, she yanked the door open and sat on the edge of the seat. She pulled her boots off and dumped the water out. Hathorne was going to be the death of her. Literally.

Nico reached for the door frame. "Why won't you talk to me?"

"I am talking to you. Please, just go home. It's not... good for you to be here."

"Why not?"

"Because it's... it's cold. And wet." Not a single part of her was dry. Her waterproof jacket was waterlogged. She shivered uncontrollably as her body succumbed to the bitter cold.

Nico ran a hand through his hair, sending a spray of water into the air. "*You're* out here."

"I had something to take care of."

"Something. Okay, how about you let me in on this thing? Let me help." He glanced around. "Is this a ghost thing?"

He knew who she was and accepted her anyway. But this was a whole new level of wild and strange, and she didn't know where to start. She threw her boots on the passenger seat floor. "You're soaked, Nico. Go home and dry off. I'm just..."

I'm freezing, can't feel my feet, and miserable in every single way possible.

"You're just what?" He raised his voice over the pounding surf.

She started the car. Her hair dripped down her face, blending in with her tears. Nico always came. "Why are you here?"

"I heard about the fire and came to check on you. You suck at checking your phone. I guess I just wanted to make sure you were okay."

"I'm fine. I've just been busy."

He glanced at the house. "Yeah, I see that. You're not staying there, are you? I think you have to make sure the smoke damage is gone first."

She leaned forward, letting her head hit the steering wheel. "You're the tenth person to tell me this. I know. I have cleaning people coming soon."

A burst of wind shook the car, and she lifted her head. Tugging his hood up, Nico shielded his eyes. "Where are you staying? Piper's?"

"Dad's place."

"And what are you doing on the beach in the middle of a storm?"

Fighting with a dead witch hunter.

She bit her lip and said nothing.

"Follow me back to my place and dry off. You look like you could use a friend. We *are* still friends, right?"

The misery kept on rolling. This was a bad day. A very bad day.

"Right. I'm fine, I'll just—" She blinked up at him through the rain blowing into the car, but he'd already started walking back to his truck.

She closed the car door as Nico pulled onto the road and drove toward his street at a snail's pace. She couldn't leave him alone, not with Hathorne's warning fresh in her mind.

A raven swooped down and perched on the hood of her car, its black eyes unblinking like it was trying to communicate a secret through its piercing gaze. The peculiar creature always trailed behind Hathorne, but never appeared menacing. It spread its broad wings and lifted off into the air, flying away.

Nico slowed to a stop along the side of the road, waiting for her. She should go to her father's, but she refused to allow Hathorne near Nico.

She followed him home.

TWENTY-THREE

Drew parked behind Nico's truck and stepped out of the car in her socked feet. The rain hit her face like needles as it turned to ice. Nico gestured for her to follow him up the stairs along the side of the garage. She hesitated by the car door as his long legs carried him to the landing at the top. He fumbled with keys under the light over the door. She didn't know what she was doing. Right now, jumping back in the car and driving downtown to her dad's would be a good idea. But when she peered down the neighborhood street to the main road, she couldn't shake Hathorne's words.

He's next.

Nico leaned back against the balcony railing and yelled for her. This time, she obliged. They were friends. Had always been friends, and she wouldn't let the blip in time when they'd been together ruin it. He was one of the good ones, and she cursed herself for running from him. She'd lost him once, and she wouldn't allow herself to lose him again.

Heat radiated as she stepped inside, pulled her socks off and moving into the small kitchen. She caught a hint of Nico's cologne from the jackets and sweaters hanging in an open closet. Nico reached past her for a blanket on the top shelf and handed it to her.

"Come sit down. Dry off." The familiar scent clung to the blanket, taking her back to their intimate moments together, and she held the blanket up to her face to hide the flush on her cheeks. The curse of being a freckled redhead.

Nico grabbed the remote from the pedestal table and turned off a hockey game playing on the wall-mounted television in the living room. He reached for two glasses from a drying rack beside the sink. Placing them upright on the counter, he opened the refrigerator near the stove, triggering a humming sound. "What do you want to drink? I've got water, soda, beer…" He trailed off as he pushed things around in the fridge. "I guess that's about it. I can run into the house and see what Mom has."

Being in the space above the garage, she couldn't help but reminisce about all the private moments she had shared with him. Her thoughts had often drifted toward leaving town, instead of being fully present with him. A pang of regret struck her. She might never be that close to him again. "Water would be great. I won't stay long." She used the blanket to absorb water from her hair, the copper red color returning as it dried.

Nico pointed to a worn L-shaped sectional. "Stay as long as you want. I've got nothing going on tonight." He filled up two glasses with water and brought one to her before taking a seat at one end of the sofa. Not wanting to be too close to him and scared of looking foolish if she chose the far end of the sofa, she settled for the middle and tucked the blanket over her legs.

Despite the warmth of the room and her flushed cheeks, she couldn't stop her body from shaking. Nico got up and headed down the narrow hallway. Her hands were trembling as she drank half the water. Nico reappeared with a large comforter, fluffing it above her head before wrapping it around her, rubbing her back with both hands. The heat produced from the friction was no match for what was growing inside her. She couldn't allow herself to want him like this, but all she wanted to do was grab him, kiss him, and feel his arms around her.

He sat back on the sofa—this time beside her. Leaning forward, he turned to her, looking through lashes that framed his brown eyes in perfection. "That look you had on the beach; I know that look. What scared you?"

There was not much she'd hidden from him, especially during the last year they'd been together. But how could she explain something she couldn't even make sense of herself?

"How long have you been staying over the garage? Will you live here and run your dad's business? It's been redone since the last time I was here."

He sat back. "I know what you're doing, Drew. I'll answer your questions, but you have to promise to answer mine, too."

This was the closest they had been in six months. *Six months.* Their connection had always been strong, but the chemistry between them as they sat beside each other was like a hurricane, unyielding and fierce. Did he feel it too, or was she the only one missing him so much it hurt? As soon as the thought popped into her head, so did his girlfriend's name. *Nicki.* She pulled the overstuffed comforter around her up to her chin. "Okay. Deal."

"I'm looking for a place of my own, but for now, it works. Dad's business can sponsor me for my apprenticeship, and I've been restoring old cars for extra money. I love doing that though. Doesn't feel like work."

"It all sounds perfect."

"Yeah, right. My life is far from perfect." He ran a hand through his wet hair, and it fell into a beautiful, tangled mess. "Dad left. Dominic Sloan—Ben, whatever his fucking name is—went to jail, but it took more than that for Dad to clear his name by association. He transferred everything to me so we could save the shop; I didn't have a choice."

She'd been so selfish. It never once crossed her mind that Nico's family was still paying the price for his father's business deals with Dominic Sloan. "I'm sorry, I thought things were okay. Last spring, you said he had everything back on track."

"I thought he did. Anyway, he's been staying at the Cliffside Motel since September."

"Do you think they can work things out?"

"Not looking good. Mom filed for divorce, but I don't know. It doesn't matter. I've just got to handle things here for now. I'm looking at moving the shop closer to town. Dad's been helping me find a space. If he's going to keep working, we can't have it on the property anymore."

"I don't know what to say, Nico. I had no idea."

Nico must've given up any possibility of exploring history or teaching as he had so often talked about. He was stuck here, and her heart broke for him. She wanted to hold him. *Kiss* him. But she continued to follow the unspoken rules of friendships, and sat on the sofa, cocooned in the soft fabric of the blanket.

"My brother's home with his girlfriend until January. Did you know he finished his degree and got into med school? I can't remember if I told you before we..." He looked away for a moment before facing her again. "I'm happy for him. I swear I am. I don't know. Maybe you got it right leaving here."

"Well, for someone who's gotten out of here, I can't seem to stay away." She smiled and let the blanket drop from her shoulders, her smile fading at the same time. "Maybe this will be it. With Gran gone now, everything is changing."

Nico reached over and squeezed her hand. "Everything doesn't have to change."

"I kind of think it does." Despite the comfort of his touch, she pulled her hand back. He had a girlfriend. But the closer she got to him, the more she wanted. She couldn't let herself get too close. "I was happy for you, Nico. I mean, I thought things were going well, and you moved on—you have a girlfriend now..."

"I thought the same about you after you went to California and moved to Boston. You're painting again. You had Shane—"

"I didn't have Shane. I don't want Shane."

He rubbed the back of his neck. "Why were you on the beach tonight? I know you. You saw something out there, didn't you?"

She untangled the knots in her damp hair with her fingers. What he'd said wasn't wrong; he did know her, and she could use another friend. Someone she could trust with the truth. After what happened to Piper, she couldn't bring herself to go anywhere near her.

The truth might be enough to drive him away, keeping him safe. Something stirred deep inside of her. A knowing.

Nothing I do will drive him away.

Pushing the thought aside, she started talking and didn't stop until she'd told him everything. It came out in a jumbled mess of words, but he didn't interrupt. That was Nico. He didn't just hear what she said, he listened. When she was done, she sank against the sofa, exhausted. She clutched her knees close to her chest under the comforter. She braced herself for Nico's reaction, holding her breath, because it felt safer than breathing—something she could control.

His calm demeanor shouldn't surprise her—he'd always been so together, even when he wasn't. The palms of her hands burned and tingled. She scratched them against her jeans. When she held them out in front of her, there was no sign of redness or a rash. The amulet's low vibration warmed her neck underneath the sweater she wore, and she plucked it out and let it rest over the soft fuzz at her neckline.

"And this ghost with the cloak—" Nico said, his face serious, like he was considering every word.

"Hathorne."

"Right. The witch hunter from the 1600s."

"According to my research, yup." Telling him was letting the air out of the proverbial balloon. She released her legs and stretched them in front of her. "You still want me to stick around, or have I completely scared you away? I'm not safe to be around. Look what he did to Piper."

"I don't scare that easy." He folded his hands together and turned his head to the side, locking eyes with her. Melting her insides into a puddle.

Do not fall in love with him again. Do not! It can't work. He's taken.

She broke eye contact and rubbed her tingling hands together. "Thanks for believing me. You know my world isn't... *normal*."

"No one's world is normal. Normal is overrated! Yours is exciting, extraordinary. Literally."

A laugh escaped her. A genuine, feel-good laugh she hadn't had in a while. The warmth from her hands felt like a sunburn with a prickling, itchy sensation, more intense than before. Her chest tightened like a cluster of sparklers on a birthday cake was lit inside her. A metal taste filled her mouth and an aroma of hot flames tinged with smoke tickled her nose.

"I'm serious! You get to see what no one else can. You solved a murder last year and helped put a man behind bars. If that isn't something to be proud of, I don't know what is."

As Nico talked, his voice grew distant, like she was trying to hear underwater. Sweat gathered at the back of her neck and down her back, but a shiver crawled over her skin and her hands turned clammy.

Clear as a cloudless summer sky, Gran's voice whispered in her ear, "Show him, dear. Like the others have shown you."

Nico touched the pendant around her neck, and everything rushed back, returning her to normal as he spoke. "It's glowing. Something's moving inside it." He brought his head close to the amulet as he studied it. She could almost hear her heart ready to burst out of her chest. A wave of warmth spread over her skin from her head to her toes and she didn't know if it was the amulet's magic, her own, or Nico. He lifted his head and their eyes connected. Her palms tingled with invisible electricity, and she raised them to his face, unsure of what she was doing. "Can I show you something?"

"Anytime."

She spun around and sat cross-legged on the sofa. She put her hands on his face like Ori did to transfer visions, and she took a deep breath like Celeste had taught her. His faint stubble rubbed against her palms, and she resisted pulling him into a kiss.

Get a damn hold of yourself! Focus and intention.

"Close your eyes," she instructed as a fuzzy caterpillar crawling sensation covered her skin.

Nico did as he was told, and it wasn't long before his eyelids fluttered. The sensation of magic pulsing through her veins was both exhilarating and confusing, leaving her with many unanswered questions. She believed the moment Gran gave her the amulet, everything changed. But maybe she had been carrying the magic inside her all along. If the magic book was accurate, her magic would follow Hathorne once she banished him back to the world from which he'd come. What would she do in an ordinary world? How would she cope if the veil between the living and the dead turned into darkened drapes, keeping her out forever? The silence was going to be the worst. The silence and the knowing of what exists without the ability to see, really *see*. Her body reacted to her thoughts the same way as it did to grief; the same horrible aching feeling she couldn't shake.

But she couldn't allow herself to dwell on what might happen. That was a future-Drew problem. For now, with her hands on his face and magic flowing between them, an invisible tie between her and Nico was stronger than any connection she'd experienced before.

As the moment ended, her hands cooled as though ice water doused them. Nico held her hands in a gentle grip, slowly removing them from his face. His eyes sprang open, and his breathing was shallow. "Stay tonight. I'm coming with you tomorrow."

He continued to hold her hands as they gazed at each other. "I saw him grab you and threaten you. He set fire to your house. It's Haven, the place you showed me. You're going back there, but I'm not letting you go alone."

"It's not safe. Every time someone I care about is near me and he shows up, something horrible happens."

Nico reached for the amulet, his fingers grazing her neck, sending goosebumps all over her skin. "This thing works, Drew. Gran wasn't messing around when she gave it to you. It's late; take my bed, I'll sleep on the sofa."

Hathorne's threat still hung in her mind; maybe if she stayed with Nico she'd be able to protect him. "Okay. I'll stay." She messaged her dad to let him know she was fine and not coming and followed Nico to his room.

He brushed aside a few clothes from the neatly made bed and dug through his drawers, handing her a gray T-shirt and sweatpants. Grabbing a hoodie from his closet shelf, he draped it over her shoulders and smiled, his dimples making their appearance once again. "Dry clothes will help. You pretty much know where everything is. There are towels in the bathroom if you want to shower. Just be comfortable here." Leaning against the door frame, his shirt lifted from his waist, exposing abs that appeared more defined than she remembered. She caught herself staring and lifted her eyes to meet his gaze, only to find he was doing the same.

He stepped into the hallway. "I'll let you change," he said before closing the door.

Alone in his room, she stripped off her wet jeans and sweater. On the wall hung two framed photos of the mustang from the summer before. She sat on the bed and slipped his T-shirt over her head, followed by the hoodie, and held the too-long sleeves against her nose. It smelled of him. Clean laundry mixed with the faintest hint of sandalwood. The sweatpants were soft against her legs, and her body relaxed underneath Nico's clothes. She stood and tied the string on the waistband tight to hold the baggy sweatpants in place. As she opened the door to leave his bedroom, a small photo perched on a tall dresser caught her eye. It was a photo of the two of them at Jupiter Cove Beach from the same day as her favorite picture of him. She still had it on her phone.

Friends. She was not good at this at all.

She joined him on the sofa, this time sitting beside him as he asked her questions about Ori and Gran, and what she'd learned so far from Celeste. She didn't hold back, telling him everything she knew.

His phone buzzed on and off and he picked it up, his fingers typing across the screen. His jaw tensed with a twitch as he focused in silence on the phone. She resisted the urge to read over his shoulder and fidgeted with the hoodie's strings. "Everything okay?"

Exhaling sharply, he put his phone down. "Yeah. It's fine. Nicki's been messaging."

"Does she know I'm here?"

"She does. I'm not lying to her, Drew." He rubbed his face and dropped his hand to his knee. "My head's all over the place right now. I've just got a lot going on—"

"Nico, I'm sorry. I can go to my dad's tonight—"

"No. I want you to stay. Maybe I'm being selfish as hell, but I miss hanging out with you and talking like this. But I want to be honest with you, so you know where I stand."

She didn't have a sweet clue where he stood, not really. But she'd gotten a glimpse into his feelings for Nicki, and they weren't as rock solid as she initially believed. Heat flushed her cheeks, and she chewed her lip in anxiety; it was hard to hold back her feelings for him.

But she couldn't let go of the fact she'd be leaving Atlas Cliffs again, putting them right back to where they were last June.

"I care about you, too. Um." She took a deep breath, feeling like her heart was trying to leap out of her chest. "I just want you to know that... I missed you, Nico. So, I guess if you're being selfish, so am I."

"I'm glad we figured that out," he said, smiling.

"Me too." Her eyes watered as she struggled to suppress a yawn.

Nico stood and reached out his hand, and without a second thought, she took it. He led her to his room and pulled the blankets back. "You're tired. Go to bed, get some sleep."

She didn't argue and sat on the bed. As she lay back, Nico pulled the blankets over her. "Good night, Drew." He squeezed her hand before heading for the door. He flipped the light off. "If you need me, I'll be out on the sofa."

Darkness suffocated her, crushing in on her from all around. Her breath turned quick and shallow. Panic clung to her chest. Why did this happen at the most inconvenient times? Being vulnerable was tough for her, but she didn't want to be alone. Asking for help was harder. "Nico?

He stepped back into the room, but she could only make out his broad figure in the dim light. "Yeah?"

"Would I be too selfish if I asked you to stay with me?"

"Would I be selfish if I said yes?"

"Maybe."

He walked over to the bed and laid down beside her, turning to his side as the mattress shifted underneath his weight. She turned to face him. His breathing was steady and his warmth palpable. She touched his face, and he placed his hand on top of hers. He threw off the blankets and pulled her into his arms. As he held her tight, she felt his chest rise and fall with each breath, listening to the comforting sound of his heartbeat. Her troubles faded away and she let her eyes shut. For the first time in months, she drifted off into a deep, undisturbed sleep.

TWENTY-FOUR

Drew rummaged through the closet in the foyer for supplies to take along for her trek to Haven. Full moon or not, she was going to find the moon gate. She grabbed a flashlight, a Swiss Army knife her father had given her, a bottle of water, and a fleece blanket, and zipped up her backpack. And unzipped it when she realized everything was on the floor around the backpack.

She kept getting distracted.

She couldn't stop thinking about falling asleep in Nico's arms. They'd woken up early, so she was home in time to meet a crew from the cleaning company, but she'd been in a daze ever since. They'd crossed the line into friends who sleep together without having sex or kissing or being naked at all. Did those friends exist? Because she was struggling to keep the lid on her feelings. The pot was boiling over.

Hums of equipment and the smell of bleach swirled amongst freshly brewed coffee all around the house as the cleaning staff worked. Gran wouldn't have it any other way. If people were helping, you make sure they had what they needed. Now and then, someone yelled out an order, or they moved back and forth between the vehicles parked outside. The owner had known Gran and frequented the Tough Cookie often. He'd promised Drew they'd have everything in order so her granddaughter could be in her home for one last Christmas. She couldn't think about it anymore or she'd start crying and never stop.

By the time she'd showered and packed a bag, it was after eleven. Nico was coming over at eleven thirty; he had to run into town for something, but he hadn't given her details. She assumed it had to do with the space his dad was looking at.

The magic book caught her eye, and a kernel of guilt nagged at her. So much for practicing with the book for spells or witch hunter killing step by steps. Nico was important to her, but she had to keep her mind on the goal. Getting rid of Hathorne. She grabbed the book and added it to her backpack, just in case.

The idea of returning to the scene where everything started a year ago overwhelmed her with anxiety. Her chest tightened as she remembered the skeletal remains left behind. The memories of finding Iris and running from Dominic had made it difficult for her to go back there, but it was time to face her fears. He was still Dominic Sloan to her, not Ben Morana. Enid and Ezra were Moranas. Jack was a Morana. She cared about them and struggled to include the man who attacked and threatened her as part of the Morana family. Her determination to get rid of Hathorne and keep her own friends and family safe took over. She'd convinced herself she'd have the upper hand if she drove to Neptune Point while it was still daylight.

Donning her jacket, she put the backpack in the entryway's corner and checked her phone. Fifteen minutes after eleven. She'd decided eleven minutes after eleven to be the magic time when the clock stopped in the morning and woke up at night. She made her way through the kitchen into the den to peek at Gran's antique clock.

The hush in the room told her all she needed to know. Eleven. The magic number Celeste had told her about. Magick spelled with a k. The eleventh letter. The eleventh hour... eleventh minute. She hadn't landed on the meaning but knew in her gut it had everything to do with Gran or Hathorne. Or both. She tapped the wooden frame of the clock and waited. Thudding and the whir of a vacuum clanged from upstairs.

Needing to get away from the clinical smell and constant noise in the house, she stepped onto the front porch and breathed in the winter air. The sun broke through clouds and warmed the cold ocean air. She tossed the backpack into her backseat and started the car, sitting in the driver's seat to wait for Nico. Her phone rang, and she fumbled to answer it without looking at the screen. If Nico was running late, she would consider leaving without him. For no other reason than to keep him at a safe distance from Hathorne. The amulet reacted to her thoughts, the cool gem heating against her skin, reminding her of its power. She'd keep him safe.

Piper's voice rambling on the other end of her phone cut off her thoughts before she could even say the word *hello*.

"You're avoiding me, Drew, and I don't like it! I told you I'm okay, it could've been worse, and I do not, I repeat, do not, want you going out there without me! I saw Nico downtown. I'm coming, too. Are you back in the house? Or are you driving? I hear a car."

She wanted to keep Piper away from the house and away from Hathorne's wrath. "I'm in my car. Nico told you?"

"Yes, but *you* should've told me. Are you going now? Why didn't you tell me? I've been messaging you all morning. You know what? Forget it. I'm on my way."

"Piper, no. I'm just taking a drive out, you know? I'm not doing anything, not really. Celeste said I need a full moon."

He's next.

Hathorne's throaty voice haunted her like he was beside her.

Turning around in her seat, she searched for any sign of him across the road, but the only movement she saw was the tips of seagrass blowing against a blanket of snow. She could've sworn she heard his voice. Her promises echoed in her mind.

She wouldn't let him hurt Nico or Piper.

The amulet's magic would protect them.

Her magic would keep them safe. It had to.

Chaotic sounds of murmured conversations and a door slamming shut rang through the phone.

"Piper?" she asked.

"I'm on my way. I want to be a part of this. All of it, the weird and the witchy. See what I did just there? Okay. I'm hanging up. I'll see you soon?"

Drew closed her eyes and dropped the phone to her lap. Piper was an unstoppable force. She lifted the phone back to her ear. "I'll meet you in the clearing by Aurora." She hung up and grasped her amulet, holding it at eye level. The vines scattered as they stretched and curled around the black stone.

"You in there. Whoever or whatever you are. I'm trusting you to show up if I need you today. Deal?" The light pulsed and the tendrils of ivy twirled faster as Nico's truck parked along the side of the road.

A vanilla leathery scent lingered as Nico leaned close, buckling his seatbelt, and her stomach erupted in butterflies. Being close to him was like taking a deep breath of fresh air amidst the chaos and noise.

"Good morning, again." His eyes held a spark of flirtation, and she smiled back.

"Good morning. Are you ready?"

"I'll go anywhere with you, anytime, Drew. Are *you* ready? When was the last time you were out there? Last summer?"

"Before prom, so... June?" She backed out onto the road and headed for Neptune Point. "I'm ready. I've got to do this."

She could feel his eyes on her, and heat built deep inside, causing her to sweat underneath the layers of clothes she wore.

"I didn't see prom night going down at all the way it did."

She glanced over at him. He tapped his fingers along his knee, and she almost reached over to grasp them. Almost. "Neither did I."

"I know. I knew you wanted out of here. It was all you talked about. I guess I didn't expect it to happen so fast. Next thing I know, you were gone. I don't think we talked after that. Not until you came home for Gran."

She'd believed that leaving her small town was the only way to satisfy her desire for more in life, whatever that might be. Maybe the same tether anchoring Nico to this town held her here, too. The haunted town, her home, and her deep and tangled feelings for him were all intertwined in a knot of emotions in her stomach. But when she imagined herself staying in the house where she'd grown up, she pictured a blank canvas, and the emptiness terrified her. Her first trip away had set her on a thrilling new path, but like gravity, Atlas Cliffs called her back home.

"I just wanted to leave here and not look back. It wasn't fair to stay with you and hold you down while I took off. The opportunity to travel was my first ticket out of here. California opened my eyes to more, you know? I didn't find my mother, or figure out a damn thing, but for the first time in a long time, I had *fun*. That trip is what convinced me to move to Boston, and school has been good for me."

Nico repositioned himself and rested his arm over the center console. She took a sharp turn a little too fast, but he said nothing as he swayed from side to side. She steadied the car as the road narrowed.

"I was happy for you to go away to school... still am. I think it's amazing. You're the most talented person I know. You hide it from the world, and I hope college finally pushes you to share your work with people." He crossed his ankle over his knee and picked at his bootlaces. "But you can still go to school and keep your house here."

"I can't keep a house I'm not living in. And if Nellie can't run the business anymore, it's got to go too. I don't see any other way to do this."

"I disagree. You can totally make this work. Keep the house for a bit and decide later. Get your dad or me to check on it when you're not here. See? Other ways. Think about it. When school is done, will you want to come back here for a bit? Maybe you're happy living in Boston, or somewhere else. If you're done with this town for real, selling is the right thing to do. But if not?" Nico turned down the heat and unzipped his coat. She had figured she was the only one burning up in this car just by sitting beside him. "You can still go to school and keep your home. Just be sure. That's all I'm saying. Unless there's more to it."

"Like what?"

"Shane is there. In Boston. And I'm not coming down on you for it, I promise. I just knew you still had a thing for him. I couldn't compete with that."

"You're wrong. The thing with Shane isn't a thing at all. I've been over him, seriously over him, since he left town and you and I got together. If I thought for a minute I still wanted him, I wouldn't..."

Be sitting here in love with you.

She shifted in her seat and glanced from the road to Nico. He observed her with an intense gaze through thick lashes, and she thought she'd chew her mouth raw. "You're biting your lip," he observed. "You wouldn't what?"

She couldn't summon the courage to say the words out loud. The fact he still had a girlfriend wasn't lost on her.

But she needed him to know the truth.

"Shane and I were hanging out because I thought with everything that happened with Dominic and his mother dying, maybe I could help him somehow. Be his friend. When I noticed his feelings were more than mine, I was going to talk to him, maybe stop seeing him." She exhaled a rush of breath between her lips. "And then I found out he lied to me. All those months I thought he was dead; he was with another girl on that boat. Friendship with him is off the table. I don't want to see or talk to him again."

"Seriously? All those months you were miserable thinking he was dead, and he was cheating on you? He doesn't deserve your friendship. He doesn't deserve anything from you." He paused. "I'm about to be selfish again."

She smiled as she kept her eyes on the road. Last night, "selfish" had ended with the two of them wrapped up in each other. "Do it."

"I'm happy you aren't with him anymore."

"That's a pretty selfish statement, considering." He had a girlfriend, and he was happy she was single? "That's as selfish as it gets." She licked her lips and reached up to touch her mouth as her stomach fluttered. She was relieved the winding road was free of traffic.

"We've known each other for so long. I think you're making a mistake selling your house. I'm not calling it Gran's because it's your home, too." He looked at her with his brown, glorious eyes lit up with a small, dimpled smile. She ignored the sneaky feelings continuing to bubble over like lava and shook her head.

"Why do you think I'm making a mistake? We aren't kids anymore, things are different now, and I think I'm doing exactly what someone should do in this situation." She slowed her speed to keep the car from veering off the road, regretting her sharp tone. But who did he think he was? He'd moved on with someone else and yet he was happy she wasn't with Shane anymore!

Nico remained unfazed by her tone. He tried to stretch his legs in the small car, but it was a challenge, and he settled with bent knees. "That's not a reason to sell everything. I think you're sad as hell and telling yourself this is the only option is just a way to cope with a decision you aren't one bit comfortable with. I know this isn't my business, and you might think I'm being an asshole, but I think you should leave and do all the things you want to do. School, travel, whatever. But if you've got to convince yourself that you're making the right decision, are you actually?"

It amazed and annoyed her how easy it was to slip back into a familiar dynamic with Nico. Maybe because they had a long history together, but he understood her in ways no one else did. She couldn't hide behind a façade; he knew her too well.

The amulet vibrated against her skin, and she reached for it, keeping one hand on the wheel. She was making the right decisions!

"First of all, it's been six months since we've been together or talked to each other. I needed to make sense of everything that happened in the past year. Leaving was the only way I could do that, and I can't explain why, just that I had to figure my shit out. I never imagined Gran would be gone. Not this soon." Tears burned her eyes, but she blinked them away, hiding them from him. He'd be upset if he thought he made her cry. And he wasn't making her cry... she was capable of that on her own. "Nico, when I see you now... You have a business and a life of your own with plans for the future. I know the way it all happened with Dominic and your dad is shitty, but you're stepping up because you're this amazing guy who doesn't let anything stop you from being happy. You're creating a life for yourself here. You have a girlfriend who adores you—"

"No, I don't."

"Oh, please. I've seen the way she looks at you." Drew couldn't look at him. Why had she even brought Nicki up?

"You're wrong." He stared at her with such intensity, she almost pulled the car over to avoid an accident from not watching the road.

"What do you mean, I'm wrong?" This time, she glanced between Nico and the winding road. The top of the lighthouse came into view in the distance.

"We broke up."

Her knuckles turned white with her death grip on the wheel. "What? When?"

"This morning. That's where I was. She didn't like that you were over, and I couldn't lie to her."

"Didn't you tell her we're just friends? She's got to understand that. Do you want me to talk to her? I can explain—"

"It wasn't her who did the breaking up, Drew. It was me."

And just like that, Nico paved the way for her to be selfish. She didn't want to be happy over the breakup of two people, but he wasn't sitting beside her with a broken heart.

The warmth of the amulet intensified as they approached Neptune Point, and her nerves heightened. She searched the sides of the road for any sign of Ori, or Heath Hathorne.

"Almost there," Nico said.

She reminded herself that this time she was going to Neptune Point to discover a veil to the other side, not to find the body of a dead woman. Her hands shook as she drove along the road toward the lighthouse. She curved around the last bend and crossed the bridge. The sea revealed its strength as the waves crashed against the rocky barrier, sending droplets of water flying into the sky.

Aurora blinked with every turn of its beacon. Her heart thudded in her chest, sending her pulse thumping in her ears. Memories of the shooting, running for her life, and Iris's body, lying in the dirt.

Damn Dominic Sloan to hell, or purgatory, or whatever inferno abyss the witch hunter was from. A prison cell was too good for that man. She rubbed the pins and needles numbing her thigh, a constant reminder of the night at the warehouse. She hated how one minute she was fine, and the next she couldn't breathe. A sight or sound could sneak up and trigger panic whenever they wanted. And now wasn't the time to lose focus.

Instinctively, Drew checked the rearview mirror for a black sedan. But he was gone, no longer a threat to her life. She'd survived Dominic Sloan—and without her, he'd still be running free. Surviving was woven into her DNA. With a little magic on her side, she was going to get through this, too. And she wouldn't do it alone.

TWENTY-FIVE

"We're here." She pulled onto the snow-covered dirt road. Fear and exhilaration crept into her heart as she processed Nico's admission about his breakup. She held back from throwing her arms around him and asking if she was the reason. Being near him, knowing he was single again, feeling the pull toward him was too hard to ignore—her inability to have him had made it easier for her to sell the house and leave Atlas Cliffs behind. But now...

Wind swirled loose snow into the air over the long, dried grass. The lighthouse stood stoic as the beacon's light spun in eerie silence. The keeper's house loomed over the hill. Boards covered the windows, hiding the secrets inside. Memories of the dark tunnel slipped from the corners of her mind. Flashes of images bombarded her like a strobe light. Finding Iris's body, forgotten and left to rot. Nothing more than a skeleton in the dirt, the torn fabric of the last dress she'd ever wear again, and fragments of hair around her skull.

Her stomach gurgled and lurched. She unbuckled her seatbelt, opening the door at the same time as she put the car in park. She swung her legs to the ground, taking deep breaths with her face in her hands.

Nico was crouched in front of her in seconds, his hands on the sides of her knees. "Look at me."

"I can't."

"You can. I'm right here." He rubbed the sides of her legs.

Raising her face from her sweating hands, she wiped a mess of tears and mascara from her face, unable to meet his eyes. She was stronger than this. She'd come so far! Her heart skipped beats—maybe she was having a heart attack. Young people could have heart attacks. She couldn't control the hyperventilating and thought she'd choke to death. Chills and sweat racked her body. She unzipped her jacket and stretched the neckline of her sweater.

"Drew, look at me." Nico's calm voice barged through her anxious haze. This time she gave in to the cursed vulnerability and allowed herself to meet his gaze. "Grab my hand and squeeze," he said, holding his hand up. She obliged and gripped it like a life preserver. "Breathe with me. Let that sea air in like we do on the water." He smiled, and she relaxed her hold on his hand as she mirrored his steady breathing. "What do you need? We can turn around and go back home right now."

She continued to hold his hand and placed her other hand on the seat, running her fingers over the fabric. The air was cool, but not the usual deep freeze of winter. Deep breath. Aurora's light rotated, glistening against the clouds in a timed beat. One. Two. Three... With each count, air filled her lungs, and the trembling eased. When she faced Nico again, the irresponsibility of her actions hit her. Once again, she was leading him into the dangerous unknown without regard for his safety.

He's next.

"I made a mistake, Nico." She released his hand. "I should never have shown you what I did last night. I didn't even know I could do that, and I was selfish dragging you into this all over again. You shouldn't be here with me. This is wrong."

"Really? Because I don't remember it that way. I wasn't giving you a choice, not really. I wanted to be part of the adventure reel you showed me." He stood, surveying the rocky cliffs. "This town is as much a part of me as it is you. I'm not scared of what you can see, or what you might be. I know *you* and that's all that matters. You decide. We can walk the path to Haven or turn around and go back home. But I'm here for whatever you want. I'm all in."

She could leave and come back alone on the full moon. The amulet pulsed over her skin, and she held it up. Vines wove a web around the soft light.

Gran's presence radiated from it, giving her a sense of security. Piper's car rounded the turn like a racecar driver; Drew had almost forgot Nico wasn't the only one who insisted on joining the fun.

"The gang's all here, I see," Ori said, appearing beside Nico who was, of course, oblivious.

"What's the plan?" Piper approached them, holding a knit hat in her hands, smoothing her pink hair into a short ponytail. "Hi, Nico. The last time the three of us were back here, we were running from guys with guns."

Drew inwardly flinched at the mention of Dominic Sloan's henchmen. Piper didn't realize how much the events of the last year still got to her. She avoided talking about it more than she had to, saving the rehashing for her therapy sessions that had dwindled to every couple of months.

Drew stood and closed the car door, grabbing her bag from the back seat. "We're just going to walk down to Haven, look around, and come right back, deal?"

"Whatever you say," Nico said, throwing a wary glance at Piper, as if Hathorne was going to appear and set a fire again.

"Or," Piper said, "we make a fire in the woods, dance around it and embrace nature?"

Drew shot Piper her best, *I can't believe you're saying that after what happened*, look.

"I'm kidding. You know how I cope when bad things happen. If I let myself sink, it gets too dark," Piper said firmly. Drew could count on her fingers how many times Piper had stayed serious in a weird situation—she knew her well, knew her flippant nature was just a front. And here, in the cold air, Drew could hear her fright underneath, masked by the seriousness of her words.

With a swift movement, a raven glided over the treetops, disappearing among the branches. It had to be the same one, but why was it fixated on her?

Ori swirled into a mist and reappeared near the path to Haven up ahead. Drew walked through the seagrass poking out of melting snow and entered the trail first, with Ori keeping pace among the trees. "Your friends are cool. I like the one with the pink hair, and he's got it bad for you," he said, pointing at Nico.

Nico's footsteps crunched in the snow behind her. "No, he doesn't. Her name's Piper, remember?" She spoke out loud without thinking.

"Piper. Right. And he does so; you'll see."

"Who are you talking to?" Nico asked, closing the gap between them, and she peered over her shoulder.

The winter jacket fit him perfectly everywhere except the shoulders, which strained against the fabric. Her cheeks flushed with heat, and she covered them with her cold hands. "I know you can't see him, but Ori's here."

"The ghost from California? Okay. Hi, Ori," Nico said into the air.

Someone who didn't know would think the whole scenario was beyond strange. People in the know probably did as well, but this was her life... For now, anyway. She shook her head to rid her thoughts and forged forward.

As she walked the path to Haven, the river rapids grew louder, and the ocean waves crashing and slamming into the rocks faded. A thin layer of snow blanketed the treetops, and the bare branches curved over the trail, creating a shadow dulling the daylight. Her hair tossed around her face as the wind picked up, and she shifted it to one side. The mild day wouldn't last. The cold, biting wind through the trees was enough to make her ears ache. She pulled up her hood and moved further down the trail, navigating over the knotted roots that protruded from the snowy ground.

She reached the clearing and approached a burned-out bonfire in the middle of deteriorated timber benches. Nico and Piper talked behind her, and she heard Taj's name mentioned, along with Celeste, but didn't turn around. She couldn't take her eyes off the raven as its haunting call echoed above her head. A rush of air tickled her cheek as the bird flew past her face and settled on a circle of rocks surrounding the fire pit. As she stepped closer, it cocked its head and stared at her.

"Who are you?" she whispered. "Are you part of *him*?"

"Definitely not Hathorne," Ori said from beside her, and she jumped.

"How do you know?"

"Has it tried to claw at you or peck your eyes out? I'd say that bird is not out for blood like he is. Look at the stone around your neck. It's on fire."

She lifted it up to her face, and a flame pulsed deep inside. "What do you think it means?"

Ori pointed toward the river's edge. "We're close. Through the trees over there." He looked back at Nico and Piper. "How do you plan on keeping them safe? You do have a plan, don't you?"

She chewed her bottom lip, trying to think of something clever, anything to reason with herself for dragging her friends back into the world of the dead again. "I won't let anything happen to them. I just have to see the moon gate, so I'll know what to do when I send him back."

"Gee, you'd think we were chasing werewolves or something," Ori said. "Drew, you're playing with fire. Be careful."

Piper sauntered over to stand beside her. "Are you scared?"

"I'm angry. If I didn't hear you scream, that fire would have—"

"But it didn't," Piper interrupted. "We'll figure this out. How many times have you told me they can't hurt us? They're dead, and so is he. That fire could've been caused by anything. Where to next?"

Drew bit her lip; she'd been wrong about the dead souls. They had the power to move between the world of the dead to the living, and not all of them wanted her help.

Drew trudged in the direction Ori had pointed, her eyes seeking the moon gate. Clouds persisted through the sky, covering what was left of the sun. The tree trunks lined the bank of the river in nature's perfection. The frothing water collided with boulders over a steep incline to the other side. Chunks of snow fell off tree branches and bounced off twigs on the way to the ground. A strange noise reverberated through the forest, and she stopped to listen, gesturing for Piper and Nico to stay behind her.

"Do you see something?" Nico said, making his way to the river's edge.

A dark figure glided between the trees.

Sweat broke out over her skin and beaded down the small of her back. Her blood raced through the veins at her temples. The sound of her breath echoed under her hood, and she pushed it off her head. As the branches broke, she hoped to see a deer or a rabbit in the trees. The sound of another crunch prompted her to spin around.

The wind caught the fabric of his long cloak, and it rippled around his tall boots. From her stance, she could make out the deep indentations in his skull and the raised patches of his ulcerated skin.

The witch hunter was here, the smell of smoke lingering in the air.

He wants you, not them, she told herself.

Piper leaned close to her ear. "He's back, isn't he? What do we do now?"

"You stay back."

"Hathorne is here to torture us," Ori said. "I told you this was a bad idea."

"I've got this, Ori. Trust me."

"Trust has nothing to do with it, my human friend. I'll stay with them. Turn your attention over there. Can you see it?"

She gritted her teeth and turned her gaze away from Hathorne, her eyes widening as she watched the tumult of the river. Waves of electric blue shimmered like a pool of water, suspended in midair between two trees. She could have sworn she heard a shriek coming from somewhere deep within. "What's that sound?"

"You don't want to know."

"Ori, I need to know!"

He covered his face with both hands, dropping them to his sides. His mouth trembled—something she'd never seen on Ori before. His sullen eyes held hers. "It's the souls who want to join him, and it's your job to keep that from happening, no matter the cost."

Nico had vanished, and she frantically searched the area near the river, listening for his voice amidst the sound of the rushing water. He lingered close to the shoreline. Too close. Terror seized her, and her palms tingled with the same intensity as they did when she showed him the visions. Before she could scream his name, the witch hunter descended upon him like a hawk and knocked him off the edge with a single, powerful shove.

TWENTY-SIX

Every sense in Drew's body heightened as she bolted for the river's edge, shaking her backpack and coat off. Piper's cry from behind her pierced the thunder of rushing water. She scoured the white-crested water, desperate for Nico to breach the surface as she hopped on one foot and tugged one boot off, and then the next. He was a much better swimmer than her.

He has to be all right!

She couldn't see him over the whitewater surging toward the ocean. She plunged into the water and the icy flow enveloped her, submerging her body.

He's next.

The witch hunter's words echoed in her mind as she fought against the current and searched for Nico to surface. Across the river, Heath Hathorne peered down at her from his reign of terror on the embankment. A twisted smile contorted across his face.

Death seeks you, fucker, not me or my family. I'm sending you into a final, forever death.

Anger exploded in her chest as she directed her death wish to him before the rapids sucked her under. Her lungs were on fire as she kicked her feet—no longer able to touch the bottom—and moved her arms to launch her upper body out of the water. Nico could swim, he had to be okay. He had to survive. Taking in a lungful of air, she screamed his name with all her strength. The forest reverberated around her with Piper's shouts.

Nico can't die! I brought him here. I did this!

"Nico! Please! Don't die, don't die, don't die!" The water crashed against two big rocks, then recoiled, and the power of the undertow dragged her back down. She opened her eyes and looked up, but the further she descended, the murkier the water stirred around her. Wasn't the amulet supposed to protect her?

The memory of their last time together on Jupiter Beach rushed back as she struggled to break the water's surface. Perched on their boards, they watched the sunset after a long day of surfing. Nightfall had come, and a bright, hot bonfire illuminated the darkness. Nico wrapped his arms around her, sharing the warmth of the blanket draped over his shoulders. "I'll love you forever," he'd whispered in her ear. She'd ended their relationship days later.

And now, he'd come back to her, and they were in the water again, but with the danger of drowning hanging over them.

Gran's melodic accent sang in her ears, quieting the rapids surrounding her. "Swim, dear. Remember the hours pretending to be a mermaid? You made me sit on that bleedin' beach watching you for hours. You're strong and brave. Magic pulses through your soul. Use it. *Find him.*"

Heat radiated around her neck and her hands throbbed with pins and needles as they warmed in the frigid water. She propelled herself upward with her feet, breaching the surface of the water. She spotted Nico holding onto a boulder further down the stream. He attempted to push himself off the boulder and reach the other side, but kept slipping back in.

"Nico!" Feeling Gran's presence, she gave a final push and swam to the other side. She needed to get to him before the river's devastating power pulled him out to sea. She ended her battle and swam with the current, getting closer to the other side until the toes of her socked feet found the muddy ground. Holding onto the low-hanging branches, like she had done the last time she'd collided with the Coda River, she guided herself to the shore. Nico bridged the gap to the shoreline but couldn't stand. As if he could sense her nearness, he glanced up, and their eyes connected as she moved through the water, stepping from one rock to the next.

She had to get to him.

"What are you doing here? You could've drowned!" he shouted between gasps for air.

She leaned forward, reaching her hand out while holding onto a boulder for support. "Look who's talking! Give me your hand!"

"I'm too heavy, you won't be able to—"

"It wasn't a question!" she yelled, stepping into the deep water again, making her way toward him. "Give me your hand, or I'll keep going and we'll both be swept out to sea!"

Bracing against the boulder with one hand, he offered her his other and their hands connected. She dragged him, engaging in a tug-of-war with the river as she slogged to the shore. The moment his toes found the bottom, the pressure relieved, and she stumbled, slipping back into the water. He seized her with both hands, pulling her up, until they stood wrapped in each other's arms, their breaths shallow and gasping.

"Thank you," he said. He was without his jacket, and he stood shivering, wearing only a drenched T-shirt. Her hands tingled with burning energy that matched her insides, and she held him tighter, resting her head on his chest as she rubbed his back. She looked up at him and he studied her face. She wanted nothing more than to crash into him. Her eyes locked on his, where the depths were full of desire, but there was something else. Something that reflected in her own.

Love.

For years, their bond had been like a boomerang, the ebb and flow creating distance, with magnetism pulling them back together. But their connection was evolving into something deeper than they'd ever had before, she could feel it.

His hands rose to her face, and when he brought his mouth to hers, she kissed him back. Energy flowed from the amulet and surrounded them with an aura of invincibility.

Piper's shouts broke the moment as she came into view on the other side of the torrential river, with Ori at her side—even if she couldn't see him. "Oh my God, are you guys okay? He came back, didn't he?"

"We're good!" Drew separated herself from Nico and swept the frozen hair icicles from her face. Once again, they'd crossed the friendship barrier. Despite all the turmoil and strange unknowns in her life, Nico soothed her fractured soul. With him, she could be unapologetically herself. Kissing him again was better than she'd expected—she'd forgotten, somehow, that being in his arms was like being home.

She tore her gaze from him, gripping his arm as she searched for the witch hunter. Heat no longer poured from her hands, and as clouds enveloped the sun, a winter chill crept in. They both stood shivering uncontrollably. Branches swung as a gust of wind blew, but Hathorne was gone. It didn't mean he wouldn't come back, and staying this close to the edge of the river wasn't wise.

Nico stared up at the river from where they'd come. "I'm not sure what happened back there. One minute I was standing, and the next I felt a hard shove and lost my balance. I didn't see anything coming, Drew. It was him, wasn't it? The thing that wants you dead?" His voice strained as his body shook with chills. He scanned the river. "Piper can find some rope, or we can walk back up toward the road and cross there."

She recalled the last time she'd been in this exact place and tried to swim across. Claudia had been her rescuer before, but this time, swimming back across to the other wasn't an option. "We're not going back into that water, and it's too far. We have to get warm, or we'll freeze to death. I have a better idea."

"What do you need me to do?" Piper hollered, holding her phone up.

"Go back and grab my backpack. My car keys and phone are in there! We're taking the tunnel to Aurora. Meet us there."

"Are you sure that's a good idea?" Piper said, her voice echoing over the rapids.

"It's better than crossing back the way we came, and it's close." She glanced at Ori, who hovered near Piper. "Stay with her!"

Piper looked around her. "Ori is here?"

"He'll keep you safe!"

He has to.

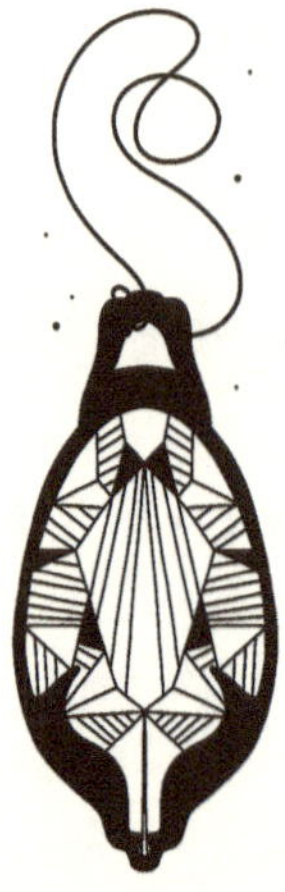

TWENTY-SEVEN

D rew navigated Nico between the trees, distancing them from the riverbank. The last time she'd been on this path was after she'd come up from the tunnel with Enid. It had been a while, but she remembered enough to locate the metal cover that was over the opening leading down into the tunnel. If they descended the ladder into the tunnel and slogged their way to the basement of the keeper's house, the car would be waiting nearby.

The raven soared ahead, landing on branches and dead-wood. It observed her, never taking its eyes off her as she moved. She resisted the urge to talk to it and ask questions.

Who are you?

Why are you following me?

Gran?

A strange tingling came from the amulet pressed underneath her wet shirt. The cold clung to her, sucking all the body heat from her skin. Her ears ached and her hands and feet burned from lack of feeling. She rubbed her hands together, wishing she could create a spark of magic, or somehow regain the strange heat in them. As they ventured closer to where the river met the ocean, the wind whipped around them, growing colder with each step.

Nico wrapped his arms around her, his body trembling in sync with hers. She pressed her body against his and hugged him back, desperate to find warmth. Their shallow breaths billowed around them. The image of him slipping below the surface made her sick to her stomach. She shuddered at the thought of Nico's lifeless body in the water. If the unthinkable had happened, she would give herself over to the witch hunter to do with her whatever he wanted, even if it meant death. The carelessness of involving him and Piper in the chaos of her world sunk deep into her bones. When would she learn to keep this part of her life a quiet whisper inside, instead of sharing it in the name of self-acceptance?

"Keep moving, Drew. We'll crank up the heat in the car. The lighthouse is right there. Where's this entrance we're looking for?"

She pulled back and looked around. The top of the lighthouse was visible above the trees on the other side of the river. The raven screeched and dove between two leaning trees, their tops arching toward each other.

"Over there," she said, grabbing his hand and stumbling over the hilly ground to where the raven landed. She dropped to the ground beside it. "This is it." The bird watched her with a sharp-eyed stare, and holding its gaze, she brushed a layer of snow away, revealing the cover of the tunnel. She balled her stinging hands into fists and tucked them against her stomach. The raven spread its wings and cried out as it launched itself above her.

Nico crouched down and helped her push the round lid off the tunnel. She couldn't recall if she'd replaced the cover, or if someone else had come since, but it didn't matter. They were getting out of there before hypothermia froze them both. Swinging her legs over the side, she pivoted around to grip the ladder. "Does your phone still work? We could use the light."

Nico reached behind him and pulled a phone from his back pocket. "It's dead."

She peered into the depths of a black hole. For all she knew, this was Hathorne's lair now, or something worse. Her foot slipped, and she caught herself. She knew this tunnel. It was the best option out of the wind and cold, and the fastest route back to the car. "Follow me."

She descended the ladder as Nico trailed behind her. He stopped for a moment to drag the lid back over the opening, plunging them into darkness. "You still there?"

"I'm here." She gasped for breath, her chest heaving, and she forced herself to stay focused before panic set in.

"One step at a time. Feel your way down. You've done this before. Breathe. I'm right here."

She descended until her feet touched the bottom. Nico dropped next. His fingers traveled along her arm until their hands interlocked, sending goosebumps over frozen skin. She placed her hand on the stone walls, her fingers sinking into the mud and moss. She tracked the tunnel until a gust of air came from above their heads, and a crack of light snuck through.

"Air vents," she said. "I remember those."

The farther along they went, the more panic built. Iris's tomb was up ahead to the left, and while her body was gone, Drew's shock and sadness at her discovery came flooding back.

"This is where you found her? Hearing about it and actually seeing this creepy place are two very different things. I'm sorry you went through that alone."

"I didn't, not really. I had help." She moved closer and closer, each step carrying her closer to Iris's temporary grave. "It's okay. I'm okay," she whispered, voice trembling and throat tight with emotion. Her palms burned, and she let go of Nico's hand, holding them up to her face. A faint blue light radiated from her palms, but she had no clue what it meant or what was happening.

The sound of a tongue clicking cut through the stale air. "You are making this too easy."

She reached behind her and pushed Nico back, searching for the disembodied voice belonging to Hathorne.

"Drew? Where the hell are you guys? Answer me!" Piper's muffled voice called out from the end of the tunnel. "I can't get the door open!"

"Piper, go to the car!"

"Not until I know you're okay!"

"Talk to me. What do you see?" Nico persisted forward.

Out of a whirl of motion, Heath Hathorne manifested himself before her. She shoved Nico forward. "Run! Go!" She pushed him again toward the end of the tunnel, but he refused to leave her side.

"I'm not leaving you here!"

Light from the amulet illuminated Hathorne's veiny, ulcerated head. He glared at her with sunken eyes no human possessed. "You float in the river, but will you breathe air if I crush your body with stones?" He interlocked his fingers and tapped his talon nails together. His snake-like pupils narrowed in on hers like they would snatch the soul from her body. "It's been centuries since I have had this much fun ridding the world of impurities."

The amulet reacted, emitting a burning spotlight in his direction. If Nico wouldn't run, she'd have to keep him safe. She yanked the amulet off her neck and held it up to the witch hunter. His cloak whipped around his legs, but no air circulated underground, and she couldn't locate the source. "I *will* send you back!"

The witch hunter bellowed a wicked laugh, and a cloud of bugs flew out of his mouth. A blast of sound echoed in the tunnel, like beetle wings clicking together and she ducked. A rush of adrenaline coursed through her like a shaken soda can being opened, and she stood, raising the amulet into the air, blasting an electric current toward the witch hunter. The nasty insects burned into ash.

"Are you still with me? Nico?" She didn't dare turn around.

"I'm not going anywhere, but I can't see him! Do we stake him with something?"

"He's not a vampire." She held her stance, willing her magic jewel to do what it did best.

Ori appeared beside her. "I locked Piper and her friend out. Would you look at this guy? Is he, or is he not, the most hideous-looking thing you've ever seen?"

"Not the time, Ori."

Electricity coursed through her, catching her breath the way a gust of icy sea air did in the middle of a storm. Her hands burned and as the amulet dangled from her fingers, faint light swirled over her palms. Magic lived inside her, and all she had to do was harness enough to keep them safe. A sudden bright flash spread around her, engulfing Nico. The witch hunter tried to lunge at her, only to be propelled back before disappearing.

"Did you see that?" she exclaimed through her panting breaths.

"I saw it, all right. See? It worked. It'll protect you." Ori touched the amulet still clutched between her fingers, and as if on cue, the vines crawled and stretched, almost blocking out the light fading in the center.

"Your ghost friend's here, isn't he?" Nico asked.

"He kept Piper out."

"What was that... burst of light?" Nico walked across the narrow pathway, searching every inch of the area in the dim light. "He was right here, threatening you. I could hear him, Drew. I heard laughing, and I could tell how scared you were, but there wasn't a goddam thing I could do."

"That's just it." She held the amulet up between the three of them, and a spark flickered inside. "This isn't for you to take care of. I have to be the one to send him back, and this is going to help me do it."

"How?" Nico said.

A scraping sound emanated from the end of the tunnel, followed by a flood of light piercing the darkness.

Ori turned to face her as he faded from his human form into the ghost version of himself. "I'm outta here, but you'll be okay for now. I'll be back."

Celeste Locke stooped and entered the opening, Piper and Taj following, each with a flashlight.

What are Celeste and Taj doing here?

Piper must've called them, but she couldn't figure out why they'd be her first phone call. Unless things were more serious between Piper and Taj than she realized.

Piper proceeded through the dim tunnel. "What the hell happened in here? We couldn't get the door open." She shined the light over her surroundings, taking in the stone walls.

Celeste headed toward Drew. She still had the amulet dangling in the air—a beacon of light among the shadows. Celeste cradled the amulet like a fragile bird. "You've got the whole sisterhood in the palm of your hand. It's no wonder you'll need the full moon."

The sisterhood?

Twenty-Eight

As Drew walked behind the rest of the group through the passage, she could almost see Iris standing near her first resting place. She took Piper's flashlight and directed it for a better view, but of course, Iris was gone now. She'd found peace on the other side of life and death. So had Enid and Ezra. But knowing they'd crossed over where they were supposed to be didn't make the loss any easier. "That's where I found her."

"You okay?" Nico said.

"Yeah." She kneeled and peered into the narrow tomb made of stones. The police had removed all evidence of Iris. If Jack still watched from Aurora and knew of Hathorne's wrath, he wouldn't tolerate him lurking at Neptune Point. Unless Jack was powerless to stop him.

"I'm ready," she said. Nico held out his hand and pulled her up.

The familiar musty smell and dim lighting of the basement hit her with a wave of déjà vu. She didn't think she'd ever come back, vowing to herself she'd leave Neptune Point and Aurora behind forever. She remembered the photo book from the attic. Aurora held childhood memories for Enid and Ezra. This place was once home to a family who loved each other and celebrated together. They had experienced the devastation of their lives together. For Drew, this place held fear and sadness.

Haven was different. Steps away from the dilapidated old house, the familiar clearing in the woods held different memories. She'd enjoyed bonfires with friends and first loves, and formed a connection with Claudia, which helped her solve Iris's murder. Drew's relationship with Neptune Point was complicated and bittersweet, and no matter how hard she tried, she couldn't stay away.

Piper and Taj stood next to each other, whispering with their faces close, confirming their connection. How much had Piper told Taj? With little cell service, he must've known they were out here before Nico had even fallen into the river. Breaking away from Taj's side, Piper handed Drew her jacket and gave Nico a blanket. "I found it in your backpack."

Drew shoved her trembling arms in the coat and zipped it up, eyeing Piper, Taj, and Celeste. "How did you know to come out here?"

Celeste adjusted her fur-trimmed hat and pulled her gloves from her pocket. She raised her eyebrow, amused. "When something terrible is happening to someone I care about, I'm not sitting idle. And clearly, it's a good thing I came. You need more help than I realized." She narrowed her gaze, placing her hands on Drew's arms. "Go home, warm up, and try to sleep. You'll come see me right away, got it?"

Celeste had a way of embracing her with words. Her sincere eyes opened into her generous soul, and if she wasn't shivering so badly, she'd hug her. "What are you going to do?" she asked through chattering teeth.

"I'm going to help you. Now, put that thing back around your neck, and don't take it off again." Celeste pulled red suede gloves over her fingers. "It's time to leave. Everyone out." Her heeled boots clicked with each creaking step, and Drew hoped the rotting wood would hold until they all ascended.

As they walked through the house toward the front door, the wind whistled through the cracks in the house. How it was still standing and what Celeste planned to do with it was beyond her, but she couldn't deny her curiosity. Maybe Celeste would burn it to the ground in honor of Enid and Ezra. Drew would want to be a part of that ceremony.

She gazed up the winding stairs to the dim hallway above. This had been Enid and Ezra's home. She bet the bedroom remained untouched from the last time she'd explored upstairs. Placing a hand on the banister, she took the first few steps.

"Are you coming?" Piper said.

Drew gazed up at the space, searching for a hint of mist, or a shadow, but only found an unbroken stillness. Emptiness hung in the air. Even Jack was nowhere to be seen. The only sound was the rattling of windows and the groaning of the floorboards as she walked.

No longer barricaded, when Drew pushed the front door of the keeper's house, it opened, swinging in the wind on its broken hinges. Night was coming, and the moon was almost at its fullest. With a solemn promise she'd return on the night of the full moon with enough magic to close the portal and keep the witch hunter inside, she passed the flashlight to Piper and stepped onto the run-down front porch. She ignored the wave of fear washing over her as she tried to figure out *how* she was going to banish him.

She licked her lips and tasted salt as the ocean crashed below and the bite of the winter air pricked her skin like needles.

Celeste shoved the front door closed and secured it like a gate with a padlock as everyone rushed for the cars.

Piper handed Taj the keys. "Can you start my car?" He chatted with his mother before hopping into Piper's car. Celeste climbed in her own vehicle, started the engine, but sat waiting. Something inside Drew knew Celeste would sit in her car until everyone else left.

Reaching for her coat pocket, she found the keys and gave them to Nico so he could start the car. Climbing into the driver's seat, he cranked up the heat as far as it would go. Piper hovered close to Drew, so she stood with the passenger door hanging open. "Something you need to tell me?"

"Taj knew I was coming out here. I told him to stay near his phone and be ready for anything."

"Why would you do that? You said you wanted to meet me out here. It frustrated you when I didn't let you know I was coming! Why bring him into this?"

Piper pulled her hood over her head and folded her arms, avoiding looking in Drew's direction.

"Piper, I'm freezing. Why did you tell Taj to be ready for anything? I don't get it."

"Remember the last time we were out here? This isn't your first time surviving the Coda River or Neptune Point."

"Then why come at all? That's why I didn't want you here!"

"I'm scared for you! No one else..." Piper rubbed her forehead and locked eyes with her. "How can we stop something we can't see? I don't want to leave you alone, ever!"

"Nico was with me—"

"And he almost drowned!"

Her throat tightened and despite trying to swallow the lump away, it clung, choking her. "You think I don't know that?" Her eyes were burning with tears. Their warmth was the only thing that could reach her.

"That night in the bedroom." Piper didn't look away this time. The silver gem in her eyebrow glittered in the headlights as her brows furrowed. "I couldn't see him, but I could hear him."

"You told me you heard him laughing." The sound of his cruel laughter reverberated inside her, filling her with disgust and terror.

"There's more to it. He said something, and I didn't want to tell you, but now I think you need to know."

Drew gripped the open doorframe. Nico sat in silence, but there was no way he couldn't hear the conversation happening. The other two vehicles idled in wait, as if Taj and Celeste both knew something Drew didn't. "Everyone is waiting for us, Piper. And you said so yourself if he comes back and I can't stop him, where does that leave us all? We need to get out of here."

She turned to leave, but Piper grabbed her arm. "He killed Gran."

She felt lightheaded, as if all her blood had drained to her feet. She grabbed onto the car's roof to brace herself. She spun around, her heart pounding. "What did you just say?"

Tears streamed down Piper's face, and her shoulders shook as she muffled her tears with her hand. "I'm so sorry. I didn't want to tell you and cause more pain, but after tonight, you need to know. I know you don't think the dead can come back and hurt you, but this one can, Drew. I can't let that happen, not to you." Sobs erupted from her, and Drew hugged her, desperate to control her own rage and grief.

Drew peered down at Nico as Piper stepped back. He had never appeared so devastated before.

"Do they know?" Drew gestured toward Celeste and Taj.

"I'm sorry, but she's the first person I could talk to about any of this who wasn't you. Please don't hate me. I didn't know what to do."

Every fiber of her being was screaming in pain. She was numb to the core. Shards of glass filled her chest as her heart shattered into a million pieces. She didn't know this level of grief existed.

But when she saw the turmoil on Piper's face, hate was the last emotion she could ever feel for her friend.

"I could never hate you. You're my family. I don't want you to worry about me. I'm going to fix this. Go with Taj and be safe. Tomorrow is Christmas Eve, you love Christmas." Drew hugged Piper one more time. "Go home. I'm going to be just fine, I promise."

"Celeste wants to help, and I think she might be able to, you know? I never believed in magic until I met you, but if you really are a witch, you'll have power, too. He won't win, Drew."

"No. He will not win."

Piper leaned down to Nico. "You'll stay with her?"

"I'm not going anywhere," he said.

Piper sprinted for the car and settled herself in the driver's seat. She made a heart with her hands before driving away. Celeste steered onto the main road to follow Piper and Taj, pulling over as she waited for Drew to leave.

Drew plopped down and slammed the car door shut. "Let's go."

Nico headed along the road toward home, neither of them saying a word. She wrapped her arms around herself, struggling to stave off the cold despite the oppressive heat coming from the vents. All she wanted was to witness the moon gate, but one selfish decision had turned into a waking nightmare.

Nico glanced over at her, and their eyes met. He dropped one hand from the wheel and held it out to her over the middle console like a lifeline. She clutched it and gazed out the window as night closed in around them.

The witch hunter was about to learn firsthand what it meant to be the one being hunted. What it was like to look over your shoulder every moment, wondering if it was going to be your last, or your friends' last. Or your family. The injustice of Gran's death burned her senses like a rush of salt water up her nose and into her lungs.

She was going to make Heath Hathorne pay.

Twenty-Nine

Nico drove up the driveway to her house and turned the car off. His truck sat at the end near the road, its windows covered with a layer of frost. Gran's colorful lights twinkled along the porch and the cleaning crew had left a light on inside. The house might be missing its heart, but it appeared less lonely and more like the home she'd always known, even without Gran. She didn't want Nico to go home yet.

The idea of being without him made her chest ache, but she couldn't bring herself to say the words. She was also struggling to leave the car and go into the house alone.

"Are you hungry?" Nico said.

The randomness of his comment surprised her, making her aware of her growling stomach. "Starving, actually."

"Come on." He climbed out of the car. "Let me start a fire and find something to eat."

She followed him up the porch steps, and he pressed the keys into her palm. She unlocked the door and Nico followed her inside. The house sheltered them with its warmth, blocking out the rest of the world.

She hung her jacket and rubbed her arms as Nico set to work with paper and kindling. "Where are the matches?"

Her hands tingled, and if exhaustion wasn't fogging her mind, she'd try to light a fire without a strike. She handed him the festive tube of matches instead of attempting that trick again; she was done with magic for the night. The fire was soon going, its warmth radiating out as it crackled and snapped. He added a few logs and placed the mesh cover in front of the fireplace, keeping the sparks from bursting free.

"I might have something of Dad's upstairs. A sweater or something."

"Don't worry about me. I'll dry off. I just hope you're okay. That's really all that matters to me right now."

He cared so much for her, and she'd pushed him aside for months. She touched her lips, and a shiver ran through her as she remembered the sensation of their kiss in the water.

"You're freezing," he said, "go change, and I'll go see what you've got in the kitchen."

"Good luck. I'm out of everything right now. Been busy with other things."

"I've noticed," he said. "I'll find something. I always do."

He headed for the kitchen, and she scurried up the stairs, ignoring Gran's closed door, and hurried to her bedroom. She hadn't checked her phone for hours, but the cleaning crew was supposed to have finished this afternoon. When she saw her reflection in the mirror, she wiped away the mascara smudges under her eyes and ran her fingers through her tangled mess of red hair.

She stripped out of her wet clothing and changed into her favorite leggings and the green sweater Piper had given her for her birthday last year. She rummaged through the spare bedroom closet, finding a navy sweatshirt and matching pants. Grabbing what she could find, she headed for the stairs, stopping before going back down.

How did Hathorne get into this house?

Celeste had told her Gran used a Safe Haven spell, placing stones at each entrance. She opened the door to Gran's bedroom, an aroma of bleach mixed with lemon filled the frigid air. The walls would have to be replaced, but the fire would've taken the entire house if she hadn't gotten there when she did. The window was open a crack, letting the whistling wind inside. Drew crossed the room and shut it with a decisive click. Two stones sitting between the windowpanes caught her eye. One black and the other a smoky brown. She ran to each of the bedrooms to find the same stones in each of the windows. She recalled the pattern of stones at the door of the Tough Cookie, and underneath the mat. If each entry point had protection, how had he gotten inside?

She tapped her foot against the floor, and the hollow sound echoed. A memory struck her; the day she'd come to live with Gran. Her mom had abandoned her, and her dad kissed her goodbye as he left for a job at sea. She'd been crying for hours and Gran had shown her a special door in the floor leading to a hidden room. She and Drew had made a fort where they read books by flashlight for hours at a time. Of course, she'd forgotten—the trap door! It led outside!

I've got to ask Celeste how to do a Safe Haven spell for the trapdoor.

She plucked a stone from each window and placed them on top of the closed door before sliding the bed over it.

"Would you just go down there already!" Ori appeared, leaning against the door frame.

"Jesus, Ori. Now is not the time."

"It's never the time, but I'm not sticking around, don't worry. I wanted to make sure you were okay."

"I'm fine, really. You don't need to worry."

"Yeah, that's a problem for me. I'm kind of stuck with you, which means you're stuck with me. When you worry, I feel it, and I worry. And I'm not going to add to your troubles right now, because—" He grinned and gestured toward the stairs, "You've got company, and I like that guy."

She exhaled hard. "Add to my troubles, Ori. Bring it."

"I won't do it. Not tonight. Have fun, my human friend." He winked and vanished, leaving her wondering what trouble he was about to add to the mountain.

Holding the clothes for Nico, she headed for the kitchen. As she walked across the living room, the lights from the tree twinkled and the heat from the fire radiated throughout the room as its flames danced within the confines of the mantle.

Nico emerged from the kitchen with two grilled cheese sandwiches, a few cookies, and two cans of ginger ale under his arm. "I hope this is all right. It was the best I could do."

"It's more than all right. Thank you." She handed him the clothes after he set the plates on the coffee table.

"Thanks." He pulled off his damp T-shirt and draped it over the back of the chair. A silver chain hung around his neck, highlighting his broad chest, and his muscles flexed as he tugged the sweatshirt onto his head. She couldn't stop thinking about the kiss they'd shared in the river and how his arms chased away the cold and soaking wet clothes. She took a seat on the sofa, propping the plate in her lap, and opened a can of ginger ale. Nico poked the fire and added another piece of wood before sitting beside her.

She was falling for him all over again, but she knew what sort of life she brought into the relationship, and it was only getting more complicated by the day. Leaning back in the seat, she pulled Gran's blanket over her legs. She pulled her phone out of her bag and glanced at the unread messages as she ate. Her dad was coming for a takeout dinner on the weekend, and Piper wanted to be sure she was all right. But when she clicked the last message from earlier in the day, she froze. Anna Tate was overflowing with enthusiasm about a lucrative offer. The buyers intended to handle the fire renovations themselves and needed a closing date of the first of February.

Drew wasn't sure if she was going to pass out, scream, or burst into tears. She should be happy, not miserable! Nico sat upright, staring at her with concern.

"What is it?" he said.

"Listen to this." She played the message on speaker for him.

"An offer." He exhaled and leaned back, picking up his can of soda. "What are you thinking? Are you going to accept it?"

"She wants to meet me this week, but I think I've got to take it. But I don't want you caught up in all my shit—"

"I'm stronger than that, Drew. Don't do this."

"Do what? Piper's right. Just hanging out with me is a risk. What if your family is next? Or Piper's? My dad? If I thought the witch hunter of death would follow me back to Boston, I'd run back and keep him away from all of you. Don't you see? I'm damaged and broken, and I think I might be what he says. A *witch*. Do you know what a witch is? I have no idea what it all means, or what Gran's superhuman power was, or why she kept me in the dark all those years." She picked at her soft sweater, avoiding his soulful, kind gaze. "Maybe you should go home."

"Is that what you want?" he said.

Sitting side by side, their legs touched, and a wave of heat spread through her. They were picking up where they'd left off months ago, but with a different level of seriousness. Her feelings for him were more than infatuation or friendship. She'd had time alone, time to heal and figure out what she wanted. Her connection with Nico was real and meaningful. He saw her scars and the ghostly part of her life and cared about her without expectations. Why couldn't she say the words?

I don't want you to go.

He leaned forward, tilting his head to face her. "I don't remember a time I didn't love you. Probably since we were kids. I've been hurt, I've moved on. And if I have to, I'll do it again, but you're not going to lose me as a friend. I wouldn't do that to us." He stood, running a hand through his hair. "I'm not scared. Your quirkiness makes you awesome. If you want me to leave, of course I'll go. But if there's a chance that this"—he gestured between them—"is something amazing and you might want to see where it goes...? Just say the word and I'll stay."

She stood, her gaze lingering on him, the warmth of the fire reflecting in his deep brown eyes—it was like she could get lost in them forever. But for the past six months, she'd been questioning so much, including her feelings for him. She was overthinking everything, and she was so tired of holding back. Why couldn't she be honest with herself? With him?

He turned toward the foyer, and she stepped forward, grabbing his arm. "I want to be selfish. Don't go."

He turned around, closing the gap between them, raking his eyes over her face. She wasn't sure what that look in his eyes was, but she knew it was more than friendship. He ran the back of his hand along her cheek, and she tilted her head against it, closing her eyes. Every ounce of tension melted away. His hand against her face sent every nerve in her body into sensory overload, like electricity to power a village. Reaching up, she held his face in her hands and stared back into his eyes. He licked his lips, and all she wanted was for him to kiss her mouth, her neck... She wanted to be as close to him as their bodies would allow. He leaned down and their lips met, sending sparks throughout her body. For the first time in months, she found herself able to breathe. Really breathe, the way she could on Jupiter Beach. Every other thought, every anxiety, and dread disappeared from her mind with each second that passed.

Her breath hitched when they parted. He held her close, and she nestled her icy hands against the warmth of his back, hidden inside his cozy sweater.

"I love you too," she whispered.

She entwined their fingers, her heart racing as she led him up the stairs to her bedroom. She'd been with Nico before, but this... this was different. This was trust and love. This was letting her guard down, allowing herself to be vulnerable without fear of loss. Their kisses became frantic as they undressed each other and slipped under the covers. They were two souls colliding in the most intimate way, mending broken pieces with an unspoken promise.

They fell into each other's embrace, and she lay with her head on his chest. She inhaled the lingering scent of his cologne as his fingers moved slowly through her hair and along her back. She drifted off to sleep, free of terror.

In Nico's arms, she'd found her haven.

THIRTY

The chimes rang out, mingling with the big band music blaring from the speakers, as Drew stepped inside Little Mysteries. Taj looked up from a book spread out on the counter.

"Hey, Drew. You here to see Mom?"

"Is she around?"

"She's upstairs." He picked up his phone and typed a message with a furrowed brow as she wandered around the shop, eyeing a display of crystals and their meanings. She picked up a jet-black stone, its obsidian surface shining in the light. It was identical to the other stones scattered around her house. The card beside it read, *Black Tourmaline, for protection from negative energy*. She turned the stone around in her fingers, feeling its rough ridges.

"She'll be down in a few minutes," Taj said, placing his phone beside his book. Drew sat on a wooden stool opposite him at the counter.

"What are you reading?"

He held the book up—a kinesiology textbook. "Studying."

"Where do you go?"

"UNE. I'm in my second year. I pick up shifts at Maze when I'm home."

He drummed his fingers along the varnished surface, keeping precise time to the beat of the music. She longed to be back at Maze with Nico and Piper, even Claudia, to listen to music and have a fun night again.

"Do you just play drums?" she asked.

"Bass, sometimes, but I'm not that good. I connect with playing drums. Drums and bass are all about keeping the beat for the group. It brings us together. The best feeling in the world. You?"

"No musical talent here. I paint. Draw."

"Nice. It's all art, my friend." He shoved the book into his backpack and pulled a red hoodie over his head. "We play every Thursday night at Maze. You should come next week. It'll be our last gig before everyone goes back to school." He moved with a mysterious appeal, like his mom, and Drew got why Piper was attracted to him.

Throwing his backpack over his shoulder, he turned to her. "I'm not like you. I don't get what you can see, but I've been around it my whole life. People judge, some of them are assholes, but you can trust my mom. She knows what's going on."

"Thanks." Drew plucked a smooth, clear stone from a bowl on the counter and stared through it. "I suppose you don't know what all these are for?"

He shook his head and smiled. "They're rocks, dude. Magical rocks."

She squinted her eyes, trying to find a spark of magic inside the stone, like her amulet, but nothing happened.

Steps echoed from the back of the room, and Celeste appeared wearing the most elegant wrap dress in a beautiful emerald green with a matching silk headband. Drew dropped the crystal stone back into the bowl with the others and sat on her hands.

Celeste raised a brow. "Clear quartz. It brings the light in. Keeps your home a haven."

"I'll catch ya later, Drew." Taj waved to his mother and headed out the front door, sending the chimes clanging. She watched through the window as he vanished among the last-minute holiday shoppers along the sidewalk.

Celeste flipped the sign to 'Closed' and shut the blinds. "Did you bring the book with you?"

Drew held up the magic book. "Right here. I've been trying to focus like you said, but the rest of the pages are still blank. I've got to figure this out, Celeste. He killed her. He killed my grandmother—the kindest, sweetest, loving person. She didn't deserve to die. It's time we get rid him."

"Sure is. Mother Nature, help me. I'm going to show you what I can. It's magic I haven't used in a very long time, but it's the only way." Celeste picked up a remote and turned off the music and dimmed the lights before reaching out her hand. A stack of beaded bracelets shimmied. "Book."

Drew gave it to her, and she flipped it upside down, opening it from the back. Placing it on the wide counter in front of Drew, she pressed the pages down, cracking the spine with the gentleness of a mother's touch to keep it from closing. She placed candles around, muttering as she lit each one. Their flickering light filled the room with a gentle glow. Wisps of smoke curled from burning incense, carrying a powdered aroma mixed with earthy grass.

"What do we do next?" Drew asked.

"We make a plan. You need a full moon to seal the gate; there's no way around it, but you can get ready. Protect yourself in the meantime. Consider this a dress rehearsal. Come, stand beside me."

Drew obliged. Her heart raced with the thrill and apprehension for what she was about to do. Magic was real, but not without caution. The page Celeste had turned to in the book was the page with the red words of warning.

This time, she placed her hand on the book and read aloud. "'The talisman bearer must surrender their mystic birthright and all magic and make peace with what no longer belongs to them to banish the specter to the soul realm and seal the moon gate.'"

Celeste leaned over the book from beside her. "Mm-hmm. Are you willing to part with your gift?"

The prospect of a calm life without dead people haunting her around every corner should have filled her with joy. But when she imagined an existence without ghostly encounters, she wanted to curl up and cry. She found purpose in helping the dead, and a few of her favorite people were those she had met after they died. "Do you think there's another way?"

"Have you always seen dead people?" Celeste asked.

"Yeah, always. It's just the magic stuff that's been new."

"Since she gave you the amulet?"

Drew tapped her fingers on the shiny countertop. Hathorne attacked her in the bathroom at school—a first, but the magic hadn't started until she received the amulet. "Do you think the only reason I can do any of this is because I have this?" Candlelight sparkled off the silver chain as she lifted the amulet to eye level.

"It appears that way."

"Will I still see ghosts? After all this goes down. Or will I lose it all?"

With her hand on her hip, the pink silk of her blouse rustled as Celeste flipped the pages, reading the gold writing Drew had conjured up while with Ori. "I don't see another way, Drew. Your gran did what she could, but it'll be your decision. You might lose it all."

I can't let him win.

Who would she be without helping the dead find their peace? The answer was simple. She'd still be Drew. An artist. A friend, a daughter... Nico's love. She would find her new normal. Somehow.

"Tell me what to do, and I'll do it," she said. She'd make sure she would have time to help Ori before losing her gift.

Celeste reached for the amulet around Drew's neck. Wrapping her hand around it, she closed her eyes and breathed deeply. Drew's skin crawled from her scalp down her spine as the amulet lit up, glowing through Celeste's grip. If she could, she'd climb out of herself to break the feeling of fireworks exploding inside her chest. "What is that—that weird feeling?" she gasped.

Celeste released the amulet like she would a breakable treasure. "They're all with you. The sisterhood of witches from centuries ago. They'll be ready, but only if you are." She clapped her hands together. "You're going to do this spell."

"*Spell?*"

"That's right." Celeste opened a cupboard and extracted a silver bottle with a pump attached to it, like an antique perfume bottle. She passed it to Drew and stepped on a step stool, reaching to the top of the cupboard, retrieving a small box with a picture of an eye on the lid. Turing the bottle over in her hand, Drew unscrewed the top, careful not to spill its contents, and inhaled. A bittersweet blend of a spicy, powdery aroma enticed her.

"Sprinkle some of this inside the bottle," Celeste said, handing Drew the small box.

The eye seemed to stare at her as she opened the lid. Dried flowers lay inside. "What is all this? What's it for?"

"Sea water, Frankincense, and Myrrh." Celeste pointed to the box. "That's Vervain. Combined with the seawater and a little dose of magic... with a k." She winked, candlelight twinkling in her amber eyes. "You're going to learn the protection of the moon with a little help from the other side."

"Vervain. Isn't that a vampire thing?" Drew sprinkled some of the dried flowers into the bottle. "Is this enough?"

"Plenty. Close it up and give it a shake. Just a little. It's been used by witches for centuries in protection spells, and also, of course, banishing rituals."

Drew recapped the bottle and shook the liquid. She was in a store making potions and protection spells by candlelight. The experience was wild, strange, and beautiful at the same time. The only way to defeat Hathorne was with magic; arming herself with whatever power Celeste offered was going to empower her. "Is this something you do often?"

"I do it when I need to. I don't broadcast it though. This town couldn't handle what we can do. I'll show you what I can, but you'll have to figure out where your strengths lie. Only you can do that part."

"You mean like I can see ghosts? Is that my strength? What's yours?"

"I'm a teacher." Celeste smiled. "And I've been known to move things from time to time."

Move things?

"Sounds interesting."

"It is, I assure you."

Drew turned the little bottle over and was about to depress the pump when Celeste stopped her. "Not here. That's for your house. Maddie must've missed somewhere. You spray every entrance—windows, doorways, all of them—and recite the spell."

Drew eyed the book and placed the bottle on the counter. "Okay. Focus and intention, right?"

"You've got it. Stand in front of the book and breathe." Celeste settled onto a stool across the counter from her.

Drew rubbed her palms together to get rid of the pins and needles reverberating through them, but the tingling only intensified. "What do I focus on, exactly?"

"Try something simple first." Celeste eyed a candle. "Make the flame dance."

Drew scrunched her face as she glanced between the row of candles and Celeste, who gestured to the candle. "That's not simple. I already tried that, and it didn't work."

What if I can't do this?

"Try again. Stop doubting and do," Celeste said.

Maybe Celeste's power was mind-reading, too.

Closing her eyes, Drew held her hands over the largest of the candles and imagined the flames moving closer to her palms—reaching and *dancing,* as Celeste put it. She cracked open an eye to peek, but the flame flickered low in the glass holder. "Nothing's happening."

"Breathe. Let go of the doubt and trust... *Believe* in what you're capable of."

Drew let her shoulders drop, and she breathed in through her nose and out through her mouth, like Piper had shown her. She held her hands over the candles, and her palm burned. Yanking it away, she opened her eyes. The flickering flames shook like they were laughing at her. "Celeste, why isn't it working?"

"Keep trying, Drew. You give up too quickly! If you keep doubting, this will all be for nothing."

I do not give up easily!

Everything she set out to do, she made happen one way or another.

"Lift your hands higher," Celeste said, her voice hushed.

Drew lifted her hands, and the heat in her palms intensified. It was happening! The heat dropped off and she glanced down. The flames refused to work for her. Work *with* her. She took a deep breath and saw the flame of a candle in her mind's eye, swaying and dancing. The burning sensation stung like a hot knife piercing her skin. Her body begged to recoil, but she breathed through it and opened her eyes instead. The flame stretched like an elastic band into the air beyond what was naturally possible.

"I'm doing it!" She tried to release the flame, but it continued to flounder close to her palms. She pulled her hands back, and it followed. "Celeste, what's happening?"

Celeste reached across the counter, taking Drew's hands. "I've got you." She exhaled sharply, and the flame obeyed, diminishing to a faint, flickering light. "Takes practice, but you can do it. Try calling the ghost that stays with you."

"Ori?"

"Focus on him. Imagine him here in the room." Celeste sat on a stool and rested her elbows on the counter.

Drew shifted her thoughts to Ori. If she mastered the ability to summon the dead, she'd bait Hathorne on the night of the full moon.

Back to Ori.

Closing her eyes again, she imagined Ori standing in front of her, visualizing his pony-tailed hair and angelic eyes when he was most ghost-like. As she concentrated, the sight of his lifeless body played out before her eyes, creating a sick feeling in her stomach. She could feel the pain radiating from his broken heart, begging for help. The comfort his presence had given her since they'd met all those months ago filled her with guilt. Guilt for not doing more to help him. As she ventured into a new world of self-discovery, she promised to do better. No one else could understand any of this the way Ori and Enid could. She'd been there for Enid, Ezra, and Iris. She would do the same for Ori and figure out what happened to him, and why he remained in limbo. She would have to figure it out quickly; the time before she lost her power was dwindling.

Focus. Ori? Please appear.

"Well, shit. If I knew you could call me whenever or wherever you wanted, we could've solved a lot more a hell of a lot sooner." Ori appeared beside Celeste, whose black curls danced as she shook her head.

Celeste gripped the counter. "I felt that one. He's here. You're catching on."

"I don't think I've ever been happier to see you than I am now," Drew said.

"Ditto, living friend."

Celeste looked around where Ori stood, but not directly at him. "Oh, honey." Her hands flew to her chest. "So much sadness. I was wrong. This is bigger than the Jo woman. He misses someone. He's not going anywhere until you reunite them."

Ori tucked loose strands behind his ears. "She's good," he said, appraising Celeste, "but we'll deal with my shit later. This first."

"This, for now. I'm going to Haven alone to send him back, Ori."

"We talked about this. You need me, I need you." Candlelight shimmered off his pale skin like glitter.

"You'll be gone. I have to help you first, before I lose every-thing. You'll be stuck if that happens."

"I trust you, Drew. There was only one other person in my life I trusted as much as you and—" Ori trailed off.

"And what? Who?"

"This first," he said, pain reflecting in his eyes.

Brilliant light shone from the amulet, illuminating the room. The book's pages fluttered by themselves like wings taking flight. Drew tensed, reaching out to touch the book as a fizzing sensation filled her mouth, extending to her face and down her arms.

"Don't touch it yet. Let it show you." Celeste rose from the stool.

A gentle breeze swirled in the room, its source a mystery as it stirred Drew's hair. Buzzing filled her ears, like a chorus of ci-cadas in the summer. The pages of the book paused, suspended in mid-air, before descending back into place. The vibrating cicadas stopped singing.

As Drew glanced over the pages, Ori and Celeste leaned in close. Gold lettering drifted across the yellowed pages.

Essence of night
Where the water flows,
The peak of the moon's power
Calling upon the ones who burned,
Vanquish harm through reflection.

Lock the door.

Seeking Haven for all, after and before.

A blue butterfly appeared, landing on the opposite page. Drew reached for it, letting her fingers graze its silken wings. The butterfly's wings flattened, allowing her touch. The vibrant blue wings fluttered like a hummingbird, sending the scent of lilac around her before it whirled above the book and disappeared.

"Gran?" she muttered. Instead of the usual unbearable ache, the warmth of grief trickled through her.

The gold lettering sped across the page as Gran's voice whispered the words. "'Please, this way come. I summon the powers of the day. Powers of the night. Oil and water, fire and air. No harm shall pass. No harm shall pass.'"

"There are your spells." Celeste clasped her hands together on the counter. The flickering candlelight made her brown skin shimmer, casting a magical glow.

"Did you hear Gran?" Drew glanced from a quiet Ori to Celeste.

"I saw her, Drew," Ori said. "She was standing beside you."

"Why couldn't I see her?"

"She didn't want to break your concentration, or the spell would vanish." Empathy crossed Celeste's gentle eyes. "I heard her thoughts. She's gone now."

Drew blew out a breath through pursed lips. Losing her gift to see the dead was going to be a whole new type of grief. Tears gathered in her eyes, and she blinked to stop them from falling, turning her attention to the words on the pages. "'Vanquish harm through reflection'… What, like a mirror?" Drew whispered.

"Mirrors." Celeste gestured toward a shelf of decorative mirrors of various sizes. She picked out three, small enough to fit into a backpack, and placed them on the counter beside the bottle of potion. "Of course! They'll drive him back through the gate. As soon as he's through, you drop them. Got it?" She plucked the two crystals Drew was toying with earlier from their bowls. "Take them all."

"How much do I owe you? I can't just take them."

"Take them." Celeste grabbed Drew's hands, holding them in her own. Warmth pulsed between them, their energy colliding together in fireworks under Drew's skin. "Consider them gifts from the sisterhood."

Dropping Drew's hands, Celeste ran a hand over the candles, extinguishing all of them in one swipe, and turned the music back on. She turned on a lamp covered with dragonflies on the counter and took a deep breath. Stretching her neck from side to side, she exhaled a deep breath. "You'll be ready."

Drew was doubtful an hour of Witch Training 101 would be enough. "What about this?" She held up the bottle and shook it. "What am I supposed to do with this, exactly?"

"That's your oil and water. Sprinkle it around your house at every entrance as you repeat that spell. The one your Gran gave you."

"What about the fire and air part? I'll end up burning my house down if I play with fire."

"Leave that to the sisterhood." Celeste winked. and patted Drew's cheeks. "Focus. Intention. Drew, you will be ready."

THIRTY-ONE

Drew headed to the restaurant, The Casting Spoon, to meet Piper and pick up takeout. She'd promised her father Christmas Eve dinner and wanted to follow through on something nice. She didn't know how to cook a turkey, ham, or any festive dish, so a meal from the best restaurant in town was the next best thing.

Memories of her time working at the Casting Spoon flooded her mind. It represented the first time she'd communicated with one of the dead, and where Dominic Sloan accosted her at that exact back door. As she drove behind the cedar building to park in the sparse parking lot, she glimpsed Jasper's broken-down Volkswagen bus.

A flurry of snow swirled around the car, and she strained to see as the wipers picked up speed. The massive patio was stripped of deck furniture, and the dock at the bottom of the steps was vacant of the usual array of yachts and sailboats.

Piper's car pulled up beside her and a flash of pink hair was a stark contrast to the dull winter day as she exited her vehicle. When she stepped out of the car, Piper embraced her in a warm hug.

"How'd it go with Celeste? I can't stop thinking about it. I just hope you're not mad at me. Are we good?" As she eyed Drew with a concerned look on her face, snow coated her hair and eyelashes, but she didn't bother to wipe it away.

"We're good. You're right; I should've been more careful. I didn't know he killed her, Piper. If only I'd been there, I could've stopped him."

"You don't know that! He would've killed you too, Drew. He wouldn't let her live and not take you. I think she saved your life."

The next time she went to Neptune Point, she'd be going alone. If she didn't help Ori and let him go soon, she feared she would lose her ability and the chance to free him. She closed her eyes and focused on the magic within her, feeling its energy pulse under her skin. She clenched her fists, determined to avenge Gran and defeat the dark spirit.

A burst of wind sent a spiral of snow spinning between her and Piper, and she shielded her face with her hand, leading the way toward the doors. A huge wreath hung over the entrance, and holiday music played as a handful of staff tended to the two remaining tables. Drew didn't recognize any of them. She walked through the waiting area and peered off to the side of the grand room, but it was empty. Her skin crawled, remembering Dominic Sloan and his Godfather-like attitude, taking over the entire town. She checked behind her, as though he might appear any moment, and struggled to swallow as her chest tightened.

Piper shook off the snow and stomped her feet on the floor mats as Drew paid for her order at the bar and sat to wait. Piper plopped beside her and leaned in. "Did Nico stay with you last night? I saw Claudia downtown today, and she told me Nicki called in sick for work yesterday. I didn't know he broke up with her! You've got to give me details."

Drew couldn't contain the smile spreading across her face.

She'd pushed Nico out of her mind to put all her focus on Celeste, but the mention of his name sent her stomach into a frenzy of butterflies. Nicki had been the last thing on her mind, and she flinched at the thought of running into her in Anna Tate's office.

Piper's mouth gaped open, and she smacked Drew's arm. "I knew it! I saw the kiss in the river like something out of the Notebook. Ya make me sick." Piper laughed. "So, are you two back together now?"

"Oh, I don't know. We haven't talked about it. It just sort of... happened."

"He's been in love with you for a while. Even before Shane. He was heartbroken last summer. I told you Nicki was just his way of trying to get over you."

"Maybe." She expected a surge of anger and resentment at the mention of Shane's name, but she felt nothing at all. He was a closed chapter in her past. With so much unknown, her future was a blur, but one thing was crystal clear; when she envisioned her future, Nico was in it. She didn't know how to deal with the tidal wave of emotions and decisions to be made as they surfaced. She loved him.

"I'm in love with him, Piper. I don't know what's going to happen, but I love him." A lump in her throat eased when she said it out loud.

Piper smiled at her. "I know you are. It's all going to come together for you. Just you wait. Stranger things have happened than a couple of best friends falling in love and hooking up. You guys just make sense, don't you think? You're like... couple goals." She stretched her legs out, revealing candy-cane striped leggings and bright red Doc Martens boots to match.

"I don't know about that. I just worry that when I leave town for good this time, we'll grow apart again. I don't want to get hurt, and I don't want things to end up like last time."

"So don't go. Keep the house for now. See what happens. Go to school, come back home when term is done. Rinse and repeat. Drop this whole, there's only one way to do things, and take a risk."

"There's an offer on the house."

Piper spun in her seat and grabbed her arm. "No! Really? Oh my God. How? When?"

Drew filled her in on Anna Tate's message. "She said it's a good offer. How can I say no?"

"You just said the word. Do it again. Say, no, I'm keeping my house. All I know is once you sign those legal documents, there's no turning back. I'm questioning your head space with these big decisions. I don't like it."

"I told her I'd let her know. We're meeting on the twenty-seventh."

The night of the full moon.

Keep the house. Hang on to her home. Those thoughts gave her a hell of a lot more comfort than selling it and leaving forever. She didn't know what to do.

"That's two days away! Think about this. Don't sign anything. At least let me give the contract to my mom to look over for you."

"I might do that. Hey, did your parents have their annual Christmas lawyer party thing?" She changed the subject to avoid further discussion about things she didn't have answers for.

"It's tonight. I wish you'd come. We always hang out on Christmas Eve. We're totally breaking tradition, and with Gran gone, I don't want you two to be alone. Bring your dad and come over."

"There's more than just one way to do things, Piper." She grinned as Piper rolled her eyes. When Piper called her out, she was usually on point.

"Oh, burn. Say whatever you want, I'm right!"

"I never said you weren't. We'll be okay. Dad sounds so sad, and I just want to be there for him. We can't go to a party." Spending Christmas Eve at the house where they both had grown up was the best way to feel connected to Gran. The house was an extension of Gran, her essence everywhere. Drew longed for another chance encounter with her. In a couple of days, she might never see another wandering soul again. If the possibility of losing sight of the dead had happened a year ago, she would've handed it over like a bad omen. She'd undergone changes far greater than she'd predicted. What she thought she wanted was changing with each passing day.

"I get it. Is he staying overnight, or will you be on your own? It's not a good idea for you to be alone in that house all night. What if *he* comes back?"

"I'll be ready. It's still my home, Piper, and if I can't be alone in my own house, I can't be anywhere. Dad likes his routine. He's always been like that, but I'm good with it. I'm not telling him what's going on. I don't want him to know—he won't get it. I think knowing I see dead people freaks him out. We'll have dinner and a drink by the fire together. Toast Gran—his idea, and I'll just go to bed early."

After I spray all the entrances with my new potion and chant a protection spell.

She fidgeted with her keys, staring at the wooden surfboard key chain she'd bought in California. Nico would love it there. Maybe they'd go together someday. She gripped the wooden board in her palm. She needed clarity on her present circumstances before she could daydream about their future together—if a future with him even existed.

"What about Nico? Have you made it social media official?" Piper nudged her arm.

"I don't care about that stuff."

"Doesn't matter. You said love. This is more than a friends with benefits deal."

Nico was a silver lining in a lot of darkness lately. "He left this morning to help his mom with stuff and take care of the shop before everything in town closes for the next couple of days. I'll see him when I see him. I'm not going to bother him."

"Are you kidding me? Bother him, trust me," Piper said.

She hesitated, the weight of jumbled emotions threatening to push her down. She couldn't come up with a coherent sentence to put her relationship with Nico in the right words.

What if loving him wasn't enough?

If she survived the looming full moon event, she'd have the conversation with Nico, but his safety came before their relationship.

Someone called out from behind the bar. "Order for Drew Harlow?"

As Drew took the bags from him, Jasper walked through the swinging doors. Dark circles lined under his eyes and his bottom lip trembled. He looked miserable, like he was about to break down. Balancing the paper bags in her arms, she moved closer as Piper hopped up and put an arm over Jasper's shoulder.

"Are you all right?" It was all she could think to say to him, even knowing he wasn't at all.

He shrugged, his eyes filling up with tears. "I don't think so. Rough day."

"Let's get out of here," Piper said.

Drew backed into the door, holding it open for them before falling in step toward the cars. It was Jasper's first holiday without the one he loved, and her heart broke for him. She stowed the bags of food in the backseat and maneuvered her way through the snow to the driver's side. Jasper opened the passenger door to Piper's car beside her and froze. He covered his face with his hands and his shoulders shook as he sobbed. Drew hugged him as Piper ran to his side. The three of them huddled together, surrounded by a flurry of snow.

Jasper dropped to the passenger seat, the door still hanging open. "I miss him so much. I'm living in this small town, in the middle of a blizzard, working at a job I hate. What do I do about it? Move back to San Francisco and open another bistro or café? I can't start all over. Everywhere I look reminds me of Orion. Everywhere." He glanced up at Drew and Piper standing over him. "You're both getting wet and I'm a freezing, blubbering mess." Rising from the car, he hugged Drew. "Drive safe getting home. See you later?"

"Yeah, sure. If you need to talk, Jasper, I'm not far. Maybe I can help."

"Thanks." Tears ran down his blotchy face, and he wiped his eyes. "Piper, we should probably get home. I told your mom I'd make those pastries for the party."

Piper pulled Drew into a quick hug. "Merry Christmas. I love you. Go home and be with your dad. We'll be all right. If I can get away later, I'll come see you." She broke free and ran to the driver's side, hopped in, and started the car. Jasper grabbed Drew's hand and squeezed, mouthing the words, thank you, before closing the door.

She got in the car and brought the engine to life as Piper drove away. The wipers picked up where they left off, moving from side to side, squealing with each swipe. She sat still, in shock.

For the first time, Jasper had said his love's name. Orion. *Ori?*

THIRTY-TWO

The flames of the tall candles wavered. Wax trickled along the sides before settling over the mosaic holders. Drew cleared the empty dishes from the kitchen table and sat back down across from her father. He raised a glass of Gran's favorite red wine.

"I miss you, Mom." He used his free hand to press his fingers against his eyes. When he dropped his hand, he clicked Drew's glass and drank, making a face.

She sipped the red liquid, savoring its sweet warmth as it traveled from her throat to her stomach. She'd never been one for wine before Gran died, but now it felt like a way to keep her memory close.

Swirling her wine, she stared into at the decorations hanging from the tree branches in the living room. Snow fell outside, melting and sliding down the window. Gran's colorful lights twinkled outside, illuminating shadows.

Is that a tree? Or has Hathorne come back? Ori?

As her father put their plates in the dishwasher, she got up from the table and moved into the living room, closer to the window.

"If you need me to stick around, I will. You gotta tell me, though. I'm not so good at reading minds." His voice trailed from behind her.

"Thanks, Dad, but I'll be fine. I'll meet you and Nellie at the Tough Cookie tomorrow."

As soon as her father left, she'd focus and call on Ori. Maybe if she reunited him with Jasper, he'd be able to cross over. She'd shoved the idea of finding her mother into the far corner of her busy mind for months, and she hoped she could help Ori without ever having to see Joelle.

Headlights crawled along the road before pulling into her driveway. The snowfall obscured her view. She gulped the last of her wine and placed her glass on the table. A log in the fire snapped, and she almost jumped out of her skin.

Her father walked into the living room, wiping his hands on a kitchen towel. "I appreciate what you did for me tonight." He tilted his head to look out the window and tossed the towel aside. "Someone's here."

Piper and Jasper got out of the car, carrying a large green bag, running for the porch. Her body tensed seeing Jasper, knowing what she had to tell him. Wondering how he'd react, and if he'd believe her at all.

"It's Piper and her cousin."

"Good. That's good. I'll leave—"

"No, Dad. You can't leave until I give you your present, and you know Piper. Stay for a bit."

He smiled. Gray streaked his overgrown red hair, hanging into his eyes. "You got me a gift?"

"Of course I did."

The doorbell rang, and when she opened the door, a gust of cold air blew in carrying snowflakes and Piper and Jasper with it.

"Last minute decision. We left the party early to come say Merry Christmas, Happy Holiday, Seasons Greetings, basically just all the things." Piper gave her a hug. "I wanted to make sure you were okay," she whispered.

"I am." She glanced outside for Hathorne before shutting the door after them. "I'm glad you came." She eyed Jasper, weighing how to tell him about Ori... and when the best time to call on Ori would be. She hadn't seen him since she'd called on him at Little Mysteries. He was staying away, but she wasn't sure why. She sensed it, like the negative ends of magnets repelling each other instead of coming together.

Piper greeted her father with a hug and introduced Jasper as Drew hustled to the kitchen to pour more wine, as much for herself as for everyone else. The wine helped soothe her frazzled nerves, its warmth calming them.

They sat around the tree talking as Piper handed out gifts to Drew, and even two to her father. He opened them, laughing as Jasper joked about some show from the 70s that he loved. Her father beamed as he opened Piper and Jasper's gifts of chocolate, and a lucky horseshoe for his next trip to sea. His eyes filled with a deep joy she had never seen before, and her own burned with tears of gratitude, but she didn't let them fall.

She handed him her gift. She'd run out of time with the wrapping part, but he didn't notice as he untied the silver bow. When he peeled back the paper, his hand covered his quivering mouth. "What are you doing to me?"

He held up the photo of the three of them she'd taken the day she'd left for Boston. It was a selfie with her standing between Gran and her father, Jupiter Beach in the background, and Gran making a silly face.

"I just thought you should have a piece of home with you."

"I'm proud of you, kid. You're not a kid anymore. I just... I don't know what to say."

"You don't have to say anything. I know how you feel."

They finished their drinks, and her father headed for the door, putting on his coat and boots. He hugged her before leaving. "If you change your mind, I'll come with you to check over that offer."

"I can do it, but thank you."

He nodded and picked up his bag of gifts. He waved to Piper and Jasper and turned to Drew as he walked out the front door. "I'll see you tomorrow, right?"

"Cross my heart," she said, drawing an 'x' over her heart. As he walked away, the amulet's light poured from the center, warming against her skin.

He'll be all right, Gran. All of us will.

And at that moment, she closed her eyes and focused. It was time to call Ori to the party and hope she could give the gift of peace to both him and Jasper, somehow.

"You're getting good at—" Ori appeared and froze as he looked behind her where Piper and Jasper sat on the sofa. "Where'd you find him?" He moved close to Jasper, who continued to sip his wine and chat with Piper about his broken van and plans for the new year. "He doesn't know I'm here." Ori turned to her, frantic. "Drew, tell him I'm here!"

"I will. I'm going to." She moved in between him and Jasper. Piper and Jasper stopped talking.

"Um, who are you talking to?" Jasper said. He leaned into Piper. "What's wrong with her?"

Piper glanced from Jasper to Drew. "Someone here, Drew?"

"One sec," she said, facing back to Ori. She handled this all wrong by getting too swept up in the sweet moment between herself and her father. She should've told Ori first. Or Jasper. But as Ori stood with his mouth gaping open and tears in his eyes, it was too late now.

She breathed, focusing on her hands as she took Ori's hands. It worked and she was able to hold them. "Look at me," she whispered.

He tore his gaze from Jasper and looked into her eyes. His pale face appeared deathlier than it usually was. "You knew? How long did you know?"

"I didn't know until today. I give you my word. Okay?"

"I... I thought J was in California. Seeing him brought it all back. It's like my soul remembered, but my brain... My absent brain neglected to communicate the details like a name or a face. I can't explain... *this*." He gestured back and forth between himself and Jasper. "You know him?"

"I met him when I went to San Francisco."

"How could I not know then?"

"Who are you talking to?" Jasper stood and straightened the collar of his pinstripe shirt.

Drew exhaled, readying her thoughts to manifest as words. "You know I can see people who've died."

Jasper's Adam's apple bobbed as he swallowed, and he rubbed his goatee.

Piper hopped to his side as his body trembled. She put an arm around him and looked at Drew with a knowing look.

"I do. Why?" he said.

"Today, in the parking lot. You said a name. For the first time, you told me his name."

"Oh God." Jasper covered his mouth with shaking hands. "Who are you talking to, Drew? Is it him? Is Orion here?"

"Orion?" Piper said with a gasp. "Ori is Orion?"

"He's here in the living room." Drew continued to hold Ori's hand and reached for Jasper with her other, joining them together through her.

"Are you holding his hand?" Jasper whispered.

"Yes."

"I never told him how I really felt," Ori said. "I loved you, Jasper. I still love you. I should've told you. You wanted to get married, and I was too scared to say yes. I should've said yes. I should've said something, anything."

Drew repeated Ori's words as a sob escaped Jasper. She could tell he was trying to suppress melting down, and her heart ached for him. The emotional pain coursing through her from Ori to Jasper was enough to tear her heart into shreds.

This was the most difficult part of bringing the living together with their dead loved ones… but it was also the gift part of her cursed ability.

"Tell him it's okay. I knew he loved me. I knew he was scared, but I'm not angry at him. I miss you, Orion. I think of you all the time, and I'm having a fucking hard time letting go." Tears streamed down Jasper's face and Piper held him with both arms. "I'd give anything to hug him. Hold him one more time. Just once. It's not possible, is it?" He begged Drew with his eyes.

If she could share visions, maybe she could share more of her magic and bring them together.

Focus. Intention.

In her mind's eye, she asked the sisterhood's energy in the amulet to wrap her in love and help her give this gift to Ori and Jasper. She didn't just ask. She *pleaded* with them. The fire roared as it suddenly rose higher. A blast of heat spun around her, and she brought Jasper's hand to Ori's. She placed a hand on each of their backs and their eyes met.

"How is this happening? I see him! I love you," Jasper said through tears.

"I love you too. This is good for you, J. Living here near your family, and Drew. I feel it. Please don't be sad."

They kissed and wrapped their arms around each other. Visions of their relationship flooded her mind. The closed sign on J's Bistro and a patio dinner by candlelight. Arguing about what color to paint Jasper's apartment, ending in laughter. Walks along the beach hand in hand. Jasper holding a book in one hand and waving to Ori surfing with the other. Driving along the coast with the top down in a vintage convertible. And the screech of tires and someone jerking forward against the wheel, followed by Ori's lifeless body on the pavement. It all came full circle in this moment, and the magic waned, fading.

"I'm losing it guys. I'm sorry, I can't hang on much more." Her legs shook, about to give out from under her.

Jasper's arms fell to his side as he collapsed to his knees in tears. Ori shifted into his ghostly silhouette, gesturing for her as he vanished. She didn't get the chance to ask him if he saw a bright light, or if he was gone forever. Panic rose in her chest, thinking of defeating Hathorne alone, but if Ori had found his own haven, she had to let him go.

As her knees buckled, she dropped to Jasper's side and Piper plopped on the floor with them. The Christmas tree lights flickered as though they'd lost the energy to continue shining, and the fire retreated to red coals.

Jasper hugged her. "You gave me my life back tonight."

She stared into the void where Ori had been standing. Had he gotten what he needed and crossed over? Was this how it ended? Sudden and cold, without a goodbye? Without knowing who killed him? Grief had become a toxic companion, suffocating her with its heavy embrace. Ori's last goodbye was supposed to be beautiful and a full circle, happy moment, but she was left empty and couldn't figure out why.

Moments like this made her gift feel more like a curse.

THIRTY-THREE

It was almost eleven o'clock when Piper and Jasper left for home. The walls creaked with each gust of wind. Drew glanced up the stairs shrouded in darkness and returned her attention to the door, staring through the window. Snow blew sideways under the streetlight across the road. She waited on close watch for Hathorne with no sign of him or the raven.

She longed for Gran to be sitting in her chair beside the tree. As she stood alone in the foyer, sadness clamped down on her like a vise. Tears burned her eyes. Her only focus had been bringing Jasper and Ori together, but she might have lost him forever, too.

She secured the deadbolt and crossed the kitchen into the den. As she picked up the little bottle of protection potion, she glanced at the clock. Its golden arms holding still at eleven minutes after the eleventh hour. She peeked at her phone. The clock would resume ticking again at precisely eleven minutes after eleven o'clock, stopping again in the morning at the same time. Either the antique clock was broken, or it was a sign. The clock stopped for twelve hours during the day. Her instincts told her there was meaning behind the time, but she couldn't figure out what. The missing link might be nothing, but what if there was a connection to Gran or Hathorne?

A chill crawled up her spine, and she rushed back to spray the entrance for the third time, repeating the protection spell. Pulling the glass knob on the small door under the stairs, she angled the flashlight from her phone to the length of the narrow space. Gran had boxes stacked as high as the sloped ceiling would allow. A ladder fastened to the wall led up to the trapdoor in Gran's room. Across from the door was a round window, reminiscent of a porthole on a ship. She didn't know much about architecture and house construction, so couldn't comprehend who could have come up with such an odd design. Her special secret hideaway had become a source of terror. If Gran had spell-protected the other entrance points, the portal window had to be how Hathorne had gained access to set the fire.

She tried to ignore any doubt she had about magic and placed the stones on the ledge and sprayed more of Celeste's concoction.

"This better work," she muttered into the silence. Her hands itched and burned as she spoke, and she held them up to her face. A soft light cascaded from her palms, and the amulet vibrated with a similar radiance. She held her trembling hands up to the little window, and sparks of electricity jumped from her fingertips as the light shone through the crystals. She'd grown used to the sensation, finding the magic comforting as it offered protection from the unexplained darkness.

When the current stopped flowing, she pulled her hands back and her phone fell, clanging against the floor. She bent down to pick it up, taking note of the time as she bounded into the hallway.

The time on her phone read five past eleven. She ran back toward the den to catch the exact moment when the clock started again but paused in the living room at the red coals left in the fireplace. If she was going to defeat Hathorne and send him back, she needed all the practice she could get. Crouching down in front of the hearth, she held her hands up, not bothering to remove the mesh screen.

She channeled her energy through her hands, attempting to rekindle the fire's dying embers. Smoke filled the firebox and curled around her. She coughed but held her ground as the tingling sensation intensified. Ribbons of flames ignited into a blazing fire.

I did it! Merry Christmas, Gran.

Her phone read eight minutes after eleven. She scurried into the den and held her phone beside the clock. Nine minutes after eleven… ten minutes… eleven. Tick. Tick. Tick.

She ran her hands along the sides of the clock, and a shock zapped through her body. She jerked her hands away. The pulse of electricity was unmistakable, the same one she had felt during her visions, but no one else was in the room, dead or alive. She placed her hands back on Gran's clock.

"Show me."

She shuddered as the vision played through her mind like a haunting melody. Gran and Celeste talking in the store, Gran's blue eyes sparkling with spilled secrets. The chimes rang out as Gran left the store carrying a white bag labeled with the store's name.

The vision changed, growing darker. She watched as Gran arranged crystals around the house, speaking the same words the book had shown Drew and Celeste. Unsteady on her feet, she prodded into the den toward the window, walking past Drew, standing with her hands clinging to the clock, but not really there. Gran placed crystals along the ledge, but as she lifted her hand away, a shadow appeared behind her. Something fell from Gran's wrinkled hands. The cloak surged up and around, engulfing her. Drew's perspective changed so she was seeing everything through Gran's eyes. Her gaze turned downward at the floor near the clock, but not before her eyes glared at the time. Eleven minutes past eleven in the morning.

Light radiated from the amulet on the floor, nestled in the carpet fibers. A brilliant flash charged out of the jewel, transforming Hathorne into a puff of dark smoke. Gran's lifeless body lay on the floor beside the clock, as the light surrounded her, bathing her in an ethereal glow. The raven flew out of nowhere, landing on the clock, keeping a watchful eye on Gran. A last glance at the clock showed the same time, but without the sun streaming through the window. An image appeared in Drew's mind, showing Gran among her flowers before the vision faded to black.

Drew released her hands from the clock and gripped the amulet. Reacting to her touch, it glowed beneath her fist, and she opened her palm to watch the vines crawl along its surface. The sisterhood had been too late to help Gran.

"Please don't be too late for me," she whispered.

The shrill ring of her phone made her almost jump out of her skin. She grabbed it from the back pocket of her jeans, scared something awful had happened, and at the same time, grateful to see Nico's name splayed across the screen.

"Nico?"

"Hey! Everything okay? You sound out of breath." His voice offered a sense of security, a nudge that she was going to be okay.

"Everything's fine. I'm glad you called."

"Good. I know it's late, but you said you were going to be alone tonight, and it's Christmas." He hesitated. "I just miss you and I wanted to see you. That's the real reason I'm calling. But if you're too tired—"

"Come over," she said, throwing practical sense out the window. She was about to move away, didn't know where home would be, and was prey for an evil witch hunter who tried to kill her best friend, and her... *love*. Her selfishness was undeniable, yet her need to be with him was too strong to resist.

Nico's truck pulled up behind her car and he ran through the snow up the porch steps. She opened the door before he could knock and threw her arms around him. Lifting her feet off the ground, he walked inside and closed the door behind them.

"That's the best greeting I've ever had," he said.

"I'm happy you're here." She gazed into his eyes, holding his chilled face in her hands, and kissed him.

Their kiss deepened, and he kicked his boots off. She pulled his jacket down and he shook it the rest of the way off, leaving it in a heap on the floor. She wanted to bury herself in him.

He held her hand as she led him to the sofa. "How long can you stay?"

"As long as I'm home for the big holiday breakfast, I can stay as long as you like. Why don't you come with me?"

"I promised my dad I'd meet him and Nellie at the Tough Cookie in the morning."

"Until then, we've got all night," Nico said.

They lay in each other's arms on the sofa, and Nico pulled a blanket over them. Unlike last night, this time they took their time exploring each other's bodies, savoring every touch and sensation. She trailed kisses along his chest, feeling his heartbeat quicken beneath her hands. He stroked her leg with his fingers, sending goosebumps over her skin. The bond between them deepened, the love palpable. She wished the night could last forever. If being with Nico, sharing themselves, and loving each other was part of her life, she never wanted to let him go. Nico was entwined in her version of what a happily ever after could be.

Thirty-Four

She followed Nico to his truck. The sun sparkled off the untouched snow from the night before.

"I have something for you," he said.

"You shouldn't have done that, Nico. I didn't get you anything."

"I don't need anything, and it isn't much, but I saw it and thought of you." He unbuttoned the front pocket on his jacket and handed her a wrapped box with a red ribbon. "Open it. I meant to give it to you last night, but..." He ran a hand through his hair, his dimples making an appearance as he smiled.

Her cheeks turned hot, and she knew they must match the color of her hair. She had nowhere to hide in the sun's glare, but this time, she didn't care. She removed the wrapping and opened the small box. A beautiful rose gold compass sparkled in the sunlight. Nico picked it up and turned it over. "I had it engraved."

Never lose sight of home.
Love, Nico.

She bit her lip as a wave of happiness overwhelmed her. She cried way too much these days and didn't want to ruin the moment with more tears—happy or not. "It's perfect. I love it."

"I love you," he said.

"I love you too." Not overthinking was a first for her. Saying the words was easy now, but it only made her choice to leave more complicated. She kept coming back to the thought of the house, sitting empty and unmaintained.

"I know there's a lot going on right now. With you and the house." He glanced at the For Sale sign stuck in the front yard. "I don't know what's next. But whatever this is? It feels right. There's no other place in the world I'd rather be than standing here with you."

She choked on emotion as a laugh escaped. "Oh, come on. There are lots of places. Hawaii, for example."

"Nope. Not even Hawaii." He rubbed the hint of stubble over his face. "Unless you're coming with me? Then sure, let's go."

"Don't tempt me!" As she daydreamed about being on a plane with Nico, her mind raced with thoughts of driving away from the house for the last time, heading back to Boston, and attending school again, cutting her fantasy short. How would they make it all work?

He kissed her goodbye and drove away. Her untied boots thumped as she hurried up the porch stairs and into the house, almost dancing. He loved her. They were getting another shot. He was her happy place. Closing the door behind her, she leaned against the cold metal, holding the amulet close. Gran might be gone, but she wasn't alone. She had her family, her friends, Nico.

Her hands tingled, and she grabbed the book of magic to practice before heading for brunch at the Tough Cookie. Placing the heavy book on the kitchen table, she opened to the blank page after her protection spell. Leaning over the table, she chewed her lip raw, contemplating what to focus her intention on next, coming up with nothing. Something was missing. The ambiance of candles and crystals. She placed a few colorful crystals around the book and lit the candles she and Ori had used, a pang of missing him smacking her in the gut.

Closing her eyes, she opened her mind and visualized pushing Hathorne through the swirling blue veil between realms.

"What if I'm not strong enough to send him back?" she muttered to herself. She opened an eye and peeked down at the book. Nothing. She exhaled and held her hands over the book, shutting both eyes again. "Okay. Haven on the full moon. I'll focus on Hathorne, enticing him back into the portal. But I can't walk through it. Will he go in without me? How am I going to do that? Focus." She let her hands fall so they were touching the rough pages. "He'll show up and I'll just... um. I'll... throw the amulet in the portal and he'll chase it?" An icy sensation covered her hands like she'd stuck them in a snowbank, and she lifted them from the pages, opening her eyes. Her fingers turned white as they numbed, and she held them under her shirt against the warmth of her skin.

As her hands thawed, she stared at the motionless book. "What am I doing wrong? Ori, if you're still stuck somewhere between the living and dead, I sure could use some help." She couldn't bring herself to believe he was actually gone until she uncovered the identity of his killer.

"Did you really think I'd leave you to fight that asshat by yourself?" Ori leaned against the door frame between the kitchen and the den.

She ran to him, hugging him as tightly as his other-worldly form would allow—it was nothing like embracing a person with flesh and bone, but it still meant something. Hugging him was like holding a feather pillow, or lighter, like he'd disappear any moment.

"You didn't leave me?" She cleared the lump in her throat and released him, stepping back. "I thought you'd crossed over to your paradise city! It would've been all right if you did. You found Jasper again, and it was so beautiful... I didn't think I'd ever see you again. I missed you."

"What? And leave all this? Please."

"Where'd you go? I had myself convinced you'd been freed."

"For a few minutes, so did I. The warmth and bright lights... All that happened, but I wound up with your mother again."

"Where?"

"A park bench. The two of us sitting side by side. Her crying and mumbling on about shit that didn't make any sense. She said your name."

Her mother was in town, and she still hadn't tried to find her. She knew where Gran's house was; why she hadn't shown up yet was beyond her comprehension. "Portal Park. I wonder where she's staying?"

"Dunno. I left her to find you. You called me and it worked. That's progress! You might be stuck with me for longer than you bargained for. You've got two days before the full moon, Drew. If you lose your ability to see me—"

"No. I'll sort it out before that happens. I have your name now—Orion Dara. There wasn't much online, and I haven't talked to the police yet, but don't worry, I will. I thought you crossed over."

"What's worrying gonna do? It doesn't change the circumstances, that's for damn sure. What's the worst that can happen? I'm already dead, Drew. And if I'm stuck in limbo, I'll find my way."

Ori was back, refueling her belief in her magic and defeating the witch hunter.

She walked back to the counter and hovered her hands over the book again. The pins and needles pricked through her palms. "I might not see you, or anyone, from the soul realm after I do this. I'm trying to figure out a way to send Hathorne back without losing my abilities."

In a flash, he was beside her. "That's a change."

"What do you mean?" She closed her eyes and took a deep breath, ready to tackle the magic book again.

"Listen to yourself. Your curse isn't a curse anymore. You don't want to lose it."

He wasn't wrong, but she kept her attention on the book and didn't respond. The amulet hummed against her skin, and she let her hands take over. She opened her eyes and glanced at the pages as they lifted with slight movement. The candle flames flickered, and she held a hand over the tallest of the pillar candles, coercing the fire to reach for her palm. It didn't stretch as far as it had with Celeste, but she was driving the magic sparking under her skin through her hands.

"It's working, Drew. Keep going."

Cursive lettering sprang through the page, the gold words twinkling as the flames danced in rhythm to the words.

Ori read the words as they appeared, one after the other. "'The gate's impenetrable passage will pull the specter against their will when a witch speaks the ancient words, forcing the lock open. The moon's power shall melt the edges, sealing the specter within the gate's veil. The witch who assumes great responsibility relinquishes the magick most closely aligned with their soul's mission.'"

"Soul's mission," Ori repeated, looking at her. "You're not giving it up. It's who you are." He flipped the pages, but the words had stopped scrawling. "Ask it again. Ask the magic to tell you another way."

She swallowed hard. "There isn't another way. There's no one else who can do this. Gran gave the amulet to me. We both know I've got to finish what I think Gran started. I can't stay locked in my house under a protection spell that may or may not hold up, and I'm not risking anyone else I love. You're right, Ori. Seeing people on the other side of life as we know it—"

"Death."

"Death. Seeing you and others who've died and are lost has been a huge part of who I am. But I will figure it out and love the other parts of myself too. I'm going to help you before it all falls apart. We've got two more days."

The phone rang, startling her. Her dad's name scrolled across the screen. She was late. Answering his call, she lied about oversleeping and hung up under a minute later, closing the book and tucking it on the table beside Gran's chair.

In two days, her gift of seeing the dead and using magic would end. And before it all disappeared, she was going to use every ounce of magic—or magick with the eleventh letter—existing within and around her. The ability she once cursed now bonded with her soul. Fear made her sick to her stomach at the thought of who would rip it from her and how. But she wasn't walking away from Hathorne, and he would not terrorize her, or her loved ones, ever again.

THIRTY-FIVE

Drew's dad and Nellie reminisced in the bakery's front café while she cleaned up their breakfast dishes in the kitchen. She'd hired the same cleaning company that took care of the fire damage to do a thorough cleaning of the bakery next week. Whenever she caught sight of the For Sale sign on the house or the bakery, her chest tightened, and a claustrophobic feeling swept over her. Her heart raced, skipping beats, and she clung to the edge of the large stainless-steel sink.

The door swung open, and her father peeked his head in. "Drew? Someone's here to see you."

Her father's calm composure suggested the person who was out front had nothing to do with Hathorne or fire. She ran a list through her mind as she dried her hands on a towel. Piper was with Taj this afternoon. She'd invited Drew for Christmas dinner, but she'd declined, and Nico was with his father. She removed the compass from the pocket of her jeans and ran her finger along the engraving.

Never lose sight of home.

Jasper held the door and stepped through, keeping it from swinging closed. He looked like a runway model with his red suit jacket and matching trousers. His wavy hair shone under the fluorescent light, and he'd trimmed his goatee to perfection. She'd never seen him look so put together.

"Can I come in?" he said.

"Yeah, of course!" She hopped up on a bar stool and pointed to one beside her. "Have a seat."

His polished shoes clicked on the floor tiles as he neared her. "I'll stand. I don't want to wrinkle."

"You look great, Jasper."

He adjusted the top button of his crisp white shirt. "Dinner with the family. Aren't you coming too?"

"No, I appreciate it, but I've got a few... things to do."

He looked around the kitchen. "Well, as superb as my aunt and uncle have been letting me stay with them, I need my own place. And a new job."

"I get that. Is there anything I can do?"

"That's what I want to talk to you about."

She straightened her posture on the backless stool. "A place or a job? Because right now, I sort of don't have either. Well, I guess I do in Boston, but a few hours a week isn't exactly paying all my bills." She rubbed her temples. "I'm sorry, what is it you want to talk about?"

He eyed the stool beside her and sighed. Unbuttoning his suit jacket, he sat down. "The other night, you told us you had no other choice but to sell everything. What if you did? Have another choice, I mean."

"I've been through it all in my head. I can't live in Atlas Cliffs and attend school. It wouldn't make sense—the cost alone would be too much. There's no other way."

"I beg to differ. Hear me out, okay?"

Jasper's entire demeanor had lifted. He had an aura of... *hope*. What did she have to lose? "I'm listening."

"You changed my life last night. Do you understand how amazing this gift you have is? You can give people what no one else can. *Peace*. It's my turn to help you."

"Jasper, I'm so happy I could help reconnect you, but—"

"What I'm trying to say is I want to help *me*, but also you." He clasped his hands together. "I have an idea that will not only be a good business decision... It'll keep your Gran's bakery alive. Please, don't brush this off. I was up all night devising a plan. It's perfect, Drew."

She glanced around the bakery, remembering the sight of the rows of cupcakes and hearing the mixer going and laughter erupting. The memories within the walls were fading away with each day Gran was gone. She pictured removing the Tough Cookie sign and shutting the doors for good. It shouldn't hurt this much, but it did. She had helped rebuild it after the fire last year and while doing so had developed a deeper appreciation for the place.

"Tell me your plan," she said.

He jumped up again, smoothing his jacket before perching on the edge of the stool. "I want to buy Nellie's half. Go into business with you, as partners. Like Nellie and your Gran. I ran a successful bistro, Drew. I'll create specials and a lunch menu—simple things like gourmet sandwiches and salads, plus luxurious cakes, seasonal cookies, and treats. I'll honor your grandmother with my own flair. I can do this and do it fucking well, I promise." He stretched his leg out as he balanced on the stool. "I can manage the books; I'm good at it. It's where I started before the numbers bored me to tears and I became a chef, but I can do it."

"What about school? I want to finish my program. Art is where my heart is."

"And art is where you shall be. We'll keep the pastry chef, who will soon be without a job if this place closes, and we can hire someone to run the counter. You come home for the summer and collect a salary working here. It's a win-win, Drew."

"You're forgetting one thing. I won't live here anymore. Soon, there won't be a house to come home to." Her mind raced as she processed Jasper's idea. She couldn't deny the excitement building inside. But it could also be too good to be true. "Can you afford Nellie's share? Sorry to get personal, but if I do this, and it's a big if, I've got to ask."

"There's money from the business I just sold sitting in the bank begging to make dreams come true, so to answer your question: hell yes, I do. I don't make deals I can't honor." He rose and placed the stool back against the counter.

Examining the kitchen, he opened the fridges and the large oven. The appliances were brand new since the fire had ravaged through the bakery last year. Another one of Dominic's threats that had come to life. She cringed, thinking about the man's icy stare as he held the gun against her head. Steadying her breathing, she tried to calm the rising panic.

She hated Dominic Sloan more than she hated the witch hunter.

Jasper glanced at her, his grin dropping as he rushed to her side. "Are you all right? You look like you're about to be sick."

Clearing her throat, she stood. "Bad memories sneak in sometimes."

"Music," he said.

"What?"

He grabbed his phone and turned on an eighties rock song she'd never heard before. "Music chases those away. Usually."

"Good to know." She smiled at him as he watched her with his kind eyes, reminding her of Piper.

He lifted his sleeve, revealing ruby cuff links to match his suit. "I better head out, so I'm not late. Piper's mom will be a flitting mess right about now, making sure everything is perfect. Say that you'll think about this. I have a proposal organized for you when you're ready."

Her mind wandered back to the living situation. "I have an offer on Gran's house, Jasper, I meet the realtor—"

"Don't accept it yet. Just think about it. Please?"

A way out of her predicament. Another way of doing things. She nodded. "I'll think about it."

"That's all I needed to hear." He gave her a quick hug before heading through the swinging door to the front café.

A burst of laughter rang out a moment later, and she opened the door, leaning against it to keep it from swinging shut.

Nellie and Jasper shared an embrace, and he waved goodbye as he raced out the front door like the happiest person alive.

"You knew about this," Drew said.

"Only since this morning. He called here looking for you, asking about the Tough Cookie. I thought he was a potential buyer until he told me he was Piper's cousin."

Her dad walked around carrying his coffee. "A lot of memories in this place. It was the happiest part of my childhood. I feel like an ass for leaving it all behind." He placed the cup on the counter and put his jacket on. "If you do this with him, I'll help out when I can. Same with the house. Or, sell the place, take the money, and enjoy your life... But if you change your mind and need someone to check on it while you're gone? When I'm home, I'll do it."

"You're gone more than you're home, Dad." His face fell and she shook her head. "I'm not angry about it, it's just the way it is."

"I'll hire someone to maintain it," he said, pulling his keys from his pocket. "I assumed you wanted to sell, but if you want to keep all this, you can. I don't get it when you've got opportunities in a big city, but maybe you keep it for a while and sell later." He kissed her forehead and tapped her nose. "Not my decision to make, but I'm here for you."

He might not be the usual doting dad, but he loved her, and she didn't doubt that he would do anything for her. They left the Tough Cookie, locking up behind them.

She entered a trance as she drove along the road overlooking Jupiter Cove Beach. She faced a new set of decisions and was uncertain of which path to take. Weighing each scenario in her mind, she kept coming back to one sincere, unapologetic conclusion. She didn't want to give up her home. Her focus blurred, and she yawned as her body spiraled into exhaustion. She hoped the protection spells held up so she could sleep the rest of the day and night.

She drove up the driveway and saw a pristine, fancy car parked near the porch. Claudia stepped out of the car and gave her a gentle wave. Drew's eyebrows knitted together as she glanced at a woman sitting on the wooden frame of the porch swing—the cushions long gone before winter. Judging by the suitcase at her feet, it was clear she wasn't dead; the dead don't come with that kind of baggage. As Drew exited the car, the realization crept up on her. The memories of the woman she knew as a five-year-old were a distant blur in her mind, but it was shocking how much had changed between those memories and now. Her mother had become like one of her ghosts, not existing among the living. Just an echo in a small corner of her mind. But here she was in front of her, as real as the snow on the ground, and the cold ocean air.

Her hair used to be long and straight but now was cut in a sharp bob and dyed so black it took on a blue hue under the sunlight. Despite the changes in appearance, she couldn't deny it.

Mom?

THIRTY-SIX

Stepping with care on the icy driveway in high-heeled boots, Claudia glanced back at Joelle as she rushed to Drew's side.

"What are you doing here? What is she doing here?" Drew couldn't keep her voice steady. "It's Christmas Day. Shouldn't you be having a ten-course dinner somewhere?" Claudia had brought Joelle to her doorstep, and she wanted to scream.

"Drew, stop. It's okay. She's got something to talk to you about. She asked me to bring her here."

"So, you just did? Without calling me, or a text?"

Claudia flung her blond hair off her shoulders. "I'm going to ignore all this attitude and anger directed at me right now. Because you are my friend and we've been through hell together"—she glanced over her shoulder—"and this woman, your *mother*, caused a massive stir at the office. Security was involved. I told my mother I'd take care of it, and here I am, at your door, taking care of this problem. As you might gather, there was no time to call or text. No time."

Claudia followed Drew's gaze to the porch, and they both stood in the driveway staring at the woman on the porch swing. Her mother was here. Ori needed her to step up and quit avoiding the woman who'd traveled across the country to find her. "I've got to do this now, don't I?" Drew said, sighing.

"I'm afraid so." Claudia squeezed her arm. "But I'm not going anywhere; I'll stay with you. She's got some... problems she's working through and she's refusing to do anything until she sees you."

"I don't understand. Why didn't she come here on her own?"

"She said she did. No one was home. The house was dark and abandoned, and there's that." Claudia pointed to the For Sale sign. "She didn't know where you lived. When I tell you it took a ton of convincing that you in fact do still live in this house, don't argue with me." Claudia's piercing blue eyes could've sliced through her.

This wasn't Claudia's fault. Claudia had left her Christmas festivities to be here with her and her estranged mother. "You don't mind staying?"

Claudia's glossy pink lips turned into a smile. Nothing about it was disingenuous; she wanted to help. "I'm not leaving you here alone with her. Let's go." She gestured to Drew who walked up the driveway to the front door.

Joelle got off the swing and stepped forward to meet her. Visible lines between her brows and the sides of her eyes appeared more defined along her thin, troubled face. The few freckles along Joelle's nose and cheeks were the only similarity between her and Drew. The thought of being anything like this woman repulsed her. She'd left her own child and never looked back. Leaving without an explanation or attempt at contact for almost fifteen years didn't give her the privilege to show up and smile at her, like she'd be welcomed in Gran's home. *Drew's* home. Claudia stayed at Drew's side as she held onto the railing with a death grip.

"You're all grown up," Joelle said, stepping onto the steps closer to Drew, who released the railing and took a huge step back. She stumbled on a patch of ice, but Claudia reached out and grabbed her before she could fall. Claudia was no stranger to family drama, and her presence was the dose of courage Drew needed to face Joelle.

"What are you doing here?" Drew's stomach churned in time with the crashing waves across the road, and a throbbing headache migrated from her neck to her temples.

Joelle smoothed her black hair behind her ears. "I wanted to see my daughter. Wish her a Merry Christmas in person."

"You're joking, right?"

Drew's breakfast revolted, and she thought she might throw up, but she held her composure. This day had hovered over her for months, ever since Ori's arrival last summer, and then ever since California had been a bust. But she owed Ori, and that promise was the only reason she didn't yell at Joelle to get off Gran's property.

Joelle's sheepskin boots scuffed against the porch as she stepped from side to side, adjusting a canvas bag slung over her shoulders. "Can I come inside? I've been traveling and living from motel room to motel room. It's been difficult."

Anger burned in Drew's stomach. She didn't want to let her inside her home. She didn't want her mother to cross the threshold back into her life. She wasn't ready for any of this. Moving past Joelle, she unlocked the door and went inside, with Claudia close behind. She eyed the suitcase as her mother picked it up. "You're not staying here."

Joelle flashed a smile and the musician charm of her youth resurfaced into her face. Claudia folded her arms across her chest and glared, practically spitting, "I can give her a drive back to town when she's done here."

Against her better judgment, and on Claudia's promise, Drew gestured for Joelle to step inside. Her mother set her luggage down and took off her coat, tossing it on top of the suitcase. Stuffing her hands into the pockets of the bulky cardigan she wore, she stepped into the living room, not waiting for an invitation.

Rage crept into Drew's chest, but she suppressed it. Locating her mother had been the most important thing to both Ori and her. They needed to figure out what the letters were about, why she wanted her to go to California, and what the connection between Ori and Joelle was. The chance to uncover every answer was walking through her living room; she had better think fast.

Claudia unbuttoned her pink wool coat, leaving it on as she stood against the mantel. With her body buzzing with energy and tingling fingers, Drew kneeled with her back to Joelle to add a log to the dead fire. She breathed through the anger threatening to boil over as she held her hands over the black coals to re-ignite the fire. Whether it was the sudden reunion with her estranged mother, or magic taking hold, intense energy flowed through her, and flames sprang to life within seconds. She trembled, her body hot and clammy at the same time. She bit her lip to keep herself from an outburst of years' worth of pent-up anger she didn't realize still lingered.

She stood as Joelle wandered around the living room. When she picked up a ceramic butterfly from the mantel, Drew snatched it from her hands. "What are you doing here?" she took a deep breath to steady her racing heart.

Joelle stepped forward and tried to hug her, but she moved out of reach. "What do you want to talk to me about? Start there." Drew stood next to Claudia, almost grabbing her arm to steady herself.

"I know. I know I haven't been around for the past ten years. But you are still my daughter. Doesn't that mean anything? It's Christmas." Joelle smiled, but her eyes remained stoic and empty.

"Ten years?" Drew scoffed. "I'm almost nineteen. It's been longer than ten years."

"Valid point." Joelle pushed her bangs from her eyes. "I'm just so happy I get to see you again. I've wanted to for so long. You just don't know... you don't know. I missed my daughter." Her voice trailed off as she looked around the living room.

Claudia squeezed Drew's arm with one hand and held her phone in the other, not taking her eyes off Joelle. Drew was grateful she stayed. Claudia's presence was her moment of sanity.

The mother she'd known from her childhood was gone. The woman in front of her was a delusional stranger. "I want to make something clear, Joelle. I'm your daughter by birth and nothing more. The woman who raised me is gone."

Don't forget about Ori.

"Madeline died?"

Hearing Joelle say Gran's name in such disbelief was like a sudden jolt to her system, throwing salt over an open wound. Joelle had traveled all this way, desperate to see her daughter, but was in the dark about Gran's death? Drew's chest burned with anger, and she took a staggering breath to compose herself. "She died a couple of weeks ago. What do you want to talk to me about, because I have questions for you, too."

Shaking off her coat, Claudia draped it over the back of the sofa and leaned against the wall. "Let me know if you need me to do anything, Drew."

Joelle chuckled, a throaty laugh with a snort. "You've made friends. That's nice. She's feisty and rich."

"Don't talk about her," Drew snapped. "Tell me why you're here."

"Drew, like it or not, we're family, and I need my daughter in my life right now."

"We are *not* family. Not anymore." Drew balled her burning palms into fists. The amulet matched the fiery heat as it warmed her skin through her sweater.

"That's so pretty. Where did you ever find something like that?" Joelle reached for the amulet, but Drew clutched the jewel before she could touch it.

"You're time's almost up, Joelle." Claudia glared at her with a cheerless grin.

Joelle paced around the room and crossed her arms. "Oh, come on. Is this how you treat your mother? Does she need to stay here? Can't we just start over?"

"This is how I treat the woman who walked out on me. I'm an adult, there's no starting over. Not for you. I want the truth. No more small talk, or I'm calling the police. Why did you send letters and call this house begging me to go to California? Who was the woman at the address on that postcard? How do you know Orion Dara?"

Claudia glanced at Drew, her grin fading with a puzzled look on her face, but she said nothing.

Joelle raised her hands. "No need to call the cops. Please, don't call the police." She sat down in Gran's chair and Drew leaped forward. "Not there. You don't sit there."

Exhaling through her teeth, Joelle moved to the sofa. "You got something to drink?"

"Answer her questions," Claudia said.

"Aren't you going to sit too? You're both making me nervous standing over me like that. Jesus, what's the matter with you? It's supposed to be the warmest time of the year. You're an ice block."

Drew didn't understand how the shittiest mother still held the power to crush their child's spirit. After years of nothing. No relationship, no contact... that power could run a country. She didn't know what she was expecting. Perhaps she'd always had hope that her mother would drop to her knees, begging for forgiveness. She had imagined their reunion to be strained, but she never expected her mother to be so cruel and calculating. She'd been foolish to have let herself be so blind.

Claudia moved close to Drew, glancing down at her before sitting on the sofa by Joelle. She crossed her long legs and waited for Drew to take the lead. Drew sat on the edge of Gran's chair, hoping it would offer some sort of comfort, but the only emotion burning inside was frustration and an invasion of space. She couldn't believe she'd struggled with finding her mother for so long. Now that she was here, she couldn't wait to get her out of the house.

"Anything happening?" Ori appeared on the arm of the chair beside her, and she almost slipped to the floor. She clasped the Amulet and didn't say a word to him.

"I searched for you in the town near San Francisco last July... Rubyvale. They didn't know who you were. It was a dead end, and I gave up. Why did you beg me to go all the way across the country?"

Joelle stopped picking at her short nails. "I knew my sweet ginger girl would come."

Ginger girl?

Breakfast might make an appearance all over the floor. She was going to lose it. Claudia made a disgusted face and rolled her eyes.

If it hadn't been for the amazing time with Piper and Jasper in San Francisco, she'd be kicking herself for ever chasing after this woman. But she wanted her to keep talking, so she bit her lip and coaxed her along. "I actually wanted to help you. When you weren't where you said you'd be, I was…"

"Worried. Concerned," Ori said from his perch beside her.

"Worried about you," she finished. The words almost got stuck in her throat with the lie, but she needed information more than she needed anything else. She widened her eyes at Claudia to play along but could tell by her scrunched nose and narrowed gaze, Claudia didn't understand.

Joelle looked from Claudia to Drew. "Does she need to be here? I want to talk to you alone."

"I can wait outside if you want, but I'm not moving until you give me the okay," Claudia said.

"Screw it," Joelle snapped. "Look. Something happened in Rubyvale. I'm so happy you got to see it. It's pretty fancy." She pulled at her baggy sweater. "It was so glamorous. I sang at a piano bar. Maybe you've heard of it? The Four-Leaf Clover?"

Drew stole a look at Ori, who looked as dumbfounded as she was. He pointed to her hands, his face, and gestured to her mother, but she ignored him. There was no way she'd be able to place her hands on her mother to get what was in her head. Could she? "Never heard of it. What happened?"

"Well, I was sort of a big deal. My career was taking off, and I met someone. We got married on a beach and built a house overlooking the ocean—"

"I'm confused. Why are you back in Atlas Cliffs again?" Drew couldn't think of a single scenario connecting her mother and Ori. This was a giant waste of time—one thing she didn't have a lot of at the moment. The last thing she wanted to do was talk about her mother's fancy lifestyle.

Claudia uncrossed her legs and leaned forward. "Okay, Joelle. It's Christmas, and we all have places to be. You're wasting time. I told you I'd take you to see Drew, but you promised to tell her what you wanted to say, and we'd leave." Claudia lit up her phone. "Answer her. What are you doing here?"

"You're very abrasive. Claudia, right? Sloan is your last name?"

"Why?" Claudia stiffened.

"I knew your father. It was a long time ago. He's in jail, now? Is that right?"

Claudia stood, straightening the white blouse she wore. Before she unleashed on Joelle, Drew stood and intervened. Her mother would never spill a word if Claudia lost it on her now.

"Claudia, can you wait outside? For just a few minutes. I'll explain later. Please?"

Swinging a finger at Joelle, Claudia started to talk and stopped herself, covering her mouth. "Okay. I'm going." She swept up her long coat and stormed outside, slamming the door behind her.

Drew sat on the edge of Gran's chair. "Last chance. How do you know Orion Dara?"

Joelle chewed her lip, shaking Drew to the core at the behavior they shared. She had to break that habit immediately.

"How do you know that name?"

"How do *you* know him?"

"I thought I could start over here, but ah. Clearly, this isn't going to work for me or for you. That house you went to, the big one with the fancy gate. That's my mom's place. She kicked me out. And that was after my husband kicked me out. Baby girl, you're all I've got. I never stopped loving you."

She touched Drew's hair and studied the red locks as she wrapped a strand around her finger. Drew jerked away, jumping out of Gran's seat as if stung by a wasp. She'd never met her other grandmother, and no part of her wanted to. But somehow, the revelation that she had encountered a woman who was her grandmother and had never reached out to her, stung deeper than she had anticipated. She was done with Joelle and her entire family. Blood wasn't a requirement for family, and she had hers in Atlas Cliffs. "I'm not your baby anything anymore, Joelle. I thought... I thought you were in trouble, and I tried to help. It was a dumb decision." When she thought back, getting out of Atlas Cliffs was all she had wanted, and taking off on a quest to find her mother across the country was as good an excuse as any. Helping Ori had always been more important than finding her mother; he was more family to her than Joelle.

Joelle sunk into the sofa looking defeated, but instead of compassion for another's pain, Drew only felt disdain and anger. If her mother was hurt, she should be. She was the one who'd abandoned her all those years ago. At least her father had tried. He'd always tried to be in her life, even when he was away, and provided as much as he could. If it wasn't his presence, it was money to help Gran and her, but the man had tried, and it was better than nothing.

"I thought maybe since I traveled all this way, I could stay for a bit. We could catch up, you know? Before you sell the place. I saw the sign."

"Catch up? So, what? Have a mother-daughter slumber party and do each other's hair or something? Move into Gran's house with me?" The anger won and bubbled over like a pot on the highest setting. Pacing back and forth, she gripped the mantel and took a deep breath, fighting back tears. She would not let herself cry in front of this woman.

Joelle stood and touched Drew's back, and she pulled away. "Don't touch me."

"I'm sorry, okay? For everything I've ever done to you! Is that what you need to hear? I'm human and make mistakes, just like you. I don't want to fight."

Drew wanted nothing more than to pick up the suitcase and throw it outside, screaming at the top of her lungs. "Leave. I need you to leave now."

"I need to talk to you about something, but I want to know I can trust you," Joelle said.

Trust? Trust! She wouldn't trust this woman to dump water over her if she was on fire. How could Joelle waltz back into her life, into her home, and demand trust! She held back the urge to hit this woman in front of her—beating people up had never been a knee jerk reaction from her before. Never. But Joelle brought something out in her she didn't like.

"Trust is a big word, Joelle."

Ori moved to Drew's side. "Let her talk. This is what we've been waiting for, right? She walked right into exactly what we need. I'm right here with you."

"Maybe I should go, then." Joelle rose and picked up her suitcase.

"Sit back down. You can trust me." The word barely made its way past her lips, and she didn't mean it, but it was the only way to help Ori.

Her mother sat back down on the sofa. She clasped her hands together and her face grew serious. "Something horrible has happened, and I made it worse."

"What did you make worse?" Drew said softly.

Joelle looked from her hands to Drew. "How do I know I can trust you? You hate me."

"I don't hate you." She questioned herself, but hate was too strong a word for what she felt toward Joelle, so it wasn't a lie.

"My family turned their back on me. I've been on the run for months. I changed everything about myself, even my name, until I came here, so I'm not recognized. But I'm running out of money... and it's eating at me."

Drew glanced at Ori, and their eyes met. His human form shifted as he slid from the arm of the chair into Gran's seat.

A vision of Ori on the pavement with headlights jerking forward and back before the screech of tires tugged at the edges of her mind. She braced herself for what was coming next. She knew what Joelle was about to tell her. She might've known all along.

"You can tell me. I went to California to find you, remember? I wanted to help. Maybe I still can." She controlled every syllable to keep from screaming or crying. Or both.

This is about Ori. I've got two days before it all goes away. I need to fix this now.

"I hit someone with my car. It was an accident, but I freaked out and drove away." Joelle's eyes filled with tears. "I shouldn't have left, Drew, but I did. I don't know what the fuck I was thinking. I just... left. Who does that?"

Ori hung his head and Drew wanted to run to him, but she couldn't. The vision she had tried to suppress for too long was real. "What happened to the person, Joelle?" Her words caught, and she cleared her throat.

"You said his name. Orion Dara. He was twenty-two. He had his whole life ahead of him, and I stole it from him." She delved into her pocket and gave Drew a wrinkled piece of newspaper. When she opened it, a photo of a smiling Ori holding a surfboard stared back at her. It was his obituary.

"It was either take a chance on you, or kill myself. I probably made the wrong decision." She wiped her nose on her sleeve as she cried.

Ori got up and sat on the coffee table across from Joelle, not taking his gleaming eyes off her. "Touch her hand. Please. I need you to *know*."

Drew closed her eyes, and tears burned as they ran along her cheeks. If Ori needed her to do this so he could be free, she would do it. Opening her eyes, she sat next to Joelle, and for the first time since she was a child, held her mother's hand.

Joelle hung on for dear life, wrapping her other hand around both, sobbing uncontrollably. She had no idea what Drew was capable of.

Drew gasped as the vision played. An SUV with darkened windows drove through the crowded streets in the pouring rain. Windshield wipers swished back and forth quickly. Horns rang out. As the light turned red, Ori stepped onto the street. Drew wanted to shout for him to turn back, but her screams were silent as the SUV slammed into him. Agonizing pain, far worse than when she'd watched Iris die, ripped through her body and she flinched in response. He lay on the pavement, the rain washing over his limp body as lightning lit up the bleak gray sky. The vehicle sped away, its tires squealing against the pavement as thunder cracked overhead.

Pulling her hand from Joelle's grip. Ori placed his hand over Drew's. "Thank you," he whispered. "I'm free. I can feel it."

She was losing him, and the understanding that this was how it was supposed to be couldn't stop the heartache.

"Turn yourself in," Drew said. "If you want any hope of a relationship with me, you'll do it. Prove to me you want me in your life."

"I can't go to jail. I'll die in there."

"It's either you do it, or I will," Drew said firmly. Ori needed justice.

"I thought you said I could trust you. I need more time—" Panic swept over her mother's face.

"Ori was... *is* a friend of mine. He was the love of someone's life. Someone I care deeply about. You've had months of freedom you don't deserve, while they've been in a living hell. Time is not something I'm willing to give you."

"How could you have known him? I don't... I don't understand. It was thousands of miles away from here, and you say you knew this young man?"

"No. I said he is my friend." Shaking, Drew held her phone up and wiped her eyes to clear her vision. She looked up the Atlas Cliffs police department and readied the number. "Make the call."

"Call the police here? And say what? They don't know me here." She got up and grabbed the suitcase. "I'll go back to California and turn myself in there. I'll run. I've been running for months. I'll do it again!"

Claudia opened the front door and stopped when her eyes connected with Drew's teary ones. She stepped into the entryway, shutting the door behind her.

"Great. Look who's back. You want me to join her father?" Joelle gestured to Claudia and she put her jacket on. "No. No way. I'll start walking, but I'm not saying here."

"Joelle, what did you expect to happen when you told me this? You killed someone! You stole another human's chance to accomplish everything life had waiting for them! His family and friends will never be the same! Make the damn call!"

"Can we take the night to talk? Just one more night? Please, I'm begging you, Drew." Joelle collapsed to her knees with her hands on her face, wailing. Begging. Drew was numb to it, numb to Joelle. She had no love for her. No more heartache or longing for a mother she never had. She had her family here, and they loved her, without conditions. She silently released her mother from the broken promises, in turn releasing herself from Joelle.

Holding her phone out, she stared at the broken woman at her feet. She took Drew's phone.

Joelle's voice listed Drew's address before hanging up. "Goodbye, Drew. You betrayed your own mother for someone you claim is a friend." She pushed past Claudia and bolted outside, down the driveway, rolling the suitcase over the ice and snow along the pavement.

Claudia followed her, stopping by her car. She shielded her eyes as she ran to the end of the driveway, watching Joelle run down the road. "You called a taxi!" Claudia shouted. "She didn't call the police, Drew!"

In the doorway, Ori placed a hand on her arm. "You could give her the night. Ask her everything you've ever wanted to know. You can find out about all her letters and postcards, and why she left. This could be your chance to heal something inside yourself. Get closure."

"I healed something tonight. I got closure. You've already given me that gift, Ori."

"I can't believe it was her. I should be enraged, but I'm surrounded by too much love to feel any anger. I don't want to be the reason you turn your mother in for murder."

She dialed the number to the Atlas Cliffs police and held the phone to her ear. "You're not the reason, Ori. *I* am."

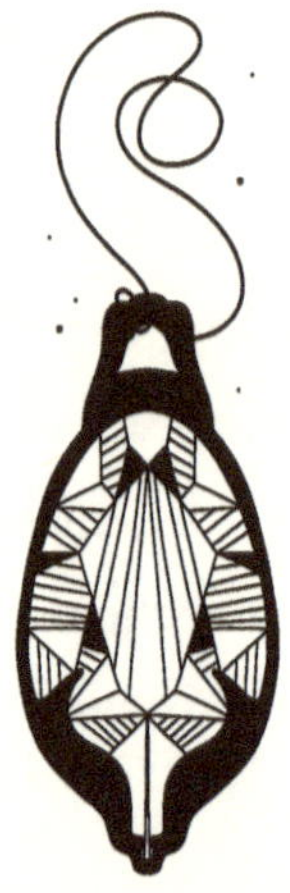

Thirty-Seven

Drew sat in a plastic chair at the police station, the hum of conversation echoing off the cement walls as she waited to talk to an officer. She peered out the window behind her. Even in the light of day, she could see the faded full moon. She burned her tongue on the hot coffee from her cardboard cup. The lack of sugar or milk didn't bother her as much as the exhaustion of the past two days since her mother's arrest. Bitter coffee was better than nothing, and with her scalded tongue, she couldn't taste it anymore, anyway.

Detective Valerie Porter unlocked the glass door with a concerned look on her face. Her hair had grown a little since the last time Drew had seen her. Her short, shiny curls framed her face, accentuating her smooth brown skin. The silver hoop earrings added a touch of elegance, but she was one of the toughest women Drew had ever met. "It's been a while. I'm sorry it's under such awful circumstances. Come in."

One year ago, Drew had been in the same office when she found out Shane was still alive. She couldn't believe how different things were—how different *she was* since the last time she'd been here. The person she used to be was gone. She hoped the strength she had gained would be enough for everything she had to tackle before the end of the day.

First things first: Joelle.

Detective Porter pushed the sleeves up—plain clothes instead of a uniform, revealing muscular forearms. Maybe she'd been called in from her holidays. She'd always struck Drew as someone who could win a fight in one minute and rock a ball gown the next. Taking a pen, she opened a leather-bound notebook. As she asked Drew a series of questions, she jotted down notes. Another officer entered the room for an official statement, and Detective Porter closed her book. When the officer left, she pushed the door closed. "You've been dealt a shit hand lately."

"I guess so. Don't you think everyone's got their own version of a shit hand?"

"You're probably right." Porter pushed her chair back.

"Where is Joelle? Is she still in town?"

"She left about an hour ago. They're escorting her back to California." The detective handed her a piece of paper with police information about where she would be processed. "In case you wanted to get in touch. Your call, obviously. I just wanted you to have it. There is something I'm curious about."

"What's that?" A question like that would've thrown her off a year ago, sending her defenses on high alert. But she was tired of shying away from the tough questions.

"You said your mother didn't tell you anything other than she hit that young man with her vehicle and took off."

"That's true."

"It happened last spring. How could you know specifics about that evening unless she told you? You described, in detail, the street, the weather... even the make and color of the vehicle. I received a copy of the case from the precinct handling this incident, and everything you said was spot on. If she didn't tell you, how'd you know all that?"

Drew hadn't taken the discrepancies into consideration. Justice for Ori and Jasper had been her only concern. She'd find a way to process the harsh reality that her mother was going to be spending time behind bars for a fatal hit and run later. That was a future Drew problem.

"Detective—"

"Call me Valerie; I think we're past the formality," she said, folding her arms across her chest as she waited for Drew to respond. There was no urgency, just patience and calm, as if she had all the time in the world, even though Drew knew that was not so.

Drew stopped chewing her bottom lip, cursing the habit. "I saw them."

"You *saw* them?"

"The same way I knew what happened to Iris. I get… visions sometimes. This is one of those times."

"Did you really see Iris?"

"I did, yes. I'm not a liar, De—Valerie. Everything I've ever told you has been, and continues to be, the truth."

Valerie sat up, smiling, lighting up her sharp eyes. Her features were still as stunning as ever, despite the stress her job must have on her. "I believe you, Drew. It's just curiosity. There are some very odd rumors about you in town, but I hate gossip and don't want any part of it. That's why I'm asking you directly. You have my word that what you say here, stays here."

"I see the dead and they communicate with me. Ori… Orion Dara is my friend, but I only met him after he died. That's how I could see the details. But I swear I didn't know it was my mother who was responsible until she showed up two days ago." She glanced at the clock on the wall. She had to make it to Tate Realty for ten, and she didn't have much time left. "I've got to get going. I have an appointment." She stood, and Valerie did the same.

"Thank you for telling me." Valerie stacked the notebook on top of a pile of files. "You ever consider a career as an investigator? I think you'd be a brilliant asset to a team."

She almost burst out laughing. She couldn't imagine such a career. "Thanks for saying that, but I'll stick to art school."

"Where?"

"Boston."

"Cool. They're opening a gallery on the waterfront. Maybe you can get your art featured."

Claudia's art gallery. She smiled, thinking about the night at Maze when her friend had offered to buy the painting off the wall. She wasn't sure yet what her career would look like, but she was making big decisions about her life. The rest would fall into place. Somehow. "I don't know about that."

"It's the Tate women. They're a force, those two. This town needs them." Valerie opened the door for Drew to leave. "If you need anything, you know how to reach me. Take care, Drew."

She waved and headed for her car, driving across town to Tate Realty.

Big things today, but I can do this.

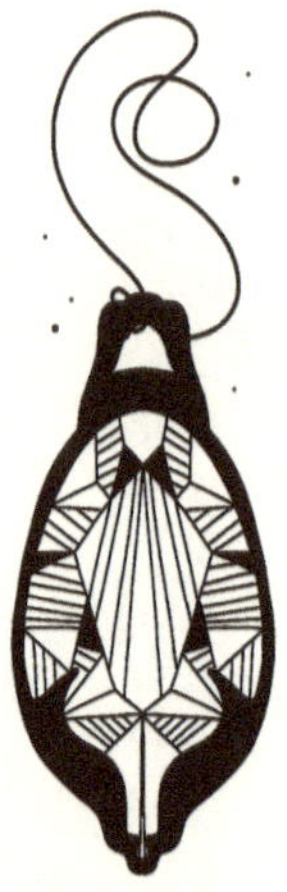

THIRTY-EIGHT

Drew sat in the waiting area of Tate Realty, her eyes drawn to the abstract art on the walls. She hadn't realized Claudia was interested in art. It had to be Anna's preference. Faint instrumental classical music drifted from the radio, playing at a low volume. The doors opened and Nicki entered, a tray of cups in one hand and a briefcase in the other. Drew wished she could sink into the floor and disappear. It could be possible Nicki didn't know about her and Nico; it hadn't been long and wasn't as though they'd gone public yet.

Nicki flung the bag onto her chair and put the tray of coffee down on the desk. When she shook her coat off and reached to hang it on the rack, she took one look at Drew and stopped. Her face reddened as she glared at her before hanging her coat up.

She knew, all right.

Nicki straightened her posture, smoothed out her blazer and spun on her heels to sit at the desk. Awkward silence hung in the air. Drew peered toward the glass doors of the office, but it was empty. Where were Anna and Claudia? She wanted to take care of the pressing matter that was Gran's business and the house. She picked up a gardening magazine from a side table and flipped through it without reading.

"I thought you were selling your house," Nicki remarked, eyeing the magazine.

Surprised by Nicki's comment, she closed the magazine. She wondered if everyone who worked in this office knew the details of the offer on her home before she did. "Why are you so interested?" She tried to not sound bitchy, but her tone had other plans.

"Just making conversation," Nicki said.

Drew diverted her attention from the desk, flipping through the magazine again. She could sense Nicki's penetrating stare.

"I know you're seeing Nico, and while your coming back to town didn't help, you weren't the reason we broke up."

"Nicki, I—"

"I don't need your pity, please. Don't even go there."

"That's not what I was going to do."

Nicki clicked the mouse beside the laptop, staring at the screen. "Whatever. I just wanted you to know it isn't always about you."

Drew didn't know her well, and what she was referring to was a mystery, but she dropped the conversation. She was learning fast; it didn't make a difference what everyone else thought. She never intended to hurt Nicki or anyone else, and not for a second had she believed she was the only reason Nico broke up with her. None of that mattered from her perspective.

Claudia sauntered across the office and beamed at her. "Hi, Drew. We've got everything ready for you."

Drew followed her into the glass office and sat in the plush desk chair across from Claudia.

"My mom's just on the phone. She'll be here soon." Claudia pulled the chair as close to the desk as her body would allow. "I have a proposition for you." She bubbled over with excitement, but all Drew heard was, *proposition*, and the art gallery Claudia had mentioned at Maze came to mind. But one proposition was plenty, and she'd pondered Jasper's for two days.

"What sort of proposition? I've got to say, I'm all out of propositions to give."

Claudia smiled. "Cute. Very cute. I'm opening an art gallery and I want to feature local artists... starting with you."

"I don't think so, Claudia. I'm not an artist, not really."

"Yes, you are, silly! Hear me out." Reaching back, Claudia held up the painting from Maze Drew had painted years earlier.

Drew took it from her and ran her hands over the canvas. The image stirred up sorrow within her for the girl she used to be. She wasn't that same lost girl anymore, and those ropes holding the swing were strong as they held her up now. "How did you get this? Did you steal it?"

"I convinced the owner of Maze to let me borrow it. But that's where you come in. I want to buy this from you for the gallery. It's opening in time for tourist season this spring, and all you have to do is give me three more to go with it. My promise to you is I will have these sold by the end of summer."

"Sounds like a business deal."

"Precisely." Claudia pointed back and forth between them. "Now our minds are on the same page. What a beautiful thing." She tossed her blond hair over her shoulder, and took the painting back, placing it carefully behind her.

"I'll have to think about this."

"What's to think about? You can still sell the house; you don't even need to live here. Go back to school and create more art! That's all you've got to do."

Claudia handed her a cheque for one thousand dollars, along with an invoice and a receipt. "What's the title of this piece? I want to get it right."

Drew's mouth dropped open. "This is too much. I can't accept this."

"Nonsense. You can and you will. Take it."

"A thousand dollars, Claudia? I'm a nobody artist."

"Not to me, you're not. Not to tourists who want to see local artists! Will you please just agree to this? Just this once. It's the easiest decision you'll ever make. You must have other pieces lying around collecting dust, I imagine?"

"Sure, but—"

"Good. It's perfect."

Drew exhaled and flopped back in her seat, exhausted. She could be a real artist, even if it was just among Atlas Cliffs. "Okay, but you're getting two more, not three."

Claudia clapped her hands together. "Deal." Her face fell. "Shane's in town, too. He came for Christmas and is staying with me for a few days... I just thought you should know. He wants to see you before he leaves."

She had been mistaken when she thought she would never have to face Shane again. "I don't have anything to say to him. We're done."

"He said you might say that. I think he just wants to apologize."

Drew glanced around for Claudia's mother and shifted in her seat.

"I know about the other girl, Drew. It scared him to tell you, but I told him he had to. So, it's partly my fault he told you."

"It's not your fault, it's his. Even if this never happened, we weren't getting back together. I thought we'd be friends, but that was it. You can tell him I don't want to talk to him, or about him, or see him. I've moved on and he should, too."

The glass door swung open, and Anna Tate walked in. "I'm so excited for you! Let's get this house sold."

Claudia's eyes widened, and she placed her hand on Drew's. "I'll handle him. Don't worry. I didn't mean to upset you. You've got bigger things going on." She got up and walked out of the office, spinning around before letting the door close. "And Drew? Thank you. I think your paintings are going to be fabulous."

She did a double take as Claudia strutted away in her grey pantsuit. How was this girl only nineteen? Valerie Porter might be correct in saying the Tate women were a force; they were building a secret empire behind closed doors.

Anna spread out documents and started talking about offers, lawyers, and other terminology Drew didn't grasp. She put her hands up to interrupt her. "I'm not selling."

Anna froze. "What? Did you see their offer? They're not requiring any renovations for the fire damage either. This is an amazing offer with a quick close, Drew."

"I don't care how much money they're willing to pay. I'm pulling the house from the market. I'm not selling."

Anna slunk into the chair across from her. "Are you sure about this? I can't guarantee you'd get such an offer again."

Drew sat up straight in the chair. Heat radiated from the amulet beneath her green cashmere sweater. The faded light of the moon made its appearance through the office window as she glanced over. The full moon would shine over Haven tonight, and she'd have to be ready. Everything she was doing to keep her home would only clear her mind for the focus and intention she'd need later.

"I've never been more sure of anything in my life. I'm also taking back the Tough Cookie. Tell me what I need to sign or do, and I'll do it, but nothing you say to me will change my mind. It's made up." She rose from the chair and Anna stood as well. Drew reached her hand over the desk. "Thank you, Ms. Tate."

"Anna. Call me Anna." She extended her hand to Drew. "If you are sure about this, I will take care of things from here. But if you change your mind, call me."

"Okay." She zipped her jacket and headed for the door.

"Oh, and Drew?"

She stopped with her hand on the door handle and turned around.

"My offer still stands. If you ever need anything, please reach out. I owe you my life, my daughter's life..." Anna trailed off, her eyes suddenly appearing haunted. She shook her head and ran her hand over her chin. "My husband was a prick and what he did to us, all of us, is unforgiveable. You've got an ally in me, and Claudia, too."

Unexpected emotions hit Drew. Anna Tate, the ex-wife of the man who tried to ruin all their lives, was mothering her. She showed compassion toward Drew like she was her own daughter, and Anna's pure act of nurturing and kindness touched her.

Relationships had bloomed in her life when she needed them most. She'd longed for a mother's love, and she found herself surrounded by it, even if she hadn't realized. Gran stepped into the role with grace. Nellie substituted as needed. And there was Celeste, who opened herself up to Drew, taking her under her wing.

Drew reached for the paperwork, and Anna handed her the cheque Claudia had given for her painting. "Don't forget this. Claudia's savvy. She won't screw you over."

Drew took the cheque from her hand. Despite being overpriced, she'd sold her first painting. She wasn't as confident in her art as the Tates, but she was unstoppable today. She'd taken care of her most nagging decisions and was ready to face Hathorne. Without Ori by her side, she had no choice but to send the witch hunter back on her own. Ori must've crossed over because she hadn't seen him since Joelle's confession and calling him wasn't working anymore. She didn't have time to let herself feel the pain of missing the brother she never had.

She passed by Nicki, ignoring her angry glare following Drew out the doors. The Atlas Cliffs sea air swept her hair up, taking her breath away. Not only was she now a business owner, but she was also keeping Gran's home. Her home.

As she crossed the parking lot toward her car, her last obstacle watched her every step with a piercing gaze from across the street.

Hathorne was on the hunt.

She kept her attention fixed on him as she got in the car. She was as prepared as she could be, but Hathorne's anticipation drifted across the street. Excitement pulsed around her like a snake about to strike its prey. He was ready for her and the tight lock on the dam of fear she'd been suppressing for two days threatened to break open.

He smirked before shifting into a tornado cloud. People walked along the sidewalk, oblivious to the dark smoke engulfing them as he vanished. Starting the car, she pulled onto the street.

The day of the full moon had arrived. She'd embraced her gift, no longer considering seeing the dead a curse, but when the night ended, she would never lay eyes on the wandering souls again. A year ago, she would've signed over her ability without another thought—a trade for the 'normal' life she'd always wished for. But losing her connection to the other side was going to feel like losing a piece of herself, and she wasn't sure how she'd go on without it. If there was any other way, she'd do it. But each time she used the magic book, the same caution reappeared on the page.

Kiss my magic and soul's purpose goodbye.

THIRTY-NINE

D rew stopped at Nico's place, but the big garage doors were closed. A high-pitched buzzing of tools rang from inside. She couldn't leave for Neptune Point without seeing him and sharing her news. If something horrible happened to her, or if she didn't make it back, he had to know how she felt about him and this place. She walked around the side of the building and knocked on the door where she could hear muffled music thumping from inside. She knocked a few more times, opening the door when he didn't answer. Nico's bent legs stuck out from underneath a car as music blared from a small speaker. He sang off tune to Queens of the Stone Age, tapping his foot.

"Nico!"

He leaned his head to the side and beamed when he saw her. Sliding out from under the car, he hopped up and wiped his hands on a rag. She'd never seen someone look so good in grease-stained coveralls. He leaned down and kissed her. "I'd hug you, but I don't want to get you dirty."

She threw her arms around him and held him tight before kissing him again. "I don't care."

"Can you stop by when I'm working every day?" He laughed.

"I have some news." Her gaze fell on the black car beside him. "What is that? It's beautiful." She ran her hand over the sleek, curved hood.

"My holiday project. It's a '69 Corvette Stingray, and you're right. It's a beautiful car, but it's almost ready to go home to its owner."

"This is what you meant when you said you restore old cars?"

"Yeah, this is one of them. I love doing it, but the more my name gets out, the busier it's getting, especially before spring."

He washed his hands in a utility sink, grabbing paper towels to dry them off.

"That's amazing, Nico."

He gave so much of himself to everything he did, giving up dreams along the way to keep his family business going. And when he loved, it was fierce and loyal. The bond between them had stretched but refused to break. They found security in their shared imperfections. She trusted him with her most private thoughts and the secrets she kept hidden from the world's judgment.

Trust. It was a big word, but Nico filled it out well. "You're amazing," she said.

He hugged her again. "So are you. I've never had a girlfriend ask me about work before. I appreciate that about you."

He called me his girlfriend.

Her heart raced for a moment before settling back into a steady beat. She used to worry she might panic if things got serious between them, or if labels like *love* and *girlfriend* came up. But her body tingled with excitement. Being with Nico warmed her chest and made her heart happy. "Girlfriend," she said, smiling. "You said, girlfriend."

"Should I not have said that? I assumed we were, you know, doing this?" He gestured between them. "If I'm wrong—"

"No. No, you're not wrong. I'm in. I don't know what's going to happen with school, but I'm in. With you, I mean."

"I'm not looking for big promises, Drew. I'm more of an in the moment type of guy, but I think you already know that." He leaned against the workbench and gazed at her with his alluring brown eyes. "With you, I'm in too. In this moment, and if I'm being honest, all the future moments. But don't freak out, okay? It's not like that. I just need you to know I'm not going anywhere. If you go to school, move away, whatever you decide. You can trust that I won't ever hurt you. That's all."

She smiled, remembering their times on surfboards at Jupiter Cove Beach. The ability to be in the moment was one of Nico's best qualities, and one she needed in her chaotic life. Stepping in front of him, she brought his arms up and around her. He clasped his hands together around her back, and she cupped his face in her hands. She kissed him, and they tumbled into each other's arms, as close as they could be in a garage surrounded by the smells of oil and grease. Giddiness overwhelmed her, and she had to resist letting it sweep her away.

It's the full moon tonight and I can't lose focus.

It took every ounce of willpower to pull away from him, but she did it.

"Now that we've got that settled, what's your big news? I'm sorry about Joelle. The last message I got, you were at the police station. How'd that go? I would've come if you called."

"I know you would, but Claudia was awesome. And I need-ed to take care of it on my own. Joelle's on her way back to California. I might call next week to find out what's next for her... maybe I won't. I don't know what I'm going to do." Her mother had killed Ori and left him for dead. Jasper's life, and Ori's family's life, wouldn't be the same again. If Ori and her mother had never crossed paths, maybe they'd be friends—ac-tual living friends. The *what if* game was a dangerous rabbit hole to fall into, and she cut herself off from allowing her thoughts to spiral. "I had to do it. I had to turn her in."

"Don't explain, I get it. You did the right thing." Nico rubbed the sides of her arms and kissed her forehead. "Have you told Jasper yet?"

"He knows." She grabbed two red chairs on wheels and pointed to one of them. "Jasper's part of my news."

He sat on the stool with his feet on the floor. Her legs weren't long enough to reach the floor, so she rested hers on the metal height adjuster.

Stop staring at his legs and focus.

"I went to see Anna Tate today about that offer."

"When do you have to be out?" His Adam's apple bobbed as he swallowed.

"That's my news. I'm keeping the house and going into business with Jasper. We're going to run the Tough Cookie together." She exhaled and chewed her lip, caught the habit and stopped at the reminder of her mother doing the same. "So? What do you think?"

Nico hopped off the stool so fast it barrelled backward as he rushed to hug her. "Are you serious? Are you sure?"

"For once, yes. I'm one hundred percent sure."

"This is the best news. But what about school? You're still gonna finish, aren't you?"

"I'm going back a week late, but I'll finish this year and next, and get my graphic design diploma. I'll just travel home on the weekends and holidays, and work at the Tough Cookie with Jasper to cover bills. Gran had some in her savings, too. I think I can make it work, for now anyway." She hadn't worked out a solid five-year plan or anything, but she was doing what settled the anxiousness inside of her. Keeping the house and the business felt... right.

"I can keep up with house stuff anytime," Nico said, his hands on her shoulders. "Just tell me what you need."

"Are you sure? Because that was going to be my next question."

"Fuck, yes, I'm sure! I'd say let's go out and do something fun, but there's one thing you haven't talked about yet." He rolled the stool beside her and sat back down.

Going back to Neptune Point to do the unthinkable. Alone.

"What's that?" she said, knowing full well what he was going to say. She wasn't bringing anyone with her. She'd told Piper

Hathorne was gone and peace had been restored in the world of the dead, but she knew she didn't buy it, and Nico wouldn't either.

"It's the full moon tonight." Nico's face turned serious. "When do we leave?"

"You're not coming with me, Nico; no one is. I can't protect you, or Piper, out there. I know what I have to do, and I'm ready. When it's over, I'll come see you, and everything will be great." Doubt escaped alongside her words, and anyone else wouldn't notice… but Nico wasn't just anyone.

He observed her through dark lashes, his eyebrows knitted tightly together. "No way. I can't let you do that."

"That isn't for you to decide. I know you're scared, but trust me when I tell you I'm ready for him. I'm going alone. Please respect my decision, Nico. Please."

"Drew—"

"*Please.*" She wheeled her stool close and took his hands in her own. He tightened his calloused fingers through hers. "You know I'm… different. This part of my world isn't for you, or Piper, or anyone I care about. There is nothing your being there could do to help me. If anything, I'll lose focus worrying about you and everything will go to shit, and I can't let that happen."

He locked eyes with her. "I can't make any promises. If I don't hear from you—"

"You will. Eleven eleven. That's the time it will all be over tonight."

He pulled his hand back, running his hand through his dishevelled hair. "I can't just sit around here and wait. What if something goes wrong? What do I tell the cops? Go save my girlfriend from a dead guy?"

She smoothed his hair with her fingers and held his face. "Celeste Locke. That's who you call if anything goes wrong, but it won't. I promise I've got this." She lowered her hands to her lap, and he moved a strand of hair away from her face. He pulled her stool between his legs and kissed her, letting his lips linger over hers. Her breath caught as she reached for the back of his neck and kissed him harder. What if this was their last kiss?

They parted, and her fingers danced along the edges of the amulet hanging on her chest. The jewel was cool to the touch, with an eerie stillness waiting deep inside, as though it was saving its energy for the full moon.

She knew what she had to do.

FORTY

Drew left her car in the clearing near Aurora and walked along the path toward Haven. The light of the full moon illuminated the night sky and her way forward. As she moved, the raven followed, flying overhead and landing on branches along the way. She didn't know why it was tracking her, but its presence gave her a strange sense of safety, as if the raven wanted to protect her.

The trail opened to the clearing where the fire pit was dormant. Powdery snow blanketed the ground, untouched by footsteps. Bare branches creaked in the icy breeze, whispering warnings as she moved deeper into the woods toward the river's edge. The raven soared past her and perched on fallen deadwood, staring at her. The river thundered, unforgiving. She shuddered as she thought of Nico floating downstream toward the ocean, grateful she'd convinced him to stay away tonight.

Stepping over protruding roots, she shook off her backpack. She'd memorized the banishing spell and had been reciting it all evening, with intention and focus, like Celeste taught her. Her hands burned with electricity as she approached the swirling veil of blues and greens hovering among the trees, close to the river. If this didn't work and Hathorne won, she'd end up inside the swirling hell or dead... Probably both. Fear's debilitating hold gripped her like a noose around her neck constricting blood flow and cutting off her air.

She crouched in the snow and hung her head between her knees.

Touch something concrete and breathe.

Picking up a handful of snow, she cupped it into a ball between her palms, sending water dripping along her fingers as it melted against her skin. She steadied her breaths, visualizing Nico in front of her with his calming eyes holding hers.

She opened her backpack, scanning for signs of an unexpected attack, like a rabbit on high alert for a wolf. He was hunting her, waiting to strike and rip the magic from her.

Death seeks you.

The words touched her ears with a clicking sound, and she jumped to her feet, spinning around.

The air was thick and hung around her as though the oxygen was being sucked away, leaving her unable to take a deep breath. An acrid stench of dark, forbidden magic pierced her nose. It smelled of rusted metal, blood mixed with burning flesh—something she'd only experienced in nightmares.

She longed for the security of Ori's presence, silently begging him to appear beside her, even though she knew he was gone. Like Enid, Ezra, and Iris, he'd found his peace. The weight of his absence filled her with a sadness, a loneliness, she couldn't ignore.

But she had no choice except to push forward without him.

The moon's light shone down through the birch trees, casting shadows over the raging river and wet stones. The radiant glow illuminated the forest, leaving no shadow unturned and no place to hide. There was no hiding from an expert hunter. Hathorne was always watching.

A gush of wind rushed over the trees, sending a scattering sound like the rustle of tiny feet through bushes. Mournful howls mimicked each other in the distance, like animals in a fairy tale. But this wasn't a fairy tale with magical princesses talking to animals or warriors saving the day. She was the witch assigned to create the happy ending in her real-life story.

The raven flew closer, perching on the root she'd climbed over. Its head cocked from side to side as it stared into the forest. She inched closer, extending a hand until she could almost touch its sleek feathers as they glimmered underneath the moon's light. She recoiled as the raven stretched its wings and flapped in place, beady eyes fixed on her.

"Who are you?" she asked. It cocked its head, answering with a harsh, grating screech, but didn't fly away.

Her heart raced as she brought a water bottle to her dry lips and drank the cool liquid. The time on her phone read eleven o'clock.

Almost time.

Rummaging through her backpack, she grabbed mirrors, the bottle of potion from Celeste, and all the stones and crystals she'd taken from the house. She trudged through the snow, carrying her magic weapons in her arms toward the swirling portal. The moon gate.

Enid and Iris had never walked through this gate. In all her times at Haven, she'd never seen anything like this before. She might never know how the gate manifested or why, but she was convinced the connection to Neptune Point ran deep. Maybe before Aurora's witch discovery.

The colors spun together like water, forming a circle. She set to work, placing crystals and spraying the contents of the antique bottle all around her. She tucked the smallest mirror into her jacket pocket. As she angled the other three mirrors toward the portal, the amulet sprang to life, vibrating against her neck. She freed the glimmering jewel from underneath her sweater, holding it outward.

Celeste's voice rang in her ear, *"You've got the whole sisterhood in the palm of your hand."*

The souls of a sisterhood of witches who were burned and hanged centuries ago were her protection now. Trembling, she dropped the amulet against her neck and lifted her hands up to the moon gate. She recited the first part of the spell.

"Essence of night. Where the water flows—" Her voice faltered, and she cleared her throat. "The peak of the moon's power. Calling upon the ones who burned."

The amulet's vibration intensified as the vines spun around with increasing speed, surrounded by a dazzling light.

She closed her eyes and tried to call the witch hunter to her, but an oppressive wall crept up from the dark corners of her mind, blocking her out. Her eyes flew open as a vice gripped her throat, clenching it closed. Fighting to catch her breath, she fell to her knees on the cold ground, clawing at her neck as she tried to break free from the invisible hands constricting with every inhale. She couldn't breathe or speak—the spell died before she could finish, the amulet's light fading.

No! Don't kill me! Someone help! Please!

Snow soaked through her jeans as she collapsed, sinking deeper into the snow. Her body shook from the cold, turning numb as she stared skyward at the twinkling stars, gasping for air.

It's not working! He's killing me.

Her breaths came in quick shallow bursts as her eyelids drooped. Liquid ice ran from inside her head through her veins down her body as she struggled to hang on to consciousness. She was dying on the ground at Haven. Claws scraped at her neck as the amulet lifted away from her body, its chain still clinging to the back of her neck as her head lifted off the ground.

A cloak enveloped her, suffocating her. Hathorne leaned down, hovering over her face, staring into her eyes. His rancid breaths held the same smell as the burning flesh.

"Mine," his sinister voice seethed in her ear.

He'd killed Gran, and he wanted her dead, but she would not let him win. She had her life to live and dreams to accomplish. She promised Nico and Piper she'd be okay. Her father would never recover if she died. She focused on moving her hands and her fingers twitched. She reached up toward her face, screaming on the inside, but unable to speak.

Are you there, Ori? I can't do this without you.

A tsunami of warmth rushed through her and Hathorne's hands released from her throat. A scream of relief broke loose, echoing throughout the forest. She filled her lungs with air until her breathing steadied, her head spinning in panic.

Ori stood over her like an angel. He wore the same clothes, but his hair cascaded over his shoulders, and his eyes glittered. She took his outstretched hand and stood on wobbly legs, wrapping her arms around him, thankful he was mortal enough she could feel his warmth under her arms. "You came!"

"You called me, didn't you?" He smiled.

"But I thought since... I assumed you—"

"Walked into the light?" he teased. "It wasn't quite like that, but yeah. You did it. You freed me. Now, it's my turn to free you."

"It didn't work." She pointed around her. "I made the protection circle and sprayed Celeste's potion. He had me on the ground before I could finish the spell!"

Ori looked up behind her and she followed his gaze toward the moon gate as Hathorne stood in front of it. He removed his cloak, letting it drop to the ground. He approached her, flames burning along his clawed hands. "It is time to burn, as the others have done before you. As more shall burn after you." He widened his mouth until a stream of bugs flew out and scattered over their heads, releasing a maniacal laugh that rose over the rushing river. Flames poured like gasoline from his hands and out from under his cloak.

They crawled toward her feet and she leaped back, untouched as the deadwood outside of her protection circle burst into flames.

It worked!

Quivering, she took a few steps toward the witch hunter until she was inches from his face. She held her hands up and called on the current of magic coursing inside of her. The taste of metal filled her mouth as it fizzed and popped like candy on her tongue. Whispers of sadness surrounded her, and images of fire and screams of death filled her mind's eye. Heath Hathorne looked on with pride as his lethal killings played out beyond the gate. Bile rose in Drew's throat, mixing with the taste of burning magic.

"You know what to do," Ori said. "I'm not leaving your side. You thought you needed me, but you didn't. You've got this, my friend."

She crossed the boundary of the protection circle and pressed forward with energy pouring from her hands. Each step forward forced the witch hunter back toward the spinning moon gate.

He hovered in front of the whirling blues and greens. An abyss of darkness, like a black hole into nothing but torment, emitted from its depths. Fear threatened to break her focus but she shook it off, shifting her eyes back to him. He reached a clawed hand for the amulet, breaking the chain and tearing it from her neck. A burst of light exploded around them, sending an array of golden sparks into the air. The souls of thousands of witches flashed forward, engulfing the witch hunter as they pushed him into the moon gate.

Drew attempted to grab the amulet, but it was out of her reach. As she tried to retreat, the witch hunter's sharp nails dug into her skin, yanking her hand into the gate with him.

"No!" She snatched the mirror from her pocket and pulled her hand back, holding him close so she could stare into his torturous eyes. "You will never kill again. You picked the wrong era to come back, asshole." She held the mirror up and a last surge of energy, like the river's current, released him from her, forcing him back through the portal.

She lifted her hand to her neck and felt nothing but her sweater. The amulet was gone.

Voices called out her name somewhere in the distance.

"It's not closing," she said to Ori through tears. If the witch hunter crossed back into her world, he would kill Piper and Nicofirst before turning his attention on her. She stepped close to the portal and held her hands up, but nothing happened.

The river rapids crashed so loudly all other sounds were muted. Drew turned around, scanning the forest. No one was there. The portal was disappearing from her vision, but she knew it was still open. Her magic was disappearing and her ability to see the dead was going with it.

"Say the spell. All is not lost," Gran's voice whispered through her mind, drowning out all the other sounds for a brief moment.

The last of her magic, just a tinge, hung in the air. When the witch hunter came back to kill them all, she wouldn't be able to see him. It was now or never.

She stood tall and closed her eyes as she let the words flow from her soul. "Essence of night. Where the water flows. The peak of the moon's power. Calling upon the ones who burned. Vanquish harm through reflection. Lock the door. Seeking Haven for all."

Vibrant light flashed from the mirrors like a lightning strike and they crumbled into dust. The sisterhood of souls soared free, surrounding her in warmth and love. A remaining glimmer of the moon gate shimmered, once, violently, before it collapsed in on itself, melting into a pinhole before disappearing.

Sirens wailed in the background as Piper and Nico's cries sounded in the distance. The only source of light was the full moon shining down on her once again. But something was wrong.

She stared at where the gate had once hung among the trees as she slumped to the ground. The amulet was gone. If Ori was still with her, she could no longer see him or feel his presence. She'd lost a part of herself, left with an emptiness deep inside her soul. A strange silence cut through her thoughts—a knowing. Her gift had evaporated. Pain and loss overwhelmed her, and she sank into the snow as tears streamed down her face. She flopped onto her back and lay still. A brand-new life was waiting for her. One without friendships with the dead. Everyone she loved would be safe now. She'd accept her fate, knowing the other side was now beyond her reach forever.

Why does it hurt so badly?

The swoosh of wings flapped an arm's length above her head. Feathers brushed against her face as the raven landed beside her, tilting its head from side to side. "Go away." She covered her face, exhaustion and grief taking over. She felt like she was trying to scream, but she was being held underwater and forced to hold her breath.

Something sharp tapped her hand, and she turned onto her side. She was face to face with the raven. Light glowed in its dark eyes as it tapped her with its beak, and she sat up against a piece of deadwood. "What do you want?"

The raven picked up something shiny from the snow and flew, landing on the deadwood. The amulet dangled from its beak. She reached a shaking hand out to the bird, opening her palm.

The raven dropped the amulet in her hand. A delicate glow radiated from the center of the black stone as a few remaining vines crawled underneath the surface. As she hung it over her head and let it dangle against her chest, a sudden shock ran through her like hands, dragging her out of the water and finally allowing her to breathe.

She scrambled off the ground as her vision cleared, showing Ori standing in front of her. Pieces fit back together one by one, making her whole again.

"You're back," she said.

"I never left; you did." He laughed. "I knew there was something up with that bird. I wanted to make sure you were safe. You did it, Drew, and you can still see me. It worked. It's over."

She wiped snow and tears off her face. "You were wrong."

"I'm never wrong." His eyes sparkled as he laughed.

"I *did* need you. Thanks, Ori."

"Well, maybe a little, but not really. You're welcome."

She threw her arms around him as fresh tears stung her eyes. "I'm not selling the house. I just wanted you to know in case you're ever back this way."

Ori hugged her back, but all she could feel was his warmth as he faded away. "Thanks for looking out for him. Let him know I'll be around."

"I will," she whispered as he disappeared. He wouldn't be back. They never came back. It was the bittersweet part that hurt the most.

The vines in the amulet swirled until they vanished. A pop of light clouded the black stone before it burned and disintegrated, falling off her neck into a puff of smoke. She patted herself down and pushed wet hair off her face. Her hands tingled, and she held them up. A faint glow winked before it too faded, leaving her magic and gift intact.

She secured the crystals in her backpack and trudged back through the path toward her car. A hum of chatter and voices yelled from the direction of the parking area. Footsteps thudded through the snow down the hill of the narrow trail, and Piper charged for her, almost knocking her over with an embrace. "Why do you always insist on doing these things alone?"

Nico climbed down after Piper. "The time passed, and I didn't hear from you. I couldn't wait."

"It's over," she said. She was so glad to see them, alive and whole. Safe.

The smell of burning smoke drifted around her and the sirens blared close. Thumping pounded in her ears as she took off up the hill. A bright orange glow filled the sky.

Fire!

"What's burning! Is he back?" She dashed closer.

"It's the keeper's house, Drew," Nico said as he caught up to her.

Dropping her backpack near her car, she kept running for the keeper's house. The house of Aurora was ablaze. Celeste stood in front of it, with a girl beside her.

Drew stumbled through the snow, and over rocks, tripping and picking herself up. She was out of breath when she reached Celeste. Her mouth gaped open, and she froze in shock.

"Enid?"

Celeste smiled. "I figured you'd be able to see her. You kept your gift. Good. You'll need it."

"You can see her?"

Celeste shook her head. "I feel her beside me, but that's enough."

Enid's face beamed with joy as she smiled at Drew. When she pressed her hand against Drew's face, she felt a pleasant warmth radiating through her fingers, like Ori's. "It's good to see you again."

"What happened? Why is the house burning?"

Enid turned back to the burning house. "It was the only way to keep the gate from ever opening again. It was my fault it returned. I tried to come back to see you and took a... wrong turn. I've learned a few things." Enid scrunched her nose and smiled. Her silhouette faded in and out, sparkling with each movement.

"Did you do this, Celeste?" Drew asked.

Celeste shrugged. "Sometimes all it takes is a little focus."

"And intention," Drew said, smiling. "Are you a witch like Aurora was, Enid?"

"We all are." Enid's voice grew quiet, and she faded away, leaving a brief swirl of light behind.

Celeste patted Drew on the shoulder and headed back up the hill. Drew crouched as the house's walls tumbled to the ground into rubble. The fire snapped and roared, and firefighters yelled commands from behind her.

The raven landed beside her.

"You again. I sure wish you'd show yourself."

"One thing about Atlas Cliffs no one else knows; all the witches who've come through here over the years," a deep voice rattled, startling Drew as she stumbled and landed on her ass in the snow.

Jack kneeled beside her.

"Jack! It was you?"

His white hair cascaded beneath his hat, and the hem of his long coat brushed against the ground. "I've tried to close that gate for months." He stood, and she rose to her feet beside him.

"You gave me back my magic."

He grunted. "You're going to need it. And when you do, I'll be here. I made a promise to keep them safe. It's what I do."

He tipped his hat and walked past the fire toward Aurora.

"Jack Morana, you are my hero."

Forty-One

Drew and Nico settled together at their usual round table near the stage at Maze. The concert would mark the end of the holidays and the return to school. With the construction underway in Gran's room, she had been spending most of the past week with Nico above the garage. They had an insatiable desire for each other, falling into a pattern where he would work while she and Jasper were busy with the relaunch of the Tough Cookie.

Across the table, Piper rested her chin on her hand, listening as Jasper talked, his hands and face animated. Their sudden burst of laughter made Drew smile. She had never known Jasper to be as light and alive as he was these days. He and Drew reminisced together about Ori sometimes; their unique understanding of Ori, which nobody else shared, strengthened their friendship. Jasper helped her through the painful loss of losing Ori. But Enid had returned and seeing her again opened Drew's eyes to possibilities she didn't know existed. She clung to the hope she'd see Enid and Ori again.

The band stepped aside, making way for Taj's impressive drum solo. The pounding of the drums thumped in her chest, as though it was her own heartbeat. Her only new year's resolution was to have more fun. Between an elaborate New Year's Eve party in Piper's grand living room and the night at Maze, she savored in accomplishment, and it had only been a week.

Nico found her hand under the table, and she leaned her head against his shoulder, feeling the solid warmth of his body against hers.

"Happy Birthday," he said.

"You already wished me a happy birthday." She ran her fingers along the pendant that was around her neck. She admired the deep blue of the butterfly on the silver chain. Nico had given it to her to remember Gran, knowing she missed the sensation of the amulet around her neck.

"You could turn it into a birthday month if you wanted."

She rolled her eyes. "I think one day is fine."

The drum solo ended, and a wave of applause was followed by the sound of Claudia's laughter as she greeted friends on her way to their table. But it was the guy walking behind her who caught Drew's attention.

Shane.

Her jaw tensed, and she bit her lip.

Nico turned around, following her gaze. "You okay?"

"Yeah. I knew he was in town, just didn't expect to see him. It's no big deal."

His eyes met hers. "Do you want to leave?"

She refused to let Shane drive her away from anywhere. "We're having fun. I'm good." She put her hand on Nico's leg and the tension melted away as he squeezed her hand.

Piper slid into the seat beside her. "Did you see who Claudia brought?" Her eyes followed Shane as he leaned down to talk to someone. "I still can't believe Shane is her brother. Did you know he was coming tonight?"

"He spent the holidays with her. It's a good thing, Piper. He needs family."

"So, you don't care that he's here?" Piper reached for her glass across the table and plopped back down, taking a drink.

Drew sat back in her seat with a smile. "This is me, not caring."

"I like this side of you. It reminds me of California Drew. We need another trip. Maybe Spring Break or something. You take Nico and I'll bring Taj. We're trying the long-distance thing, get to know each other more. Nothing serious."

"You say that now." Drew laughed.

"You're one to talk. Speaking of serious." Piper nodded toward Nico.

A few of Nico's friends arrived and pulled up chairs beside him as they talked.

"I think I might be... *happy*," she said.

Piper feigned shock as she placed the back of her hand on her forehead. "Happy? *God*." She laughed and nodded to Nico. "It looks good on you. I'm happy you're keeping the house. Jasper is over the moon about the new business deal. I was worried about him but he's like a new human."

Drew narrowed her eyes at Piper. "Over the moon? You've been spending too much time with Jasper. You're talking like him."

Piper puffed out a breath, blowing her pink bangs away from her eyes. "Just wait, it'll happen to you, too!"

"It already has, my friend. It already has," Drew said. "If it weren't for him, I probably would've sold it all. I owe him a lot."

Taj gave Piper's shoulders a quick squeeze. His tight curls bounced as he leaned down and kissed the top of Piper's head. He stood talking to a few people who stopped by.

Piper leaned over and lowered her voice. "Truth? I'm going to miss him."

"I know you are. When do you leave?" She was going to miss Piper, and the more time passed, the more she realized how important it was to stay in touch with each other.

"Three days left. This Sunday. I've got a class on Monday. How about you?"

"Not for another week. I have a few things left to finish up here. Gran's estate stuff. I'm going back late, but I'll catch up."

"I have no doubt you will do amazing things." Piper draped an arm across her shoulders. "You're a witch who sees dead people. You're unstoppable, Drew Harlow."

Witch. The word had a whole new meaning now. To her, it meant the light in the darkness, helping lost souls, love, and magic.

There was a tapping on her arm, and she turned around to see Shane standing behind her. His eyes appeared bloodshot as he glanced at Nico, who was already watching him. "Can we talk?" he asked her.

She folded her arms across her chest prepared to shut him down and send him away from her. "I don't have anything to say to you."

Piper spun around in her seat. "What are you doing here, Shane? She doesn't want to see you."

Shane swayed and gripped a chair with one hand. He stuffed his other hand in the pocket of his leather jacket. "Please, Drew. Five minutes?"

He was drunk. If it weren't for the pained expression on his face and the way he hung his head downward, she would have told him no. Rising from her chair, she glanced from Piper to Nico. "Five minutes, Shane." She placed a hand on Nico's, stopping him from getting up. "I'll be right back. It's okay."

"Can we go outside?" Shane asked.

"It's freezing out."

"It's loud in here."

"Fine." She'd give him a few minutes to hear what he had to say and put their relationship behind them. Signaling for him to lead the way, she followed him outside. She crossed her arms over her soft sweater and paced back and forth in the frigid, January air.

Shane started to take his jacket off, and she put her hand up. Outside was an icebox, but she'd freeze to death before wearing his clothes. "I don't need it. What did you want to talk about?"

He shrugged it back on. "Right. Five minutes."

"And counting," she said.

"Happy Birthday."

"Thank you."

"I'm feeling like shit about the last time we were together. I never wanted you to find out about Leah. It doesn't matter, and I knew it would just hurt you." He staggered on his feet and leaned against the lamppost across from Maze's entrance.

"You're drunk."

He pinched his thumb and index finger together. "Just a little. I miss you, Drew. I needed to tell you how I felt. I'm going back to Boston this weekend. Maybe I can give you a ride?" His words slurred together.

"What is it you want from me out here, Shane? I'm not mad about Leah anymore. We were done before I found out about her. We were never getting back together. I didn't love you anymore."

"But you did... *love* me, didn't you?" He stumbled close to the building and placed a hand on the brick.

She stayed close to the entrance, moving out of the way as people came and went. "Of course I did! I loved you so much it hurt."

She'd lost herself in that love and wouldn't let that happen again.

"I want to kill my—my *father*. If it weren't for what he did, you and me would still be together. D'you ever think about that?"

She sighed and dropped her hands to her sides. Seeing Shane in such a state, despite his betrayal, made her heart heavy.

"Killing him won't change what happened. It'll only hurt you more. He's not worth it. Go back to Boston, become a paramedic, and make yourself proud."

"Do you think about us?"

"I don't think about us in the way you mean, but I don't regret us either. We were so young, Shane, I was sixteen. It's taken a lot to heal, but I've moved on. Please, leave. I'll go inside and find Claudia—"

"I knew you'd come running back to him. Does he know he's second choice? You're giving up a life in Boston to stay... here? Really? With that guy? Fuck."

Anger burned in her chest, flushing her cheeks. "You're an asshole!" She spun around to leave, but Shane's firm grip on her arm stopped her in her tracks. Visions of Dominic Sloan pointing a gun at her flooded her mind, and she froze. "Let go."

"Look, I'm sorry."

She struggled to free her arm. A tingling sensation pricked her hands, but she would not use magic here. Not against Shane. "Let me go!"

A sharp jab of a fist connected with Shane's face, and an arm moved between them, gently pulling her back. Shane stumbled back to the ground, grabbing his bleeding nose. He tried to get up as Claudia ran to his side. "Jesus, Nico!"

"I didn't hit him hard," Nico said.

"Hard enough!" Claudia swore under her breath as she helped Shane stand. Pushing away from Claudia, he ran toward Nico, fists flying. Drew's hands burned to release the magic under her skin, but Nico grabbed Shane's wrist before she could do anything.

Shane tried to pull away as Nico guided his hand down. "We're not doing this, Shane," Nico said. "Let your sister take you home."

Claudia called two of her friends to her side, and they helped her keep Shane steady. He narrowed his eyes at Nico and pointed a finger at him as he mumbled incoherent curse words.

"Come on," Claudia said. She looked over her shoulder as she led him away. "Really, Nico?" She walked away, shaking her head as they disappeared down the alleyway toward the back parking lot.

Nico hugged Drew. She hadn't seen him throw a punch since the second grade. Her bully wouldn't stop harassing her, poking a stick through her bike spokes. She'd fallen off that damn bike so many times, her knees were still scarred.

"I want him to be happy. I've never seen him like that—so angry. I shouldn't have frozen. It just brought up some old stuff I thought I'd buried."

"I wasn't letting him get away with that. He'll be fine." He rubbed his swelling knuckles. "Claudia, on the other hand. I won't hear the end of this for a while."

She took his hand, kissing his reddened knuckles, and led him to the doors. "Let's go back inside. I can talk to Claudia."

Nico held her hand as they walked back to the table. The chaos of her life took a sharp turn, settling into fine dust, but it would take time for her to stop looking over her shoulder for the next threat to appear, waiting for the other shoe to drop. But never in her wildest dreams could she have imagined herself in this moment with Nico, happier than she'd ever been. And for now, this was all that mattered.

FORTY-TWO

Drew stretched to release her aching muscles as she moved crates and boxes around to create an appealing display at the front of the Tough Cookie. She arranged cupcakes and cookies in the glass cabinet under the counter, while Jasper was on the phone back in the kitchen on his quest to find an apartment. She held up the new lunch menu, admiring its glossy laminate and rose gold trim. Jasper had hired a cake decorator, venturing into the world of party planning. He had skills; Gran would be proud of the changes.

The music resumed, and Jasper's voice from the back fell silent. She pushed through the yellow swinging door and entered the kitchen. As Jasper stirred the large pot on the stove, the aroma of chicken soup wafted through the room. The familiar smell of Gran's recipes brought back memories of childhood and filled her with warmth. Jasper wiped his hands on the Tough Cookie apron he wore, which was embroidered with the bakery's logo he'd designed. In a clever twist, the 'o' in cookie resembled an iced shortbread cookie donning a chef's hat and sunglasses.

"Any luck?" she asked.

"Luck isn't even in the realm of possibility right now. The apartments I've seen are dumps, and the new condos by the water are ridiculously expensive."

"Did you go see Claudia? She said she had a list."

"She sure does. Her list is the ridiculously expensive category. It's a lovely list of beautiful new developments in an up-and-coming part of town along the boardwalk."

"Did you memorize that?" Drew scooted beside him and hovered over the pot. "Can I try it?"

"Of course you can." He beamed and scooped a bowlful with the ladle and handed it to her. She grabbed a spoon and took a seat on the stool at the counter.

She had a brilliant idea for Jasper's housing situation. He was desperate to find a place to live that wasn't in Piper's parents' home. Piper was back at school, and he'd started dating again. Drew's solution was perfection... or at least, she thought it was.

"I've got a proposal for you." She blew on the hot soup before tasting it. She closed her eyes and her shoulders slumped. "My God, this is amazing, J! Will there be biscuits?"

He placed the ladle on Gran's spoon holder. "Two kinds. Herb and cheese, and buttery goodness. Well, plain, but we're not calling them *that*."

"I like it." She ate another mouthful, flinching as her lips burned.

"It's hot, Drew. When steam is rising off, it's a burn risk."
She laughed. "You sound like Ori."
His face dropped. "I miss him."
She held the spoon over the bowl. Losing Ori had left a void in her life. As much as she tried to fill the hole with the business, comfort food, and Nico, she never realized how much of a light he'd been in the darkness until he was gone. The pain felt like losing a beloved family member. A brother. "I miss him too."

Jasper sniffed and clapped his hands together. "Tell me. What's your proposal? More business? Because you're leaving for school this weekend, and I don't think we can fit in any-thing else."

"No business. This is personal, sort of."

Jasper leaned over the counter with his chin in his hands. "I'm listening."

"You need a place to stay, and I live alone in a house that's too big for one person."

"I love that house. It's right across from a beach." He tilted his head to the side as he daydreamed. "I miss the beach."

"I know you do. That's why I'm offering you a room in my home. My haven can become your haven."

Jasper stood and tapped his fingers over the counter before turning off the burner on the stove. "Are you sure? Would I be in your way?"

"Not at all. I'll be at school during the week, and Nico offered to help, but I'd feel better if someone was living there. And I welcome the company. I can't think of better company than you."

"Um... yeah, you can. He's tall, with dark hair, glorious eyes, and his name rhymes with Rico."

Her cheeks flushed with heat as she smiled. Love had a way of doing that to a person. "Yes, Nico is definitely glorious company. But Nico and I aren't ready to move in together." She'd thought about it but wanted to give their relationship time to develop on its own, with no pressure. "Even if we were ready to move in together, it wouldn't change my mind. I'm having Gran's room renovated, so you might cross paths with the contractors, but the spare bedroom is furnished and empty. You can bring your J flair to the room and decorate it however you like."

"You're serious," Jasper said.

"Dead serious."

"Let's not use that word."

He had a point. "Okay, but yes, I'm serious," she said, laughing.

"I'll pay you rent."

"That's fair, but nothing in the ridiculously expensive category." She ate another spoonful of the soup, savoring the rosemary and dumplings.

Jasper appeared thoughtful as he looked around the kitchen for a moment. "When can I move in?"

"Whenever you like."

Jasper came around the counter and side-hugged her. "I freaking love you, Drew."

She grinned at him. "I love you, too."

"Can we get a dog?" he asked.

She had never entertained the idea of owning a pet before, assuming she would always be on the move. The changes happening and the family surrounding her brought a renewed sense of happiness into her life. "I'd be open to that."

The Tough Cookie family was growing, and Jasper's enthusiasm filled the air with a special charm.

I miss you, Gran, but you'd be proud.

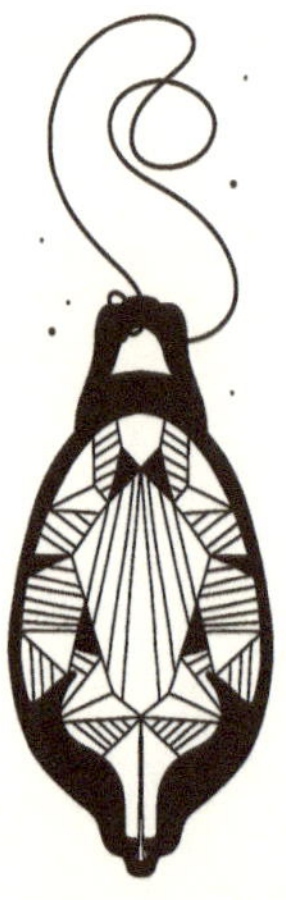

FORTY-THREE

With their surfboards stuck in the sand, Drew settled onto a towel of Jupiter Cove Beach with Nico at her side, pulling their wetsuits down around their waists. Seagulls ran over the wet sand, fighting over a small fish until it separated into two revolting pieces to share. Despite the unusually hot May sun beating down on her fair skin, she was too excited about being back home from school to mind the burn.

She'd been counting the days until the spring term ended for summer and she could come home for longer than a weekend. The next four months promised time with Nico, working at the Tough Cookie, and catching up with her friends.

Nico's fingers traced the curve along her hot shoulders, sending a shiver from her neck down her back. "You're sunburned."

"I know." Her skin mirrored the fire burning inside her.

"Want me to barbecue? I can do it at your place or mine. Will Jasper be home tonight?"

"He's got a date. It's just us," she said, smiling at him as she shielded her eyes from the sun's glare.

He stood up and stretched. God, she loved him. Being with Nico was bliss, and she never wanted to let him go. They'd found a natural rhythm with each other, and she could be herself around him, flaws, insecurities, and all her unique strangeness. She trusted him with the most vulnerable, hidden part of her, and he shared his own fears about his father, the business, the future. They were moving into a new chapter, a different path. Only this time, together.

She picked up her board and followed him barefoot up the steps and across the road, the pavement warm under her feet. Storing their boards in the shed, they rinsed the sand off their feet with the hose before stepping inside the house.

She hung their wetsuits up to dry on the hook behind the bathroom door and took her swimsuit off, wrapping herself in a towel. She combed her wet hair with her fingers as Nico came up the stairs, stopping when he saw her. "You're beautiful." He stepped closer and gazed into her eyes.

"So are you." She plucked a thick eyelash from his cheek, closed her eyes and blew it off her finger.

"What'd you wish for?" His dimple appeared as he smiled.

"I'll never tell."

Cupping his face with her hands, she stood on her tiptoes and kissed him. He wrapped an arm around her waist and led her into her room, where they ended up tangled in each other's arms on her bed. Entwined in the sheets, he propped up on his elbow and kissed her. "I love you. I'm glad you're home."

"Me too." She wrapped her arms around his neck and hugged him tight.

Drew showered and dressed, leaving her wet hair to dry on its own. Nico leaned against the door frame, looking into Gran's room. She'd had the room converted into an art studio, and Nico stocked it with a list of supplies before her arrival home. Claudia's gallery was thriving, and she was aiming for more of Drew's artwork, lighting a fire under her to get painting over the summer break. She shuddered at the reminder of Gran's room on fire and regretted her thought.

"It looks great, doesn't it?" He pulled a T-shirt over his head and ran a hand through his hair.

"It's perfect."

He prodded into the room. "Did I forget anything?"

"Not a thing. Thank you."

He pulled his phone from the back pocket of his jeans. "I've got a customer coming to the garage in a few. I'll be back later."

"I'm counting on it." She smiled. She'd been doing the smiling thing a lot more these days.

He kissed her goodbye before heading down the stairs, letting the door click shut behind him. She entered Gran's room and sat in the loveseat she had moved from up from the den.

She'd positioned crystals along the window ledge and the trapdoor on the floor. She'd placed a protective spell on the entire house after the night at Neptune Point. In a short time, she'd woven herself in among Celeste's most loyal customers at Little Mysteries, sometimes spending a couple of hours at a time talking to her. It surprised her how many customers came into the store with stories and interest in the unknown.

She picked up the Book of Spells—her name for it, since a title had never existed—from the floor to ceiling bookshelf she'd had built. Placing it on her lap, she opened it to a blank page.

Closing her eyes, she held her hands over the page. Focus and intention. She'd been trying to connect with Gran for days, coming up with nothing, but refusing to give up.

I miss you, Gran. Where are you?

Gold lettering spelled out two lines. Today was the magic day.

The butterfly is in the garden.

She shut the book, leaping from the seat and down the stairs. Bounding outside to the backyard, she walked through Gran's garden. The sweet fragrance of blooming flowers filled the air, and every color of the rainbow had popped up from the ground. Gran had dedicated many years to these gardens, and the silence hanging in the air this spring was a reminder of her absence to care for the new blooms. Drew sat on the grass, surrounded by the flowers, magnolia trees and cedars.

The tulips suddenly opened as a vibrant blue butterfly fluttered above the newly sprouted plants, its wings glistening in the light. She stretched out onto her stomach with her chin in her hands, staring at the beautiful insect, unlike any she'd ever seen.

An icy breeze cut through the warmth of the day, and the butterfly shifted and swirled in a mist of blue. She pushed herself up from the ground and waited, gripping the butterfly pendant around her neck. Someone was coming, and the sudden scent of lilacs meant one person.

Gran materialized in front of her. As she moved, her white hair and flowing sundress created a beautiful, otherworldly effect.

"Gran!" Drew threw herself into Gran's arms. Gran stroked her hair as she sobbed. "I didn't think I'd see you again."

"I'd never leave without saying goodbye. It might take a little time to find my way back, but I always will. I'm some proud of you for taking care of what I couldn't."

"I wish I could've been there when he came for you. I'm having a hard time letting it go."

"No, dear. You were exactly where you were supposed to be. As was I. Let it go."

She held onto Gran with all the magic inside of her. The sweetness of the sparkling magic popped along her tongue and pulsed underneath the surface of her skin. She didn't want to let Gran go. "I miss you."

"I know you do. But I get to dance with your grandfather again. Look around you; everything is as it should be. And I'm not far. Keep an eye out for the butterfly." Gran winked as her silhouette started to fade away.

"Please, don't go. Not yet."

Gran placed her hand on Drew's face and smiled. "I love you, dear."

She vanished, leaving the blue butterfly behind. It flew up into the air and disappeared into the bushes. A flock of tiny birds fled a nearby tree in unison, leaving the branch swaying. The ocean's gentle waves echoed from across the road.

"Hello?" a melodic voice sounded.

Drew turned around, searching for where the voice came from. Her hands prickled with energy when a ghost was near, and the person the voice belonged to was indeed, dead. "Who's there?"

A young woman emerged from between the magnolia trees. Her short hair was long enough to sweep to the side, revealing dried blood along the side of her face.

"Finally! I need your help." The girl paced through the garden. She didn't have shoes on and leaned down to roll her pants up at the ankles. "I don't want my feet to get wet."

"There's no water here." Drew didn't know what she was talking about; the beach was across the road, and the girl was walking on grass.

The girl glanced around. "Oh. I thought I was... Where am I?"

"You're in my backyard, but otherwise, I'm not sure." Drew had yet to discover the different realm possibilities where the dead ended up. She might never discover them, but she'd try.

The girl's eyes widened, and she tapped her fingertips together. "I don't know where I am, but I want to go home."

"Where's home?" Drew asked, feeling sick to her stomach. Did the girl not realize she was dead?

"Atlas Cliffs. Do you know it?"

Shit.

Drew moved until she was in front of the girl. "What's your name?"

"Jules. What's yours?"

"Drew Harlow."

"I don't know you," Jules said. "Can you take me home?"

"Jules, this is Atlas Cliffs, but I can help you cross over, find your home."

"Cross over where? I don't know what you're talking about."

Drew struggled to find the right words to tell the girl she was no longer among the living. "Crossing over" had been the closest way to explain it in her own mind. Perhaps she needed to come up with a new phrase. "I'm not sure how else to say this."

The girl stood with her hands on her hips. Blood stains lined the neck of her T-shirt. "Say what? I don't like fluff. If there's something you have to say, say it."

No fluff. Got it.

"Jules, I'm sorry to be the one to tell you, but you're not alive."

The girl burst out laughing, grabbing her sides. "What do you mean, I'm not alive? What's wrong with you?"

Drew chewed her bottom lip. Damn, she could not break the habit. "What I mean is... you're dead."

The girl's smile dropped, and she glared at Drew. "That's not funny."

Drew didn't know how to respond, so she didn't. She just stared at the girl, hoping her eyes conveyed how serious she was. After a moment, the girl brought her hands to her face, shaking her head as she faded into the air.

Standing alone in the garden, a heavy weight of sadness settled in Drew's chest. The poor girl had no idea. She took a deep breath in, then let it out slowly, feeling the tension in her body release like air from a balloon. Finding the balance between helping the dead and living her life had become a priority, and she couldn't take on this ghost's pain as her own. As she walked back toward the house, she repeated the girl's name, so she didn't forget it.

Jules from Atlas Cliffs.

Inside the kitchen, she grabbed a notepad and pen and scribbled the name across the page with an abrupt underline. She tapped the pen on the counter before tucking the notepad into a drawer. This was a future Drew problem to be added to her summer list.

The sharp strike of the clock echoed from the den, and the pen slipped from her fingers, bouncing off the floor. The clock's hands might work again, but the chime had been silent for years. As she approached the swinging door leading to the den, blood pulsed in her ears and sweat gathered at the back of her neck. She took a deep breath, focused her energy like she'd been practicing, and summoned her magic to shield herself from the unknown on the other side. Her hands tingled and burned, and she placed them on the door, ready to push it open. Hathorne was gone, and the portal had been sealed. Maybe Ori was back!

Shoving the door open, she burst into the den, her heart sinking when she found the room empty as the door swung shut behind her. She'd never give up hope of seeing Ori and Enid again. The chimes stopped, leaving a steady ticking as the second hand clicked past eleven minutes after eleven. A cloud of dust danced in the breeze from the open window as a beam of sun reflected sparkles along the wall.

Where are they coming from?

She crouched down and peered under the desk and along the baseboard until she'd searched the room. As she turned back to the pedestal the clock rested on, her gaze landed on the source reflecting light. The amulet!

Dropping to her knees, she picked up the ebony jewel and its warmth spread over her hands. She held it against her chest and closed her eyes. She didn't know if Gran sent it, or how it found its way home, but the amulet was back in her hands again.

"You're mine," she whispered as she placed the silver chain around her neck. A radiant glow from the amulet's center surrounded her before fading to black. The vines had broken free from the stunning gem. She was part of the sisterhood, and their magic lived inside her now. Love surrounded her, giving her the safe space she needed to embrace all the weird and wonderful parts of herself.

As she stood, a gust of wind tossed her hair across her face. She reached over to shut the window and came face to face with the raven perched on a nearby branch outside. It watched her with unblinking eyes, and she smiled back.

"Thanks, Jack."

The raven let out a screech and flapped its wings before flying away.

Wrapping her fingers around the amulet, she made her way back to the kitchen. *Jules.* The ghost who didn't know she was dead would return soon enough, and the pendulum would shift once again as Drew helped another soul find their haven.

Acknowledgements

"There is freedom waiting for you, On the breezes of the sky, and you ask, "What if I fall?" Oh, but my darling, what if you fly?" Quote by Erin Hanson.

My beautiful friend Krista Scott shares my love for motivational quotes. Whenever I experience self-doubt, this quote always comes to mind. Thank you for being up for a road trip with live music, or a heart-to-heart chat. I treasure our unfiltered, guards-down, say-anything friendship.

Natasha MacKenzie, my dream cover designer! Thank you for surpassing the vision I had in my head and bringing to life a stunning cover for Seeking Haven. I'm excited to work together in 2024 to do it all over again for book 3 of the Atlas Cliffs series!

My editor and proofreader, Kayla Ramoutar. I love our full-on honesty and openness. Your dedication to elevate and bring out the best in my writing is palpable. You push me to take it a step further and give the story more depth than I think possible. I'm grateful to you for keeping it authentic and real, but also for your unwavering encouragement and belief in me as an author.

My writing critique partner, Kamy Lavin, if there was an award for Indie Author Cheerleader, you'd win it hands down every time. I appreciate you taking the time to read and re-read my draft and revisions, offering story advice along the way. (Kudos goes to you for the Nico and Drew one-bed scene idea!) I can't thank you enough for sharing my books with the world through your own social media and giveaways. I've had the honor of reading Kamy's work, and I look forward to holding her book in my hands one day!

Thank you to everyone who beta read Seeking Haven in its early stages, offering priceless feedback. And to my street team of ARC readers—reviews make a tremendous difference for an author, and I appreciate each of you for being part of my journey.

I can confirm that magic happens outside my comfort zone. A year ago, I pushed past the fear of putting myself out in the world as an author and created a TikTok account in search of Booktok. This community has been pivotal in my Indie author journey, and I don't think I could have made it this far without the connections I've made. To my Booktok friends, how do I thank you? You've welcomed this newbie author, took a chance on Wandering Souls, and encouraged me to keep writing. The gratitude I feel is humbling. Thank you to those who've reached out and booked me on their Lives for author interviews. Thanks to the amazing Booktokers who took the time to create content for my books. Every time I see those tags, I feel exhilarated! Thank you to the readers who have sent me messages—I will always love hearing from you.

Sara Flanagan, you're a total ray of sunshine and I'm happy to know you. Your turn is next! Tess Watters, thanks for reminding me to never quit our daydream. I admire you. Jaclyn Kot, you've been my sounding board for all things indie author and writing. I'm grateful for your advice, pep talks, and our kindred spirit connection. Thank you all for your friendship. My wish is for all writers to have these beautiful connections.

My writing friend, Keegan Eichelman. Your passion to help others by sharing tips and encouragement while designing your own dream life is admirable. You once said that people might think we're always happy-go-lucky, glass half full people, but we are this way because we've seen the dark stuff, and we know the importance of sharing light and kindness with others who need it, too.

My husband, Roman. Thanks for making me laugh when I'm ready to pull my hair out in my writing cave. I "appreciates" you, and your full attention when I need to brainstorm plot holes, story details, and develop villains. Side note, Next of Kin is a nod to the band Roman played drums for years ago.

My son, Ro Jr. You inspire people more than you realize. Don't ever lose your passion to motivate and accomplish amazing things in this life! It will never steer you wrong. I'm proud of you.

Lucien, I've dedicated this book to you. Just when I think I can't, you push me to keep going.

Cheers to my family, and friends who are family. You always show up, no matter what. Sarah and Pat, thank you for listening to my "talking book" on your road trips. Your friendship and support mean the world to me, and I can't wait for our next travel adventure!

I'll breathe relief for now, knowing I still get to hang out with Drew, Nico, and the characters in Atlas Cliffs for one more book. But don't worry! I've got a new cast brewing for my next project and look forward to daydreaming the next story onto the pages!

Angela never dreamed of being an author until she started writing Wandering Souls. She always has music playing when writing and creates a playlist for each book. Supernatural ghost stories keep life interesting, but after Seeking Haven, she discovered a love for writing romance. Be prepared for more in future books!

She lives on the east coast of Canada in New Brunswick with her family and their beloved dog, Harley, who she calls 'Pippy' and 'Harley-Quinn'. A lover of the ocean, full moons, and sunsets, she'd choose to be barefoot on a beach in a small coastal town any day over big city life.

Book three of the Atlas Cliffs series is her priority, but a standalone with a fresh cast of characters is in the works... unless she can't bring herself to let go and that novel turns into another series.

Follow for writing updates, book playlists and more!
https://linktr.ee/angeladvl